A DUCHESS OF MYSTERY

The Mismatched Lovers
Book Three

Fil Reid

ARE YOU SIGNED UP FOR DRAGONBLADE'S BLOG?

You'll get the latest news and information on exclusive giveaways, exclusive excerpts, coming releases, sales, free books, cover reveals and more.

Check out our complete list of authors, too!

No spam, no junk. That's a promise!

Sign Up Here

www.dragonbladepublishing.com

Dearest Reader;

Thank you for your support of a small press. At Dragonblade Publishing, we strive to bring you the highest quality Historical Romance from some of the best authors in the business. Without your support, there is no 'us', so we sincerely hope you adore these stories and find some new favorite authors along the way.

Happy Reading!

CEO, Dragonblade Publishing

Additional Dragonblade books by Author Fil Reid

The Mismatched Lovers Series
A Sham Engagement (Book 1)
A Hint of Scandal (Book 2)
A Duchess of Mystery (Book 3)

The Cornish Ladies Series
The Cornish Mermaid (Book 1)
The Cornish Bride (Book 2)
The Cornish Inheritance (Book 3)
The Cornish Widow (Book 4)

Guinevere Series
The Dragon Ring (Book 1)
The Bear's Heart (Book 2)
The Sword (Book 3)
Warrior Queen (Book 4)
The Quest for Excalibur (Book 5)
The Road to Avalon (Book 6)

CHAPTER ONE

MAJOR RICHARD CARSTAIRS, Diccon to his closest friends, of the 2nd Battalion of the 95th Foot, looked up from cleaning his Baker rifle as the shape of an orderly blocked out the merciless Portuguese sun for a moment. The man, dressed in the red jacket of the main army rather than the green of the Rifle Brigade, the regiment in which Richard was an officer, saluted smartly.

"Yes?" Richard asked, pausing in his pleasurable task. His soldier servant, Corporal Baxter, could have cleaned his rifle for him, but Richard had always maintained that a good rifleman, whatever his rank, looked after his own weapon, and he wasn't about to change now, tired as he was. Besides which, Baxter had enough to do.

"Major Carstairs, sir. Message for you to report to the Commander of the Light Brigade, sir." The man barked out his message as he stood to attention and saluted. He had the puny, underfed look about him of a man who'd grown up stunted and hungry in the slums of London. Many of the ordinary soldiers under Richard's command shared that appearance. However, if they joined young enough, some of them had been known to flourish and grow both upwards and outwards. Not this little man though, with his narrow, ratty face and scrawny shoulders. Probably fast on his feet, which would be why he was being used as a messenger.

Baxter, a similarly short, but in his case sturdy, grizzled man a few years older than Richard, glanced up in curiosity from where he was occupied in darning his master's stockings, a task at which he excelled. The needle in his horny hand stilled above the darning mushroom on his knee, and his eyes narrowed to slits against the sun's glare. His sharp gaze traveled from his master's face to that of the orderly, then back again, no doubt weighing up the import of this order and how it would affect him.

Richard set down the oily rag he'd been using on his rifle. He knew better than to ask a lowly orderly the reason for this summons. Leaning his rifle against the tree under whose inadequate boughs he'd been sheltering, he rose to his feet, something that enabled him to tower over the little infantryman. Flexing his stiff shoulders, he gave the man a nod. "Lead on, soldier."

Out of the tree's meager shade, the unrelenting heat of Portugal's late summer sun beat down on his back as he fastened his far-too-hot woolen uniform jacket and retied his red waist sash. Despite the much easier relationships amongst the riflemen, it wouldn't do at all to present himself to Brigadier General Fane in anything approaching undress.

All around him, the men of the 95th, many of them his own particular men of whom he was justly proud, sat about just as he'd been doing, resting in the aftermath of the intense battle they'd been part of on the preceding day. A good few of them were nursing wounds. The battle had taken place at Roliça, some eleven miles to the north, where they'd put the outnumbered French to flight and captured three of their five guns. A resounding success, although the combined British and Portuguese forces had suffered four hundred and eighty-seven casualties—more than half from the 29th Foot who'd rashly stormed a too-well-guarded hill. However, they could all rest satisfied that the French had suffered much heavier losses and run off with their tails between their legs.

Richard felt his customary glow of pride as he surveyed

where his men sat at ease, crammed into whatever shade they'd been able to find. The trees here were nothing like the spreading oaks of England, neither in height nor in spread. For himself, he was glad to have seen action so swiftly after his regiment's arrival in Portugal, and proud to have been a party to the first shots fired. He had confidence his men felt the same, and nothing about their cheerful dispositions gave the lie to that. Their first engagement had happened on August 15th, only days after their disembarkation at Figueira da Foz, when the 95th and the Royal American Regiment had encountered the French rearguard and pounced on it. The only sad adjunct to that was that they'd also suffered the first loss of the campaign, when young Lieutenant Ralph Bunbury, a man Richard had known well, had been killed.

Despite nearly twenty years of soldiering under his belt, having taken up a commission as a raw ensign at only fifteen years of age, it never failed to upset Richard when one of his men died. They were like family to him—taking the place of the family he'd never had. He doubted he'd ever get used to losing one of them.

Brigadier General Fane had set up his tent on the far side of the camp, amongst the cluster of tents belonging to the other commanding officers of the sizeable force now gathered near the hilltop village of Vimeiro. As a major, Richard could quite reasonably have set his own tent up on the outskirts of that group, as many of the officers of the other regiments had done. However, like the rest of the 95th's officers, he preferred to remain amongst his own men, where they could see him. After all, they were all riflemen first and foremost, and officers only secondarily.

A few officers from some of the other regiments, sitting in their shirt sleeves on their folding chairs outside their tents, legs outstretched in relaxation, called out to him as he passed or raised languid hands. Today was a day of hard-earned rest, save for the men rostered on sentry duty. It never did to take things for granted. The French had proved many times over that they could be slippery customers.

The little orderly led him to where the largest tents had been erected, near a scattering of trees on a rise, a spot from which the whole of the camp could be observed. Without exception, all of them had their flaps pinned back in an effort to persuade whatever breeze there might be to enter in. The orderly halted outside one of them and stood back, at attention again. "Major Carstairs all present and correct, sir," he almost shouted through the flimsy, sun-bleached canvas, without making any attempt to enter.

Richard ducked his head as he passed through the open doorway to go inside.

Brigadier General Fane, whom Richard knew quite well, was standing beside his campaign desk. This was because someone else was occupying his folding campaign chair and had taken his place behind the desk.

Richard, a little taken aback at the sight of the second man, stood to attention and saluted. "Lieutenant General Wellesley, sir."

Sir Arthur Wellesley, the overall commander of the expedition and victor at Roliça, was an unmistakable man, with his majestic bearing, prominent nose, and stern blue eyes. Unlike Fane, who was rapidly going bald, Wellesley still possessed a fine head of hair. He was only four years older than Richard, but his rise had been nothing less than meteoric, and every soldier serving under him had unassailable respect for him. Richard included.

"At ease, Major Carstairs," Wellesley said, waving at the folding seat in front of the desk. "I'd sit down, if I were you. What I have to tell you is going to come as quite a shock, I imagine."

After a quick glance at his own commanding officer, Richard did as he was told, attempting to look as much at ease as possible. What on earth could Wellesley be about to tell him that would come as a shock? Racking his brain brought nothing to mind.

Wellesley picked up a folded piece of paper from his desk and held it out. "You'd better read this for yourself."

Curious, Richard took the paper and opened it out, annoyed to discover a slight tremor of trepidation in his fingers, even though there was nothing anyone could possibly tell him that could cause him any upset. After all, his parents had both died when he was a small child and he had no brothers or sisters, nor a wife or children, nor anyone to whom he had any kind of attachment. Save for his men, of course.

He read the note. It was very short.

Request return to Britain immediately of Major Richard Carstairs. 7th Duke of Stourbridge deceased. Carstairs now 8th Duke. Essential he return with all haste.

What?

He had to read the note a second time before it fully sank in. Marcus was dead. Marcus, with his iron grip on life made fiercer by his huge strength and determination. Dead. No more. Gone. But he'd only been three years Richard's senior. How could he be dead so young? Men of thirty-eight didn't just up and die for no reason. Perhaps he'd been ill, or suffered an accident, or even been killed in a duel. His lifestyle, even as the very young man Richard remembered, had always been of the most hedonistic. He shook his head to clear it. However his cousin Marcus had died, he was definitely dead, or this message would not have arrived. And if Marcus were dead… then the message was right. He was now the Duke of Stourbridge. Something he'd never expected to be if he'd lived to be a hundred.

Good God. The weight of this news began to slowly sink in.

"You see our quandary?" Wellesley said.

Richard met his level gaze. "I do, sir."

Fane nodded. "We're loath to lose a good officer like yourself at a time like this, but that comes from the Prince of Wales's office itself. We'll have to let you go."

Richard resisted the temptation to squirm in his seat, at the same time wondering what on earth the Prince of Wales's office was doing sending messages about the inheritance of dukedoms.

"What if I don't want to go?"

"Don't want to, man?" Wellesley said. "Wanting to has nothing to do with it. You have to go, and that's an order. From on high. You are the last male Carstairs and owe it to the estate and title you're inheriting not to allow it to fall into abeyance."

Saying he possessed no inclination to inherit his cousin's title and become a blasted duke didn't seem quite the right thing under the circumstances. The temptation to spit out the truth blossomed, however. Why would he want anything that evil bastard Marcus had possessed? Not his title nor his house nor his money. None of it. However, he held his tongue. This was Wellesley he was talking to. He couldn't object to anything he ordered him to do. Especially not if it came from the offices of the Prince of Wales.

A little protest might not go amiss though. "Why is it so important that I go back? I'm sure the inheritance will take care of itself. My cousin probably had an excellent estate manager and the same man of business my uncle had. They should be able to take care of everything until I find time to return. Until the fighting here in Portugal is done with."

Fane shook his head. "I know you want to stay here, lad, but you can't." His voice had softened in sympathy. He glanced at Wellesley. "I suppose we'd better show him the other message."

Wellesley nodded. "You're right. We have to." He reached into the leather messages pouch that lay on the desktop and withdrew a second folded sheet of paper. "Have a look at this and you'll see why you have to go back. Aside from the fact it's your duty as a Duke of Great Britain, as I just said, to not allow the title to fall into abeyance. A serving duke with no male heir is not approved of in the military. What if you were to be killed? Look at what happened to young Bunbury. One can't predict matters like that."

More curious than ever, Richard reached for this second message, his fingers no longer shaking. He unfolded it.

Duke dead under suspicious circumstances. Duchess of Stourbridge under suspicion of murder. Estate in an uproar. Imperative you order Major Carstairs to return and clear her name.

"Same origin as the first message," Fane said. "Only this one was marked 'personal.'"

Richard looked up again. "Ah." Not that he'd even known Marcus had a wife, and especially not a wife the Prince of Wales might show an interest in. Why would he have? As far as he knew, his cousin had always been more of a man to keep a stable of mistresses than one wife. Although, if she were suspected of his murder, perhaps Marcus had been as vile to her as he had been to Richard when he was an orphaned child living at Stourbridge Castle. Any woman who'd had the foolishness to marry Marcus surely had to be pitied, not pilloried. There was no denying that the world would be a better place without his cousin in it.

"You see?" Fane said. "We have to send you home. For more than one reason. If a duchess were to be openly accused of murdering her husband, it would throw the reputation of Britain's nobility into chaos. Those eager to move against them, as has happened in France, would seize upon it. You will need to clear her name."

Wellesley nodded. "There's the inheritance, too. We usually get younger brothers in the army, or more distant relatives. Just as you were until today. Peers tend to be the ones who stay at home and let others do the fighting. Preserving the bloodline. You'll want to get yourself a duchess and a son in the nursery before you think of doing any more fighting. Perhaps two heirs, just to be on the safe side. If you even wish to return at all, by that time."

Not return at all? Richard fixated on those words, heedless of the suggestion that he should find himself a wife and beget a child which was not something he'd ever seen himself doing.

Not return to the life he'd lived since he was a boy of fifteen and a lowly ensign in the 42nd Foot, a commission bought for him by his beloved grandmother, partly to save him from Marcus's ever-increasing bullying. Since that moment, he'd never looked back, never visited Stourbridge Castle, never thought about the family he'd left behind. Except perhaps for his cousin Dora. But she'd be married now, with a family of her own. Stourbridge Castle would be empty of all the people he'd known there as a boy, nearly twenty years ago. The one overriding benefit, however, would be that it would be empty of Marcus.

Richard waved the paper at Wellesley. "Do you know what happened to the duke that has led to his wife being under suspicion?"

Wellesley shook his head. "No more than you've read here. No other word came with these messages that have been following us around without catching us for a while. Henry and I have discussed this at length, and we are ordering you home to put your affairs in order. No doubt you'll find out soon enough what's befallen your cousin. I'm afraid your days of soldiering are over, Richard, at least for the foreseeable future. You leave for the coast in the morning. There you'll take one of the ships returning to London. Is that understood?"

The use of first names struck Richard. Wellesley was no longer addressing a fellow officer but a civilian. Whatever happened next, he was not going to be fighting against the French for some time. Not unless he married with undue haste and provided the necessary heir. A male one, at that. And getting married was not something he'd ever considered. Not something he wanted to do at all. He was happy the way he was right now, wasn't he? Anger at Marcus for getting himself killed welled up and had to be controlled. Bloody man. Affecting his life from beyond the grave.

He rose to his feet and saluted. "Yes, sir."

Wellesley's serious mouth quirked in a rueful smile. "Although I think that we'd best address you as Your Grace now, hadn't we, my boy?"

Baxter had finished his darning by the time Richard returned to their camping spot and was stirring a pot of stew over the little campfire he'd lit. The meaty aroma wafted enticingly to Richard's nostrils, but he had more important things to think about that filling his stomach.

He halted in the shade. "You'd best pack your things. We're going back to England."

His man raised his bushy eyebrows and grimaced. "All of us? We only just got here. Them in charge need to make their bloody minds up."

Richard shook his head. "Not all of us, no. Just you and me. Well, just me technically, but I'd like to take you with me. No one'll object to that, I'm sure. We've grown accustomed to one another's ways, over the years, and I don't want to lose you. You won't mind the change, will you?"

Baxter shifted the pot away from the heat and rubbed the side of his sizeable, and decidedly crooked, nose. "I go where you go, Major. You know that. But why just us? If you don't mind me asking, that is? What've we done to deserve being shipped back to England, I'd like to know? I was lookin' forward to a bit more Johnny Crapaud bashing."

Richard took off his jacket and lowered himself back into the spot he'd so recently vacated. "I've been recalled on a personal matter, Baxter. I might as well tell you as you'll find out soon enough." He considered his soldier servant's puzzled but trusting face. They might have been officer and servant for years, and indeed Richard considered Baxter a friend, but he'd never felt the need to divulge any of his personal history and neither had Baxter. He was going to have to now, though. "I suppose I must tell you something of my history at last. I have—I mean I had—a cousin of whom I was not at all fond."

He licked his lips. How long had it been since he'd even thought of any of them, especially not Marcus, the bane of his boyhood? "It appears he has died childless, and I am his heir. We have to return, because I am to inherit his title and estate. Lieutenant General Wellesley, no less, has ordered me back to

England, after a message from the office of the Prince of Wales." He gave an uncertain laugh. "I am, if I wish to return to the army, to provide myself with a wife and an heir with some alacrity. Something, I fear, that might take a lot longer than Sir Arthur thinks."

Baxter scratched his head, his fingers running through the stiff bristles of his hair. "So we're to go back to his estate that's now yours?"

Richard nodded.

"An estate what was once your cousin's?"

Another nod. Richard's inner reticence was keeping his mouth shut, although memories swarmed through his brain: of the terror he'd felt aged only seven when the bullying Marcus had laughed with glee as he held Richard under in the lake, of running with wild abandon with Dora, hand in hand through the woods, and of the warm safe feeling of his grandmother smiling with benevolence as he pressed his small body against her knees.

Baxter sat up a bit straighter. "And what is it that I'll be calling you, Major, now you've inherited a title? If I'm to come with you, then I'll have to be minding my manners a bit more than I've had to in the Rifles, I'm thinking."

Richard's lips quirked upward in a half smile. "I'm rather taking a leap to the top of the pile, title-wise. You see before you, dusty and unshaven and, I have to admit, a bit smelly, the eighth Duke of Stourbridge." He let his smile spread into a grin. "And before you say anything, let me tell you that no one could be more surprised by this than I am."

CHAPTER TWO

I SABELLA CARSTAIRS, THE Duchess of Stourbridge, always made it her habit to arrive late at any social event she was invited to. She liked to create an impression on the already present guests and the only way to do that was to make sure they'd all arrived before her. So they could fully appreciate her theatrical entrance.

Tonight she was wearing black, something she'd been forced to do since the death of her husband, although, apart from the color, the appearance of the silk gown she'd chosen made no homage whatsoever to the duke's loss. It was lowcut, revealing the alluring curve of Isabella's pert breasts, an attribute she felt ought not to be camouflaged beneath a somber fichu. In fact, she'd taken the mourning color to extremes and was clad entirely in that shade from her dainty black kid slippers upwards via the ornate black silk gown and its overlaying of fine lace to her long black gloves and the black feathers that adorned her magnificent auburn hair. Black pearls sparkled at her throat and had also been affixed to the fine netting that the black feathers sat amongst. All of this set off the pale alabaster of her skin to great effect—as it was intended to do. If she had to wear black for a year, something she had no intention of doing, then for now let it complement her beauty. It did.

She paused at the top of the steps that led down into the ballroom of Bembridge House exactly long enough to make sure every eye was on her, before setting an elegant hand on her escort's arm and descending with well-perfected languid disdain, the train of her gown sweeping the marble steps behind her.

Another reason for all eyes to be upon her was her choice of escort: Lord Rupert Wyndham, that epitome of elegance and toast of the *ton*, the man whose approval every mama sought to gain for their daughter. The man society, and in particular the bejeweled old hens now watching her descend the staircase, believed to be her lover. Let them think that. What did she care for their approval? They'd made it quite clear when she'd married Marcus ten years ago that they thought her beneath their notice. Well, now they were all beneath hers.

If she'd deigned to glance to her right, she'd have been able to feast her eyes on Lord Rupert's much admired Hellenic beauty from the top of his perfectly coiffured, falsely disarrayed curls down to the high points of his collar, his immaculately-cut, figure-hugging coat and his tight satin breeches. However, she had no need to do so, for she'd already approved his turnout as her escort before they left Stourbridge House, when she'd received him in her boudoir.

"Stap me, Bella," Wyndham now said, under his breath and leaning closer to her. "If there ain't a surfeit of ugly girls coming out this Season. You'll have to tell me if you spot a pretty face amongst them because I certainly don't. Faces like the backsides of those monkeys at the Exeter 'Change. Just like their mothers."

Isabella smiled sweetly, despite her inclination to burst out laughing at this gross exaggeration. Part of the reason she liked Sir Rupert so much was his acerbic wit and sharp-tongued descriptions of the people who flocked to fawn over him. The same people who ten years ago had looked down their aristocratic noses at her when Stourbridge had chosen her, the daughter of a rich tradesman, as his bride. "Surely there must be a few pretty girls here somewhere. I can't believe that the poor queen will have to receive a parade of plain ones when the Season begins. And such wonders can be done with hair and cosmetics if a girl has a clever maid."

"None so pretty as you, of course," Wyndham said, as they reached the dance floor and Lady Brocklebank, their hostess for the evening, swept up to them.

"My dear Isabella, and Lord Rupert. How charming of you to grace my little gathering."

That it was not a "little gathering" was obvious, as the ballroom was packed and a great deal of trouble had been gone to in order to decorate the house. Chandeliers sparkled, an orchestra played, floral arrangements abounded, and anyone who had any claim to being anyone in Berkshire or Hampshire, or possibly even further afield, had been invited. Lady Brocklebank was not someone who ever did things by halves.

Wyndham swept her a flamboyant bow but Isabella bestowed on her only the merest of curtseys. She was a girl who never forgot a slight, and this woman had been one of her most vociferous and spiteful critics when she'd first assumed the mantle of duchess. When Marcus had first become betrothed to her, even, as if that event had anything to do with anyone but them. That he'd done so with an eye to the fact that not only was her father, in Marcus's words, filthy rich, but that she was his only child, had not escaped any member of the disapproving ton, who themselves were frequently on their uppers. Her wealth, combined with her having been the most beautiful debutante of that year, had not endeared her to them one whit. And neither had their behavior endeared any of them to Isabella. But she kept that fact well hidden. Most of the time.

"Maria, how charming you look," Isabella lied, keeping that sweet smile she liked to affect stitched onto her face. She flattered herself that she was very good at wearing masks. In truth, Maria looked anything but charming, for she was a lady grown stout with age and the bearing of many children, many of whom had predeceased her.

Lady Brocklebank, whom experience had long ago taught Isabella was nothing if not gullible, preened as though she were a young debutante at her first ball. "How kind of you to say so. My dressmaker in London has fashioned matching gowns for both me and Honoria. Lord Brocklebank's clever idea. He says we look like sisters, not mother and daughter. You must know that she is newly engaged to be married to Sir William Cholmondeley? She was quite the success of last Season. Eligible young men came calling every day while we were residing at our London town house."

"How fortuitous for her. I wish her all the happiness I have derived from my marriage." Lord Brocklebank must be as blind as his wife was gullible. And Honoria must either be completely mad to be persuaded to dress identically to her mother, or sufficiently under her thumb to have offered no protests. Isabella made a mental note to sniff out the unfortunate girl and see if she looked worse than her mother. Not something one would think feasible, but then, if one thought that, one had not lain eyes on the young Honoria. She had been presented at the start of the last Season, and it seemed with the right result, and this ball, no doubt, was an opportunity for her parents to show off their own success in marrying her off. Weren't there two more girls at home still, twins if Isabella's memory served her, needing to make their debuts shortly? Lady Brocklebank must be relieved to have got one of her daughters out of the way with such speed.

As Lady Brocklebank moved away, a puzzled frown on her face at Isabella's last words, Wyndham leaned closer. "Let us hope that before the Season starts, someone will have instilled a modicum of taste into Maria's dressmaker or her two younger daughters will be the the butt of every joke."

Isabella raised her fan to cover her mouth in a vain attempt to suppress her laughter. "I doubt it possible." She fluttered her fan as a gentleman approached. "Oh good heavens, it's Lord Amersham. I fear he's about to ask me to dance. Quickly, Rupert. Lead me onto the floor. I can't abide the thought of that man pawing at me again."

With consummate dexterity, Wyndham whirled her out onto the floor to join the dance, which, as luck would have it, was a country dance performed by couples rather than in sets. Isabella had the briefest of glances at Lord Amersham's heavy-jowled, disappointed expression before she was engulfed in the crowd of lively dancers. What a bore it was having to avoid suitors now she was a widow. Not that she'd been short of them even before Marcus died. Being married did not seem to be considered a barrier where love affairs were concerned. And many men had shown a satisfying inclination to become her lover. One of the reasons she kept Wyndham so close. Her perfect undemanding escort. Let everyone think he'd succeeded where they had failed, when being her lover could not have been further from his intentions.

"You know," Wyndham said, keeping his voice low as they came together a short while later, "now you are a widow, you could marry again very advantageously if you so wished and could bring yourself to offer some of your suitors decent encouragement, instead of just leading them on the way you do."

She shook her head. "Not that one though. He might be a member of the aristocracy, but he sweats like a canal navvie at the least little exercise and his face when he dances takes on the color of a ripe plum. Most unattractive. Nothing is worse, I declare, than a man who has to keep wiping the moisture off his brow with his own sweat-dampened hands." She gave a shudder. "I manage to keep myself away from him as much as possible and have administered some cutting putdowns, and yet he returns, ever hopeful, as though he believes that one day I will give in to his attentions. Such is hope, I suppose."

"Has he asked you to marry him?"

She twirled around. "I fear it would be impolite of me to reveal that."

"You can tell me anything, you know."

She laughed. "Not when it involves the feelings of someone else, however much I may not care for him."

The dance moves took them apart. When they came back together again she'd assumed a serious expression more befitting her current status. "I think I may tell you, though, that I have assured Lord Amersham that as a recent widow I could not possibly entertain the attentions of any man for at least a year." She had to admit that wearing mourning was useful when it came to putting off ardent gentlemen.

His turn to laugh. How handsome he was when he did so, and how wasted his beauty. A shame he didn't like ladies, as he was the one man she might have considered. The one man she didn't find a threat, but that was most likely due to his predilection. "A fiction you will find hard to maintain when the whole world believes you are scandalously involved with me."

She gave a toss of her head. "What do I care what the world thinks of me?" And the dance snatched them away from one another again.

The dance was a long one, as each couple performed their own part to the end of the line, and it was some time before it reached its close and allowed all the dancers to retire, flushed and laughing, to the edge of the dance floor. As if from nowhere, as though drawn by a magnet, a coterie of eager gentlemen assembled to surround Isabella. Of course, the determined Amersham, his face shiny with sweat despite not having danced, numbered amongst them, but so too did the despised Lady Brocklebank's only son, Giles Worthing, a young man who, as luck would have it, resembled his ageing father more than his stout mother and thus was as long and thin as a string bean.

Isabella, aware of the delicious disapproval of so many mamas, wives, and mistresses, opened her dance card and took the greatest of pleasure in filling it with the names of all these admiring gentlemen. She took care to reserve the dance before supper for young Giles, at whom she batted her long eyelashes more than anyone, so she could be sure he would escort her in and dance attendance on her while they ate. The only thing more fun than flirting was to flirt with a young man whose mother, despite her present professions of friendship, hated you. And on top of that, who also happened to be a close friend of the now dispossessed and jealous mistress of your dead husband. *Touché, Lady Brocklebank.*

Having filled her card, and with the possibility of having been able to fill it twice over, she spun out onto the dance floor for a cotillion with Lord Alfred Ponsonby, whose wife, she well knew, had been unable to attend the Bembridge Ball due to having just produced their third child—yet another daughter. Lord Alfred, whose small country seat lay less than ten miles from Stourbridge Castle, must be feeling the usual neglect of a man sidelined in his wife's attentions by a small baby, and was most attentive to Isabella's needs. Which meant he told her frequently how beautiful she was, squeezed her hand suggestively every time the dance brought them together, and took any opportunity that presented itself to squeeze her waist as well. At least he wasn't the overly sweaty Lord Amersham. She'd managed to avoid a dance with him altogether. And at least because this was a country ball, there was very little possibility of the Prince of Wales attending, as he, like Amersham, could get a sight too familiar. That he fully intended to make her his mistress, if he could, she knew all too well. It was only this present inconvenience of Marcus's death that was holding him at bay. Thank goodness.

Suppertime with Giles arrived, and very pleasant it proved to be. There was so much one could do while seated at the supper table beside the gentleman of your choice, and so little he could do. Although she did allow him to put his hand, which proved to be as hot as Lord Amersham's, on her thigh beneath the table, but that was as far as she was prepared to allow this puppy to go, even though he several times tried to sneak it somewhere slightly more intimate, the naughty, forward boy. That was a place no one was allowed to go.

Without ever having to glance at his mother, she was able to ascertain her icy, disapproving stare just by the feel of the woman's eyes boring into her. To make her worry that little bit more, she leaned in close to young Giles and whispered into his ear. "I do declare I find you more and more attractive as the evening progresses."

This produced the desired effect. Poor Giles, rendered quite speechless by such praise, blushed scarlet and turned eyes brimming with hope, and lust, on Isabella, prompting her to kiss her hand to him. Was that a snort of indignation from further up the table. She didn't look but felt satisfied her behavior was having the desired effect.

All too soon though, Wyndham was seeking her out and informing her their carriage was awaiting them at the front doors of Bembridge House. Just as she preferred to arrive fashionably late, Isabella also made a habit of leaving early. Not too early, for she didn't want to be thought straightlaced in any way. But as much as she liked her entrances to be observed, she also liked the same for her exits, and she liked to leave the men who attended her wanting more.

To this end, she made great play of wishing all the gentlemen who had spent the evening dancing attendance on her a fond farewell, particularly young Giles, with a weather eye kept on his mother's reaction. This young man, fortified by a few more seductive looks directed his way, had by then taken on the appearance of a lovesick spaniel. Something that had not gone unnoticed by his adoring mama. Good.

Isabella extended her hand to Giles to allow him to kiss it, pleased by the lustful heat in his eyes. What fun it was to keep a man dangling like this, especially when he was the son of one's enemy. To allow him to work himself up into a frenzy of desire and yet to relinquish nothing to him. She'd become quite expert at that over the years, and Wyndham's presence as her escort was enough to keep her would-be lovers at a safe enough distance. Lusting after her but unfulfilled. The perfect revenge on the male fraternity from which Marcus had emerged.

Taking Wyndham's arm, she allowed him to help her into her carriage and settled herself on the velvet upholstery, facing forwards. Wyndham climbed in after her and took the seat opposite, as was his custom. The carriage rocked for a moment then moved off into the darkness of the night. An hour's drive and they would be back at the castle.

Wyndham stretched his long legs. "You are quite incorrigible, you know, Bella."

A single oil lamp illumined the interior of the carriage. Isabella copied him by stretching her own legs out and rubbing her foot against his ankle. "My feet ache terribly from all that dancing." She wrinkled her nose and kicked off her shoe. "I swear young Giles Worthy possesses two left feet. If he trod on me once, he trod on me a dozen times. My toes will be quite black and blue."

For answer, Wyndham lifted her foot and set it on his lap, his slender fingers beginning the massage she so liked. "Not black and blue. A little red, perhaps." He had more uses than just as an escort and buffer between her and the men who would like to go a lot further than kissing her hand.

She sighed. "That's better. You always know just what I need."

He chuckled. "Which is the only reason you tolerate my presence."

"Nonsense. I love you. How could I not?"

"Shameless hussy."

The carriage rumbled on, and Isabella remained silent for a while, relishing the relief for her poor feet. Thank goodness for dear Rupert.

"You know," he said after a bit. "You probably shouldn't tease so many of those men the way you do. Your reputation is quite ruined. And one of these days you're going to find yourself in a situation you can't escape from. Men will only take so much teasing, and some of them would not be above taking for themselves that which they think they are owed."

She shrugged. "I can take care of myself, thank you. And as for a reputation, did I ever have one that was worth ruining?"

"Of course you did. Once."

She shook her head. "You know very well that I didn't. Those old harpies and their lecherous husbands had me pegged as the daughter of a cit out to buy myself a title from the moment I showed my nose in Town. Every single one of them looked down their aristocratic, interbred noses at me in disgust when Marcus married me. And as for Lady Brocklebank, she hated me from the outset because she'd been after Marcus for Verity, her oldest daughter. And don't forget, she's friends with that dreadful woman. At least I can be grateful she wasn't at the ball tonight."

"You're like the elephant that never forgets, Bella. That was ten years ago now, and they only looked down their noses at you because half of them, the half with daughters to marry off, had wanted Marcus themselves. Including, as you say, Lady Brocklebank. Don't forget that Verity had to put up with marrying that frightful Sir Algernon Chase." He gave an eloquent shiver.

She snatched back her foot. "That's as may be, but not a one of them has changed their opinion. They all still see me as an upstart, despite the fact that I'm a duchess, and have been these last ten years."

"They might not be quite so judgmental if you behaved differently towards them. Forgave them for their past sins, for example. Stopped flirting so outrageously with their sons and husbands."

She scowled. "This isn't at all like you. Are you out to vex me, or did I miss when you were cornered by Lady Brocklebank and converted to her side? I do hope you're not going to be a bore. I don't like you when you come over holier than thou. Do you want me to class you with the rest of them, or do you want to remain my friend?"

He sighed. "I want to remain your friend, darling Bella. You know I do. I couldn't live without you as my friend."

"Well then, stop proselytizing and tell me the funniest thing you saw tonight. Make me laugh. I feel I need to after this."

He rubbed his temples. "That has to have been the old Earl of Manville with his new young wife. Fat as a hog with features a hog would be proud of, and seventy-eight if he's a day. Him, not her. He's married the youngest daughter of old Clyde, straight out of the schoolroom. I hear Clyde was much in need of the readies, so he virtually sold his daughter to the highest bidder. Didn't you see her? That petite little blonde with the belly she couldn't hide. Looks like a miracle has happened, and Manville will finally get himself an heir. He'll probably be dead before it's out of petticoats though. He's already looking exhausted by the exertions incurred in getting the girl in foal."

Isabella frowned. "That's not at all funny." In truth, it reminded her all too sharply of how she had been bartered by her own father for money. And her father had lived only a year after her marriage to bask in the glory of having a duchess for a daughter. Serve him right. Her mother, God rest her soul, would never have allowed him to do it. But titles were something that had long fascinated Josiah Hope, so when the arrival of a handsome young duke in dire financial straits had presented itself, he'd been quick to take advantage. Isabella felt nothing but pity for Lord Clyde's youngest daughter. She'd seen the Earl of Manville on many occasions, and he made Lord Amersham look positively attractive.

"If you can't entertain me properly," she snapped, slipping her foot back into her slipper, "then don't speak at all. I am quite fatigued and intend to close my eyes."

Wyndham, well used to her putdowns, did as he was told.

CHAPTER THREE

ONE OF THE horses Richard had bought for himself and Baxter in Canterbury, for an eye wateringly exorbitant sum even for a soon-to-be duke, threw a shoe on the third day of their journey to Hampshire. The road they'd been following being little more than a potholed, stony track, he was forced to detour into the nearest village in search of a farrier's shop. With evening falling, and no doubt his dinner awaiting him at home, the man was just packing up and not at all happy to be asked to put a set of shoes on the beast of someone he'd never set eyes on before. Begrudgingly, and for a princely sum, he offered to do the two front shoes only, as it was a front shoe that had been lost and the other one looked not only worn thin but had also begun to make that clattery sound that is a precursor to true looseness.

Richard had to be satisfied with that and cross his fingers that the back shoes would not decide to part company with the sorry horse's hooves before he reached his destination.

So it was already quite late when the farrier took the coins he'd demanded and stowed them away in the pocket of his trews, and Richard and Baxter could mount up and continue on their way again. They had a long distance left to cover, on already tired horses, and Richard was determined to make this their last day in the saddle. As riflemen, they weren't accustomed to riding everywhere, and Baxter, not a great horseman and ever one to give voice to his woes, was already complaining of having a sore behind and being made permanently bandy-legged.

As a consequence of this determination, harnessed to the increasingly slow gait of the horses and the worry their footwear might give up the ghost, Richard and his trusty manservant didn't arrive at the gates of Stourbridge Park until well after midnight.

However, it was early September, and the night was balmy with just a light breeze stirring the trees beside the road as they approached the wrought iron gates into the Park. These were set between twin, sandstone gatehouses, the occupiers of which would perforce be sound asleep at this time of night. Richard leaned over in the saddle and slid back the well-oiled latch, pulling one side of the gates open wide enough to allow him to nudge his horse through the gap, and Baxter, less accustomed to the skill of mounted gate opening, followed.

Having been brought up in the country, Richard knew better than to leave the gates open, and took care to slide the latch back into place with as little noise as possible. No need to waken the family living in the gatehouse. A high wall surrounded the wide acres of the Home Park they were entering for most of the perimeter, with the intention of keeping in the large herd of red deer. It wouldn't do at all to go letting them out onto the farmland where they could wreak untold damage on the crops. His first act as duke must not be to antagonize his tenants.

He was pleased to observe that the driveway was in far better condition than the public highway had been as Baxter brought his horse up beside him once more. A childhood spent playing in the Park ensured that he knew it would take some time to traverse the long drive up to where Stourbridge Castle sat, like a particularly fat spider at the center of its web. As a boy he'd always had to walk it, and now, with his horse so tired, he might as well do the same and stretch his aching legs. Three days of unaccustomed riding had produced a similar effect on him as it had on Baxter. Walking would give them both some much needed relief.

"Not much longer now," he said to his unfortunate servant, who'd been trying to adjust his position on his horse for some time now, to no effect. Neither of the saddles they'd purchased with their mounts had proved to be even a little comfortable. "We could probably get off and walk these unfortunate animals the last bit."

Baxter was off his horse in a trice. "About bloody time too. I'll not be able to sit down for a week after this. Bloody horses. Now I know why I joined the Rifle Brigade."

Richard, too, slid down from the saddle and hooked the reins over his horse's head. Did it give as hearty a sigh of relief as Baxter had? It wasn't such a bad horse, really, just that it hadn't been well looked after prior to sale, nor well-schooled. A bit of work might turn it into a tolerable hack. Enough for him, at any rate. He harbored no pretensions about his horse-riding skills.

However, he'd learned their care from a master horseman and had taken a look at both horses' teeth before handing over his money. Both were probably only eight or nine years of age and probably ex-coach horses. Young enough to be changed. He'd also run his hands down their legs and found them unblemished, which was unusual. He probably wouldn't have bought either of them, though, had not the thought of taking the stagecoach firstly into London, then out again along the Great West Road been so repugnant. That would have included not just traveling with strangers he might not have liked, but also several nights in busy, noisy inns between what would probably have been damp sheets. Riding home had seemed as if it would be both quicker and a more pleasant experience.

If it hadn't been for the lost shoe.

The woodland they were walking through began to thin, and the sweeping curves of the open parkland he remembered came into view, bathed in gentle moonlight, and here and there dotted with the stately cedars his great-grandfather had caused to be planted over a century ago. There was no doubting the magnificence of the place, even in the dark. And now, unexpectedly, it was all his.

"Blimey, Major," Baxter muttered from close by his side,

forgetting yet again that Richard was no longer a major but a *Your Grace*. "Bit posh this place, isn't it? And you was a boy here and never thought to tell me? I'd've had more standing amongst the other soldier-servants if I could've boasted about where my officer hailed from." But he didn't sound at all resentful.

Richard chuckled. "It wasn't a part of my life I wanted to remember, old friend. I thought I'd left it all behind and would never have to see it again. But the winds of fate have blown me back to it, if a little against my will." He smiled. "But at least my tormentor won't be here. I suppose I owe him thanks for having died and left it to me."

Baxter snorted. "No thanks owed to that bastard, from what you've told me, Major. I wouldn't be feeling in no way grateful, if I was you. Best thing he could've done was turning up his toes."

Richard shrugged. He still couldn't quite believe it. Who would have thought Marcus, who as far as he knew had always been strong and healthy, would die before he even turned forty? And without an heir. He frowned. But with a wife. Perhaps they hadn't been married long. It was always possible she was actually with child even now, and that child, if it were a boy, might dislodge him in the blink of an eye from what he'd grudgingly begin to acknowledge might be his inheritance.

His inheritance. Not for a single moment in his childhood, nor since, had he ever considered what it might be like if fate carried off Marcus. More than a few times he'd wished a sticky end on his cousin, although his thoughts had gone no further than considering the relief of being free of his incessant bullying. The bullying that had sent him to his grandmother to beg her to intercede with his uncle, the duke, and persuade him to purchase his unwanted nuisance of a nephew a commission. Which had been the means by which he'd escaped Marcus's clutches, as his uncle had been more than glad to see the back of him.

Now, he was returning from the army which he'd expected to have been his life until he was too old to fight and had perhaps become a general, in order to step into Marcus's shoes. And not only that, but he was stepping into something that promised to have the makings of a scandal. Because, as Lieutenant General Wellesley had said, his cousin's wife was suspected of not being blameless in the death of her husband. And it was up to him to exonerate her.

How much of this was true, or just plain speculation on the part of gossips, Richard had no idea, but he intended to find out. But one thing he could be sure of was that there must be a reason behind the rumor. Marcus could not have died peacefully in his bed.

He was also more than curious about the sort of woman who had attached herself in marriage to a man like Marcus. She must have known what she would be getting, so she had to be similar to him, surely. And even if she were quite innocent of the gossip surrounding her, she would have to be paid off in some way. There was no way he wanted his hated cousin's cast-off wife brooding over Stourbridge Castle. Especially not if he were to do as he'd been commanded—find a wife and get himself an heir. The presence of the previous châtelaine was a big *no* to that. There was going to be a lot for him to sort out even before he could think of finding that blasted theoretical wife.

The looming bulk of the castle came into view on the slight rise above the lake. Richard allowed his horse to halt for a rest, as he stared across the shadowy parkland at his new home. His old home, in fact, if you could ever have called it that.

"Bloody hell," Baxter said, exhaling in a low whistle. "It's even bigger than I thought it would be."

Despite its name, it was not a true castle but rather an immense, square edifice with towers in all four corners and, at its center, a courtyard enclosed on all four sides by the house. To one side, a lane led down through a double row of cottages and a few larger houses where the staff who didn't live in and the estate workers lived, but these were invisible from where Richard was standing. The moonlight illuminated the snaking, sandy-colored drive as it approached the sweeping front courtyard. A place he'd been forbidden to play as a child, as he was considered nothing but a nuisance. Now he could do whatever he wanted anywhere on the estate. The impulse to do some of the many things he'd been banned from doing as a child rose. He chuckled.

Baxter snorted. "Glad you like it, sir, but to me it just looks like a blooming palace. A bit too big and grand for the likes of us, if you don't mind me saying so."

Richard patted his horse's warm neck. "Just what I thought when I first came here as a child of six, after my parents died. You'll get used to it, have no fear. I did." But was he telling the truth? Or was he desperate to convince himself he could fit in here as, of all things, a duke? Only time would tell.

For answer, Baxter gave another snort. "You might, but I don't think I ever will."

They set off again, only the crunch of the gravel under their feet intruding on the enveloping silence of the night, now they were away from the trees. Far off, an owl called, but, apart from that, the world appeared abandoned by all living things. This did nothing to improve the way Richard was feeling about the castle.

Who would be there to greet him at this time of night? All the servants would be abed. If his cousin's murderous wife were there, she would be asleep as well. He'd have to waken someone to let him in. The grooms had always slept in rooms above the stables, so they would be easiest to raise. He'd head around the back to the stableyard and try knocking them up. He was the new duke, after all, so they couldn't complain. But nevertheless, he didn't feel that confident. He couldn't shake off the feeling of being the same six-year-old boy arriving there for the first time, after the death of his parents.

Duke. How silly that sounded when he said it to himself. No, he was plain Major Carstairs. He could never think of himself as a duke. Let Baxter still keep calling him *major*—that would suit him well.

The moon slipped behind a cloud, plunging the landscape into deeper shadow, as he neared the back of the house. All was silent. Not a light showed in any of the windows. The house was asleep.

The stable courtyard was built as a large square with wide gates at one side, under an arch with a clock tower he knew all too well on the top. A clock tower he'd climbed to as a child in order to change the time it read, for a dare. Luckily, the gates were unlocked, so he opened one side and led his horse through, Baxter following, muttering to himself under his breath. The horses' still-shod feet clattered on the cobbles, so different from the crunching gravel of the drive. Baxter closed the gate again, and they emerged into the stableyard to the welcoming whinnies of more than a few horses in the long, enclosed stable blocks to either side.

The double doors of the block on the right stood open, so they led the horses across the yard and in through them. Both blocks were of similar construction, with a wide corridor along the front and doors to outside at either end. Inside, a row of large looseboxes housed the inhabitants. Unfortunately, out of the moonlight it was impossible to tell which were occupied.

Help was at hand.

"Who goes there?" a gruff voice called from out in the yard. Did it sound familiar?

Leaving Baxter, Richard looped his horse's reins through a tethering ring and stepped back out into the light. "Your master." Where was the fellow?

For a moment, whoever had challenged him stayed silent, probably digesting this news. Then he found his voice again. "My master is dead."

Richard peered into the shadows, trying to make out who was speaking. "Your old master might be dead, indeed, but I am your new master. Who are you? Show yourself."

A man in a long nightgown that gave him an alarming spectral appearance emerged from a shadowy corner, a musket gripped in his hands. His bald head, fringed by a straggle of thin gray hair, shone in the moonlight. "Master Diccon?" His voice quavered as though he couldn't quite believe his eyes.

"Amos?" Richard's own voice also shook. "Amos Rowan? Is it you?"

The old man, heedless of his state of extreme undress, lowered the musket and hurried forward, his face wreathed in the widest smile Richard had seen in many a long year, if a bit lacking in teeth. "It is indeed your old Amos," he stammered, as though he couldn't get the words out for grinning with delight. "And it's you, it is, my Master Diccon, come home to us at last." Tears glistened in the old man's rheumy eyes, catching the pale moonlight.

They might have been a returning duke and humble groom, but when Richard had been a friendless child and had resorted to the stableyard to escape Marcus's unwanted and vicious attentions, Amos had taken him under his wing. On an impulse, Richard enfolded the old man in his arms, disturbed by how thin and frail he felt. In his memory, Amos had always been a giant of protective strength, yet now he seemed small and shrunken, and not just by age. The old man hugged him back.

"You've come back to us," he managed, as soon as Richard released him. "I knew you would one day, even when His Grace said as you were probably already killed in battle and that we'd just not been notified. I knew you'd come back to us one day."

"I am indeed back, and must apologize for disturbing you in the middle of the night," Richard said. Perhaps it would be best not to discuss the reason for his return. Not yet, anyway. The middle of the night was not the time, and the stableyard was not the place. And anyway, Amos would only know the gossip. Richard wanted the facts before he heard the tittle-tattle of the servants' hall. "And I've brought my good soldier servant and a couple of horses we purchased for our journey. It's black as Satan's pit in the stable block, and we can't see what we're doing. Could you help us, do you think?"

Amos nodded with enthusiasm. "I can that, Master—I mean, Your Grace. Just let me go and stow away my musket and find some breeches and boots. And you didn't disturb me. I don't sleep so well no more on account of my old bones, and I hadn't been abed long when I heared the sound of your horses on the cobbles. Me and the grooms, we've not long dealt with Her Grace's carriage."

So Marcus's mysterious widow was in residence here at the moment and had been out in the carriage. Was that going to be a problem?

The old man nodded his head at the far range of stables. "I won't be more than a minute, Your Grace. And I'll tell Mrs. Rowan to go back to sleep because you're not a horse thief come trying your hand at Sultan."

"Sultan?"

"His Grace's new horse. Your Grace. The one what he won for that wager he made."

He must have seen the confusion on Richard's face. "I've a lot to tell you if you'll let me get me breeches."

Three minutes later, longer than Amos had promised probably due to him being interrogated by his wife, he was back with a lantern, his nightshirt tucked lumpily into his breeches and a pair of stout work boots on his feet. Together, he and Richard, after a suspicious Baxter had been introduced, found a couple of empty looseboxes for their tired horses, unsaddled them, and gave them both a good measure of corn and a wad of hay to eat. Amos insisted on carrying Richard's saddle and bridle along to the tackroom while Richard carried the lantern. Baxter, with a definite bowing to his legs as though in pain, trailed behind.

From the number of occupied loose boxes, the rows of saddles and the pegs of harness, it seemed Marcus had kept a large stable. Larger than his father ever had. Interesting. Presumably the cattle were all now Richard's to do with as he pleased. Including the horse from the wager, whatever that had been for— Sultan. Not that Richard had ever been particularly interested in horses, which had been one of the reasons he'd opted for an infantry regiment as a fifteen-year-old.

"Now," Amos said. "What about you, Your Grace? The house is all locked up at this time o' night, but I think I could rouse them for you."

Richard shook his head. "I don't want them disturbed. In truth, I'm sorry I got you out of bed, old friend. You must still have the ears of a hawk. Baxter and I could quite happily have settled down for the night in the hayloft or an empty stable. We're used to far worse beds than that on campaign." He smiled. "However, if you could provide real beds for the night, we'd be more than content, and I can make my official arrival in the morning. I can tell you, both of us are so tired we could happily sleep on the bare floor."

"The bare floor? For our new duke?" Amos nearly choked. "I've a couple of spare beds my sons used to sleep in before they married and went off to find employment elsewhere. But they ain't good enough for Your Grace, not now you're a duke."

"Your son Joseph, you mean?" They'd often played together as boys. "I'd love to see him again, and be honored to sleep in his bed for the night."

Amos shook his head, clearly troubled by this turn up for the books. "But you're the *duke* now, Your Grace, so I don't think as it'd be wise to be taking up some of your old friendships. Not that my Joe wouldn't be honored to shake your hand. But things've changed now, and we'll all have to remember it."

Richard gave a wry smile. Amos had missed the irony of his statement when given to the man he'd just invited to sleep in his spare bed, the spare bed of one of the stable staff. Up until this moment, the full import of Marcus's death and his own inheritance of the title and property had not quite sunk in. He'd thought he'd be returning to the home of his childhood, but he wouldn't be. Not really. Because his childhood as the indigent orphaned relation had been spent running wild with the children of the servants and tenants. And now he would be the man in charge. Things were not going to be easy to adjust to.

CHAPTER FOUR

D ESPITE HAVING ARRIVED home from the Bembridge House ball long after midnight, Isabella had no intention of allowing her mere few hours of sleep to stand in the way of keeping to her normal morning routine. And that routine had included, ever since the early days of her marriage to Marcus, an early morning gallop around the park. Away from the ties of being a duchess and, when he had been in residence, the odious company of her husband, these rides had given her room to breathe and a fleeting sense of otherwise unattainable freedom. Since his death, she'd continued with the rides. She refused to acknowledge that even after all these weeks, his presence continued to haunt the house as though his unquiet, vengeful spirit refused to leave.

She'd only discovered the joys of horses after her marriage, when Old Amos, the head groom, had very kindly taken her under his wing and taught her to ride on Sapphire, Marcus's late grandmother's old gray mare, who had been brought out of retirement especially. Sapphire had been a gentle introduction to riding, but Isabella had not taken long to realize that gentle was not what she required of a horse. Sweet Sapphire was returned to her retirement for her declining years, and Marcus, who at that time had been feeling more generous than was his wont, had bought her a much more challenging mount. In a moment of unexpected camaraderie, which could have been a veiled insult, of course, he'd also compared her to her horse. It was true they shared the same hair coloring, but Isabella's husband had probably meant they also shared their temperamental personalities.

As usual, her maid, the redoubtable Hawkins, arrived in good time to help dress her mistress in her customary deep-green riding habit, bringing with her a cup of hot chocolate to fortify her until she might return for breakfast. Before long, Isabella was able to give herself a once over in her cheval mirror. Having found her image as pleasing as she always did, especially as perforce her riding habit wasn't that dreadful dreary black, she descended the grand staircase to the wide entrance hall of the castle.

At this time of the morning dear Wyndham, who never liked to rise early, would still be snoring in his bed, so the only other people at large were the servants, all scuttling to keep out of her way while going about their morning duties. Isabella, her gown swishing as she walked, crossed the hallway, and took the corridor that would lead her to the stableyard. She was not just a lover of riding. She was also a lover of horses. And that meant she liked to prepare her own horse herself, rather than have someone else do it. She held that if you just turned up to a ready-groomed and saddled horse, you were missing out on cementing that bond of rider and horse. Why should the grooms be the only ones to experience that bond? So she prepared her own horse whenever she could. And this morning she intended to ride Sultan, the showy dun Arabian Marcus had won at cards a matter of weeks before he died, and which she now considered hers.

Jem Whitaker, one of the younger grooms, was busy sweeping the yard as she emerged. He kept his head down, but she knew he was watching her. All men watched her, even those in the lowliest of positions. How could they not? She was beautiful, and she knew it, which only served to enhance her beauty as she moved with the inborn confidence of one aware of her own charms. Jem watched her surreptitiously every time she ventured into the stableyard. Which was every morning while she was resident at the castle.

He was a good-looking lad with a mop of dark curly hair and bulging biceps. A much more presentable young man than their other young groom, the recently arrived Jack Watkins, who always had his mouth open as though he couldn't breathe through his nose, a part of him which always had a drip on the end of it.

Flashing an appreciative smile at Jem, just because he was handsome and she could, Isabella strode across the sparkling cobbles to the left-hand run of stables, whose outer door stood open in welcome. This was where the riding horses were kept, plus those who didn't, in fact, do much work at all, unless the grooms took them out for exercise. The carriage horses occupied the right-hand run of stables, and, to either side of the archway, large doors indicated where Marcus's wide array of carriages were kept. Jem, like all the other stable staff, had accommodation in the lofts above the loose boxes.

After the bright sunshine of the early morning, the interior of the stable block was gloomy and it took a moment or two before Isabella's eyes grew accustomed. Sultan occupied the loosebox right beside the tackroom, which meant she had to walk down the tiled corridor past all the other stables. Thinking she'd be riding her own horse, Amos would have left her customary wooden box of grooming tools outside the mare's door, so she needed to collect them.

However, before she reached Sultan's loosebox, her attention was caught by a strange horse in the third box along, and beyond that, a second one. With a committed horsewoman's obsessive nature, Isabella knew every horse on the estate, be it the garden pony, the farm workhorses, or those that drew her carriages. And this horse was not one of them. Neither was its companion.

She stopped outside the first stable and ran her experienced eye over its occupant. The horse, a bony bay, was engaged in snatching hay from the iron hayrack in the corner of the box with a gusto that suggested it had been starved most of its life. Bigger than Sultan, and a gelding as well, he had the look of an animal that had recently fallen on hard times. She couldn't precisely count his ribs, but she could see them clearly beneath his rough coat, and his hips stood out from his not at all rounded quarters with distinct lines of poverty to either side of his tail. A tail that had been docked.

Isabella abhorred the practice of docking, and had long since decreed that none of the horses at Stourbridge should have that mutilation carried out. The carriage horses could have their tails tied up out of the way for safety, she argued, and that would be every bit as effective as cutting their tails right off part way down the bone in such a barbaric fashion. And they would still have something left to swish to keep away the summer flies.

The horse turned its head and looked at her out of wide, intelligent eyes. Yes, some good food and beneficial exercise to build up some muscle and this poor creature might blossom. "Hello," she said, keeping her voice soft and low. "And who might you be?"

"Richard," said a voice that surely couldn't emanate from the horse. "But you may call me Diccon."

Isabella couldn't help herself. She jumped back from the stable door as the man who must have been sitting in the corner of the stable, hidden by the wall, got to his feet.

She stared.

He was tall. Taller than Marcus had been, but his superficial likeness to her late and unlamented husband was striking enough to render her breathless, for a moment, with fear. Then common sense took over. This man wasn't Marcus, but, by the look of him, he might be some by-blow of Marcus's late father, a man whom she'd never met. It wasn't unheard of for illegitimate sons to be employed on the estates of their fathers.

The fact that he was wearing a not-all-that clean shirt, open at the neck to show the curling dark hairs on his chest, and had his sleeves rolled up above the elbow, inclined her to suspect he had arrived seeking work, at the same time as setting her heart a-fluttering. Which, she had to admit, was an odd reaction.

She took a better look at him. The man had a look of whipcord strength about him that Marcus had never had, as though in a moment he might transform himself into a beast of prey. And this was not an unattractive trait. Handsome, it was true, but a rough diamond of a man. What a shame he wouldn't be gracing any of the ballrooms she frequented, as it would have been fun to have flirted with him. Just a bit.

Yet what was his horse, for it must be his, doing snugly tucked up in one of her stables? Had this man also spent the night there? He did appear to have bits of straw sticking to him. A few even decorated his attractively tousled hair. Hair it might have been pleasurable to run one's hands through. Her heart gave another little flutter. And he didn't appear to have shaved in several days, for his firm jaw was covered in a generous growth of dark beard which gave him a rather swashbuckling appearance. Which in turn further enhanced his allure.

No. She must control her heart and not think of any man like this, and definitely not someone who had come seeking a position in the stables or the garden and looked unnervingly like Marcus. It was fun to toss a careless smile at a handsome servant from time to time, but that was all she could ever do, and if anyone found out she had done it, that would only add grist to the mill of disapproval. Although the idea of seeing this man working in either location, with his muscles rippling beneath his tanned skin, kept pushing its unwelcome way back into her mind.

He smiled at her. Yes, he had Marcus's dark eyes, although something in this man's gaze felt very different to her late husband's. However, she was not about to be won over by the smile of a potential groom, however handsome he was. No, she was not. Absolutely not. Never.

She drew herself up as tall as she could, which wasn't particularly high, even in her heeled riding boots. "What are you doing here?"

He made no move to come out of the loose box. "I was communing with this sad example of a horse." He had an unusually refined, deep voice that yet again gave her heart a little unwelcome flutter.

She frowned, her natural instinct to defend anything remotely equine leaping to the fore. "I believe he is only sad due to his previous mistreatment, which I presume I can lay at your door. It is a bad horseman who blames his horse for not being strong enough when he has clearly not been fed adequately."

The man, Diccon, shook his head. "Happily, you cannot lay the blame for his condition on me. I only bought him and his companion a few short days ago, and believe me, they were the best of the bunch." He patted the horse's sunken quarters. "Although once he's been stabled here for a while, I trust he'll begin to look as sleek and well-fed as the rest of the residents."

She bristled. How dare he assume he would find not just employment here but also stabling for his horse. Although of the two, she would rather keep the horse than a man so rude and presumptuous. "What makes you think either of you will be staying?"

He grinned, showing even, white teeth, those dark eyes twinkling in a most beguiling fashion that was playing havoc with her disobedient heart. "I think you will find I'm going to be hard to get rid of."

Heavens. He had the appearance of a man who was finding their conversation both funny and pleasurable. In fact, he was looking her up and down, at least the part he could see of her, as if he were weighing her up and finding her somewhat wanting.

The cheek of it. She glared at him. "I can assure you, that whatever you were led to believe, I will not take into my employ a man with as much effrontery as you have just displayed. Whoever you are, you had best take your horse and be on your way." She glanced at the second horse, which was also eating her hay. "And your other horse, although why you have two, I have no idea." She paused. "And this is not a household that employs the by-blows of any past duke. So you may take yourself off immediately."

He laughed. He possessed a deep, full-throated laugh that suited his rough appearance, and he gave in to it with abandon. The horse looked back at him, ears pricked, still chomping on the hay that belonged to the Stourbridge estate. To her, in fact, until the inheritance could be established, which could take a long time as there had so far been no sign of any heir appearing. A far as she knew, there was only the one who had died abroad, with the remote possibility he had been father to a son who might inherit. But unlikely.

She stamped her foot, something she'd not done since her last altercation with Marcus. The fatal altercation. "Stop laughing this instant and take yourself off, or I'll call the grooms to throw you out." She eyed his size. "And the footmen."

He finally got his laughter under control. "I think you mistake me, madam. I am here to stay, and there's nothing you can do about it. Although I do believe I'm going to find it interesting living with you."

"Living with me?" Her voice rose in indignation. "Your impudence knows no bounds. I will not be spoken to like this." And she turned towards the doors. Jem must still be out there. He could fetch Amos and the other two grooms and they could overpower this madman.

The man calling himself Diccon was through the stable door in a flash, his hand on her arm pulling her back.

Furious, she rounded on him and before she could stop herself, had slapped him across the face. Hard. "Unhand me this instant."

He didn't let go. Instead, his dark brows met in a heavy frown. "Would you do to me what you did to Marcus, then?" His teeth bared. "Yes. I've heard all the rumors. I know the talk is that you wanted him dead and your wish came true."

She stopped struggling as there was clearly no point, and it seemed to be what he wanted. And somehow she didn't think this strange man, whom she could now see wore expensive, but mud-spattered top boots and finely cut breeches, was about to assault her person.

He released her arm.

She resisted the temptation to rub it. No need to let him see he'd hurt her. "How dare you insinuate such a thing." But she wasn't quite so confident now. Who was this man, whom she'd at first taken for a would-be groom but who now appeared to be wearing at least some of the apparel of a gentleman? Not the sort of gentleman who frequented the parties and balls she liked, but a gentleman, nevertheless. And of course, his voice implied that as well. Not a hint of a Berkshire accent about it.

He was staring down at her from his vastly superior height. He must be nearly a foot taller than she was. "So, you didn't do it? You had no hand in the death of your husband?" His voice was challenging, his eyes boring into her as if to extract the truth from her very core.

She met his gaze, furious that she was being asked to justify herself to a stranger. "Of course I had nothing to do with my husband's death." She paused, a nub of worry that she couldn't shake off forming. "But if I did, what is it to you?"

It was at that moment that the second stranger appeared, and he was even rougher than this Diccon. A short but sturdy individual, also with several days' growth of beard, his grizzled, on his chin, he wore what appeared to be some sort of green army uniform, the jacket buttons undone and a red neckerchief about his throat. Due to the gloom of the stables and the dazzling sunlight, he must not have spotted Isabella, for he spoke only to Diccon. "Mrs. Rowan says as she's got breakfast ready and to come in and get it, Major." And then his eyes narrowed as they took in Isabella's presence. "Begging your pardon, Miss. I didn't know as the Major had company." His small brown eyes ran over her attire before his gaze returned to the man who must be his master, the major, brows asking a question.

For a moment his master remained silent, before giving his

servant a brief nod. "Thank you, Baxter. The grooms have taken care of our horses for us. You may go and take your breakfast. I think I will be taking mine in the castle."

The lure of that breakfast must have been great, because the man Baxter gave a shrug and departed, however, not without glancing back over his shoulder at Isabella as he went, curiosity in his stare.

Isabella bristled all over. In the castle? Who did this upstart think he was? She fixed him with her best hard stare, waiting for him to tell her more.

It worked. He heaved in a breath as though resigning himself to having to say something.

"I will tell you what it is to me, as you have so politely asked." His voice was heavy with sarcasm. "If you did have a hand in your husband's death, then I suppose I should be thanking you. For without his demise I would not be here. I would, instead, be bivouacking in Portugal somewhere, trying to keep out of the scorching sun. With my men. Instead, I'm here, transformed by the hand of fate, which many suspect might equate with your hand, into a duke."

Her eyes widened and her breath caught in her throat. "A duke?" Her voice came out more than a little hoarse. "*You* are the lost heir? The one whom Marcus told me had probably died? The one people have been looking for?"

Diccon laughed. "I know he hated me, but he could at least have got his facts right. If he told you I was dead, it was only his wishful thinking. And, as you can see, I am not dead at all, but very much alive." He smiled again, a little mirthlessly. "And you, I take it, must be his widow." This time his gaze ran from her head down to her toes. "I see you are much as has been described to me."

Why did she get the feeling this wasn't meant as a compliment, despite the admiration in his eyes? She gave him a harder look. So that was why he looked so much like Marcus. They were cousins. Hadn't Dora told her this Diccon had been brought up here at Stourbridge after his parents died? This must be like coming home to him. Although with Marcus only his own age, he must never have expected to inherit the title. And it seemed as though he'd been soldiering on the Continent until quite recently. Which went a long way to explaining the appearance of his servant.

A horrible thought swept over her. Now he was home to claim his title and his inheritance, he would be wanting to install a wife of his own here at Stourbridge. He might well already have one, somewhere. Some woman who would turn her elegant nose up at the incumbent duchess much as the society ladies Isabella despised had and still did. She might, horror of horrors, be some Portuguese or Spanish woman he'd met in Europe who barely spoke any English. She only had the vaguest idea of the war going on there, but as he had mentioned Portugal, this was a reasonable suspicion. If he had, this woman would be the duchess, and she, Isabella, would be nothing again. Less than nothing, for Marcus had sewn up her father's money along with his, and none of it was coming to her. He'd taken malicious pleasure in telling her that, not long after Papa had died.

She glanced sideways along the corridor at where her own horse was looking over her stable door. Her beloved horse would belong to this unknown woman too, and Sultan, whom she'd planned to ride this morning, would be this interloper's to do with as he wished.

Resolution washed over her. Perhaps she'd better begin by being nice to him. She turned back to the new duke. "Well, Cousin, I had planned to take my customary ride this morning around the park. However, now that you have finally deigned to identify yourself, I feel I should welcome you to the castle and forego that ride. For now. I presume you are in need of some breakfast as you have just turned down Mrs. Rowan's generous offer to eat with her and your servant." She had a struggle to keep the sarcasm out of her voice.

Diccon's handsome face broke into the most friendly smile

she'd seen so far, as though he'd chosen to ignore the implication that he had been ready to eat with his servants. He looked the sort of man who would not object to that at all. "I should like that very much, Your Grace." And he held out his arm to her. A bare arm as the sleeves were rolled up to above the elbow.

Isabella hesitated. No man in her entire life had ever offered her what amounted to a nearly naked arm to take. Disturbing dark hairs ran across his tanned forearm and the back of his hand, and she would have to touch his actual skin. Swallowing her reticence down, she slipped her hand into the crook of his arm, all too aware of the warmth radiating through the thin fabric of his shirt. She felt altogether too close to him for comfort.

He bestowed another smile on her. "Shall we go inside?"

CHAPTER FIVE

RICHARD ALLOWED THE intriguing young woman who had been his cousin's duchess to lead him across the stableyard to the back door he'd been accustomed to using as a child. Clearly, she was as at ease entering the stableyard this way as he had been, which was a little surprising for a duchess. There was more to her, it seemed, than he'd expected, and possibly some of it might be rather interesting.

He had to release her arm to open the door, and, without a glance at him, she swept through it with an air of supreme entitlement, the train of her bottle-green riding habit trailing on the uneven paving slabs. She certainly comported herself as though born to the role.

The door gave, as he had known it would, onto a long, gloomy passageway, unchanged since the last time he'd seen it, that led into the main part of the house by way of the servants' hall and the kitchens. Now, why did a duchess appear so much at home in this part of the house, and why would she use it to go to and from the stables? His grandmother had in all probability never entered the stableyard in her entire life. Surely this pampered young lady could have commanded her horse to be brought around, ready-saddled, to the front of the house, as the rest of the family had always done? A mystery. Not that Richard had much experience of the nobility other than those he'd known as fellow army officers, and that had been a leveling experience for all concerned.

As she led him along the stone-flagged passage, he took a surreptitious sideways look at her. A petite little thing with a strong sense of her own importance. Pretty, too. Maybe even beautiful if she could wipe that petulant pout off her face and stop looking down her elegant nose at everything. It didn't sit well with smug superiority, although she'd managed to divest herself of that to a degree once she'd discovered his identity. It must be true that redheaded females, like chestnut mares, possessed fiery, difficult personalities.

She made no move to take his arm again as they progressed down the corridor, so he didn't offer it. Up until the moment Amos had mentioned her last night, he'd not even considered that his cousin's widow might be in residence at Stourbridge. Maybe he'd thought she would be at the town house in Hanover Square, doing whatever it was young ladies of quality did to entertain themselves, or maybe he just hadn't considered her at all. How long, even, had Marcus and she been married? She looked very young. Impossible to imagine the man who'd been the bane of his childhood being married to anyone. Not happily, at any rate.

And rumor had it that this young lady, beautiful as she was, had somehow been involved in Marcus's early demise. Rumor sufficient to reach as far as the Prince of Wales's office, and from there across the sea to Portugal. He needed to find out all about that straightaway. It wouldn't be such a good idea to be harboring a murderess in the house, even one who had aroused the interest of the Prince of Wales. Not conducive to a good night's sleep, that was for certain. He knew all too well, being a soldier, that one's hardest kill was the first one, and that successive kills came all the more easily.

Did that make him as bad as rumor had it she was? Might people class killing men on the battlefield the same as murdering a husband one hated? If she'd hated him. He was rather jumping to conclusions here in assuming their marriage had been a bad one just because of his own turbulent relationship with Marcus. Best not to do that. She might have loved her late husband. Or not...

They reached the front hall, where the butler was just unlocking the front door, and as this worthy turned, Richard saw to his delight that it was none other than Atkins, the butler of his boyhood. He must be well over sixty now, and his hair had gone thin and snowy white, but he still had the unmistakable upright stance of the man Richard remembered. Although perhaps not the eyesight.

He peered with narrowed eyes at the two newcomers, a puzzled frown settling on his wrinkled forehead and furrowing it still further. "Your Grace." He made a bow to the young duchess. "I'm sorry, I didn't expect to see you yet." His gaze ran over her riding habit, a garment which showed off to perfection her pale skin and auburn curls. "I trust there is nothing amiss with the horses?" He peered once again at Richard, clearly unsettled by being unable to place him.

The duchess shook her head. "They are quite well but will have to wait until later today for some exercise. I thought I had better escort this gentleman inside. You will be wanting to make his acquaintance forthwith, I suspect."

Atkins took a few steps across the wide hall, bringing himself close enough, probably, to have a better look at Richard. His mouth fell open, his eyes brimming with shock, before realization appeared to dawn. "M-master Diccon?" His voice held incredulity. Unsurprising if he'd been told the same faradiddle as Isabella and Amos.

Which might explain why everyone was so taken aback to see him. He'd only been off in the army in Europe, not on the far side of the world. Communications did exist. Although if Marcus had been going round telling everyone he was dead, he must have wanted to believe it himself, so perhaps no one had ever thought to check. He'd never quite understood his cousin's hatred for him. After all, Marcus had always been the elder by three years, the taller, the stronger, and the one destined to inherit the dukedom. Back then, Richard had been nothing but the poor relation with nothing to inherit, and yet Marcus had gone out of his way to make his life a misery. Right from the moment they'd first met.

"I have indeed returned," he said to Atkins, with a wide smile, for want of any other answer. He must put on a cheerful face about this with the servants. Best not to give them any intimation of how daunted he was feeling about taking on his inheritance.

Atkins's tired, serious old face suddenly dissolved into a wide smile. "Master Diccon come back to us after all these years. Well I never. I didn't think I'd live to see the day."

Richard held out his hand. "That makes two of us, Atkins. I didn't think I'd ever be returning, and certainly not like this."

Atkins took the offered hand. His was bony and thin, much like that of Old Amos, the skin dry and wrinkled. Perhaps he was nearer to seventy than sixty. Richard swallowed an unaccustomed lump in his throat. Everyone he'd known had grown old in his absence. A sobering thought. As a boy Richard had never pondered the ages of the servants; he and Dora had dismissed them all as old, Atkins in particular. Now, returning as an adult, Richard couldn't help but recognize how the years had not been kind to the old butler, who seemed suddenly ancient and shrunken. Closer inspection revealed how his dark suit hung on his bony frame.

They shook.

After a moment, Atkins remembered his position and gently drew his hand back. He made a deep bow. "Please allow me to welcome you home, Your Grace. It's a true honor to be able to welcome you once again." The fact that his new master was attired in muddy boots, had his shirt sleeves rolled up above his elbows and bits of straw adhering here and there to his person didn't seem to have put him off at all. Perhaps he remembered the boy Richard had been.

Richard smiled again, this time with genuine pleasure. How

good it was to have been presented with two such familiar faces on his return, as well as the decidedly unwelcoming, although very pretty, one of the young duchess. What was her actual name? He couldn't really call her just *Duchess* or *Your Grace*, as they were on level footing, and, after all, closely related by marriage now. He'd have to ask her. But not just now. What he wanted now was some breakfast.

Used to rising early in the army, he'd been up at the same time as Old Amos and his wife, but they'd both had to get about their morning chores, so he and Baxter had gone to see to the horses and take a look in daylight at the property that was now his. After all, horses and dogs had to come first, especially at Stourbridge. People were only secondary.

The duchess must have been thinking along the same lines as he was, regarding food, that was. "Atkins," she said with crisp authority. "Can you please inform Cook that we shall be requiring breakfast directly. I have foregone my morning ride and shall be breakfasting with the… duke."

Was that a slight hesitation before she used his title? If she'd been used to calling her husband by that title, then she might find it difficult to have to apply it to another. Unless, of course, those rumors were true and she was glad to see the back of him. Might she also nurture a desire to see the back of his successor? There was that distinct possibility. A possibility that could be worrying.

Atkins bowed to her. "Straightaway, Your Grace. I fear it might take her a short while to prepare it, as she assumed you would be taking your usual morning exercise, but I'll tell her we are welcoming the new duke and ask her to hurry."

The duchess nodded, a slight frown on her brow. "Very well. A quarter of an hour, if she can manage it. The duke and I will wait in the morning room."

As Atkins hurried away, she turned back to Richard, her nose wrinkling a little at his apparel. "Unless you would care to change before you eat?" Even with a look of distaste on her face, she had to be the most beautiful young lady he'd ever seen. Shame about her haughtiness, and the suspicions surrounding her. Not to mention the Prince of Wales's obvious interest in her.

Her haughtiness could be dealt with, though. Richard began by grinning at her obvious discomfiture. That he was making her feel awkward pleased him. For some reason he had rapidly become convinced on meeting her that she was a woman who deserved to be made to feel uncomfortable in order to soften her. There was too much of the air of the self-satisfied about her, as with many devastatingly beautiful women. She was probably far too used to getting her own way with men because of her looks, although that might well not have worked with Marcus.

It wasn't going to work with him if he could help it. Although he had to admit that of all the women who'd ever crossed his path, she was the only one he'd ever felt a stirring for. Which might be because she was the only one he couldn't have.

He gave himself a mental shake. Beautiful she might be, but if she had taken a hand in the demise of her husband, her demeanor didn't suggest any fear that she would be caught for it. He wiped his hands on the legs of his breeches. "I've eaten in worse states than this before. I shall manage." He let his gaze run over her riding attire. "Unless, of course, you wish to change out of your *green* habit?" If she had any respect for tradition and custom, her gown should be black, not green. Black for a year after a husband's death. Green was not considered acceptable by society. At least, he wanted her to think he was of that opinion. He himself had no intention whatsoever of sporting the required black armband of mourning, as that would be too hypocritical.

"Not at all," she said, nothing in her tone betraying annoyance at his inference. "I have eaten many times whilst wearing my riding habit. Come. Let us repair to the morning room." For a moment, she let her eyes linger on his rolled-up sleeves. Had she never seen a man's forearms before? He had to smother a chuckle.

The morning room had always been the domain of Richard's grandmother, the Dowager Duchess of Stourbridge, and for a short while of her daughter-in-law, Marcus's mother, until she'd faded away after the birth of Richard's youngest cousin, Grace.

It had not changed at all in the nineteen years Richard had been away.

Silk Turkish rugs adorned the polished oak floor and a sparkling chandelier hung from the stuccoed ceiling. Above the marble fireplace hung the portrait of some long-gone generation of Carstairs children clustered around a shaggy terrier under the benevolent gaze of their lace-capped mother. And on other walls hung portraits that might or might not have been of more distant ancestors in old-fashioned apparel. The comfortable, if faded, wingback chair his grandmother had favored still had pride of place beside the empty hearth, but no one occupied it. She must have been dead now for over twelve years, and Aunt Cressida, of whom he had only the vaguest of memories, for longer still. Delicate green silk wallpaper, a little faded in places by time, covered the walls, and matching, heavy green drapes, their folds a little faded here and there by sunlight, were held back from the windows by thick gold cords. However, nothing could remove the melancholy chill from the room, as though ghosts lurked in every corner, whispering their secrets together. Might Marcus's now be amongst them?

The duchess took a seat beside the fireplace, settling into it with regal grace and inclining her pretty head towards the Louis XV settee beside her.

Smothering a smile, Richard did as she'd indicated was her pleasure and sat down, leaning back, stretching his long legs out, and crossing his ankles. For some reason he wasn't sure of, it seemed imperative that he should make this pretty, possible murderess realize that this was his property, not hers, and he was here to not just visit but to take over. She must understand that she was no longer in charge here, and that the house was not hers to command. And neither was he.

The duchess folded her hands in her lap and fixed him with a direct stare. A curious stare. She clearly had questions she wished to ask, just as he did. Well, he would start.

"You have the advantage of me, madam, in that you know my name already and I do not know yours."

Her expression didn't alter in the least. "Why," she said, her eyes fixed on his face with calmly confident hauteur, probably enhanced by the fact that she was dressed to the nines and he was not, "I am the Duchess of Stourbridge, of course. Who else did you think I might be?"

She was being deliberately obtuse. Straight faced at it, as well. Was there any humor lurking in her to be found and teased out? It might be fun to do that. Despite her haughty manner, the thought of fencing words with her was an attractive one. A pity she'd been married to his cousin.

Richard brushed a stray strand of his unruly hair out of his eyes. "Your given name is what I require, for I can't go on calling you madam, can I? And as you are living in what is now my house, and we are cousins by marriage, I feel we should be on Christian name terms."

She pursed her lips as though considering his words. "Perhaps you are right." She smoothed her already smooth skirt. "My name, Your Grace, is Isabella."

Richard smiled. "Thank you, Isabella. But please, call me Richard—or Diccon if you prefer, as I invited you to while we were in the stables, and meant it. I don't think I shall get used to being addressed as 'Your Grace' for quite some time, and it's such a mouthful. Christian names are much to be preferred between cousins."

A little frown furrowed her brow as though she thought him very forward, or perhaps for some other reason. "Very well. To oblige you, I will do so… Richard."

So she didn't want to use the nickname by which everyone had known him all his life. As though in doing so she feared becoming too familiar, too close, and wanted to maintain the solid barrier that lay between them. Well, let her keep her barrier up if she wanted.

He smiled. "Thank you… Isabella." The music of her name on his lips pleased him. A name only a young lady as beautiful as she should own.

Silence fell between them. Richard could think of nothing more to say to her that wouldn't come out as some sort of interrogation and be considered rude on such new acquaintance. There was much he wanted to know, especially about his cousin's death, but that would all have to come later, and small talk with a lady of her caliber seemed beyond him. He'd grown far too used to the rough campfire talk of his fellow officers, and often of his men as well. Nearly twenty years in the army had forged rough edges on him, and he knew it. Rough edges that would be difficult to rub off.

She, on the other hand, seemed itching to pose a question. Eventually it burst out of her. "Marcus told me that you were a soldier, and yet you present yourself here in the attire of a…" She paused as though searching for the right words, which must have been hard. "The attire of a country gentleman."

He could answer that. "I have resigned my commission. I might one day go back, if I'm needed, but my commanding officer's orders to me were to return to claim my inheritance. and to swiftly find myself both a bride and an heir, or he would not have me back." He gave her an apologetic smile.

Her delicate eyebrows rose. Had he shocked her with his talk of marrying quickly and getting an heir? Probably it wasn't the sort of thing you discussed in polite company. But then, was she polite company? She hadn't so far shown herself up as being of the most polite. He considered those delicate brows, still raised in an unspoken question. They were a few shades darker than her auburn hair and arched over her hazel eyes in a perfection that suggested artistry might be involved. Damn it, though, she was the prettiest thing he'd ever seen. It was going to be difficult not to fall under her spell.

Finally, she spoke, her voice just a little brittle. "I see. So you are here at Stourbridge to find yourself this bride in haste?" A little smile played about her mouth, but he couldn't trace the cause of it. "Have you never heard of the saying 'marry in haste and repent at leisure'? I feel it is an adage you should pay heed to."

Was that a hint of bitterness in her tone? Her mouth had set itself in a hard line that implied his suspicion was correct. Had she herself done what she was now warning him against? Had she not suspected Marcus's true nature when she'd agreed to marry him? Poor fool. He had to feel sorry for her if that was the case.

He bowed his head. "I shall endeavor to follow your advice."

The opening of the door saved him from further efforts at conversation. On the threshold, Atkins bowed. "Breakfast is served, Your Graces."

Good. He was starving. He'd have to find out more later, but preferably not from Isabella, Duchess of Stourbridge. He had a feeling that anything she told him should be taken with a pinch, a very sizeable pinch, of salt.

As they stepped out into the hallway, movement on the wide staircase caught Richard's eye. A woman was descending the stairs, aided by a cane that was tapping with every step she made. Not a young woman, but not an old one either. Rather, she was of indeterminate age and indeterminate appearance, having rather dull brown hair confined in a plain bun, sallow skin and a thin, shapeless body on which her gown hung as though thrown on with no thought to appearance. She came to a halt on the half landing just above them.

Richard ground to a similar halt, staring. Could it be? No, surely not. She'd have been married off by either her father or brother years ago. But this woman had the same decided limp, a limp that had been caused by a Marcus-induced accident in her early childhood, if she was indeed who he thought she was.

Their eyes met across the wide hall. Recognition, quickly followed by shock, dawned on the woman's face and her brown eyes widened, her mouth opening in a wordless gasp.

"Dora." Richard, forgetful of Isabella, was across the hallway in a few long strides, holding out his hands to her. "Tell me it's really you."

The woman's hand shot to her mouth and she almost staggered. "Diccon. It can't be. I don't believe it. Marcus told me you were dead."

Richard ran up the stairs, two at a time, and as he reached her, caught her in a tight embrace, pressing her slight body against his. "Dora. I'm back. I told you I'd come back for you, and I have."

The cane clattered onto the stairs as Dora wrapped her arms around him. "I knew you would, if I waited. I knew you would."

CHAPTER SIX

Lady Dora Carstairs extricated herself from Diccon's embrace and, swinging her arm back, slapped him hard across the face. "But did you have to leave it for nearly twenty years?" The words exploded from her lips uncontrollably. Yes, she was overjoyed to see him, but she was also wild with fury, a condition most unusual for her. "We all thought you were dead!"

The man who Diccon, her best friend, her partner in so many childhood scrapes, and her protector from Marcus's violent temper, had become put a rueful hand to his reddening cheek. "What's wrong with all you ladies today? I keep getting slapped, and I could swear I haven't done anything to deserve it. You can hardly say it's my fault that Marcus told everyone I was dead." He paused, his eyes taking on a mischievous twinkle. "And when did you learn to hit so hard?"

With fury still quivering through her, emotion, never far from the surface, finally took hold of Dora. She burst into tears and threw her arms around her Diccon again, burying her face against his shirt front. "And you smell like you've been sleeping in the stables." The words came out muffled. But really, she felt as though he might vanish away again if she were to let go of him.

A discreet cough brought her back to reality. Dora lifted her head to peer over Diccon's admirably broad shoulder. Bella was standing at the foot of the stairs and gazing up at where they stood locked together on the half-landing, an expression of astonishment on her face. That she was here, in her riding habit, the one Dora had tried to persuade her to dye black, and had not gone out riding, was a surprise in itself.

Bella set her hands on her hips. "If you two have quite finished with your emotional reunion, perhaps we can have breakfast? Cook has especially prepared it early in order to welcome our new duke to Stourbridge, and I don't want to appear ungrateful. You know how she can get in a huff."

Diccon released Dora and took her hand instead. She clung onto it. How tall he'd grown, and how very manly. So far from the boy she'd known. Her own head didn't even reach his chin, and she was two inches taller than Bella. In her head all these years he'd remained the skinny, awkward boy of fifteen who'd packed his bag one day, kissed her on either cheek, and told her he was off to join the army. To see him transformed into a man of what must be five and thirty had upended her vision of him in her head. Although his face had hardly changed. Filled out, possessed of what looked like a burgeoning beard, but still the face she'd loved since early childhood.

He bent to retrieve her cane for her, and they descended the stairs together.

Bella smiled, but it was the brittle, mirthless smile Dora knew all too well of late; a smile that might well match her own. Ever since Marcus's death, which she really didn't want to think about, she'd seen little else on her sister-in-law's face. Well, if she thought back to before that landmark, she had to admit that even then, if Marcus was around, Bella had scarcely smiled. Not properly, anyway.

Dora held out her free hand to Bella. "You must know, Bella, that Diccon and I were children together until he left to be a soldier. We grew up together, close in age, were instructed in the schoolroom together, and kept company constantly."

Diccon nodded, a wide smile on his handsome face. At least *he* looked truly happy. Someone deserved to be. Perhaps. He nodded. "Not just us, but we played with some of the servants' children as well. Old Amos has already told me how Joe Rowan is now head groom at Bembridge House. A shame, as I would've liked to have seen him again. But as I recall, Bembridge isn't above ten miles distant."

Oh, those distant halcyon days of sundrenched childhood, a childhood shared with her beloved Diccon. The glow of contentment inside her threatened to come spilling out, strong enough, just for one glorious moment, to shoulder aside the nagging fears that still lingered from that terrible night nearly two months since. The night she fought daily to forget. The night that haunted her nightmares.

"I don't think it would do," Bella said, with a warning frown, "to be going to visit the head groom at one of our neighbor's homes. Not now our cousin is a duke. He needs to remember his position in society, even if it isn't one he's accustomed to."

She was right, of course, even though she was being unreasonably haughty. She always was. Dora nodded, a little downcast by this approbation. "I fear that's so."

Diccon laughed, reminding her sharply of how devil-may-care his attitude had always been as a boy. "As a duke, I think I can do exactly what I like now, don't you? I had enough of being told what to do here as a child. I have no intention of allowing anyone to do that to me again."

Oh dear. That sounded more than a little confrontational. And Bella seemed to have interpreted it that way as well, because her delicately drawn eyebrows had formed themselves into a perfect *V* of displeasure. If only these two, the people she loved most in all the world, should not get off to a bad start and take it into their silly heads to dislike each other. Her glow of contentment flickered a little at the worry, and her worst memories came thundering back into her head as though that worry had opened the door for them. "Are-are you on your way into breakfast?" she tried, hoping to deflect what might develop into an argument. There'd been too many arguments over the years here at Stourbridge for her liking. She would do anything to prevent another starting. Anything.

"Of course we were," Bella snapped, her tone more tart than needed. She did not like to be thwarted in even the smallest way. "I already told you we were. Come along, both of you, else it will be cold." She spun on her heel and pushed open the breakfast room door with her customary determination.

Dora leaned close to Diccon. "Have no fear. She's just saying that. It won't be cold, you know, for the footmen have it on heated plates. It stays hot for quite some time."

His deep laugh rumbled. "I guessed as much. But thank you for the heads up, for it's a long time since I had the pleasure of eating in a proper breakfast room. More often than not it's been last night's supper heated up in my mess tin, seated on a rock in the middle of nowhere."

Dora squeezed his hand, a warm feeling of relief creeping over her. With Diccon home, surely everything would now be all right and she could perhaps stop worrying. If that were possible. "There'll be none of that here," she whispered. "You're home now. Home and safe."

They followed Bella into the breakfast room, where a footman stood to one side of a row of domed, silver cloches on the long sideboard. The enticing smell of savory food filled the room, mingling with the strong aroma of freshly brewed coffee, Bella's favorite morning beverage. Bella had already taken her seat and was pouring the coffee.

Diccon held out a chair for Dora, and she sat down beside Bella. The seat at the head of the table stood vacant, but he hesitated, standing immobile for several pregnant seconds, staring at it.

Bella broke the silence. "You will find that is your place, Cousin Richard, so the sooner you occupy it, the better. Then we can all begin eating. I confess myself quite famished even though I had to forego my morning gallop."

Dora bit her lip. Why was Bella behaving so coldly? Anyone would think she wasn't pleased to have dear Diccon home. But of course, she didn't know him and how wonderful he was. How easy it was to forget that for Bella, Diccon's return might not mean the same as it did for her.

Richard put a hand on the back of the seat Marcus had occupied until so recently. "I suppose it is. When I was a boy, my place was at the very bottom of the table."

"With me," Dora put in. "And Grace, of course, when she was allowed to breakfast here instead of in the nursery."

Diccon grinned. "And we only did that for the last year I lived here, as I recall. Before that it was nursery breakfasts for all of us. Except Marcus, of course." She well remembered that.

As though he expected the chair to bite him, Diccon took his place at the head of the table. Might sitting in Marcus's seat be like when one of the dogs went into a new kennel and cocked its leg on everything it found? Dora shocked herself at the irreverent thought. She should not be comparing two dukes to a pair of hounds.

"Coffee?" Bella asked, her tone airy, as though she welcomed strangers who turned out to be long-lost heirs into her home every day of the week. Her cousin certainly possessed admirable sangfroid. But then, she'd already known that.

Richard nodded. "Thank you." And Bella poured him a cup.

She set down the silver coffee pot. "I discovered our new duke in the strangest of places, Dora. You will not guess."

Judging by the bits of straw adhering to his clothing, Dora suspected she might well have been able to do just that. But she liked to humor Bella, so she didn't say anything.

"In the stables. And I mean *in* them. I think he'd spent the night sleeping with his horse."

Diccon laughed. "You malign me. I actually spent what remained of the night after my late arrival in Joe Rowan's old bed, with my servant, Baxter, on the other bed. I was merely having a morning conversation with the somewhat dejected beast who brought me here, and waiting for the house to waken so I could make myself known. I had no idea the duchess was partial to an early-morning ride and that we would so opportunely meet."

Bella's laugh tinkled. "I took him for someone come hoping for employment. How amusing was that? We spoke at odds for some time before he owned up to who he was." Another brittle little laugh. "When he finally revealed his identity to me, of course I had to welcome him to Stourbridge. It would have been quite thoughtless of me to have gone on with my ride and left him by himself to find his way inside. I had assumed he didn't know his way about here, but as I see you are old friends, I realize I'd forgotten that he's been here before."

Dora patted Richard's bare forearm, a brief memory of his slender limbs as a boy intruding. "Of course he knows his way about, Bella. We were childhood companions so he knows the castle and grounds well." She glanced up at Diccon, unable to keep the accusation out of her voice. "Until he left us all and went off to be a soldier, that is, when he was still but half a boy."

Bella's frown suggested she might still be puzzled by much about the newly arrived duke, even though a little the wiser concerning his origins. "So, you are our long-lost cousin returned to us. There's no mistaking the Carstairs features. Tell me. Are there more of your family I have heard nothing about? Marcus never mentioned he had a living cousin, although I knew there was one who might be deceased, and who had to be located because of the inheritance."

"I am an only child."

Dora nodded. "His own mama and papa died in some epidemic which fortuitously didn't touch dear Diccon. He came here when he was six years old, all alone. I remember the day well, for Marcus had taken it into his head to tie my plaits to my seat in the schoolroom. When he jumped up to look out of the window to see the carriage arriving, and I followed, my chair came with me and left me with painful bruises across the backs of my legs." She frowned at the memory.

Marcus had insisted, once her attachment to the chair had been undone, on going down to the hallway to see who the visitor was. He'd been disgusted the carriage had only divested one small, frightened little boy. Dora could see him now, in his little navy suit of frock coat and breeches, with a small, cocked hat on his head and his eyes as big as saucers. Her own eyes had met his, and despite Marcus's jeering, she'd smiled, and the little newcomer had smiled back, their friendship of the nine years to come sealed in that instant.

Bella's eyes hardened. "How very typical of Marcus. No doubt he found your discomfort amusing."

This did not require an answer. Bella knew as well as Dora how mean Marcus's actions had been at every opportunity. How he found pleasure in small, or sometimes larger, acts of violence and bullying. She didn't need to share what both of them already knew. They shared enough, already.

"Well," Bella said into the silence, "at least we don't have to look forward to a crowd of your brothers and sisters appearing." She shot a glance at Dora. "And not a wife, either. Our new duke is here not just to inspect his inheritance but also to find himself a wife and soon, thereafter, an heir. Or so he hopes."

Good heavens. Bella must have been questioning him closely to have ascertained all this information already. For herself, Dora would never have entertained exacting such facts from someone she had only just met. But Bella had always been different, from the first day Marcus brought her back here to Stourbridge as a blushing bride, and Dora loved her for it and would change nothing about her. She and Bella were bound by more than the ordinary bonds of friendship and sisterhood.

It was at this opportune moment that the door opened and Bella's visiting friend, of whom Dora was not fond, made an entry. Lord Rupert Wyndham was, as usual, perfectly coiffured and dressed, which made a sharp contrast with the roughness of Diccon's appearance. He paused with his elegant, long-fingered hand still on the door, staring up the room at where Diccon was sitting, delicate eyebrows arched in surprise. "Well, stap me, Bella, but I thought it was Stourbridge back to haunt us." And he gave an uneasy laugh.

Diccon had risen to his feet, curiosity in his eyes. As well he might have. "I'm afraid I don't have the pleasure of your name, sir."

Wyndham came in and closed the door. He was wearing an absurd lilac tailcoat with a matching embroidered waistcoat that gave him a decided look of the dandy, which was what he intended, of course, as he was one. Aiding that impression were his cream pantaloons and his highly polished hessians, and an intricately tied cravat nestling between the far-too-high points of his collar. How he would be able to turn his head was anybody's guess. His appearance was not at all to Dora's taste, but she tolerated him if only because her dear Bella liked him so much, and also because he was not at heart an unpleasant fellow. Well, at least he dressed to match his personality. Much as Diccon appeared to. Two more different men it would have been hard to imagine.

"Lord Rupert Wyndham, sir," Rupert said, making one of his flamboyant bows. "And I think I might have surmised your identity for myself. Your Grace. You have about you a certain familial resemblance to the last duke. I can't say that I was expecting to meet you while I was visiting dear Bella and Dora, though. I count myself honored."

Diccon smiled, but it was not an altogether friendly smile. More the smile of a dog who has just found another canine on his territory. "You are correct in your supposition. I have returned to Stourbridge from Portugal to claim my inheritance, and to survey it for myself." He waved a hand at the table. "Please, do feel free to join us for breakfast."

Wyndham took his seat opposite Bella and Dora. "I only like to take a little toast at breakfast, but I will have some of that coffee, thank you. I would not usually make my appearance before eleven, but, alas, I am thinking of returning to Town today, so necessity calls for me to breakfast early."

Bella wrinkled her nose. "Surely not so soon, Rupert? You

know how much I value your companionship."

"Yes," Diccon said. "Pray don't hasten your departure on my account."

Lord Rupert pursed his lips before bestowing a smile on Bella and a nod to Diccon. "Thank you, Your Graces. I think I could be persuaded to extend my visit by a day or two, if you insist."

Dora hastened to pour the coffee for him and smiled at Diccon, aware that with the arrival of Wyndham the atmosphere had subtly changed. Was Diccon suspicious of a strange man in his house, a man on first name terms with his womenfolk? Best to divert the conversation.

She smiled at Wyndham. "Diccon has been away in the army these past nineteen years, Lord Rupert." She turned to her cousin. "You must have a great deal to tell us about your adventures." She dabbed her mouth with her napkin. "I, for one, should very much like to hear about them. We lead such dull lives here at Stourbridge, that anything you might have experienced will be a boon to us and allow us to vicariously live your life." She had past experience of peacemaking.

Diccon shrugged. "I doubt what I've been up to since I left here would make much of a story. And I'm sorry to say I'm not a great storyteller, even if it would. I've been soldiering for my country, and that's all there is to say for it."

Wyndham took a sip of his coffee. "Come, come, sir. Surely you won't disappoint the ladies by belittling your accomplishments. What rank did you hold, and in which regiment did you hold it? Hussars? I believe most gentlemen favor them for their splendid uniforms."

"Not every gentleman," Diccon said, a little stiffly. "I was never a passionate horseman and therefore chose a foot regiment. My last was the Rifle Brigade."

"The Rifle Brigade?" Rupert said, and Dora sensed with a sinking heart one of his putdowns coming up. "Ain't they rather a Johnny-come-lately bunch? Newly formed? Not one of the old traditional regiments."

Dora, devoid of any appetite now, quickly interrupted. "You must excuse Lord Rupert as he knows so little about army customs and etiquette." And, it seemed, the etiquette of not being openly rude to your host. Bella might love him for his wit and repartee, but it could go too far. One day it would get him a much-deserved punch on the nose.

However, darling Diccon just smiled. "In a way you're right, Wyndham. The Rifle Brigade is very new, but that doesn't mean it's not good. In fact it's one of the best. We were at the Battle of Copenhagen and helped capture the Danish fleet to prevent the French getting their hands on it. And our name betrays the fact that we are equipped with the modern Baker Rifle. A wonderfully useful weapon. We're rightly proud of our green uniforms and our rifles."

Bella set down her toast. "Rupert was my escort last night to the ball at Bembridge House. He's been staying here a few days. Such a shame he has to leave today."

Dora bit her lip. What was Diccon going to think of that statement? They were supposed to be in mourning, and yet Bella was right now wearing green, and she was now confessing to having been out to a ball with an exquisitely handsome gentleman as her escort. Beau Wyndham, no less. A man who was staying in a house where until this morning there had been no master present. That did not look good. Especially not when Dora knew very well that society assumed Wyndham was her lover. Might Diccon have heard these rumors? They weren't the only ones circulating about Bella, however.

"Was it a pleasant evening?" she asked, with a tinge of desperation.

"As much as a country ball can be," Bella snapped, with more asperity than she might have intended. She must have guessed at Dora's own embarrassment.

Diccon, who had fetched himself a plate of Cook's best kedgeree, raised a laconic eyebrow, but said nothing, a fact which clearly riled Bella, who took a forceful bite of her toast and glared at him.

Dora began to fervently wish she were better at reading people. That something was going on here, she could tell, but what it was escaped her. Telltale sweat began to prickle out down her back and across her forehead. What had Diccon heard about Marcus's demise? The rumors were rife and he could well have picked them up on his long journey back here. Did he think their household lacking in respect to his cousin, a man he'd hated? Confusion mingled with the anxiety that already occupied Dora's heart. Surely he must be glad Marcus was dead, dreadful as even thinking those words was.

"Committed army man, are you, then?" Rupert asked.

Richard nodded. "I am, or rather I was. I've resigned my commission on my commanding officer's orders."

Rupert, with probably as small a morning appetite as she and Bella due to his night of excesses, not to mention the direction the conversation was taking, sipped his coffee. "Been fighting Boney, I take it?"

Richard nodded again, and swallowed a mouthful of the kedgeree. He appeared to be the only one with any appetite at all. "That's what I was doing in Portugal, until I received a garbled message that I had to return to England." He waved his fork. "This is fine kedgeree. Do we still have the same cook as when I left, I wonder? I remember Mrs. Burton well for the food she was able to provide to fuel a hungry boy."

"Mrs. Burton retired to live in one of the estate cottages a few years ago," Dora said, in a hurry, and glad of the change of subject. "She's very old now, and arthritic, but I know she'd love to see you if you have time, Diccon. You could ride or walk over there. It's not far. I could come with you." Did she sound as desperate as she felt?

He nodded. "And I to see her. I have a lot to do now I'm here, but first I think I must see Marcus's man of business to make sure all the formalities have been gone through. I'm sure he'll have papers for me to sign." He paused. "Would you happen to know who this is? I left so long ago, I have no idea of the way the estate is run, nor who Marcus used for his legal work."

Bella set down her coffee cup. "I don't have the least idea. Marcus never allowed me to become involved in business or estate matters." There was a definite rebellious jut to her jaw. "He said women do not have a head for figures." She gave a huff at the end of this utterance, a frown settling over her face that implied his opinion was erroneous.

Dora interceded again. "I think he still uses Allsop and Crichton in Newbury. Those were Papa's men of business, although I think Mr. Allsop senior is no more, and Mr. Crichton has retired. But, as far as I know, others have taken on their mantle. I believe there is a Young Mr. Allsop."

Dora ignored the hard stare Bella was directing at her. "I know who will be able to tell you for certain. Mr. Sanders will." Telltale heat crept slowly from her throat up to her cheeks. She looked down at her empty plate. If only she could keep her emotions in check in the way Bella could. "He is, I mean he was, my brother's land agent. Well, yours now, I suppose." She could only pray no one had noticed her blush. Although Bella knew already how she felt about Philip, but was sworn to secrecy.

"Then that's who I shall visit first," Richard said. "When I've eaten my fill of this wonderful kedgeree." He beamed at his audience of three. "I think I'll have a second helping. We never ate as well as this on campaign."

CHAPTER SEVEN

AFTER BREAKFAST WAS over, Richard went in search of Philip Sanders. When he'd been a boy here, the land agent had been a Mr. Hamilton, who'd been white haired and bent with arthritis back then. Little wonder a new one was in residence nowadays. Despite having had as little to do with old Mr. Hamilton, whom he and Dora had thought intimidating and scary, as possible, Richard had not forgotten the way to the estate office. Having found his coat and picked off the straw he'd deliberately left in his hair and on his clothes during breakfast, with the rather childish intention of annoying Isabella, he knocked on the stout office door.

A deep voice bade him enter.

Philip Sanders was neither a young man nor an old one, but of the sort of indeterminate age that fits between those two definitions without being a part of either of them. His fluffy brown hair, thinning a little on top and combed upwards to disguise this, was matched by impressive side-whiskers and bushy eyebrows. It could have been said that his head hair was in the process of migrating south.

His face when he saw Richard gave away the fact that no one had as yet thought to inform him of the arrival of the new duke. His eyes widened, his jaw dropped, and one hand went to his heart as if to still its palpitations. It took him a few moments to find his breath and voice. "Good heavens, sir. You gave me quite a shock. You look just like our late duke." The bushy brows met in a puzzled frown as realization began to dawn. "Oh my goodness. You can be no one but the *new* duke. How could I not have known." He sprang to his feet, almost knocking over his chair, and executed a hasty bow. "Please forgive me, Your Grace. We were not expecting you at all. In fact, I understood that you were presumed dead, and your possible heirs were being searched for abroad right now."

Richard waved him back into his seat. "I am found, as you can see, and I am very much alive and without heirs of any sort. And I'm here to take up my inheritance. I'm told you are the man to come to for advice. So that is what I'm doing." He smiled. "I must also ask you to forgive me, Mr. Sanders, for having given you such a shock. I know I look all too much like Marcus, and that's enough to frighten some people. Or to make them think they're seeing a ghost."

Philip Sanders settled back into his seat, his face flushed. "It's just we had no idea you would be arriving." He shook his head. "No idea you were even still alive. There seems to have been some confusion about your continued existence."

"So I gather. However, let that not come between us. What I'd like from you today is some details about my cousin's man of business. There will be papers for me to sign as regards the inheritance, and I'd like to get all that over with as quickly as possible." He didn't add that he also needed to get finding a wife and begetting an heir over with as well. That might well shock the apparently easily shockable Mr. Sanders.

That gentleman nodded. "Of course, of course, Your Grace. I understand. And may I assure you that I am at your service for anything you may need over the coming weeks and months. But the man you need to see first is Mr. Thomas Allsop of Allsop and Crichton. Their offices are at the head of the high street in Newbury. I'm sure you will know the town, as I gather from my conversations with Lady Dora that you once lived here." He blushed. "She has told me a lot about you. She was—is—clearly very fond of you." He smiled a little uncertainly. "I'm sure she must be delighted at your return from the dead."

Richard nodded. "She is, although she seems somewhat changed since I last saw her. Her happiness will be one of my priorities, you can rest assured of that. And now, I must leave you and ride into Newbury. I'm sorry this meeting has been so brief, but I anticipate spending much more time in your company in the weeks to come." He held out his hand. "I trust we will rub along together well enough, Sanders."

They shook, and Richard departed in the direction of the stables. Well, that was good. If Dora was in love with Sanders, it seemed from the man's telltale blush that her feelings might well be reciprocated. Although how far that courtship could have progressed under Marcus's tyrannical overlordship was another thing entirely. Probably nowhere at all. He wondered again why Dora was not already married off with a family of her own. Her injured leg should have been no barrier to marriage. He'd have to find that out. She must be thirty-four by now, on the old side for marriage, but in theory still young enough to have children of her own. Perhaps a talk to Sanders about that was in order, once he'd found his bearings. If it would make Dora happy, it would make him happy as well.

In the stableyard, Amos provided him with what he described, a little scornfully it had to be said, as a "reliable mount." He'd wanted Richard to take one of Marcus's hunters, a huge bay with a wild eye, but Richard firmly informed him that quiet was what he preferred. And so he was equipped with a sturdy gray cob with the rather unusual name of Douglas. Marcus had always been an accomplished horseman, despite his other failings, and although horses with spirit might have suited him, Richard held no illusions about his own lack of riding capabilities.

The offices of Allsop and Crichton were located, as Philip Sanders had described, at the very top of Northbrook Street, the main thoroughfare of the small market town of Newbury. As Richard could only once remember having been into the town as a boy, and that had been to take the coach to London when he'd gone to join his first regiment, this was very much a journey of exploration. Philip had informed him that the building he required stood on the left, where Northbrook Street widened to meet the Great Bath Road as it entered on its way westwards towards its namesake city.

Approaching the small town from the south, along a graveled and potholed road, he found none of it looked in the least bit familiar. When he'd left, he'd been only fifteen, desperate to escape the bullying of his older cousin, excited by the prospect of a career in the army, and careless as only a boy of fifteen can be of those he'd be leaving behind. Consequently, he'd paid but scant attention to his surroundings. He'd been concentrating on not missing the London coach, and Newbury and its charms had been lost on him.

As he rode down the hill into the wide river valley, the little town spread out before him, its long arms running out as they did upon the major crossroads it was set on. To east and west lay the Great Bath Road, to the north and south ran the route from Winchester to Oxford and beyond, on which he was riding. Beyond the town he could just make out the crumbling ruins of the keep of an ancient, medieval castle, peeking out of the trees that surrounded it, and far beyond that to the north lay the downs of the Vale of the White Horse. In the center of the town, glimmering in the morning sunshine, lay the River Kennet, currently, according to Philip who seemed very well-informed on local goings on, in the process of being transformed into a much-needed canal link from London to Bristol.

Douglas, the horse Richard was riding, not being the under-fed creature he'd arrived on the night before, was still fresh and lively. He slowed him to a trot and then a walk to negotiate the hill down into the town, where the tall spire of a large church pointed skywards just above the river. The town possessed an altogether welcoming air, combining bustling business and friendliness as people he passed doffed their hats to him in cheerful greeting.

He soon discovered this was because it was market day, and the square about the rather-dilapidated-looking Guildhall thronged with busy stalls and crowds of people. He chose the coaching inn from which he remembered catching the London stage, because he knew it had stables, and, having paid an ostler of almost frighteningly early youth to take care of his horse for an hour or two, set off for the north end of the town on foot.

He soon found the offices he was seeking in a building whose lopsidedness indicated its extreme age. Having pushed open the heavy oak door, he climbed rickety spiral stairs to the rooms above. On pushing open another door, he discovered a middle-aged, ruddy-cheeked man seated at a huge desk piled with papers, his back to the low, leaded window that gave onto the street below. Most of the walls of the room were lined with shelves of hefty books, and any spare surface boasted piles of more papers that did not have the comforting appearance of having been well filed and docketed. Richard forbore from commenting on this, although he formed the immediate, private opinion that Mr. Allsop might not be quite as efficient as Mr. Sanders.

The man looked up at Richard's entry into the room. He was small and rather rodent-like in appearance, with a long nose on the end of which balanced half-moon spectacles. And he was a lot balder than Mr. Sanders.

Like most people who met Richard and had also known Marcus, he started in surprise. "Good heavens. You have to be the long-lost cousin. I mean, the new duke. We all thought you were dead." He rose to his feet and made a rather chaotic bow as bits of paper cascaded to the floor around him. "Delighted to see you are alive, and to make your acquaintance, Your Grace. Please, do sit down."

This entailed a foray around his desk to remove yet more papers from the only other chair in the room. Richard sat down once this had been done. "Mr. Allsop, I presume." For someone described as "young Mr. Allsop," he seemed surprisingly aged.

Surely he couldn't be a day younger than fifty.

Mr. Allsop nodded, fighting his way back to his own seat. "I am indeed he, Your Grace."

Richard was finding it hard to quell his desire to stare around himself at the state of the office. Instead, he fixed his gaze on his own hands for a moment. "I'm told by Philip Sanders, my land agent, that you still act as man of business for the estate—that you acted for my cousin while he was alive. I assume you will have papers that need my signature."

Mr. Allsop nodded with vigor. "Please don't think that because I am a little behind with my paperwork that my work for the seventh duke was anything but of the first quality. I have just recently lost my most excellent young clerk to consumption, poor man, and have yet to employ, and perforce to train, his replacement. It was his one of his jobs to file all the papers away where they belong. I must admit to not having realized just how much work that entailed."

"I trust you will swiftly find another clerk," Richard said. "Or I might have to find myself a new man of business." He didn't know the fellow, so he felt no constraint in speaking his mind and risking offending him. He needed a kick in the pants, and had he been one of his soldiers, Richard would have had no hesitation in doing so. Best to start as he meant to go on, by expecting the best of service. He would be paying for it, after all.

Mr. Allsop blustered for a moment. "Of course, of course. Yes, I shall make it my priority, Your Grace." His face brightened a fraction. "I assume you have come here to ascertain the extent of your inheritance?"

Richard nodded. "And for you to answer some questions for me."

Mr. Allsop began to look a little less enthusiastic. What did he imagine Richard was about to ask him? "I am at your disposal, Your Grace." His voice lacked a certain gusto now.

On his ride in, Richard had already decided the best plan was to be blunt. "Firstly, I think it important that I should know the circumstances of my cousin's demise, as it has led to my unexpected elevation. As far as I knew, he was in robust good health when last I saw him. Although I'll grant that was nineteen years ago. I assume you know the details?" He tapped his fingers on his knee, a feeling of impatience surfacing.

Mr. Allsop's face paled a shade and his Adam's apple bobbed. "I believe," he said, with even less enthusiasm, "I believe His Grace died from a gunshot wound to the head."

Richard couldn't help his eyes widening and his breath catching in his throat. So not from natural causes. Still, he hadn't really expected Marcus to have died in his bed of some illness, or the rumor mill would not be suggesting his wife had a hand in it. "Self inflicted?"

Mr. Allsop swallowed again and licked his lips. "As far as I know, Your Grace, that was the assumption." This did not sound like a definitive answer.

"I would have thought it would have been glaringly obvious if he'd done it himself, don't you?" Richard paused. "Where did this unfortunate event take place? Here or in his townhouse—I mean *my* townhouse?"

"Here. Or rather at Stourbridge Castle, Your Grace. I believe he was found in the library. In the middle of the night. By his wife. The duchess."

So she'd been first on the scene to discover her husband dead. Or had she been the one to kill him, and then pretend she'd found him? No wonder she'd come under suspicion and was the subject of rumor.

"Could it have been a burglary gone wrong, that he disturbed?"

"As far as I know, nothing was taken and all the windows were still shut. If there'd been a burglar, one would have expected him to have made off with at least the money His Grace kept in his desk in the library, and to have left a trace of his presence behind. But there was nothing. So I've heard. I was not there that day and did not see His Grace's body. I was not called until three days later."

"Where was the wound?"

"In his head."

Richard scowled. Was the man being deliberately obtuse? "I assumed that, man. Where in the head?"

Mr. Allsop grimaced. "I am told he'd been shot with one of his dueling pistols. In the temple."

That sounded self-inflicted to Richard, which made him wonder why the rumors had gained any credence. As a soldier he'd seen one or two suicides by young men who'd been so traumatized by warfare they couldn't keep going. And they'd invariably set their pistols to their temples, or in their mouths. Nevertheless, it would not have been a pretty sight. A dueling pistol took a large ball, and, being lead, it would flatten on impact. It would have made a relatively small hole where it had entered, but left the other side of his head along with most of his brains by a much more cavernous orifice. And if Isabella hadn't done it herself, she'd have had the horrifying experience of finding her husband lying so mutilated. He made a mental note to go into the library and see where Marcus had met his end. Someone, Atkins probably, would be able to fill him in on the details.

"Did my cousin have any enemies?" Silly question. Better to ask if he'd had any friends as the answer would probably have been a resounding no. Although no doubt he would have been surrounded by the usual crowd of sycophants he'd liked to encourage.

Mr. Allsop shrugged in apology. "I am afraid I was not party to His Grace's social life. He visited me infrequently, being content to trust in me and in Mr. Sanders, his land agent, to run the estate and supply him with a sizeable income. Which is now yours, Your Grace, of course."

So he was getting nothing from Allsop, who probably knew more than he was willing to divulge. The rumor mill in this town would have been working overtime after Marcus's death and probably still was. The fellow must have heard all the speculation.

He tried again. "Did he have any creditors to whom he owed any outstanding amounts? I remember he was fond of a wager when we were boys together." His brow furrowed. That made them sound as though they'd got on.

"His Grace was fond of horse racing, I gather."

"And yet his finances are healthy?"

"Ah." Allsop ran his hand across the top of his shiny bald pate as though he expected to find hair there. "There is something you should know."

Richard's ears pricked. "Which is?"

"When His Grace, the seventh duke, inherited Stourbridge and all it entails from his father, the sixth duke, back in ninety-five, he was himself but twenty-five years old. He rather ran up a few debts with his gambling. I had this from my own late father, who was much more in his confidence than I am. In view of these debts, he took it upon himself to seek out an heiress to marry."

He licked his lips, plainly of the opinion that he was passing on salacious gossip and not all that happy about it. "The richest he found happened to be the daughter of a nabob who'd made his fortune in the Indies. His description, not mine. The girl had never been to India but had been educated in England and had all the mannerisms of the nobility, despite not being a part of it. The father had aspirations, and she was his only child. She stood to inherit everything."

He paused again, shifting uneasily in his seat. "His Grace's eye lit upon her and he struck a bargain with her father for her hand."

Richard could sniff out a problem at fifty yards distance. "And what kind of a bargain did my cousin make for this girl's hand?"

Allsop squirmed. "The father, a Mr. Josiah Hope, very much wished to have a duke as a son-in-law and make his only child a duchess. He settled a substantial dowry on his daughter, with which your cousin was able to rid himself of all his creditors and set his finances on a more than healthy footing. You would perhaps have imagined the young lady was to inherit all her father's wealth on his death, but you would be wrong. His Grace insisted that it should be he who was named in Mr. Hope's will. He inherited the fortune that some might say should have been Her Grace's. Mr. Hope's money now forms a part of the estate you have inherited. It is a part of the entail."

"Do you mean to say my cousin pocketed the lot when the duchess's father died? That now she's his widow, she's been left with not a penny to her name?"

Mr. Allsop gave an apologetic shrug. "I do indeed, and I must inform you that it is much to your advantage, for, as I said, you will inherit that fortune, most of which is still in existence. It was my father who drew up the agreement between His Grace and Mr. Hope, and made Mr. Hope's will for him. I can assure you there are no loopholes. The money is yours."

CHAPTER EIGHT

SULTAN CANTERED WITH his easy, long-striding lope along the path up towards the Hampshire Downs, the breeze of his speed blowing Isabella's abundant curls out behind her. The dun Arabian was bounding with more than his usual energy, having been deprived of his customary early-morning ride, and every so often his back end rose in an impudent buck. But Isabella didn't mind. Sultan's wild and fiery nature was one of the reasons they got on so well together and why she'd taken over riding him since Marcus's death. She would have had it no other way. And probably Sultan preferred her lighter style of riding to Marcus's heavy-handedness. At least, she liked to think he did.

At the end of the track stood a crenellated tower, one of the previous, long-dead dukes having taken it into his head to provide the estate with a large number of follies. This one, unlike most follies, served good use as staff accommodation. Mrs. Crump, wife of the elderly gardener who was its present tenant, was engaged in spreading her washing over the bushes in the garden as Isabella approached. Sultan, taking advantage of something as untoward as an array of sheet-covered bushes, skipped sideways as though he'd never seen such a thing before.

Unfazed, Isabella applied her left leg and a flick of her whip and brought him back under control as Mrs. Crump, having set her washing basket on the ground at her feet, bobbed a hurried curtsey. "Beg pardon, Your Grace. I didn't see you coming.

You're usually about much earlier than this."

Isabella waved a hand in casual dismissal. "Don't worry. I'm much later than is my habit. And as for this firebrand, he takes umbrage at the least little thing in a ditch, so I'm always on the look out for things he won't like." She patted Sultan's sweat-damp neck and laughed. "But I'm not embarrassed to admit that I love him for it. My rides would be quite boring were my horses to be plodding hacks."

Mrs. Crump's brow furrowed. Probably she'd never ridden a horse in her life, nor had much to do with them. "Crump has often said to me as you're the bravest rider he's ever laid eyes on. Not just for a lady, neither. From the gentlemen he's seen too. And plenty of them."

This wasn't the first time Isabella had heard such praise, but, susceptible as she was to praise, it didn't stop her from mentally preening herself. After all, she'd only come to riding after her marriage, as her papa, bless him, had not thought riding a skill a young lady about town needed. Consequently, it pleased her every time someone commented on her prowess on a horse, and right now this inclined her to further conversation with Mrs. Crump, whom she liked.

"I thought I'd ride up over the farm track and come down through the woods on the far side, by Heaven's Gate. I feel Sultan and I both need to stretch our legs this morning, and that track is so invitingly grassy and smooth. Perfect for a gallop."

Mrs. Crump's frown deepened. "Mind how you go up there, Your Grace, if you don't mind me saying so. If you was my daughter, I'd be worrying after you out on your own like this on a horse as excitable and wild as that one looks. It's a long way from anywhere if that horse of yours should skip sideways like it just did and toss you in a hedge."

Isabella laughed. "If he skips sideways again, I shan't be ending in any hedges. You mark my words. I shall be fine. And besides which," she paused, tilting her head to one side, "should I not return home you'll be able to tell a search party where to look for me." She turned Sultan away, making her final remark over her shoulder. "Not that you'll need to."

Leaving Mrs. Crump standing next to her still-piled washing basket, Isabella turned Sultan onto the farm track, edged on one side by woodland and the other by a low hawthorn hedge. As she'd told Mrs. Crump, the grass between the wheel tracks was invitingly soft and springy, and Sultan, who knew all the places he was allowed to gallop, pranced under her firm hold of the reins. Yes, she would let him gallop.

A mile and a half later, as the track started to head downhill, Isabella brought a sweaty Sultan down to a walk and loosened the reins to let him stretch his neck. Totally alone at last, and with the morning's disturbing cobwebs blown away, now was as good a time as any to consider the new arrival at Stourbridge and what had brought him here. The warming sun beat down on the back of her neck, and, in the sky directly over her head, larks were calling. Away from the castle and all the worries it contained, this was where she'd always felt at peace.

Her mind slipped back to Marcus, as it so often had done in the last eight weeks. Indeed, she'd thought more about him in this time than she had in the whole of her marriage. In the ten years she'd been his wife, he'd never once mentioned he had a cousin to her. It had taken Dora to reveal this fact. This in itself was not surprising, as, in truth, Marcus had shared very little with her. In fact, after their first year together, he'd had as little to do with her as possible.

Isabella was under no illusion that this change in his attitude had not been because once her father had died and he'd inherited the fortune he'd married her to get his hands on, she'd served her use. While her papa had lived, he'd been civil to her, although never loving. As soon as Josiah Hope had succumbed to his final illness, that civility had evaporated like snow on a hot summer's day. But even in those first months of their marriage, when he'd been pretending to like her, he'd told her nothing of his childhood, nor even of what he liked or disliked.

Dora had filled all that in, and because Marcus had told Dora their cousin had died abroad, both women had believed this and Dora had rarely spoken of him.

Dora.

Dear, vulnerable, frightened Dora.

Isabella guided Sultan onto the track into the woods that would lead down the hill, past the brick-built, arched folly called Heaven's Gate, and back into the park. Up here on the Downs, stretching away into the distance, all the land was part of the estate, as productive farmland, all of it tenanted out to produce an income. She would have had to ride a long way to leave Stourbridge land behind her.

Her thoughts returned to Dora. She'd first met Dora when Marcus had brought her to Stourbridge, after her father's death. Their first year of marriage had been spent in London, close to her father, and she'd been more than surprised to find the castle already occupied by a woman six years older than herself. But she need not have feared, for Dora, whom she'd discovered to be a quiet, gentle creature, had taken her under her wing and made a friend of her. She'd needed one back then, when Marcus had abandoned her like an old coat he no longer wanted and returned to London without her.

She'd been a different young woman then. Just a girl, heartbroken her beloved papa had died leaving her alone in a strange world she didn't feel part of. Now, though, she'd forced her way into that world and taken it by the horns with a vigor that would have shocked her gentle papa. It had taken a while, but as she'd grown older, she'd learned to assert herself and deal with the people who'd sneered at her origins when Marcus had married her. And it had been a pleasure to learn how to make them feel as small and insignificant as they'd made her feel. Isabella was not a young lady who forgot a slight.

But not Dora. No, dear Dora had never been in the least bit condescending to the daughter of a nabob who'd made his money on trade in the Indies. She'd been as kind to Isabella as if she'd been the mother who'd died so long ago Isabella could recall nothing about her.

The path began to head more steeply downhill, passing the tumbledown folly and threading its way through tall trees where the sun slanting between the leaves made a greenway for Sultan to follow.

On occasion, Dora had divulged little snippets about Richard, the childhood playmate she'd thought forever lost. Isabella could see it now. They'd been sitting together in the walled garden one warm summer's day. Birds had been singing. Marcus had been in London so the house and gardens were happy and peaceful... and safe.

"Diccon came to us when I was five years old," Dora said, her gentle smile lighting her plain face. "He was one year older than me. His mama and papa had died, of what, I never found out. Some sickness took them both at the same time. My own papa was his uncle, but Diccon was considered nothing but a poor relation by Marcus. He took his lead from my papa, who I found out from Marcus had never liked Diccon's papa, his younger brother. My unfortunate uncle had gone off and married the girl he loved, you see, against the wishes of his father. A girl Marcus took great pleasure in saying was a nobody, and our papa could not forgive him for it."

"Like me," Isabella had said. "In Marcus's view, I'm a nobody."

"Not to me you're not." Dora took her hand and squeezed it. "You are my dearest friend, even though I sometimes think you are quite mad in the things you do and the ways you provoke Marcus's ire. There's such a thing as being too brave, you know."

"What happened to this Diccon?"

Dora shrugged. "Marcus never liked him. He was three years older than Diccon, but for some reason saw him as a rival. For what, I don't know." She gave a little shrug. "I sometimes wonder if it was because Diccon and I were such friends. Not that Marcus wanted me as his friend. He just didn't want Diccon to have that pleasure. Who knows? He went out of his way to be as unpleasant as he could to Diccon. Terrible things. He is a bully, as you well know. As we both know…"

Isabella nodded. She could vouch for that.

"However, our grandmother doted on Diccon. Another thing that incurred Marcus's rage. I think Grandmama had favored Diccon's father, her younger son, and so, quite naturally, she favored his child. When he was old enough, he went to her and asked if she'd purchase him a commission in the army. She took some persuading, but in the end she did, or, rather, she persuaded my father to do so. And one day, off he went. I never saw him again. Marcus says he died in battle. I like to think as a hero, as he was always my hero, and saved me more than once from Marcus's anger."

Only it seemed he hadn't died at all. Marcus, being Marcus and probably just because he enjoyed hurting his sister, had told her that her beloved cousin had perished. A fresh wave of hatred for Marcus welled up in Isabella's chest so violently that if she weren't careful it was going to come spewing out of her mouth. She clamped it shut, just in case.

The path slewed sideways on the steepest part of the hill, the parkland beginning to appear between the trees. A herd of red deer were browsing where the woodland joined the meadows.

So, what did she think of the prodigal son so far? That he looked far too much like Marcus for comfort. A bit taller, maybe, with a face more weatherworn than Marcus's had ever been, which was only to be expected after half a lifetime of soldiering. A tougher, more careworn version of Marcus, perhaps. Rougher, his edges not so sharp, and with a twinkle in his eye that Marcus had never had.

A decidedly attractive twinkle.

That he was attractive, she couldn't deny, but it was in an entirely different way to Marcus. And she wasn't the impressionable girl she'd been at eighteen, when Marcus had come wooing her and her father with his suave good looks and his persuasive, loving words that had all been lies. He'd promised her and Papa the world, and delivered none of it. And his good looks, thanks in part to his excesses, had soon begun to wane, slurring into the appearance of what he truly was—a dissipate rake.

She also couldn't deny that there was much she wanted to discover about this strange newcomer. That in truth, she was fascinated by him. That her unruly heart had quivered with something she'd never felt before when she regarded him. Apart from at breakfast she'd had little chance to pose any questions, and for once, she'd felt an unaccustomed reticence. Whether it was because of his resemblance to Marcus, she couldn't be sure. Was she wary of him because she feared he might have more in common with his cousin than just his looks? Possibly.

The track headed off along an avenue of lime trees towards the house, but to her right the parkland lay open and inviting. A canter, this time perhaps. She didn't want to bring Sultan back to his stable dripping with sweat. A canter towards the north gates followed by a gentle walk back through the woods and past the lake to cool her horse off would be fun.

As luck would have it, she and Sultan arrived at the north gates just as Richard passed through them on his return from Newbury.

He was riding Douglas, the cob who was often used to pull the market cart. Why on earth would he want to ride a staid old cob when he had his choice of every horse in the stables? Her brow wrinkled in puzzlement.

She slowed Sultan to a walk. She'd have to be polite and speak to him, but that wouldn't be too much of a chore. There was nowhere for her to go and he'd definitely seen her so she could hardly just ride off. She waited for him to draw level. Of course, Douglas was his cob now, as were all the horses. Everything that had been Marcus's was now his, including everything that had once been her father's and should, if the world were not upside down, be hers now. If only her father hadn't been so impressed that a duke had offered for his only child. In her heart, if she were honest with herself, she knew her father had been an easily impressed old fool. Only he'd not had to suffer the consequences of his quest to climb the social ladder. She had.

"Good afternoon, Isabella." Richard doffed his hat to her, the expression on his face hinting that he was pleased to see her. Or if not that, at least not annoyed by her presence, as Marcus had so often been. If only he didn't so strongly remind her of Marcus, liking him would be much easier. He was certainly handsome, but she well knew the old adage about beauty only being skin deep was all too true. When her papa had told her she was to become engaged to a handsome young duke, she'd been fooled all too easily. But not for long. And she certainly wasn't about to allow herself to be fooled a second time, even if he did make her heart flutter in the most delicious way.

"Good afternoon… Richard." Why was saying his name so hard? She shied well away from addressing him as Diccon, in the familiar way Dora had. But then, Dora had known him when they both were children. He'd been Diccon to her then and clearly still was. She eyed him with a touch of suspicion. How had his meeting with the man of business gone? Allsop. Well, by the look on his face. But then, she'd never expected it to do anything else. After all, what was there to go wrong with it? He'd inherited the highest order of the nobility and a fortune in one fell swoop. He would be the envy of most people.

He fell in beside her and smiled, suddenly looking nothing like Marcus and positively boyish. "I see you've been taking advantage of the sunshine to take that ride I interrupted this morning."

She nodded. "Sultan becomes a nightmare if he isn't ridden every day."

His gaze settled on her horse. "An Arabian?"

"Yes."

Out of the corner of her eye she watched his riding style. He sat Douglas well enough, but there was something about him that suggested riding wasn't something he was used to doing. But of course. He'd been an infantry officer. Which would be why he didn't have the look of a cavalryman.

"I can see you're not accustomed to riding every day."

"Is it that obvious?"

She let herself smile at his discomfort. "Yes. It is."

He shrugged, letting the cob walk on a long rein. "Riding is not a passion of mine, and when I joined the army I'd already decided I wanted to be in an infantry regiment. I've served in a succession of foot regiments. I was firstly an ensign in the 42nd Foot and then later moved on to the 81st when I became a lieutenant. It was only six years ago that I joined the 95th. As your friend Wyndham pointed out, the 95th is a very new construction."

He spoke with a hint of regret in his tone. "Will you miss it?" The words were out of her mouth before she could stop herself. One thing she did not want to do was connect in any way emotionally with this man, handsome as he was. And now she'd offered him sympathy.

He nodded. "I will. It's all I've known since I was little more than a boy. It's been my life, and I thought it always would be. If I ever considered what it would lead to, I suppose it was to perhaps becoming a general or dying in battle on some foreign field. I never thought I'd be leaving on my own two feet at five and thirty, as a major. And returning to Stourbridge." His voice dropped and his eyes took on a troubled expression.

Was it so awful for him to be returning home? She gazed about herself for a moment. Despite Marcus, she loved Stourbridge, and it was beyond her ken to picture someone not liking it at all.

The castle had come into view, its four stout, truncated towers rising above the brow of the hill they were riding up, the land undulating away into the distance, tree covered and green.

She had a sudden itch between her shoulder blades that she couldn't shake off. She didn't want to be exchanging pleasantries with the man who would usurp her beloved home and the fortune that should have been hers, whatever her heart was trying to tell her. It was all too much. "I'm sorry. I find I must hurry." She set her heel to Sultan's side, and urged him into a canter for the last few hundred yards, leaving Richard behind her. To her relief, he made no move to follow.

Chapter Nine

A FTER LEAVING THE reliable Douglas in the capable of hands of Baxter, whom he found helping Old Amos in the stableyard, Richard repaired to the estate office. He found Philip still there, seated at his large oak desk and working over the estate accounts, a rather harassed expression on his face. No doubt the paperwork involved in a change of ownership was substantial, and, on top of that, the accounts would require a lot of work right now, as the Michaelmas quarter day was fast approaching at the end of the month. All the tenants would be coming into the office before long to pay their quarterly rents, and Philip would have to be ready for them.

"Your Grace." Philip rose to his feet, but Richard waved him down again.

"No need to get up nor to call me 'Your Grace' every time you clap eyes on me. My name's Richard, and, as I believe we two will be working closely together from now on, I think I'd rather you called me that. It's going to take a long time for me to get used to being a duke."

Philip inclined his head in what could have been a bow. Well, probably was. The habits of a lifetime would be hard to overcome. "Of course, Your—Richard." He sounded a little awkward as he said Richard's name. He was going to have to get used to it. Although the army had possessed a strict hierarchical structure, the men of the 95th always referred to themselves, whatever their rank, as just riflemen. And the officers had known each other by their first names when relaxing.

Richard nodded back in affirmation. "I've just come back to tell you my visit to Mr. Allsop went well, and that I'm back, a little more informed than I was before, a whole heap of papers signed, and ready for whatever introduction you might think necessary for becoming a duke so unexpectedly."

Philip settled back into his seat, a look of relief on his face. Perhaps he'd expected a new duke to want a new land agent, or at any rate, to be more trouble than Richard was proving to be. "Mr. Allsop's a good man. He knows the estate well. He should, as he took over management of the legal side from his late father. The estate has been in their hands for several generations now."

Richard had no intention of upsetting the running of the estate, although he did want to learn a little more about it. Had Marcus shown any interest in it beyond pocketing a tidy income from it? Most likely not. "I found Mr. Allsop a little disorganized, I thought. Apparently his clerk has had the temerity to die, and he hasn't yet appointed another in his place."

Philip raised his bushy eyebrows. "Really? I hadn't heard. It may not be that easy for him to find a replacement of such caliber in so small a town as Newbury. Although it has a good grammar school. St Bartholomew's. I was there myself and received an excellent education."

Richard, not really interested, at this point in time, in the availability of grammar school education for local boys, settled into the leather-upholstered seat on his side of Philip's desk and leaned back in it. "He was able to tell me a little of what went on when my cousin died. However, as he wasn't there that day and didn't even see the body, I find myself in need of further clarification. I take it you yourself were present? And that you saw the body?"

Was he mistaken, or did this question cause Philip to shift in his seat as though uncomfortable? Richard was a master at disguising his true thoughts though, and he maintained his lazy lounge as he leaned further back in his chair. He'd perfected this appearance of disassociation a long time ago, courtesy of Marcus. The last thing he'd wanted to do with his bully of a cousin was show him how he was feeling.

Philip wetted his lips. "It's true. I was there. Later on. And I did see the body." His dislike of having to admit this was obvious. "Mr. Atkins had locked the library door, but he let me in to see."

Richard stretched his legs out, eyeing the mud that still bespattered his boots. He needed to get Baxter installed as his valet as quickly as possible, not to mention provided with a suit of clothes suitable to his new role in life. Both of them needed to get used to his being a duke and having to look their parts. "Later on? How much later?"

Philip clasped his hands on the table, the whitening of his knuckles betraying the tension in his body. "Several hours later. The duke, His Grace… Marcus… was killed about three in the morning, I believe. No one called me until some time after seven."

Richard allowed his eyebrows to form the next question.

Philip shrugged. "I think they were all too shocked, and panic prevented them from acting as efficiently as they should have done. Also, he was very definitely dead, so I suppose they saw no need for haste. It wasn't as if a doctor was required."

A sensible reaction, or one that would have given time for them to think up a good cover story. "Who is 'they'?"

Philip shifted in his seat again. "Mr. Atkins, Mrs. Barnes, the housekeeper. Old Amos."

Three of them? But not Isabella, who was supposed to have been the one who'd discovered the body. Where was she at seven in the morning when Sanders had been woken up and told what had happened? And one of them had been Amos? Why had he been involved in this? Surely out in his accommodation in the stable courtyard he wouldn't have heard the report of a gun. Or maybe he had due to the stillness of the night. Although, if he had, surely all the servants would also have heard it, and there would have been more than the three of them there. A bit of a mystery to be unraveled here, if he was to do his duty by the Prince of Wales's office.

Richard pressed on. "But you know what happened? You must all have talked about it? Someone must have sent for the constable? A magistrate, perhaps?"

Philip licked his lips again and regarded his hands. "Her Grace was the one who found the duke, after he…" Hesitating, he looked up. "I believe Mr. Atkins also heard the shot, but being of advanced years, was slow to react. When he came up from the servants' quarters, he found the duke lying on the floor in the library. Dead. It was already too late to help him."

This was like getting blood out of a stone. There was something here Sanders wasn't revealing. Something he knew, or suspected, but didn't wish to divulge. No one Richard had spoken to so far seemed to want to tell him what had happened. Were they all hiding something? "I gather he'd been shot." That, at least, couldn't be hidden.

Philip nodded, a look of determination sliding across his face. "He'd shot himself in the head." He grimaced. "It was not a pretty sight. I took a quick look only, to verify it was indeed His Grace. It was, as far as I could tell…"

"And you concluded he had inflicted the injury himself? It was that clear?"

Philip shifted in his seat again, color rising to his cheeks. "The pistol, one of a pair of dueling pistols he had, was still in his hand when I saw the body. Well, just beside his hand as though he'd dropped it as he died. I can assure you that the duke had shot himself."

Richard raised his eyebrows again. "If you say so."

Philip's shoulders sagged as he exhaled. "It's the truth."

Was it? Something about Philip Sanders whole disposition shouted out that he was hiding something. Perhaps something unimportant, but definitely something he didn't want to share. Richard tried a commiserative smile. "But you were not shown the body for several hours? When was a constable sent for?"

"As I'm the land agent, they waited for me before that was done. I sent for Hooper, that's our local constable, once I'd verified it was indeed His Grace. I also sent for our nearest magistrate—Colonel Jarvis. He's one of the three that serve Newbury. As there was no urgency, we waited until a reasonable hour to do that. Nothing would have been gained by getting either of those gentlemen out of bed in the middle of the night."

"I understood it was the duchess who discovered the body. Where was Her Grace when you arrived?"

Sanders fidgeted again. "Mr. Atkins and Mrs. Barnes had sent Her Grace and Lady Dora upstairs to their bedrooms. I believe they both went to Lady Dora's room. They were deeply shocked by what they'd seen. Understandably so. I myself shall never unsee it. Mrs. Barnes said it was best if they both took some laudanum to help them sleep. She had gone with them and administered it. They were both sleeping when I arrived. Mr. Atkins had taken charge of the house. He is a very capable man despite his advanced years, or perhaps because of them."

"Did you have any opportunity to ask Her Grace how she came to be the one who found him?"

Philip's face took on a defensive expression, a little hounded. "I did, but not until later in the day, when the constable had been, and Colonel Jarvis. They weren't with us until the middle of the morning, when the ladies were still sleeping. And of course, the body had been removed and the room cleaned." He shook his head. "I couldn't have the ladies seeing the mess on the rug. Atkins had it burned. You will see there's a new one there now if you care to examine the study."

So they had called in the authorities in the end. Sander was probably right in saying there'd been no necessity to do so until daylight hours, but all the same... "And when you did speak to her, what did the duchess say had made her come downstairs?"

He was very defensive now. "She heard the shot, of course. I hope you aren't about to suggest she had anything to do with it, because if you are, you don't know her. She is a gentle soul who would never harm any living creature. She doesn't have it in her to have killed her husband, despite what he put her through. And if you've been listening to the rumors, then you should know them for what they are. Poppycock. Pure gossip-mongering. An unexpected death like that brings out all the worst in people. They are more than glad to speculate and spread untrue allegations, particularly about their betters. They should be locked up for doing so." His voice had risen throughout his speech and now he clamped his lips together as though indicating that was the end of this line of conversation.

Richard ignored his angry expression. Now they were finally getting somewhere. Why was he not surprised? That Marcus could ever have made a loving husband was an impossibility. And Philip had been all too quick to jump to Isabella's defense when he'd not even suggested Isabella might have played any part in her husband's death. Philip was clearly well aware of the rumors and might even suspect they held a grain of truth. Could that be what he was hiding, or was it something else entirely? "You said 'what he put her through'? What do you mean by that?" As if he couldn't hazard a guess.

Philip pressed his lips together even more firmly and spoke through gritted teeth, glaring down at his clasped hands. "I've said enough. You will have to speak to the duchess herself if you wish to know more. And Lady Dora. It's not my place to talk about that."

Richard sighed. "You forget. I grew up with Marcus. I know what he was capable of."

Philip's eyes rose. They were the gray of a stormy day, and full of anguish. "As do I."

Good God. Had he witnessed what Marcus had probably done to Isabella? To Dora as well? The cruelties, the bullying, and undoubtedly the violence. The treatment which he, Richard, had blithely abandoned Dora to. Guilt welled up in his heart.

Could Philip's story be taken as evidence that Isabella was

innocent? Not that Richard saw himself as any kind of a sleuth, but Philip might well be classed as biased in Isabella and Dora's favor. Was he as in love with Dora as she was with him? The expression on his face when he'd said her name suggested he was. And if so, why had he done nothing to save her from Marcus's cruelty?

"I will do as you suggest and address my questions to the duchess," Richard said, rising from his seat. "But not today. I had a long ride yesterday and another today. I think what I require is a bath, or the ladies will be complaining that I smell, which I undoubtedly do. I shall fetch my manservant in from the stableyard, and he can organize that for me."

Philip's face brightened at what must be a point he could help with. "If you require a valet, Mr. Hopkins, His Grace's man, has remained here. He was ever hopeful of a living heir being discovered who would need his services." He tapped his fingers on the blotter on his desk. "We were all told you'd left the castle many years ago to join the army. I presume you must have taken some finding, as at first the search was carried out amongst the records of deceased officers, hoping to locate someone who was, in turn, your heir. Mr. Hopkins approached me this morning to enquire whether you would require the services of a valet. He's been acting as footman, a little unwillingly as he regards it as a step down, since the duke's death."

Richard nodded. "You may inform him that I have brought my own man with me, whom I am well used to, and who is more than capable of performing a valet's duties." Although this might be a slight exaggeration of Baxter's mixture of talents. The thought of being looked after by a man who had served Marcus sent a chill to Richard's stomach. He didn't want anything that had been Marcus's, if he could help it. It was bad enough having to inherit his house and fortune. He gave himself a shake, in the hopes of dispelling the chill. It didn't work.

"I'll go out now and retrieve Baxter from the stableyard my-self, and at the same time he can call into the kitchen and ask the housekeeper, Mrs. Barnes, you said, to send the housemaids to bring hot water to my room for a bath." He paused, with a short laugh. "Although this reminds me that I have no idea where I am to sleep." He paused again, fixing Philip with a quizzical gaze. "Do I take it I will be accommodated in the room my uncle used to occupy when I was a boy?"

This foxed the still-uneasy Philip. "His Grace slept in the largest bedroom in the west wing. If that is the one his predecessor, the sixth duke, was accustomed to using, then I would say yes, that should be your room now, unless you require a change. I'm afraid I wasn't here when the sixth duke was still living."

"Sounds correct to me," Richard said, heading towards the door, biting down the feeling of trepidation at having to sleep in Marcus's bed. "I'll go up there after I've found Baxter." He paused. "One other thing. Where is Her Grace's room located? It might be awkward if it adjoins my own."

Philip's face gave nothing away. "Her Grace sleeps in the east wing."

Mulling over that interesting piece of information, as it showed Isabella slept as far away from the ducal apartments as she could get, Richard departed in search of his new quarters. He was pleased to find nineteen years' absence had not dimmed his memory of the house, and he found his way with no problem back to the hall and up the stairs to the galleried landing. With a brief glance in the direction of the east wing, where Isabella might be right now, he headed into the corridor that led to the west wing, and the room he'd never once been in as a boy. His uncle's, then his cousin's, and now his room.

He halted outside the door, for a moment back to being the frightened little boy who'd arrived at Stourbridge all those years ago. Or even the rebellious, angry youth who'd packed his bags and taken off with nothing in his head except escaping the house that had felt like his prison. Then he turned the handle and let himself in.

The ostentatiously decorated room before him was dominated by an enormous four-poster bed with opulent covers and hangings, like something out of a gothic novel. Not that he was all that familiar with gothic novels, but he did possess an imagination.

Two long windows proved to open onto a vista of the parkland, revealing in the distance a folly in the style of a Greek temple. A folly he and Dora had played in as children and pretended was Camelot. There were going to be good memories to stumble on here, as well as the bad ones. When Marcus had gone away to school at thirteen, he and Dora's lives had been transformed. Until the holidays, of course.

Richard stood at the window in silence for a few minutes, staring out at the spread of meadows and woodland, at the cedars his great-grandfather had planted, at the glimmer of the ornamental lake in the distance near the temple. The lake Marcus had tried to drown him in. Underfoot, the Persian rug felt thick and soft, but he felt no guilt at walking on it in his dirty boots. With a wry grin, he went to the bed and threw himself down on it, legs outstretched. Marcus's bed. His bed now. Marcus was gone and would never be coming back. All of this was now his.

A tap on the door preceded its opening to reveal Baxter carrying a tin bath. Behind him followed three young maids, each carrying a couple of buckets of hot water. "Here we are, Major," Baxter said with a conspiratorial grin.

Richard got up. "Ah, that was quick. Thank you all very much."

Baxter set down the bath by the empty fireplace and the maids, having also set down their buckets, bobbed nervous curtsies to their new lord and master, eyes round as saucers and no doubt bubbling over with curiosity.

Richard gave them a once over. None could have been more than twenty, and all were dressed in gray with starched white aprons and mob caps. But they all had something else in common. They were afraid. Of him.

That Marcus had practiced a reign of terror on him as a boy

was without a doubt true, but that he'd never been allowed by his strict father to be rude or cruel to the servants was also true. Perhaps achieving his inheritance had freed him to give vent to his true nature at last. Each girl kept her eyes lowered as though afraid to look him in the eye.

This had to stop.

Richard sat down again on the edge of the bed and smiled in his most friendly manner. "I much appreciate you carrying those heavy buckets up the stairs for me, girls. I intend to be a good master to all my servants and to reward good service as it deserves." One of them dared a peek at him. "As a consequence, I would like to know all your names. No doubt you've already made the acquaintance of my trusty manservant, Albert Baxter." He grinned. "Do not be taken in by his charms for he is a scoundrel at heart, although a kind one." He winked at Baxter. "So, what are you all called?"

The girl who'd dared to peek at him looked up, her eyes wary. "Ethel, Your Grace. And these two are Betsy and Maud." Not quite so afraid now. Good.

"I trust that you will find me a fair master," Richard said. "And the water will do me well. You may all go now, back to whatever chores you were about before I disturbed you. I thank you again."

With more hurried curtsies, the three housemaids hastened away, no doubt to report back about their new master to the servants' hall.

Baxter tipped the water into the bathtub. "Your cousin must have been a tyrant. Those girls were fairly quaking when I asked 'em to bring up the water for your bath."

Richard kicked off his boots. "He was, I can assure you. But I never remember seeing the maids afraid of him when we were boys. Not like that. No doubt they thought that, as his cousin, I might be cut from the same cloth."

"It's a rum spot you've brought me to," Baxter said, picking up the discarded boots. "Something's odd about it, I'm not afraid to say. Seems to me like everyone here's a-walking on eggshells."

Richard pulled his shirt over his head. "You're right, of course. And I can only conjecture it must have more than a little to do with the death of my cousin. As far as I can see, every person here within the castle walls seems to have had a motive for wanting him dead, from the maids upwards. I would not be at all surprised to find rumor is correct and he was murdered, but by whom it would be hard to say."

Baxter opened the large armoire. It was full of clothes. "If he was the same size as you, though, these should suffice to smarten you up enough to look the part of duke. At least until you can visit a tailor."

"You want me smart?" Richard took off his breeches and stepped into the bath. It could have done with more water in it, but at least what was there was still hot. "I'm a soldier, Baxter, and dressing like a dandy doesn't come naturally to me. As you should know." He grinned. "Unless you wish to transform me into Beau Stourbridge?"

Baxter was rifling through the contents of the armoire, a faint sneer on his face, probably at the array of finery. "I'm sure we can find something a bit plainer that would meet with your approval." He glanced over. "Your Grace."

Richard sank down as low as he could into the water, which wasn't anywhere near enough to be covered. "And you can stop calling me that. I've always just been 'Major' to you, and I'd like to continue in the same way."

By the armoire, Baxter grinned as he pulled out a pair of buff-colored breeches and a clean shirt. "These aren't too bad, I suppose. He was a bit larger around the waist than you are, but braces will hold these up. And they're plain enough. Don't want to turn you out looking like the fop I saw downstairs in the hallway. Never seen the like of it. Nor sniffed it. He were wearing perfume."

Richard chuckled. Baxter must have crossed passed with the fragrant Sir Rupert Wyndham. "I suppose you'll want a raise in wages now you're to be my valet. And a new suit of clothes yourself."

Baxter also chuckled as he laid the clean clothes on the bed. "Wages at all would be a step up. I don't believe you've paid me since we quit Portugal." He glanced down at his faded Rifle Brigade uniform. "And I have to own to being fond of these duds."

"We'll put all of that right tomorrow. And we shall rub along well enough here. I should warn you that there's a footman here who was my cousin's valet, and he can either stay a footman or leave for other employ. He's bound not to like you stepping into his shoes, as that's how he'll see it, so it might be best if he goes. I don't want a man nannying me as if I were a child in petticoats. You know what I like, and that will do for me. Something of a change since our army days, but I'm sure it'll work out."

Baxter picked up the boots again. "I'll get these polished for you."

Richard laughed. "No need. We've always had a boot boy here. You need to learn to delegate a bit yourself, and get him to do them. Like I said, it's going to be a bit different to the army."

Having a valet to attend to his every need, not to mention a boy to polish his boots, was going to take some getting used to, as was having the luxury of a bath at his daily disposal. Perhaps no longer being in the army was going to turn out not to be so bad. And if he could find out a bit more about Isabella, that would also be good. Although it didn't look as though anyone here was going to tell him. He'd have to get it from the horse's mouth and ask her. He'd do that tomorrow. Clearly she liked to ride early every morning. Well, she'd find she had a companion tomorrow.

CHAPTER TEN

THE NEXT MORNING, when Isabella went into the stable block to groom her horse, she discovered someone was there before her. Richard was in the next stable to Sultan's, grooming Douglas, the cob he'd ridden the day before. Further down the row, the scrawny animals he and his man had arrived on were busy enjoying a breakfast of boiled barley, a feed that she herself had suggested to Amos would put weight on them.

In addition to taking to riding with gusto, Isabella had put herself out to learn as much as she could about the care of her horses as well, something Marcus had regularly poked fun at her for. With determination, she tried to shut out the memory of his mocking voice as he'd berated her, a sneer on his face as he spoke. "I have servants to do that, and yet you manage to show me up every day by behaving like a common farm girl, which I suppose I shouldn't be surprised at considering your origins." He'd never been able to understand her newly discovered love for everything to do with horses. For him, they'd always been a means to an end, something to gamble on, to drive at breakneck speed for a dare, or to leap enormous fences with on the hunting field. For her, they were creatures of gentle beauty and elegance who allowed her to share their friendship and speed.

For a moment, the contrast between Marcus and Richard, in his shirt sleeves yet again and with his dark hair flopping forward over his eyes in a far too attractive manner, couldn't have been greater. It had been a long time since she'd thought her late husband handsome, but his cousin, well, he was different. Here was a man whose rugged good looks could warm a girl's ardor if she weren't careful. They were certainly making her heart flutter all over again as she watched him grooming Douglas.

At least this morning he was wearing clean clothes as he looked up from brushing under the cob's belly. "Good morning, Isabella." How cheerful he sounded, as though he didn't have a care in the world, which he probably didn't. How wonderful it would be to be like that.

He grinned. "I hope you don't mind, but I thought I would emulate you and take a morning ride around the estate. I need to get a better look at it, I think, and more used to being on a horse. It's a long time since I was a boy here, and my memory is a little hazy."

She stopped outside his stable, unsure if she was annoyed at his presumption or flattered, and regarded his casual dress. Did he have no sense of how a duke should be attired? Marcus would never have been seen dead anywhere unless dressed appropriately, and would never have been seen dead in the stables. Although, now she thought about it, he had indeed died without his coat on. That would teach him. He hadn't been ready for that, had he? She pushed out of her head the unwelcome memory of his body lying on the library rug in a pool of blood and something else she hadn't wanted to look at. "Do you normally groom your own horse?"

"I noted that you did, so I thought it would be good if I did too. Yesterday, one of the grooms prepared Douglas for me." He patted Douglas's solid gray neck. "Today, I thought I should get to know him a little better, and what better way to do that than to get him ready to be ridden myself. Having been in an infantry regiment, I need all the experience I can get with horses."

"An admirable sentiment, and one to which I adhere." Isabella went into Sultan's stable and slipped a halter onto him. "I always think that if I were a man and had to fight, I should be sure and join a cavalry regiment. Why would anyone want to walk everywhere when they could be riding?" She tied Sultan up and ran an appraising hand over his back where the saddle would go, checking for any lumps and bumps, something Old Amos had taught her early on. Just smooth, silky coat under her hand with never a blemish.

Richard's laugh, a little muffled, came from somewhere under Douglas's belly where he was picking out his horse's hooves. "Perhaps you're correct. I never did much riding as a boy, though, and have no pretensions to being called a horseman. Which was why I chose the infantry as my career."

Isabella began to brush Sultan's already clean coat, which was just beginning to lose its shine as his winter coat pushed through, a sure sign cold weather wasn't far off. "Did you not have your own pony as a child? I know Marcus did, because there's a painting of him on it in the dining room above the fireplace." The urge to run inside and snatch it down and put her fist through the young rider's smug expression almost overwhelmed her. A chuckle escaped her lips at the thought of what Atkins might say if he were to see her do that. The possibility that he would help her in her vandalism existed, though.

"Dora and I rode the garden pony," Richard said. "There, feet all picked out. Would you like me to carry your saddle down from the tack room. I know which it is, because I asked Amos."

Isabella straightened up, aware of a sensation of being strong armed into something. However, he had offered, so she might as well let him. She inclined her head with all the graciousness she'd learned as a duchess. "Thank you. I have to admit, it is quite heavy so that would be very kind of you." She paused. "I like to do this all by myself, usually, but I won't say no to a little help from time to time." There. She'd been polite to him. Not so hard. And she had her heart firmly under control.

His face appeared at the vertical bars separating the two loose boxes. He was smiling, and to her surprise, contrived to look nothing like Marcus. Perhaps because the only time Marcus had ever smiled was when he was thinking of doing something horrible. Not a nice smile. Ever. Unless, of course, he'd had a different smile for his mistress. That woman. He pushed a stray lock of hair out of his eyes in a gesture that went a long way to breaking her resolution not to let her heart take over. "I'll only be a minute."

She'd smiled back before she could think of a reason not to. "Thank you." He was far too handsome with his unruly, over-long dark hair, the kindness in his brown eyes and a mouth that seemed to want to do nothing but smile. Or kiss. For a moment, as she watched him walk down the corridor and into the tackroom, she let herself wonder what it would be like to be kissed by a man like him. A real man. Not an effete member of the ton. Not a man who'd bought her from her father and considered her his property to do with as he wished. Not a fat and sweaty man with lust in his eyes who just wanted a quick fumble in an alcove at a ball when his wife wasn't looking.

Five minutes later she was leading Sultan out into the yard. Over on the far side, where the carriage horses were stabled, Amos and Jem, with the help of Jack Watkins, a relatively new arrival to the stable courtyard whom Amos had somewhat uncharitably described as a horseshoe short of a set, were sweeping up after themselves. Both young men cast surreptitious glances in her direction as they worked, when they thought themselves unobserved. Amos leaned his broom against the wall and hurried over. "Shall I give you a leg up, Your Grace?"

"Thank you, Amos. That would be lovely." Bending, he offered his cupped hands, she set her foot in them, and a moment later she was settling herself in the saddle, while Richard mounted Douglas. Amos, who could worry like an old woman at times, would no doubt be glad she had someone to ride out with. He strongly disapproved of her habit of not having one of the grooms accompany her.

She flashed a quick smile in their direction and had the pleasure of seeing the younger one, Jack, color hotly. He was a thickset youth with a shock of untidy hair and a large nose that always seemed to be running. Not very prepossessing, but she was nothing if not liberal with her smiles. Always a good idea to have men in all walks of life ready to perform favors for her. One never knew when one would need something.

Watching Richard mount brought an unwelcome memory of Marcus and the only time he'd ridden out with her in the ten years of their marriage. Her shoulder blades twitched in sympathy as she remembered the sting of the whip's blow across her back when she'd done something he'd perceived as stupid. He'd been quick to inform her of his opinion of her riding skills, or rather lack of them, and even quicker with the punishment.

That had been early in their relationship, and she'd cried real tears at the pain and humiliation. However, from then on, it hadn't taken her long to overcome that reaction and turn a cold, unmoved face to the way he treated her. The love she'd foolishly allowed herself to feel on her wedding day had rapidly turned to fear, and that, in its turn, had morphed to the hatred she'd had for him at the end. A hatred she'd done her best to keep secret, too ashamed to allow anyone to discover the truth about how she felt about him.

Pushing those memories away, she bestowed a grateful smile on the head groom as he checked her girth for her and tightened it another hole or two.

Richard turned Douglas towards the yard gates, totally unaware of the thoughts jostling through her mind, and she urged Sultan after him. She must remember that he wasn't Marcus. He was someone quite different, even though he had the misfortune to resemble his late and unlamented cousin.

"You'd better choose which way to go," he said, as they emerged onto the rear driveway. "My memories are all of paths suitable for walking, rather than riding. Dora and I were forced to explore far and wide on foot."

Isabella raised her eyebrows. This was news to her, as Dora had never been further than the gardens in all the time Isabella had been married. And that she'd only done with a stick to help her. As far as she knew, that was. "Did not her twisted leg impede her?"

Richard shrugged. "Not overly. We were children and children are resilient. I think she must have suffered from it less, back then. And we were fit from walking everywhere every day."

"Why didn't you have ponies, like Marcus?" She knew the answer to this, or thought she did, especially if Marcus and Dora's father had been anything like Marcus himself.

"We were not thought worthy of equine transport," Richard said, his words light, but with an undercurrent of resentment. "I was the poor relation, and the old duke, my uncle, declared a girl with a leg like Dora's would not be able to ride. We did manage to obtain the garden pony though, from time to time. Grace was given her own pony, of course. She was always everyone's favorite. Even Marcus's."

"I've scarcely met Grace. She was married the year before my own marriage and does not come up to London for the Season. Too busy with her brood of children in Hertfordshire, Dora says."

"She has children?" He sounded surprised.

Isabella nodded. "Four, I believe. Don't ask me their names, because I don't know. Dora probably does. I believe she corresponds with her sister. She never says, but I think she misses her still, even though she has me." As if she would want to know about someone else's brats. She scowled and urged Sultan into a trot up the track towards the Downs. "If we go this way," she called over her shoulder, "we can gallop along the ridgeway path. You can ride for miles up there. It's glorious on a day like today."

Richard brought Douglas in beside her. "Being so close in age, Dora and I were friends from the beginning. But Grace, because she was so much younger, was outside of our friendship, and I think resented us for it. But I suppose it would be nice to see her again. If I'm back here at Stourbridge for the foreseeable future, I feel I should reconnect with all my family. Don't you?"

Isabella shrugged. From her few meetings with Grace, she

had no reason to believe her younger sister-in-law was any more pleasant than Marcus had been. A spoilt and indulged child. "You will be creating your own family here, though." She smiled, a little awkwardly. "Finding yourself a wife, I think you said. Do you have anyone in mind as yet?" Why was the thought of him with a wife so disturbing? It wasn't as if she wanted to fulfill that role herself, was it? Despite his rugged good looks, she didn't know him, and he might yet turn out to be just like Marcus.

He laughed, a happy, carefree laugh, as un-Marcuslike as it was possible to be. If only she could laugh like that, but she would probably never laugh again. Not properly. "No, I have no one in mind. How could I? You forget that I'm newly back from Portugal where the number of suitable young ladies for marriage to anyone, never mind a duke, was very low. There must have been young ladies of good breeding somewhere, I'll grant, but I never had the opportunity to meet any of them. Can you imagine what the reaction would have been here and in society had I brought a Portuguese farm girl back to be my duchess?"

As this was something Isabella had initially worried about herself, she had the grace to blush, and turned her face away for a moment lest he would see.

At least, however, it meant no strange woman would be arriving at Stourbridge and attempting to lord it over her in the near future. If he were to marry a girl straight out of the schoolroom, then she, Isabella, might be able to mold her into a suitably biddable duchess. With Dora's help. Not that Dora had ever had any success in molding Isabella herself.

He chuckled. "Did you think I would be already married, then?"

She made a moue. "You are of an age when most men are."

"You forget I was in the army."

"Soldiers marry. Especially officers."

"Not this one."

She frowned. "You are not inclined in the same way as Rupert, are you?"

"Rupert?"

"My friend."

"Oh. Him. The dandy."

"Yes, him. I mean…" She hesitated. "He is what they call a 'confirmed bachelor.'"

"He is?"

She nodded. "Which makes him an ideal escort for me."

"It does?"

"Quite without danger to me." She paused, wondering at his obtuseness. How much more clearly did he need it put? "You understand?"

His frown mirrored hers. "I think so. Your Lord Rupert Wyndham does not care for young ladies."

"Well he does, because he likes me. But not in the way people think. He is not of the marrying kind. I was wondering if you might also not be, as you are five and thirty and not yet married. Rupert doesn't need to marry, you see, as his older brother has sons to carry on the Wyndham name. Although you do need to, as the last of the male Carstairs."

His brows rose towards his hairline, but he looked as though he was going to laugh again. "Are you asking me if I prefer men to women?"

Sultan tossed his head and she smiled sweetly. "I suppose I am."

Now he did laugh. "Well, you can rest easy on that count. I shall not be fooling some poor young thing into marrying me and then showing no interest in her because I prefer her brother. When I marry, I would have liked it to be for love, but I fear necessity will indicate that I should wed with speed and get myself the required heir. Being, as you so succinctly put it, the last of the male Carstairs." He eyed her up and down, his gaze lingering for a moment on her stomach. "However, as we are discussing delicate and indelicate matters, I feel obligated to pose one to you, I'm afraid. It's not intended to offend you, but I have to ask it."

Puzzled, she inclined her head. "Ask away. You will find it hard to offend me."

He nodded, bit his bottom lip, then spoke. "There is no chance that you are… increasing? It can only be a little less than two months since Marcus's death, and you might not know if you are, as yet." He grinned, more than a little awkwardly, and she was satisfied to see color in his cheeks. Always fun to let a man embarrass himself, even if she was a little herself. He cleared his throat. "A pretty fix it would put me in if you were to produce a baby boy to knock me off my perch. After I've relinquished my commission and traveled all this way to claim my inheritance."

She shook her head, aware of hot color surging up her cheeks at the abhorrent implication she'd been intimate with Marcus shortly before his death. At the implication she'd ever been intimate with a man she'd loathed so much. "Not the least chance of that." She looked away, battling to compose herself. How very true her words were. Marcus could have died any time in the last five or six years, and there would have been no chance of him leaving an heir. Not a legitimate one, at any rate. God alone knew how many baseborn brats he'd fathered. Like the little boy she'd once seen running barefoot outside one of the estate cottages, his presence having explained the rapid departure of one of the housemaids a few years ago.

He must have sensed her discomfort. "I'm sorry. I didn't mean to cause embarrassment. I'm too used to the blunt ways of soldiers. I'm going to have to learn to think before I speak."

She waved her hand. "I'm not offended. You have no need to modify your words for me. I would rather you said what you thought than dissembled. Or lied." She bit her lip, aware of the bitterness in her voice.

His brows rose again. "Your husband… my cousin. He lied to you?"

She gave a brittle laugh. "You could say so."

His eyes softened. "Rest assured, Isabella, that I shall never lie to you."

The sincerity in his voice, as well as the use of her name, brought an unexpected lump to her throat. He meant it. Good God, were those tears forming in the corners of her eyes? He mustn't see that. She had a front to maintain, and if she gave in now and let her guard down, who knew where that might lead? Nowhere she wanted to go, that was certain.

Sultan pranced under her as she inadvertently tightened her reins, giving her the perfect excuse. "Our horses are restless. Let's gallop." Without waiting for a reply, she shortened her reins and set heel, even as she spoke, to Sultan's side. The two horses bounded up the track towards the top of the Downs, the wind blowing in Isabella's face. That was better. Let the bright autumn day blow away her memories. Only the glorious day and the horse under her mattered.

But the gallop had to come to an inevitable end, and they finally brought their sweating horses down to a trot and then a walk. They were on the high ridge of the Downs now, with wide open fields rolling away to the southern horizon, dotted by the small white shapes of sheep grazing. A fresh breeze blew, and skylarks soared overhead on thermals, their song sweet to her ears. She glanced at Richard. Did she really want to share this special place with anyone? Especially a man who, depending on his mood, could look so unnervingly like Marcus, yet threatened to undo her with his kindness.

As if aware of her scrutiny, he turned to regard her out of eyes that might well have shown honesty, had her battered soul been prepared to believe it possible. "I also have a favor to ask of you."

Wary of what this might be, she answered with a raise of her eyebrows.

He smiled. No. His smile was nothing like Marcus's. She'd thought it before and now she was certain. His eyes had narrowed against the glare of the sun, a flare of lines at their corners. Nothing like Marcus's mean eyes. No. These were beautiful eyes she could have drowned in had she been a different person and this a different set of circumstances.

"As you know," he said, "I have no wife, and I have to confess little inclination to find one. But I understand from my commanding officer that if I wish to return to the Peninsula, which I do, before this war with Boney is done with, I need to get myself one in a hurry, and provide the estate with an heir. Things that cannot be done with the haste I would prefer."

This was such an unexpected statement, that Isabella couldn't control her chuckle. Why would he want to return to soldiering when he had all this estate at his fingertips? And her father's fortune to spend. "At least you are honest." Not that Marcus ever had been. "So, you wish to return to your soldiering?" A little nub of disappointment kindled in her heart. He might only have been here a day, but somehow, she'd already grown used to his presence.

He nodded. "I do. It has been my life for so long, I feel like a fish flapping on the edge of the pond, unable to return to the water. But I'm no longer just plain Major Richard Carstairs now, and I have a responsibility to the estate and title, as well as to the people who are now my tenants, and in my employ."

She laughed at his naivety. "I don't know if you know much about babies, but you need to understand, I think, that these things do not happen to order. Easier to breed horses than to breed children. And one cannot be sure to produce the boy you think you need." How odd he was with his ideas that once he'd got a son he could just march back off to war and abandon his wife and child. Although that was what Marcus had done, wasn't it? Not precisely, but very near. He'd only gone as far as London to join his gambling cronies, but he might as well have been as far away as the Continent. That sentiment must run in the family. The run-off-and-leave-the-wife sentiment.

"My commander, Lieutenant General Wellesley, won't have me back until I have an heir. He said the nobility of Britain must be preserved. I find I must do as he asks."

She pushed aside the awkward memory of when Marcus had

abandoned her lest it sour her too much. "Well, in that case, you had better do it. However, the London Season doesn't start for some time, although here in Berkshire we have a lively social life that should suit you well."

Did she really want to see him married to some girl just out of the schoolroom?

He frowned. "The trouble is, I am not at all used to socializing. I joined the army at fifteen. I have been on active duty for nineteen years, and soldiering has been my life. I know many officers do manage to attend balls and parties, but I have never done so. I didn't want to. So I am a social novice." His dark eyes implored in the most winning of ways, making her heart do yet another flutter. "I was rather hoping you might be able to assist me with this. I mean… in finding a wife."

She stiffened. He wanted her to choose him a wife? "You will remember that I am in mourning and should be for a full year."

His mouth quirked in another smile. "Your friend, Lord Rupert Wyndham, hinted that you have not let your mourning curb your enjoyment of entertainment."

Damn Rupert. There could be no denying this. "Perhaps he is right. But I fear I must admit to you that I am considered fast for my attitude to the mourning of my late husband, and other matters… The matrons frown on me and call me frivolous and shocking. I do not meet with their approval." She smiled. "Not that I give a fig for what they think of me."

"I am sure we can overcome that. What I need from you will be advice. Which young debutante would suit me best. Which to avoid. Whose mother is a harpy and should never be considered a potential mother-in-law. That sort of thing."

Why was she feeling so disappointed? She'd wanted to have a hand in the selection of the next duchess, hadn't she? And yet… the thought of seeing this man, a man whom she'd only just met but who had already wormed his way into her… her what? Surely not her heart? Not with him looking so much like bloody Marcus. Only he wasn't like Marcus at all, or if he was, he was like a mirror version of him, an opposite.

Of course, she could play along with this and never find him a potential wife. Yes. That was the thing to do. As soon as he got himself a wife, he would cease to be her friend, and she didn't want that. Let him believe she had good intentions.

She smiled. This might be quite fun, and another opportunity to cut a few enemies dead. Revenge would be sweet. "I can tell you all that, of course." She eyed him up and down. "And you do have the advantage of not already being known. You are the great inconnu. A mystery man with a title. Even with me as your sponsor, I foresee your inevitable popularity with the mamas who fancy their daughters as duchesses. Perhaps you and I should discuss what you require in a wife, and make ourselves a list?"

This made him laugh. "That feels a little formal, but it would do no harm for me to tell you what I do *not* require in a wife. That list, I feel, might be longer than one listing what I do require." He swiped his unruly hair out of his eyes, the gesture boyish and making her wish there was a portrait of him as a boy at the castle instead of one of Marcus.

She had to laugh. "You are a fussy bridegroom then?"

"I think I might be."

She could play along with this. "So what is at the top of your list of dislikes in a young lady?"

"Stupidity. I could not bear to be married to an empty-headed girl. Nor one that cannot hold an intelligent conversation. I will require intelligent children, you see, not dunderheads."

"Then that will cancel out at least half of the girls I could have suggested. I'm afraid most of them are not brought up to be intelligent conversationalists. They've been groomed to flirt, to flatter, to simper, and to make a man feel superior in all things. Most of them are, alas, dunderheads, as you put it. Although I think we'd better not tell anyone of our conclusions."

"And you were not brought up like that?"

She shook her head. "You guess right. I arrived late in my parents' marriage and was their only child. My father wanted me to have the sort of education he would have given a son." She met his gaze. "I speak half a dozen languages, and if you did not have Mr. Sanders, I could manage the estate books with no trouble, although I've never been allowed anywhere near them. I was brought up to understand trading and how to make money."

His brows rose. Perhaps he'd never met a young lady like her before.

Good. It would be fun to spar with him a little. If only he didn't keep reminding her of Marcus, everything would be fine. She could delay the finding of a suitable wife as long as possible, for the arrival of some slip of a girl, thinking she could lord it over her, would spoil her fun. Eventually, in a year or two perhaps, she would choose him a nice biddable one, who'd do as she was told while Richard was off playing at being a soldier. Or perhaps by then he might have decided not to go back. The realization that she would like it if he stayed settled over her like a warm blanket. Yes, she would like that very much.

They were riding downhill now, towards the road to Winchester. She'd given away enough about herself. "If we take that track up ahead we can ride through that farm and return to the parkland. I feel an urge for breakfast. Shall we trot?"

CHAPTER ELEVEN

O N THEIR RETURN from their ride, Richard went straight into breakfast, while Isabella went upstairs to change into a day dress. He found that delicate flower of London society, Lord Rupert Wyndham, already ensconced in the breakfast room consuming a large plate of devilled kidneys. This morning Lord Rupert sported a coat of a delicate pale blue over a matching waistcoat and had a cravat tied with the most intricate of designs. Unimpressed by this vision of beauty, Richard eyed the absurd height of the fellow's collar points. If he tried turning his head, he risked taking an eye out on them.

Wyndham rose to his feet with consummate elegance. "Stourbridge. I hope you don't mind, but I was famished and couldn't wait. That butler of yours told me you and Bella had gone off for a morning ride, and I thought I'd have fainted from starvation if I'd had to wait for you to return. I know Bella all too well and her liking for long rides." A frown of past memory furrowed his brow. "One early morning ride with her was enough for me. Never again. The early morning is not a time of day at which I function properly."

"She's gone to change," Richard said, spooning kedgeree onto his own plate. "I don't think she'll be long, but like you, I'm hungry, so please sit down and we'll eat together." He waved a hand at the footman waiting by the sideboard. "You may go. We'll serve ourselves." A little private conversation with Lord

Rupert would not go amiss.

The footman bowed and departed, and Richard took his seat at the head of the table, still awkward at the thought of occupying what he mainly remembered as his uncle's place, while Wyndham regained his. For a few moments they ate in silence before Richard set down his fork and fixed Wyndham with a penetrating stare. The one he'd used when one of his riflemen was brought before him for a supposed misdemeanor.

Wyndham stopped eating, a furtive expression on his face. Much like one of the guilty riflemen. "Anything wrong with the kedgeree?"

Richard shook his head. "Nothing. I was just engaged in thought. In wondering about something. And I wondered if you might enlighten me."

"Be my pleasure to." Wyndham didn't sound overly confident this was true. He, like everyone else here, seemed inclined to nervousness when questioned. And reticence.

Richard leaned forward. Plain speaking was called for here, or, before they knew it, Isabella would be downstairs again. "Did she do it?"

Wyndham's eyes widened and his Adam's apple bobbed. "Did who do what?" It was plain he knew exactly what Richard meant, though.

"Did Isabella kill her husband?" No point in hedging around the subject. If he were to live in close proximity to Isabella, to trust her with helping him find a wife, then he needed to know if she was guilty of what rumor said she was, and if possible exonerate her—for the Prince of Wales. And besides which, he rather liked her. The thought that if he discovered she had killed her husband he might still be prepared to like her surfaced. A bit more than liked her, as well. Even though she had departed upstairs, he was finding it hard to remove the image of her face from his thoughts.

Wyndham swallowed, color rising to his cheeks. "Of course she didn't kill him. What kind of a question is that?" He sounded offended. "You've been listening to too much gossip."

"Maybe I have. But gossip is often founded on fact. And as far as I've gathered, the facts are not explicit in clearing her of involvement."

"Rubbish," Wyndham managed, now sounding as though he were blustering. "Anyone who knows her would know she couldn't have done it."

"So, you are basing your opinion on the fact that you know her, not on any evidence you might have seen?"

Wyndham's eyes shot from side to side as though he were seeking a means of escape. "There is no evidence that she had anything to do with it." He was doing a very good job of making Richard more suspicious.

"I hear there is some evidence that might suggest she did." This wasn't strictly true, but he wanted to see Wyndham's reaction to this statement.

Wyndham shook his head with vigor. "Total nonsense. Gossips have been putting it about. No evidence whatsoever." He poked his devilled kidneys in a less than enthusiastic manner. Perhaps his claimed hunger had fled under Richard's catechism.

Richard persisted. "I gather it was she who found him."

Wyndham nodded, maybe thinking he was on safer ground here. "She did, the poor thing. Such a shock to her system. Horrifying, I'm told. I was so glad I wasn't here when it happened." He shuddered. "Nothing would induce me to go into the library now, even though there's a new rug there. By chance, I was away from home and didn't receive her invitation to visit."

"Her invitation?"

Wyndham took on the expression of a man who has just realized he's said too much. If he'd not been holding his knife and fork he might well have clapped his hand to his mouth. "Oh, er, I, well, the, er, the one to stay here for a few days to escort her to the ball…" The words squeezed between his teeth as though he'd far rather have kept them in.

"She had invited you here for a few days? Why?" Richard

raised his brows. "I rather was under the opinion that you only visited when her husband was away."

More hot blushing from Wyndham. "Oh, good heavens, no. Well, I mean yes. But not in the way you're implying. No, not at all." He set his knife down and dabbed at his shiny forehead with his napkin. "I mean, I was only friends with Isabella, not with Marcus."

Enjoying making Wyndham this uncomfortable, Richard merely raised his brows a second time. A lot could be conveyed by such a simple move. He'd done it a good few times when interrogating recalcitrant riflemen.

"I mean," Wyndham said with some determination, "that we were just that. Friends. Nothing more. And I was not friends with Marcus. So when Isabella had a local ball or dinner to go to, she would invite me to stay and I would act as her escort. As I did two nights ago when we went to the Brocklebank's ball at Bembridge House." He began to assume a more confident mask. "I'll have you know that my opinion carries a great deal of weight in society. I have been able to advise Isabella on many aspects of being a duchess." He glared at Richard. "But on this occasion when she sent me an invitation, as I have already explained, I was not at home, so did not receive it."

"You implied she only invited you if Marcus was not here?"

He nodded, seemingly glad to be on solid ground, and pushed away his half-eaten breakfast.

"So why, in that case, was Marcus here? Do you know?"

"I have no idea. He must have come down unexpectedly. It would have been most unfortunate had I been here at the same time as him. I would not have enjoyed the ball they attended. Marcus did not like me."

"So they'd been to a ball that night?"

Wyndham nodded. "I believe they had. That was why she invited me. She wanted me as her escort. I believe, from what I have heard, that she was forced to go with Marcus when he turned up."

Now they were getting somewhere. So the duke and duchess had gone out together to a ball somewhere presumably not too far away from Stourbridge, and, on returning, Marcus had met his end. Richard pushed his own plate away as well. "I gather that the 'accident' happened at about three in the morning."

"You have it right. That is exactly what I've heard." Wyndham fiddled with the handle of his coffee cup. "Although of course, we do not talk about it. I wouldn't be so ungentlemanly as to broach the subject." He shot Richard a meaningful glance implying he was finding this conversation sat under that same description.

Richard was not about to let this go. "So what was she doing up at that time of the morning? Or were they back that late? Did it happen as soon as they returned, perhaps?"

Consternation returned to Wyndham's face. "No, no, no. I think she was upstairs in her room. Yes, I'm positive she was." His eyes darted back and forth like those of a cornered animal. "The shot disturbed her. Yes, that was it. She heard the shot and came downstairs and found him. He'd taken his own life." His face clouded. "The poor girl."

"She was there first? You're certain? Did no one else hear the shot and get there sooner? None of the servants? What about Lady Dora? Didn't she hear anything?"

Wyndham wriggled in his seat. "The servants mainly sleep in the attics, of course. If they heard anything, then I daresay they would have been slower to react and descend to the library, and perhaps afraid to do so. Besides which, the butler heard. Atkins. He was second on the scene. I know that because he told me." There was a note of "so there" to this final statement.

"And what was Isabella wearing?" What Richard wanted to discover here was whether she was in her night attire or not.

Wyndham's eyes narrowed as though he suspected he was being tricked into giving away something he didn't want to. "How should I know? I wasn't even in the house. If you want to know something like that, then I suggest you ask the butler. I assume he would know." He paused, puffing his chest out. "However, I also suggest most heartily that you don't pester poor Bella with your questions. I would not like to see her further upset. She is just beginning to recover from the shock and questions from you might set her back. She is more delicate than she seems."

"You are very concerned for her welfare."

"Of course I am. She's my friend."

"And as her friend, no doubt you would defend her whatever she had done."

Wyndham set his cup down with a clatter, entirely missing the saucer and nearly upending coffee all over the table. "Of course I would. Just as she would for me. That is what friends are for. I can see you can never have had any, or you would know." He got to his feet. "I find my appetite has quite vanished. I must leave you to breakfast alone. Good day to you, Stourbridge." And he was gone.

Richard regarded his three-quarters full plate of cooling kedgeree for a long minute. That had been interesting. As far as he could tell, Wyndham did indeed think Isabella had killed her husband, despite his protestations to the contrary. They were far too insistent. He clearly knew next to nothing but believed the rumors true, and thought Isabella capable of such an act. But just as clear was the fact that the man had no intention of ratting on her to the authorities, such as they were. Because she was his friend.

But did he, Richard, agree with Wyndham? And did he really want to know? The answer to the latter question had to be yes. As far as he had made out from his interview with Mr. Allsop, she was now a penniless widow. Anything that had come from her father was part of the estate he himself had inherited from Marcus. None of it was to go to her. She was in the position of indigent poor relation, much as he had been as a boy, and he was cast as her possible benefactor. And beautiful as she was, the possibility that she might be a dangerous opponent still existed. A rather exciting possibility.

The estate already possessed one single woman in his cousin Dora, but she was a different type of person to Isabella. For a start, he knew her and trusted her. She'd been his childhood friend and companion, the only person he'd missed after he'd left to join the army. He could live with her, but could he live in a house occupied by someone who had killed his predecessor in what might have been cold blood? Even someone who looked like Isabella and had such a disturbing effect upon his equilibrium?

The question was, why had she killed Marcus, if indeed she had? She must have known she'd be left penniless if he died. Why would she be willing to risk that?

His cogitations were interrupted by the sound of the door opening, accompanied by the tap of a stick, and girlish laughter. Dora and Isabella came into the breakfast room together, both clad in what should have been somber black day dresses. Although Dora's was demure and unadorned, Isabella's had about it the look of a dress that didn't want to be classed as mourning. The black showed off her ivory skin to perfection, and her auburn hair gave a splash of color to her ensemble. His stomach gave a disturbing flip. Was he falling for her all too evident charms?

ISABELLA, SPURRED ON by her usual morning appetite for breakfast after her ride, had spent no more than a few minutes in changing from her riding habit into something more becoming for daywear. Hawkins, her maid, who was used to her mistress's habits, made no objection to the speed and merely buttoned her into one of the requisite black mourning dresses Isabella had designed herself and had made by the local dressmaker in Newbury—Miss Chaloner. That they were black was the only concession to true mourning, as Hawkins had more than once pointed out, but now knew better than to comment on. She knew all too well that Isabella always did what she wanted, especially since the death of the duke.

Once changed, Isabella emerged onto the galleried landing

where she encountered Dora, much more demurely clad. Her best friend's solemn face softened into a smile of welcome, but nevertheless didn't lose its perpetual worried frown. "Bella, are you going down to breakfast? Perhaps you will lend me your hand on the stairs? My leg is troubling me more than usual this morning. I must have slept awkwardly on it."

"Of course." Isabella held out her arm and Dora linked hers through it. They descended the stairs together, Dora's cane tapping on the dark oak of the treads with every step, just as Wyndham strode across the hall and disappeared into the drawing room looking as though he was in a huff. The staircase was the one thing in the house that threatened to daily defeat Dora, and Isabella had helped her up or down the flight many times.

Dora squeezed her arm. "And what do you think of our prodigal returned?"

Isabella shrugged. She would need to be careful what she said here. "He looks a sight too much like Marcus for my liking, although as far as I can tell, he doesn't seem to share his personality. Thank goodness." She chuckled. "And I can tell you he's no horseman. We had a lovely ride, but he could do with some pointers on his seat."

Dora pulled her friend to a halt on the half-landing. "Never mind the way he sits a horse. Trust you to think that the most important thing about him. Does it bother you that he's a little like Marcus? I know there is a familial resemblance, but I've never thought it overly worrying. Although when last I saw them side by side, Marcus was a man grown and Diccon still very much a boy."

Isabella frowned. "I suppose when he smiles he is nothing like Marcus, but every time I look at him, I admit to finding myself seeing Marcus before me again. It's like seeing a ghost, or maybe a blurred reflection. I'm not sure I like it." She shook her head. "I've a mind to suggest to him that you and I should go and live in the Dower House. Then I wouldn't have to keep looking at him." Which might be a very good idea considering how looking at him was really making her feel. Most confusing.

Dora nodded, a tinge of relief in her eyes. "That sounds an excellent idea. As for me, I would give anything to be away from this house with its unwelcome memories." She shuddered. "We could do so, but I fear we would have to ask his permission and would need him to provide us with an allowance. Neither of us are in possession of an income that would furnish the required servants nor cover our living expenses. We would be, in fact, we are, very much beholden to our cousin for our living."

Isabella's frown deepened into a scowl. "And that in itself is enough reason for me to take an active dislike to this interloper." She paused, Richard's undeniably handsome face dancing before her eyes. Most annoying. "And he's had the infernal cheek to ask me to help him find a wife. A woman who will come here and take over the running of the house and… and…"

"Take your place. I understand your annoyance. But if you are to choose him a wife, you can choose someone who will suit both of us, as well. Better to have a new friend installed here than a potential enemy."

"I already thought of that."

"So you told him you would?"

"Sort of."

Dora smiled again. "Then perhaps we'd better take on this task between us. I feel it might be a two-woman job. He will need to be steered well clear of any young lady who might have ideas above her station in life. Or who might hold the purse strings so tightly you and I will be discomfited. If we intend to eventually take on the Dower House, we will need to train Diccon's wife-to-be so that she puts us first, or at any rate, not last."

Isabella nodded. "I could not have put it better myself. We need to think of ourselves, and how a new duke with a new duchess will affect us. He can't be allowed to let delusions of grandeur overtake him. We will have to try to manage him far better than either of us ever could manage Marcus." She gave a shiver. No one had ever been able to manage Marcus. She lowered her voice. "Although, I will tell you now that I have no intention of finding him a wife for quite some time. My objections to each young lady will be of the most imaginative." She chuckled.

They descended the last few steps into the hallway and crossed to the breakfast room, arms still linked.

Dora nodded. "He won't know what's hit him," she whispered, as Isabella pushed the door open.

Richard was seated at the head of the table, his coffee cup in his hand.

"Good morning, Diccon." Dora disengaged her arm from Isabella's and came over to plant a kiss on his cheek as he rose to his feet. "Isabella has been telling me about your morning ride." She sighed. "I do sometimes wish I was able to ride myself and enjoy the mornings with her. And now with you as well. Perhaps I shall take the carriage out later on while the sun is shining."

She sat down at the table, but Isabella went over to the sideboard where the breakfast was laid out. "What shall I fetch you?"

Dora's sniffed, her nose quivering. "I find I'm rather hungry today, for once. Could I have eggs, do you think, and a slice or two of the bacon?"

Isabella brought this for Dora before returning to fill her own plate with the same. Glancing up, she caught Richard looking at her a little quizzically and smiled. "What? You think I would not help my best friend?"

Dora smiled as well. "Don't chide him, Bella. He doesn't know our ways."

No, he didn't know them at all, and they were going to make sure it stayed that way, then he wouldn't be able to work out what they were up to. Poor sap. Poor handsome sap. He had no idea what was coming to him.

Richard pushed his own plate away. "My food has gone cold,

and my appetite has vanished. Shall I pour you both some coffee?"

Isabella bestowed her sweetest smile on him. "That would be lovely, thank you."

CHAPTER TWELVE

"WE SHOULD HOLD a ball here at Stourbridge," Isabella said to Richard and Dora. "To introduce Richard to our neighbors." They were seated opposite her in the drawing room taking afternoon tea. Wyndham had taken a rather precipitate leave several days since, straight after his breakfast encounter with Richard, but neither Dora nor Isabella knew why he'd gone, to Richard's relief. Isabella set down her cup. "We can invite everyone who is anyone, and Dora and I can advise you on which are the most suitable of the local young ladies for you to consider as brides." A glint showed in her eyes. "If there are any, which I seriously doubt. But, nevertheless, it will be fun to show you off."

Richard frowned. So did Dora, but probably for a different reason.

"Should we be actually holding a ball of our own?" Dora asked, it had to be said, with a certain degree of timidity. "I mean, what with being in mourning still. You know. People might think it an inappropriate thing to do. They might not want to attend."

Isabella shook her head with determination. She was fast becoming the most determined person Richard had ever met, and she had the look about her right now of a horse with the bit between its teeth. Not that he didn't find this assertiveness attractive, because he did. Although he wasn't about to let on. She might become uncontrollable if he did.

She shot Dora a hard stare, something she seemed very good at. "Nonsense. Of course people will come if we invite them. They won't be able to resist. And what is more, they'll bring their eligible daughters in their droves, because they will all know by now that the new Duke of Stourbridge has returned from the Continent and is in the happy state, for them, of being unmarried. You know what the local gossips are like. Heaven knows how the news gets out, but it always does. And pooh to it being inappropriate. When have I ever cared for that?"

Dora pursed her lips, that worried frown deeper than usual. "You may not care for your own inappropriateness and reputation, nor mine, but I'm sure Diccon might for his own." She glanced sideways at her cousin. "Do you not?"

Richard did his best to look stern, disguising the fact that he, too, didn't give a fig for what others thought of him. Although the idea of being the host of what could be a large gathering of the cream of local society disturbed him more than he cared to admit. It wasn't as if he'd ever even attended a ball. He would be a complete ball novice, and was sure it would show. Having learned so long ago as a child, he wasn't sure he could even remember how to dance. But he didn't want either of them guessing this. Well, not Isabella, at any rate. He didn't mind what Dora thought of him, but, somehow, in a relatively short time it had come to matter to him what Isabella thought. He swallowed down his nerves. "I suspect Isabella might well be correct in her summing up of our neighbors' attitudes. I gather nothing is more alluring to the mamas of society than the prospect of an unmarried duke."

Dora laughed, the frown lessening. "You are paraphrasing Bella; I know it. She used those self-same words to me just yesterday."

"What if he is?" Isabella said, with a resigned sigh. "Come, Dora, we have to consider how things here are changing. We are not so much a house in mourning now, as a house that is preparing for that change. We have a new duke amongst us, and he requires our assistance." She paused, a decidedly naughty twinkle in her eyes that sent an unexpected current of electricity through Richard. Damn it. She was far too attractive a young widow to have to share his new home with. Perhaps he should suggest she, too, look for a new marriage partner, to get the temptation of her out from under his feet. And from inside his head, a space she had begun to occupy more than he liked over the last few days.

She made a moue, which only served to render her more attractive and him more uncomfortable. "And besides which, haven't I been attending all the balls and parties held by our neighbors? I think they would find it most odd if we didn't hold some sort of entertainment of our own, in return for all the events they've hosted. They'll all be expecting us to present our new duke to them, post haste. And it would be manifestly unfair of us to keep him to ourselves." She turned those beautiful eyes on him and held his gaze for a few long seconds before looking back at Dora as though she hadn't just seared him to the heart.

Dora frowned. She'd always been the most conservative of Richard's three cousins, with an inclination not to rock whatever boat she found herself in. A peacemaker, sandwiched between the more volatile Marcus and Grace, not a troublemaker. "You know how I cautioned you about attending balls whilst in mourning," she said, giving Isabella a reproving stare. Or at least, as reproving a stare as she was capable of, which was probably nothing compared with Isabella's.

Isabella narrowed her eyes. "Oh pooh to that. You know I don't give a fig for what others think of me."

Yes, they all knew that. There was no need for her to repeat herself.

She glanced at Richard as though for support. "And anyway, it is our new duke who will have the final say, is it not?" She raised her delicate brows at him. "What say you... Diccon?"

She let his nickname roll off her tongue in a purr that almost made him laugh out loud at its evident intention to beguile and win him to her side. What a flirt she was. And it was working, despite his disinclination to fall for it. He began to think she might have been a good match for Marcus. Whatever she was, murderer or innocent widow, she was not someone who could be browbeaten by convention. And probably not by a man.

She batted her eyelashes, which were long and thick, at him, eyes wide and brimming with fake innocence. "Well? Shall we hold a ball here at Stourbridge and invite all the young ladies from far and wide to see if any of them meet with our approval? Although I fear they might be a rather motley bunch from what I've seen of them so far this autumn."

Richard suppressed the impulse to laugh, once again, at her use of "our." That she thought she was going to be the one to choose his wife-to-be was obvious. He wasn't the idiot she took him for. That he needed her help in steering clear of the unsuitable ones was true, but the final choice would be his. He wouldn't divulge this as yet, though. Let her continue to believe she could choose him a wife who would suit her purpose. That was evidently what she thought she was going to do. And it was unlikely that either of them were going to come across the sort of wife he was beginning to think he wanted. Not unless Isabella looked in the mirror, that was. And that could never be.

"Yes," he said, with determination. "Mourning be damned. None of us had any love for Marcus, so we shouldn't be feeling guilty at throwing off our weeds." Not that he'd ever worn mourning, anyway. Not even a black armband. No one had suggested it and, like Isabella, he had no love lost for Marcus. However, maybe someone here *should* be feeling guilty. If they'd had a hand in Marcus's demise, that was.

He put that unwelcome thought out of his mind. "Let us hold the biggest and best ball of the autumn. No, of the year. Isabella is right, Dora. The local gentry will want to meet their new duke, odd as it still seems to me that he and I are one and the same. I owe it to them to put myself up for their inspection. And as Isabella already knows, I do indeed wish to be married as soon as possible." No need to repeat what he'd already told Isabella, and now rather regretted having done, that once he had an heir he intended returning to his regiment. Dora might be upset and Isabella might crow with triumph, thinking herself destined to return to power at Stourbridge in his absence. She probably thought a wife of her choice would be easy to browbeat into submission.

Isabella clapped her hands, shooting Dora a somewhat smug grin. "I knew you would see it my way. Now, which day shall we have it? There's so much we have to do. We'll need to send invitations out immediately and engage an orchestra for the dancing. It's an age since there was a ball here at Stourbridge. Marcus was never here long enough to host one. And of course, both Dora and I will need new gowns, and everything that goes with them."

Would they? Surely they both had armoircs full of suitable gowns? Richard looked from one woman to the other in perplexity.

"Oh no," Dora, who must have similar sensibilities to his, interrupted. "I shall be quite all right in my black silk. I've barely worn it. I don't need a new gown."

Isabella's expression of disgust was enough to make Richard have to fight to control his laughter. She was in full flow now, obviously didn't agree with Dora, and nothing was about to stop her informing them of this fact. He had to admire her determination.

She shook her head at poor Dora. "Nonsense. You will need a new gown for this splendid ball Richard is to host or people will think him a penny-pincher. And you cannot have another black one. There is to be no arguing." As Dora opened her mouth, Isabella held up a hand to silence her and fixed her gaze on Richard. "And you will need a new suit of evening clothes. You can't keep on wearing Marcus's old things. I confess, I would rather give them all away than have to keep seeing you in them. Just the sight of them sends a shiver down my spine. And besides which, you are nowhere near as portly as he was so the clothes rather hang on you." She flashed a wicked smile. "And you already look enough like Marcus to make me quite uncomfortable without going about the castle in his clothes for evermore."

Richard shrugged. "I have little else, I'm afraid. An army officer on campaign doesn't have much use for evening wear. His uniform has to do him." Especially not a Rifle Brigade officer.

Isabella bestowed a suddenly much sweeter smile on him, and changed her tune. "I am not criticizing you, dear Coz. I quite understand that you're not as used to tricking yourself out in as much finery as we are. And I know you haven't had time yet to even poke your nose through the door of a tailor's shop." She tilted her head to one side as though deep in thought. "Of course, it would be better for you to go to Weston's in Bond Street, but think how tiresome it would be to have to travel up to Town just to be fitted for a coat and breeches. No, there is a perfectly adequate tailor in Newbury we can take you to. Chalke's. I know Mr. Sanders goes there, and he always looks the ticket, for a land agent, of course."

Dora, throwing an annoyed frown at Isabella perhaps for her dismissal of Mr. Sanders's position and sartorial appearance, pursed her lips and frowned at Richard, who was wondering if it would be quite the thing to be decked out in clothes more suited to a land agent for his debut ball. "If you are sure this is what you want, Diccon. I mean, the ball, not the new suit of clothes from Mr. Chalke. I suppose you and Bella may have your way. Far be it from me to stand in the path of either of you. Not that it would do me any good as Isabella would run me down." She shot another frown at Isabella. "But let it be known that I still feel it is too soon after… after Marcus's death to be celebrating with a ball, even if half the countryside is keen to make your acquaintance." The worried frown was back, and something more he couldn't put his finger on.

Isabella patted Dora's hand in a conciliatory fashion. "You are a silly, sometimes. Rest assured. No one will care what we wear.

Well, they won't care what you wear. They'll all be looking at what I wear, of course. They always do. But other things will distract them this time. Not only will they be keen to meet with Richard and snare him for one of their daughters, but they'll also be full of morbid curiosity to see the house Marcus died in. And besides which, we don't want them thinking we have something to hide." Her smile, this time, was brittle. Despite her words, she was definitely hiding something.

Dora gripped Isabella's hand. "Won't they want to poke about and be nosy? I couldn't bear that." Her voice trembled, unshed tears glistened in her eyes and her frown deepened. Her face had paled so much, she looked as though she might be about to faint. "Do you think it might be a good idea to lock the library to prevent gawkers sneaking in there looking for...for things...like...?" Her voice trailed off, and she had to visibly pull herself together. "We don't want them doing that, do we?" She fixed her gaze on her clasped hands in her lap as though afraid to meet anyone's eyes. Her voice dropped to barely above a whisper. "That would not at all be a good thing." She twisted her fingers together.

Did she know something too? In fact, did everyone in this house have a secret about that night they weren't sharing? From Isabella down to the servants? Richard looked from one woman to the other but was none the wiser.

Isabella squeezed Dora's hand and gave a shrug that was as artificial as her smile. "Who cares? There's nothing for them to see. Let them come and look in the corners and they'll come to the right conclusions. That Marcus took his own life while in one of his black humors. That will kill the rumors as dead as he is."

That both of them were well aware of the rumors surrounding his cousin's untimely death was obvious. But what was it they weren't divulging? Instinct told him they probably knew a lot more than they were letting on. Should he investigate further? If he did, he might find something he didn't like. So, instead, he slapped on a bland smile. "It's settled then. No further arguments.

You ladies choose a date and begin with the preparations. So long as I don't have to do any of them, I shall be happy. I delegate it all to you."

Isabella visibly brightened at that. "Splendid. And the first thing we must attend to is our apparel. Once that is ordered, we can get on with the rest of our preparations. Can't we, Dora?"

Dora glanced up from her study of her hands, the nervous expression on her face surely not due only to what the local gentry would think of them holding a ball whilst supposedly still in mourning. Something else lurked there in her wide, frightened eyes, unspoken, yet tangible.

CHAPTER THIRTEEN

ISABELLA DISCOVERED THAT, now they'd decided on it, the day of the ball appeared to be coming around far more quickly than she'd thought it would. Dora was reticent about it, of course, which was only understandable. However, Isabella considered herself an expert at sweeping unwanted things under the proverbial rug, and told herself as firmly as possible that what was in the past was meant to stay in the past. Until she almost believed it herself.

She prided herself in being a great proponent of her old nurse's adage—"there's no use crying over spilt milk." And as the milk had most definitely been spilled, and they could do nothing to change it, it was best to get on with matters and stop dwelling on it.

Don't look back. That was her motto, and she had no intention of changing it.

Despite these self assurances, she was under no illusions about how Dora really felt, and even, although she wouldn't admit it to anyone, harbored a few doubts of her own about the propriety of holding a ball so soon after Marcus's death. Even a duchess can sometimes worry about what people might say about her. However, she dismissed these thoughts as soon as they surfaced and wasn't about to share them with either Richard or Dora. No. She would not allow herself or Dora, or Richard, to be influenced by the dictates of polite society. And besides which, there was always the fact that if they invited their neighbors into their house it would surely imply they had nothing to hide and nothing to be ashamed of.

Wouldn't it?

She had a lot of planning to do. Many things would have to be undertaken in order for the ball to run smoothly, some of which could be delegated to the servants. Although things like the menu had to be approved, as did the choice of orchestra for the dancing, and the floral decorations for the rooms they would be using. Isabella couldn't recall when last anything like this had been held at Stourbridge. She'd held a few dinner parties herself, but never a full-scale ball, of the sort she was fond of attending, and on occasion holding, when in Town.

She decided this would be different to anything she'd organized in the past.

It would be a joyous occasion, and she would make it so. Marcus was gone. He could no longer threaten her happiness in any way. Nor Dora's, although, from her demeanor, you would have been forgiven for thinking Dora still thought he could. She frequently had the sort of expression on her face that hinted at a fear of Marcus's ghost waiting for her around every corner. Pooh to that. Isabella was determined they would have the fun they so deserved after her ten years of being married to Marcus, and Dora's lifetime of being his put-upon and bullied sister.

Resolved that the recalcitrant Dora would look the part, she finally succeeded in convincing her that she needed the suggested new gown, the expense be damned. Richard, whom she was airily convinced she could twist around her little finger, would pay. He might not know it yet, but he would. So with that in mind, the afternoon after they'd decided to hold the ball, she sweetly asked him if they could take the carriage into Newbury to visit Miss Chaloner's dressmaking establishment.

Richard had spent the morning shut away in the estate office with Mr. Sanders, something Marcus had never done once to her knowledge, and she encountered him in the front hall on his way upstairs. For a moment, despite having broached the subject the day before, she thought he might ask her why she and Dora needed new gowns. Marcus would have, particularly towards the end, when he'd begrudged any penny he had to spend on her or his sister. But he didn't. Instead, he turned his so-un-Marcus-like smile on her and nodded as though it was something that gave him the greatest pleasure in the world, making her unruly heart give a little, not unpleasant, flip, for which it would need reprimanding. "Why not. As you so astutely pointed out yesterday, I have need of some new clothes myself if I'm to host a ball, so I think I'll accompany you. If you don't mind. You said there's a tailor in the town who could oblige me, I think?" His eyes twinkled with what could have been mischief, making him more attractive than ever, which only served to make Isabella all the crosser. "The one Mr. Sanders goes to?"

"Chalke's. It's perfectly adequate, I think you will find." She couldn't keep the snap out of her voice. Damn it. Why was it his niceness vexed her so?

He nodded, the corner of his mouth quirking in a half smile. "Splendid. I shall be quite happy to be perfectly adequate in a suit my land agent might wear."

Was he laughing at her? She tried to frown at him, but that smile… What was there about him that rendered him so annoyingly charming, even when she wanted to be cross with him. Try as she might, despite his resemblance to Marcus, which daily seemed to be lessening, her anger just melted away at that smile. Most frustrating.

She nodded. "Just so. We will visit Mr. Chalke's establishment as well." Not that Marcus would have gone anywhere near him for his clothes. No, his had all come from his London tailor, Weston's.

"That will suit me well." Richard benefited her with another dazzling smile. He really shouldn't be doing that. "We shall ride into town together, then." His eyes narrowed as though he'd divined her intention. "And I suppose I should come into your dressmaker's and pay?"

This time she had to smile back at him, firstly because his smile was so damned infectious, and secondly because he had it quite right. "I admit, that was indeed what I was hoping. I had intended to ask her to send you the bill, but if you are the sort of gentleman who likes to pay his bills promptly, I'm sure she'll be your friend for life." The cost of her gowns had been an ever-increasing bone of constant contention between herself and Marcus, but she wasn't about to tell Richard that. Nor did she feel that now was the right time to inform him that Marcus had left her penniless. And besides which, with everything he'd inherited, including the money from her own dear papa, which should by rights have been hers, he could well afford some new gowns. A lot of new gowns. She had no qualms about exploiting his generosity.

So, leaving the servants to begin working on arrangements for the ball, she and Dora, with Richard as their escort, had the carriage take them into Newbury to Isabella's dressmaker, the accomplished Miss Chaloner. Of course, they could have asked her to come out to Stourbridge, but, as Isabella so wisely pointed out, they could do with being away from the castle, and it wouldn't all fall to pieces in their absence. In fact, it would be a good idea to leave the servants to their preparations without fear of being interrupted.

The dressmaker's stood halfway down Northbrook Street, several hundred yards from the office of Mr. Allsop. The day was fine and warm for September, so the hood on the carriage had been down for their journey. When it halted outside the establishment of Miss Chaloner, Jem, the groom who'd been riding on the back, jumped off and let down the step.

Taking this young man's offered hand, with a smile guaranteed to keep him as one of her admirers even though he was only a servant, Isabella descended onto the pavement and surveyed the small-paned bow window showcasing Miss Chaloner's wares with interest. Several attractive hats adorned the display, as Miss

Chaloner had recently branched out into millinery. Perhaps she would order one for herself. That green bonnet would so suit her coloring, and her hair. What a bore it was to have to always wear black. On the spot, she determined to put an end to that forthwith. Richard himself had said he was fed up with mourning and they should not be ashamed of holding the ball. Well she, and Dora as well, would henceforth no longer wear this dreadful, boring black.

Richard nodded to Dickens, their coachman, and he and Jem took the coach off up towards the end of the street where there was room to turn it and bring it back facing the right way to wait outside the shop.

"I'm still not sure we should be doing this," Dora whispered, her hand tucked into the crook of Isabella's arm. "I feel as though everyone is staring. They must all know we're in mourning just from looking at us. They probably all know who we are."

Isabella glanced along the street. There were indeed a fair number of other people to be seen, going about their daily business, and some of them appeared to be surreptitiously glancing their way. As if she cared. She patted Dora's hand. "They are of no importance, and besides which, they have no idea what color gowns we are about to order from Miss Chaloner, you goose. Whereas our gowns are of the utmost importance, unless you want to go to the ball in your dowdy old gown. And anyway, they are all looking at Richard, not us. No doubt more than a few are wondering about his looks and thinking they're seeing a ghost come to haunt them. Let them. What do we care? Come along." And she whisked Dora in through the door, with Richard following.

As the door closed behind them, the fact that they were not Miss Chaloner's only customers dawned on Isabella with alarming speed. Another lady was seated in one of the special chairs Miss Chaloner kept for her most favored clients. A lady Isabella knew all too well but had not expected to find here. Only she was not really a lady, not in Isabella's eyes. Cold indignation welled up in her heart and for a moment she feared she might disgrace herself by letting it show. But no, she had herself swiftly under control again. Years of practice had readied her for this encounter.

"Your Grace." Miss Chaloner curtsied. "Lady Dora." She had to stop there, her expression anxious, because no one had introduced Richard. By the look on her face, though, she had divined his identity for herself.

The occupant of the chair of honor, ignoring Miss Chaloner, now turned her head with languid grace and fixed cold, hard eyes, the color of wet pebbles on a beach, on Isabella and Dora. Her full lips curled and she gave a dismissive shrug, as her gaze slid past them to fix on Richard's face. Isabella had the pleasure of seeing those eyes widen in shock. Even in the comparative gloom of the dressmaker's shop, Richard's likeness to Marcus was astonishing, perhaps more so than it would have been in plain daylight.

Lady Barbara Dangerfield, wife of the renowned whip, Sir Sutton Dangerfield, baronet, and until very recently long-time mistress of Marcus, seventh Duke of Stourbridge, and sworn enemy of Isabella, curled her lips into a smile that could only be described as condescending. "Why," she drawled in what had to be mock surprise, "if it isn't little Isabella Hope and Marcus's poor little spinster sister. And..." she paused as her eyes ran up and down Richard's tall form, probably taking in his military bearing, "...keeping company with the new duke, if I'm not mistaken." Her eyes, when she rested them on Richard, were anything but cold. She was drinking him in from the top of his rather-tousled head, through his casual wearing of Marcus's overlarge tailcoat and breeches, down over his well-muscled legs to his shiny boots. From the look on her face, she liked what she saw.

Isabella bristled inside. Did that dreadful woman think addressing her by her maiden name and looking at Richard as though she would like to eat him up would annoy her? It had, but it wasn't about to work. Isabella drew herself up to her full height of five feet and three inches. "Lady Dangerfield, have you decided to ape my style by visiting my dressmaker? I am quite flattered by your unexpected attentions." She kept her voice pleasant, but had no intention of introducing Richard to this woman. The greedy way she was looking at him had quite turned her stomach. Hopefully it had produced the same effect on him, but one never knew with men.

Lady Dangerfield's supercilious face took on an expression of scorn. "Whatever gave you the idea that you have style, my dear? And as for me, using the services of a provincial dressmaker? Of course not. I would as soon shop here as go into the slums of London for my clothing."

A look of horrified indignation replaced the one of anxiety that poor Miss Chaloner had been wearing. She dropped a sheaf of dress designs all over the floor where they scattered like dead leaves.

Dora bent to gather them up.

Isabella's eyes narrowed. "My mistake. I had thought that must be where you had found the gown you are wearing right now." She ended the sentence with a smile that was meant to add "so there," and had the pleasure of seeing her enemy's smug expression falter.

Richard, clearing his throat rather more loudly than she deemed necessary, stepped forward, a placatory smile on his face that made her want to kick him in the shins to warn him not to go near the poisonous creature currently making doe eyes at him. And then he bowed to that woman. Bowed, as though she were someone who merited a modicum of respect. Could the nincompoop not tell from their exchange that he was not meant to be polite to her? "Delighted to make your acquaintance, Lady Dangerfield. And you are correct in your surmise. I am the new duke. Richard Carstairs, at your service."

Isabella, who was having trouble not flooring that woman, kept her face expressionless, something living with Marcus for ten years had taught her. Inside, however, she was seething. Men.

Why were they always so susceptible to the charms of fast women? The irony of this thought was lost on her.

Dora stood up and deposited the now gathered designs on the table, her frightened gaze flicking between Isabella and that woman. Isabella ignored her.

Lady Dangerfield also ignored her. And Isabella. Instead, she held out her elegant, gloved hand to Richard, who could do nothing other than take it. Clearly she meant for him to kiss it. And damn, damn, damn the man, but he obliged. If only she herself were a man. If only both of them were, so she could plant the shameless creature a facer, as Lord Rupert might put it. Draw her cork. Maybe even challenge her to a duel, with swords, and run her through. She was adept with a sword, it having been one of the things her dear papa had allowed her to learn. But she was a woman, and custom dictated that she should keep that smile fixed on her face and grin and bear everything that came her way. Well, perhaps not quite everything.

"Your Grace," the dreadful woman purred at Richard, oozing the sort of feline attractiveness and allure Isabella knew all too well that men liked. "It is such an honor to make your acquaintance." Oh, please don't let him emulate Marcus and fall for the hussy. That would be too much to bear.

Miss Chaloner, a thin stick of a woman who must have been engaged in showing Lady Dangerfield the prints now back on her desk, giving the lie to her declaration of not wanting to order a gown here, looked about to expire on the spot. Her face had gone as pale as the paper the designs were drawn on. "Your Grace," she managed, as though she thought it possible to redeem the situation. "What an honor to see you here today." Her voice sounded thready and thin in the heavy air of the shop.

"I did not think Lady Dangerfield possessed the taste to bring her business to Miss Chaloner's," Isabella said, to no one in particular, trying hard to prize her teeth, which were wanting to clamp tight shut, apart. "I would say the designs here are a little on the modest side for her."

Lady Dangerfield's expression barely changed, only the slight indentation between her eyes betraying her annoyance at Isabella's swift repartee. "If I had known this was your dressmaker of choice, I can assure you, I would not have come." She rose to her feet, all five feet eight inches of Amazonian womanhood, and bestowed the sort of look on Richard that said she would very much like to engage him in something other than conversation. Isabella was all too familiar with that look, as it was of the sort men so often gave her.

Lady Dangerfield sighed. "In fact, I'm afraid I find nothing here *in the way of dresses* that interests me after all. Goodbye, Miss Chaloner. I wish you luck in dressing the daughter of a cit. That must be so difficult for you." Her smile increased as she looked at Richard again, and her tongue darted out to moisten her lips, a trick Isabella herself had often tried. "Perhaps we shall meet again soon, Your Grace. I do hope so."

And without a second glance for poor Miss Chaloner, who only a short time ago must have thought her new customer about to make a substantial purchase, she swept out of the shop. Not, however, without leaning close to Isabella as she passed and hissing, "Do not attempt to cross me, tradesman's daughter."

The door banged shut behind her.

With some difficulty, Isabella turned a beatific smile upon Dora and Miss Chaloner. "Well, I can only say good riddance to that creature." She nodded at the dressmaker. "I can assure you, Miss Chaloner, that she is not the sort you would want to advertise as frequenting your establishment." She advanced further into the shop. "Whereas my dear sister-in-law and I are about to make purchases here that will make your eyes water. Courtesy of my cousin, the new duke. May I formally introduce His Grace, the new Duke of Stourbridge?" How hard it was to pretend equanimity, but she could do it.

Miss Chaloner, who had sufficiently recovered herself to stand up, swept a wobbly curtsey to the new arrivals. "Your Graces, I'm honored that you've chosen to visit my humble establishment." Her gaze fixed on Isabella's face. "And had I been aware of your feelings about that lady, I would not, of course, have agreed to serve her. Please rest assured of that."

Richard was watching this exchange with a glint of amusement in his dark eyes. Had he found the whole confrontation funny? Had he guessed the reason for the distinct lack of amity between herself and the ghastly Lady Dangerfield? Let him ponder. She would make sure he knew for certain before he had a chance to make the same mistake Marcus had made. The thought of him falling into the clutches of that woman was enough to make her blood boil again. Which was very odd, as surely he meant nothing to her? She'd think about that puzzler later.

Dora sat herself down in the seat Lady Dangerfield had so recently vacated and fanned herself with her hand. "I feel quite faint with the shock of seeing her here. What can that dreadful woman be doing in Newbury? I thought her husband's estate was in Gloucestershire."

Isabella took the other chair. "I don't know and I don't care. Let us not sully our afternoon of pleasure by discussing that odious woman. We are here to order new gowns for our ball, so that is what I intend to do, with no interruptions." She glanced up at Richard, who was still looking most amused. Not for the first time, she had cause to reflect on how gentlemen could be most odd.

Miss Chaloner fluttered her hands. For a woman who had been running her own establishment for longer than Isabella knew, she was remarkably flighty in nature, and it didn't take much to upset her. But she knew when to rise to the occasion and pretend nothing had happened, "Of course, of course. I presume you will want them in black again?"

"We will," Dora said. "Out of respect for my late brother, even though we require them because we are holding a ball at Stourbridge. In my cousin's honor, of course, to introduce him to all our neighbors." Her gaze slid sideways to Isabella, and their eyes met.

"Oh poppycock," Isabella snapped, not in the mood for obliging anyone, not now she'd encountered her nemesis. "Why are we pretending we're sad he's gone when we're not? Let those who had feelings for him wear black. I refuse to any longer." No doubt Lady Dangerfield would have liked to advertise her sorrows, although as she happened to be married to someone else, she couldn't. A feeling of delightful smugness crept over Isabella. Maybe she *would* wear black again, just to annoy that woman.

Dora's shocked eyes regarded her. Most likely due to the fact that she was unguarded enough to say all of this in front of a tradesperson. Isabella scowled. "It's quite ridiculous. Miss Chaloner knows full well that my husband was not a popular man, neither with his tenants, nor with his servants and certainly not with his family."

Dora laid a restraining hand on her arm. Her fingers dug into the soft flesh. "Bella, no."

Isabella glared, too angry now to curb her tongue. "I have had my fill of black. I require a gown of color for our ball. I declare our mourning is over. For you, too. And Richard, I know, is in agreement."

"Bella, we can't. What will people say? It's bad enough that we're holding a ball without also doing away with our mourning."

"They will say that we are sensible and not a pair of hypocrites pretending to mourn someone we hated. That's what." She eyed Miss Chaloner. "Do you not agree?"

Poor Miss Chaloner. Isabella hadn't meant to draw her into this but her heart was aching to wear something that wasn't black, despite the brief but satisfying idea of keeping to black to annoy her enemy. Let Dora pretend she was mourning if she wanted to. She would not be a hypocrite any longer. "Gold," she said with determination. "I shall have a gown of embroidered gold satin. It will look well with my hair."

Miss Chaloner nodded with alacrity. She also knew when it

was a good idea to humor a duchess. "Whatever you wish, Your Grace. You will look lovely in whatever you choose to wear. Gold is such a rich color."

Isabella turned to Dora again. "And blue for Lady Dora, I think. Yes, blue will suit her very well."

A snort of laughter came from behind them. Really, why did Richard find this all so funny? The only thing to do was to ignore him. But at least he'd shown he had some common sense by not insisting on them remaining in mourning.

⚜

CHAPTER FOURTEEN

ON THE DAY of the ball, with the invitations all long since dispatched and almost all of them back with eager acceptances, Richard had assumed that Isabella, and perhaps Dora, too, could afford to sit back and feel satisfied. Their new gowns had arrived from Miss Chaloner with a full day to spare and were now hanging, wrapped in delicate tissue so no one could see what they looked like, in their bedrooms. And Isabella had browbeaten poor Dora into agreeing to wear hers rather than the old black one she'd tried to get out of her armoire. In fact, Isabella had gone through Dora's gowns while she was otherwise employed and removed every black dress. Determination was her middle name.

However, Isabella, determined or not, was clearly not a young lady inclined to inaction and resting on her laurels. With the servants, wearing hunted expressions on their faces, preparing the rooms with extravagant displays of hothouse flowers and candlelit chandeliers, and an orchestra to supervise, she swept around the house like a small whirlwind, checking this and fiddling with that. Little wonder that when he searched, Richard found Dora had wisely retreated out to the gardens with a book to take shelter in the summerhouse.

She looked up as he entered, her expression a curious mixture of pleasure and acute wariness. Blaming her years at Marcus's mercy for this nervous wariness was the easiest thing to do, and yet, just because it was easy to do so, it didn't mean he wasn't correct. However, it was logical to assume Marcus had become the sort of adult he'd promised to be as a youth.

Dora laid the book in her lap, her whitened knuckles betraying how tightly she was clasping it. "Good afternoon, Diccon." Her smile didn't reach her eyes.

Returning a smile he hoped was reassuring, Richard sat beside her. How often had they played in here as children? Especially when they'd been trying to hide from Marcus. "I wondered if I might find you out here. Our bolt hole. It seems old habits are hard to break. From whom are you hiding today?"

She managed a more genuine smile this time. "From Isabella, of course, lest she finds me a job to do that someone else has already done, and makes me irritate them. Much as they love her, the servants don't like to have her breathing down their necks. She should know by now they're quite capable of preparing for a ball without her help."

He smiled back. "A wise move. And, I have to admit, it's the reason I'm out here. She seems to want my advice on everything about this ball. Do I like the flowers in the entrance hall? Should the platform for the orchestra be higher, or moved nearer the windows? Will I look at the supper menu again?" He chuckled. "I was forced to beat a tactical retreat. Hopefully she won't find us here."

Dora's grip on her book slackened as though his commiserative words had made her relax. "She doesn't mean to annoy. It's just her way. She likes to be in charge. She so often has had her way here at Stourbridge, because Marcus's habit was to remain mostly in Town. It was why she preferred being here to being in London. Marcus was in London, and, of course, here she could be with her precious horses."

Richard stretched out his booted legs. He was wearing the new everyday breeches the tailor had made for him, but tonight he'd have to don true evening wear of silk breeches, tailcoat, and stockings. Not something he was used to doing, nor relishing.

The informality of an army on campaign was looking more attractive by the minute. He pushed that worry aside, content that it was something he wouldn't have to do very often. "I'm glad I have you to myself for once. I must admit that I'm more than curious about Isabella's marriage to my cousin. Perhaps you might be able to fill me in."

"Oh." How taken aback she sounded. She caught her breath and her eyes flew wide with what looked like alarm. Again. Despite their problems with Marcus as children, he'd never known her as frightened as she appeared nowadays. What was going on with her? Perhaps he could persuade her to confide in him. She always had in the past.

"Come," Richard said, keeping his voice gentle and persuasive. "You must know more than most. You seem very close. Like sisters."

She swallowed. "I'm sorry. I can't. I feel if I were to disclose details of Bella's marriage I would be betraying her confidence. You must allow me to keep her secrets for her. If she wishes you to know, she will no doubt tell you herself."

Good God, what did she think he wanted to know? He reached out a hand and patted hers, which was icy cold despite the warmth of the autumn day, feeling her startle like a frightened deer. That she was hiding something was obvious. But what? And was it the same thing Isabella was concealing? And, even, should he be so intent on digging it out, despite his mission to find out the truth? Might his curiosity only make matters worse?

He tried another smile, keeping his voice gentle and a little apologetic. "I only wanted to know if it's true how she came to marry him." And some more, but perhaps he could wheedle that out of her once he had this.

"Oh." Her eyes darted sideways as though she might be considering flight. If she'd been a bird, her wings would have been fluttering in a panicked attempt to escape. "She was only a child, straight out of the schoolroom, when Marcus took it into his head to marry her."

This was better. But he knew some of this already. "Is it true he was in dire financial straits and needed to find himself an heiress?"

She shrugged, perhaps feeling herself on more solid ground— the solid ground of honestly pleading ignorance. "I have no idea. He would not have told me. Philip might know. He was working here then as assistant to the old estate manager, Mr. Burrows. You probably remember him. He died a few years ago now, after he'd retired. Yes, Philip would know more of the estate finances than I do. Don't forget, I am but a woman and not considered able to understand things like money. That is the domain of men." Those last words were said with such a strong hint of sarcasm that Richard was reminded of the old Dora he used to know.

"You are one of the cleverest women I've ever met, Dora. Even as a child you surpassed both Marcus and me in your studies. I believe that was one of the reasons he so despised you." A thought buzzed into his head. "Does his dislike of you, and me, have anything to do with why you yourself aren't married? If you don't mind me asking, that is." Asking her to reveal her own story might make her more willing to tell Isabella's.

She gave an eloquent shrug. "You may be right." She paused. "I should tell you that when Papa died, some thirteen years ago now, I was in the happy position of being engaged to be married to Sir Francis Litchfield, a fine gentleman who was one of Marcus's old friends. He'd met me while visiting Marcus, and we had formed an attachment to one another." She blushed. "I...I will admit to having cared for him, and Papa was prepared to settle a handsome dowry on me which no doubt rendered me more attractive in Sir Francis's eyes. So he asked Papa for my hand. The money might have lured him to begin with, but I think he truly cared for me, because he didn't give a jot about my leg." She patted the offending limb. "He even told me that in no way had it prevented him from offering for me."

Her eyes had taken on a faraway expression, as she gazed back down the tunnel of time. For a moment, once again, she was the Dora he remembered.

He patted her hand. "So why are you not now married to him?"

Her jaw set and anger kindled in her eyes, banishing the wariness and fear for a moment. She spoke through almost gritted teeth. "Because when Marcus became duke, he refused to sanction our marriage, and, of course, to pay any dowry out. In part, it was because he wanted to keep the money for himself. I was still only twenty, so he had a perfect right to do so. It meant he fell out with Francis, but he said he didn't care. He said Francis could go to hell, but he was not marrying the sister of a duke." She patted her leg again. "He told me I was damaged stock and should not be allowed to breed. But I knew that what he really wanted was me here, at Stourbridge, where he could continue to torment me. It was one of his favorite pastimes… after you left."

How bitter her words were. Under his hand he felt the tension in her grip on the book increase. She met his eyes, hers brimming with pain. "He took pleasure in it."

What could he say? That as a thoughtless boy he'd given no consideration to how it would be for her, abandoned by her only friend? He swallowed. "I'm so very sorry, Dora."

She shook her head. "It's done now, and you can change nothing. Perhaps if you had not gone, things would be very different. I might even now be married, with children of my own… and Marcus would not be lying in his grave…" Her voice trailed off, and she gave an eloquent shrug. "I do not wish to become maudlin. Let us speak of other things."

He nodded, glad to push aside the guilt. "Don't think of it. Neither of us can change the past, much as we would like to. So instead, tell me how it was that Isabella came to join you here."

She sighed. "I was alone here for ten years, Diccon. Alone with that monster… And then Isabella came, and I was no longer lonely." A little smile hovered on her lips as she dropped her gaze to the book in her lap and his large, tanned hand covering her own pale ones.

The pathos of her words struck at Richard's heart. A lump formed in his throat for the girl he'd so casually abandoned to her fate, while he, being male, had been able to escape to a new life. He'd waited until he was fifteen before he left. She'd been fourteen. Marcus had been eighteen and about to go up to Oxford. He'd comforted himself with the thought that with Marcus becoming a man he would spend less time at Stourbridge and she'd be safe. Perhaps he'd been wrong. But he'd been young, and the army had become everything to him. He hated to have to admit it, even to himself, but he'd scarcely thought of Dora in all of the last nineteen years.

Guilt colored his words now. "How can you ever forgive me for leaving you with him? It was heartless of me."

She looked up, tears sparkling unshed in her eyes. "What for? You have nothing to apologize for, my Diccon. You had to save yourself. You were in far more danger than I ever was. I think if he could have got away with it, Marcus would have killed you one day. And everyone would have said it was an accident..." Her words trailed away again, and she looked down, as if afraid to look him in the eye.

Richard nodded. "You're right. He came close enough times."

A vivid image leapt into his head of himself tied to a tree with an apple on his head and Marcus standing twenty yards off with a full-size bow and arrow in his hands. *"I'm William Tell and I'm going to split that apple in two."* Marcus had been fourteen, Richard just eleven. Ten-year-old Dora had been leaping up and down, desperate to get Marcus to abandon his game. Marcus had knocked her down before continuing.

He must have given himself away by touching his hand to the top of his head. "You're remembering when he wanted to be like William Tell, aren't you?"

He nodded. "I suppose I was lucky he was a bad shot and didn't even hit the tree."

She turned her hand over under his so she could thread her fingers through his. "And that time he made you be Little John by the river, while he was Robin Hood. And you had to fight with staves. I thought he'd knocked you out and you'd drowned."

He gave a chuckle, although it wasn't a pleasant memory. "I thought I had too."

"Things would only have got worse if you'd been there when he became duke. I was glad you'd gone. Sad, of course, to lose you, but glad you were safe. If the army can ever be seen as safe." Her eyes wandered again. "Or I was glad, until he told me you were dead."

This time his chuckle held more bitterness. "How typical of him to torture you that way, knowing how much we meant to one another." He shook his head. "But you're right. I was safer in the army than I would have been remaining here with him in charge." He closed his other hand over hers. "Now, tell me about Isabella." The fact that she fascinated him was not something he wanted to reveal to even Dora. He'd had women enough in his time in the army, but none of them had been ladies, and even though Isabella had been born the daughter of a tradesman, she was a lady now. But was she a Lucrezia Borgia or just a young woman in a bad marriage that fate had freed her from? He pushed aside the thought that the Prince of Wales himself appeared to be interested in her.

Dora sighed again. "She has been a godsend to me. When they married... oh, I suppose I must tell you how that came about."

"I know a little, from what Mr. Allsop told me when I went to his office in Newbury."

She nodded. "Her papa was one of the richest of merchants in the city. I think the term 'rich as Croesus' would have fitted him to perfection. Added to this, he was not young, his wife was already long dead, and Isabella was his only child. His sole heir. He had ambitions for her, believing that money such as he possessed could buy her way into high society. He was right, of course. Although many turned up their noses at him, and her, at the balls of the Season, a large number of the most eligible young men come from families where they are land rich but money poor, and a girl with a fortune such as she had drew them like the proverbial bees to a honeypot." She gave a watery smile. "And of course, it helped that she was quite the most beautiful debutante of the Season."

He could believe that. At eighteen she must have been a delicate, newly opened flower. At twenty-eight her looks had ripened into the true beauty of a woman grown.

Why were his cheeks warming? He spoke quickly to cover his embarrassment, hoping she wouldn't notice. "Of course it would. But how did her foolish father allow her to marry someone like Marcus? There must surely have been more suitable matches on offer?" A girl with her looks and fortune must have had men queuing up to court her. If he'd been in their situation, he couldn't deny that he'd have been dancing attendance on her himself. Before she'd become the damaged goods she was today.

Dora curled her upper lip. "Not a duke among them. Remember how few dukes there are in Britain, and how infrequently they enter the marriage mart. I think most of the others are old codgers, as Isabella would say. Her father had set his eyes on Marcus from afar, and all unbeknownst to him, Marcus had also set his eyes on the Hope fortune. He meant to have it for himself. By any means."

"No need to tell me he succeeded. Mr. Allsop filled me in on the allocation of Mr. Hope's fortune after his death."

Dora bowed her head. "Marcus took great pleasure in telling both me and Isabella how he managed it. After the marriage, of course. When it was too late for her to escape."

"How did he persuade the old man to cut his daughter out of his will?"

She sighed. "He was clever in his wooing. He pretended disinterest in her. He pursued other young ladies of smaller fortune but better breeding. He let it be known he could never sully the Stourbridge blood and title with a shopkeeper's daughter. He drove her father, who I should point out was not a shopkeeper, to despair, for the more he found obstacles in his way, neatly laid by Marcus, the more he wanted his daughter to be a duchess. Just as Marcus intended."

"And was the girl fooled?"

Dora shrugged. "Marcus could be quite charming when he wanted to be, so I suppose he used that charm to win her over. Perhaps she thought she loved him. For a short while." She paused. "No. I know she thought that, because she told me. It didn't last long, though. She soon realized what she'd married." She shook her head. "But by then it was too late, for Marcus had persuaded her father to leave him, not her, his entire fortune in his will." She leaned closer. "And very shortly after that the old man died." She dropped her voice still lower as though she thought the walls of the summerhouse might have ears. "I have it in me to wonder if his death was quite natural."

What? Another possible murder? Or was this suggestion made to justify Marcus's death? Did Dora know how he'd died? Well, the truth of it. Perhaps.

"Were they never a happy couple?"

Another shrug. "Perhaps for the first few months. I believe it is intoxicating to a man to be worshipped by a beautiful woman, and that was what Isabella did when she was first married." She hesitated, her eyes darting from side to side. She dropped her voice even lower. "If I tell you this, please don't let Bella know I told you."

Aha. A secret was about to be revealed. At last. "I won't. I promise."

"Very shortly after they were married she found she... she was increasing. You understand?"

"A baby?" Yet there was no child at Stourbridge.

"Yes. A baby. Marcus seemed quite pleased. An heir, he said. For once he seemed in a better mood with her and she was not quite so frightened of him."

A hollow feeling opened in Richard's stomach, but he had to ask. "What happened to the baby?"

More hesitation. "As you might expect with a lady in that condition, Bella grew large and ungainly, and Marcus grew angrier with her with each passing day, as though it were her fault. I heard him calling her a… a cow, an elephant, a hippopotamus. I heard him tell her how she repulsed him with her swollen belly." She put her free hand to her eyes and the book slid unnoticed from her lap. "I know I should not have listened, but his voice was so loud, and he made no effort to disguise his feelings. He spoke like this in front of everyone, servants included."

"I see." But did he? He'd come back here to claim his inheritance, marry and beget an heir, and if his unknown wife-to-be obliged, he would surely relish her growing belly and look forward to the birth of his son, or daughter, not harangue her for something she couldn't help. Or would he? Might he be more like Marcus than he thought, horrible as that idea was? The thought sent a cold shiver of dread through his body.

"Then, one day…" Her voice had gone low and small, scarcely above a whisper now, as though conjuring up the memory was abhorrent to her. "One day at the top of the stairs they fought. He struck her across the face, and she lost her balance. She fell to the foot of the stairs." Her voice shook. "The baby came. She was in her eighth month. It lived an hour only. A little girl. Perfect in every way, but tiny. She died in my arms, for Isabella was unconscious." Tears trickled down Dora's wan cheeks.

"Good God." A turmoil of emotions washed about inside Richard's head like wild waves on the Bay of Biscay. Marcus had brought about the death of his own child, and perhaps nearly of his wife, as well. He might, if Dora were to be believed, have also had a hand in killing his own father-in-law to get his hands on the man's fortune. Isabella, that brittle, bright, determined, and rather wild young woman, had gone through hell at Marcus's hands. His heart went out to her, prepared, on an instant, to forgive her anything, even murder of the man who'd done that to her.

But Dora hadn't finished. "Marcus was furious. Not for any reason other than that the child had been a girl. He'd wanted an heir, and a girl didn't count. He didn't care that the baby was dead. No female has ever counted for Marcus. As soon as he saw the baby was a girl, a dead girl, he took himself off to London for the next six months to his mistress. We didn't see him at Stourbridge once in all that time. Isabella was ill for weeks, and took months to recover completely, if she ever has. Not once in all that time did he send her his condolences. Nothing. It was as if she, too, were dead to him."

The suspicion that Marcus might have been mad washed over Richard. Surely his actions were not those of a sane man. He'd always been cruel, but this was taking it too far. Leaving his sick wife and going off to join his mistress. Inspiration seized Richard, as the pieces of a puzzle dropped into place. "And would that mistress possibly be called Lady Dangerfield?"

Dora nodded. "It would."

Richard grit his teeth together. No wonder Isabella had been so cold, so downright rude, to the woman. And out of politeness and adherence to the mores of society, he'd kissed her treacherous hand. "Isabella goes a long way to wearing her heart on her sleeve. She would do well to be less obvious in her dislike. Lady Dangerfield has about her the air of someone who would make a bad enemy."

Dora sucked in her lips. "You must remember your promise and mention nothing of this to my darling Bella." Her eyes met Richard's. "And whatever you do, you must not separate her from me. We need to keep each other safe, just as we always have. She's like my little sister. More so than Grace ever was. We are forever linked."

Richard gazed into Dora's eyes. Yes, there was something she was keeping from him. Some secret still between her and her Bella. A pressing necessity to keep each other safe even though Marcus was gone.

Chapter Fifteen

ISABELLA STOOD IN front of her cheval mirror admiring her reflection with some satisfaction. The gold gown, in satin with an embroidered bodice and an overlay of richly embroidered gold net, suited her alabaster skin to perfection. She patted her hair, which had been piled on her head in curls by Hawkins in a style of artful disarray. Pearls, on the heads of the pins which held her curls in place, sparkled amongst the rich auburn. Yes, she looked as near perfect as it was possible to be.

Wait until Richard saw her. All the other girls would fade into the background compared to her and hopefully he would have eyes for no one else. Of course, she only wanted him to notice her because she couldn't bear to be anything but the most admired woman in the room. Didn't she? No other possible reason. Nothing to do with how handsome he was and how much she... No. Not at all. She stamped her foot as though to put an end to such thoughts.

It didn't quite work.

To distract herself, she did a little twirl. How wonderful it was not to be wearing black. There was a limit to what could be done with such a dull color, if you could even call it a color. It was more a non-color, an emptiness, a shadow, that even lace and fine jewelry couldn't truly garnish enough to make it beautiful, although she'd tried hard to do so for the last two months. But this... now this dress was divine. And as a duchess, what did she care what people thought or said behind their hands? Having to pretend to mourn a husband she'd both hated and at times feared had been an almost unbearable burden. Now she'd made the decision to end that mourning, nothing was going to change her mind. At least, this was what she was telling herself, although her pounding heart told another story. No. Determination to stand her ground was everything. She could brazen this out.

Hawkins passed over her long silk gloves, pale gold of course, and she put them on, smoothing out the wrinkles in the delicate fabric and taking the time to admire her slender arms and long-fingered hands. The gloves reached above her elbows and left only a short section of pale skin visible below the off-the-shoulder elegance of her gown. Gazing at her decolletage a little ruefully, she gave her small breasts a helping hand, pushing them upwards to gain a little more visibility. Not that she had any doubt about her attractions for men. No, she was used to being the honeypot her coterie of bees liked to buzz around, and tonight would be no different. Let Richard see how very popular she was. And how beautiful. That would be sure to make him... What? What was it she wanted him to do? No. There she was again imagining quite the wrong thing. No man, still less another Carstairs, was ever coming near her again.

She spotted Hawkins's purse-lipped expression in the mirror, half pride and half reproval. Her maid had made it clear that she thought mourning a husband, even a hated one, should go on for at least a year and had huffed her not-quite-silent disapproval more than a few times as she helped her mistress into the gown. Having been with Isabella since before she married, she considered her length of service meant she had a right to air her views. Isabella, of course, had ignored her. And not only because a part of Hawkins had also obviously been delighted to be dressing her mistress in something pretty again at last. Silly creature with her old-fashioned fancies.

Isabella glanced at the clock on the mantlepiece. Eight o'clock already. Their guests had been invited for nine, although a select few, mainly those living closest, had been invited earlier for drinks in the drawing room and to meet Richard before anyone else, as though he were a new animal on display at the Exeter 'Change. They would be arriving soon. She'd best take herself down to the hallway to greet them. And let Richard view her in her splendor. A small nub of satisfaction burgeoned in her breast. What fun it would be when he had eyes for no one but her, when all the ambitious, and jealous, mamas would be after him for their daughters.

With a last satisfied smile at her reflection, she glided across the room to the door which Hawkins already had open for her, and stepped out onto the soft red carpeting of the galleried landing. Downstairs glowed with light, and even up here, where it could be shadowy and gloomy, had been illuminated more brightly than usual. Well aware of the light dancing over her glimmering gown and her russet hair, Isabella set her hand on the banister at the top of the stairs and paused, looking down into the hall, waiting to be noticed.

Richard and Dora were already down there, standing together near the doors, Dora looking awkward in the blue gown Isabella had chosen for her. Neither were looking in her direction.

Isabella coughed as discreetly as possible.

Nothing. They had their heads together, talking.

She coughed again, more loudly this time.

Dora turned her head and broke into a delighted smile. "Bella."

Richard swung around, his eyes widening in the most satisfactory fashion as he stared at where she stood at the head of the wide oak staircase.

Good. Exactly the sort of entrance she liked to make. Long years of maintaining a façade of not caring, of femme fatale, of hauteur, and and of aloofness had ingrained themselves into Isabella's being so deeply, she was almost unaware of their effect and how much she'd changed since she'd been an innocent eighteen-year-old bride.

Taking a step down, the silken skirts of her gown rustling about her, her dainty slipper pointed, she met Richard's eyes with an open challenge, certain he would never have seen anyone as beautiful as she was. Enough men had told her that over the past ten years for her to be convinced of their veracity.

And it worked. He was staring at her as though he'd never seen her before, his eyes wide and full of what could only be admiration. She'd seen enough of that before in the eyes of her admirers, and she knew it now when she saw it in the eyes of her late husband's dashing cousin.

She allowed herself the smallest of smiles, a little more than pleased. She'd formed a habit over the years, as a reaction to her husband's infidelities, of requiring all men to be her admirers from the most callow youths to their wrinkled, gray-haired grandfathers. Perhaps because she'd known from almost the start that her own husband was never going to be amongst their number, and she'd wanted, with all the fury of pent-up jealousy, to teach him a lesson. To show him that whatever he thought of her, other men wanted her. Starved of his love, she'd set about to win the love of every man she met. The unrequited love.

And now Richard was about to be added to that number. It would suit her very well to have him dancing at her beck and call and ignoring the daughters of those women who'd looked down their aristocratic noses at her for so long.

Restraining the impulse to widen her smile, she continued on down the stairs, supremely conscious of the impression she must be making in this beautiful gown. A gown fit for a princess or even a queen, not just a duchess.

He watched her all the way down, and she, well aware of her own allure, kept her eyes fixed on his. She'd learned a long time ago that men liked to think they were the only one in the room you could be interested in. Granted, he was the only man in this room, but that didn't stop her from making the same moves she always made towards a new conquest.

Yet was he the same as her other conquests? Her legions of

devoted, lust-filled men, all of whom thought they might be the lucky one to breach her barriers and inveigle her into bed. For despite rumor, her conquests remained exactly what they were when they started out—conquests waiting on her hand and foot, for nothing but a smile or a dance in return, and perhaps, if they were lucky, a squeeze of her waist or her thigh. She'd never even bestowed a kiss on any of them. Not that many of them hadn't tried, of course.

How handsome he looked in his new evening suit, even though it had been made by Philip Sanders's tailor and not at Weston's. Mr. Chalke might be just a small-town maker of gentleman's apparel, but he had a rare skill with both his eye and the needle, and Richard's military bearing lent itself to looking good in anything. His tailcoat fitted his well-muscled body like the proverbial glove, hugging his broad shoulders and tapering to a waist that was neither too narrow nor too wide. His silk breeches and stockings left her in no doubt about the power of his lower body. Infantry, of course. No wonder he had strong legs. She suppressed a chuckle. He was used to having to walk everywhere.

But it was his face that caught her attention. Gone were the rather rough edges that had shouted soldier, and in their place was a man of elegance, his military bearing only adding to that impression. Clean shaven, hair arranged with casual artistry by goodness knows who, the scent of cologne about him, and even his hands had been transformed, the nails scrubbed, trimmed, and filed. Had his soldier servant done all that for him? If he had, he must be excellent at his job. Who'd have thought a common soldier could make such a grand job of a gentleman's appearance.

If she'd imagined this sort of a transformation would make him look more like his predecessor, she'd been wrong. Somehow, despite being attired very much as Marcus had been fond of dressing, Richard had contrived to look quite different to his late cousin. It was as if his face had changed, and his body had driven the change. Marcus, at thirty-eight, had been starting to get a small pot belly thanks to his excesses. Richard had about him a whipcord strength as though not an ounce of fat adhered to him. For a single moment, the thought that he would look good naked flashed into her head before vanishing.

Not quickly enough. Heat rose from her breasts, up her throat to her cheeks. How vexing.

"Isabella," Richard said, a smile hovering on his lips as though, heaven forbid, he knew exactly what she was thinking, the admiration still hot in his dark eyes. Eyes like peaty pools. No, she must stop thinking like that. Her flirtations had always worked best because despite the ardor of her admirers, her own feelings had never been engaged with any of them. Richard was just like all the others. Wasn't he? She would not allow herself to engage with him other than to hook him like a prize fish.

He took her hands in his. Whatever for? She would have liked to snatch them back, but that would have looked rude. She might be a tease and a flirt, but she was not rude. Not very, anyway. Well… not all that often. She made him a curtsy. "Your Grace."

Dora moved close enough to whisper. "I wish you had not made me wear this gown. I would rather be in my mourning black still. What will people think of me with my brother hardly cold in his grave?"

Isabella dragged her eyes away from Richard's. More difficult than she'd thought it would be. Damn him. He had no right to have changed the way he looked. With his appearance too much like Marcus, he'd been easier to disregard. "Nonsense. Marcus is definitely nicely cold and forgotten. We have a new duke to celebrate, and we can't be looking like a pair of old crows at his ball. No one will think badly of you, Dora. You are far too nice for them to do that." She tossed her head, wishing with all her heart Dora didn't look so damned guilty all the time. Even her eyes looked more sunken and shadowed than usual. If only she could forget what was past in the same way she, Isabella, could. "And what do I care if people whisper behind my back? You know I don't give a jot." If she said it enough, it would be true.

Richard at last transferred his grip on her hands and drew her arm through his. "Come, I think I hear the wheels of a carriage outside on the gravel. Our first guests are arriving." He smiled at Dora. "Isabella is correct. No one could possibly think badly of you. And you do look quite beautiful in blue."

Isabella frowned, a little miffed that he hadn't said that about her.

She let Richard usher her nearer to the doors, just as Atkins swung them open. Outside, dusk had already fallen and with it had come an unmistakable chill, but lamps flickered in brackets on the pillared portico, and two of the footmen were in place on the steps, resplendent in their best livery.

A large carriage drawn by four matching bays was just circling to a halt on the gravel, the crest on the door announcing that this was the chosen vehicle of the Brocklebanks of Bembridge House, their nearest neighbor. Having to be polite to Lady Brocklebank still rankled with Isabella after all these years, but they'd had to feature on the list of early invitees due to their close proximity to Stourbridge Park. Unfortunately.

The two liveried footmen riding on the back of the carriage jumped down, one going to hold the leading horse's head and the other to let down the step and open the carriage door for its occupants. He offered his hand in support, and the imposing figure of Maria Worthing, Lady Brocklebank, descended to the gravel drive.

Tonight, she'd chosen to bedeck herself in a magnificent gown of the deepest puce, amply embellished with dark green, neither of which choices were flattering to her ample figure. Her grizzled hair was piled high on her head to give added inches, and decorated with a sizeable, and, in Isabella's opinion, far too ostentatious, tiara that glittered with diamonds. Was this in honor of meeting the duke? After all, she did have three daughters of marriageable age, although strictly speaking one was already spoken for. No doubt she considered that if a better offer came along, that engagement could easily be broken.

However, it was not the daughters who descended behind her. Isabella's heart skipped an unruly beat as Lady Dangerfield, resplendent in a gown of deep immodest red, stepped onto the gravel with the air of one who thought she should own the castle.

Isabella drew in a steadying breath. Whoever had invited her to the pre-ball reception? She certainly hadn't featured on the guest list for either the reception or the ball afterwards, and if anyone had suggested her, Isabella would have put her foot down. She had to fight to keep her smile, false though it had been in the first place, fixed on her face as Lady Brocklebank passed through the wide-open doors with Lady Dangerfield, stately and superior, on her heels. She had the look of someone assessing the value of all she beheld. Taking an inventory, perhaps.

"Lady Brocklebank, Your Grace," Atkins said, and Isabella thought she surmised an expression of distaste in his eyes, quickly hidden, as he, too, spotted Lady Dangerfield. The senior servants all knew about Marcus's mistress. They could hardly have avoided knowing, as he'd brought the creature here to the castle when Isabella had been in Town.

No Lord Dangerfield though. No surprise in that, as he was elderly, gouty, and spent most of his time at his estate in Warwickshire, hunting and shooting, which had led to the ease with which his wife had been able to carry on her affair with Marcus in full view of the public eye. Lady Brocklebank's husband, the portly viscount, and his three unprepossessing daughters followed the ladies inside. No Giles this time.

Isabella snatched her attention back, with a little difficulty, to her duties as hostess and returned Lady Brocklebank's curtsy. The one she gave to Lady Dangerfield she kept as minimal as possible, scarcely bending her knees at all. And to be fair, that was all she received in return.

The three girls came forward. Like their mother, they were inclined to plainness, but all possessed a look of pillowy kindness their mother lacked, with wide brown eyes beneath carefully plucked brows and excited but nervous smiles on their faces.

What age were they? Not yet twenty, surely? And from the look of them, the younger two were twins. Identical twins. Isabella searched her memory but could find nothing in it about them. Not even their names. Remembering her own debut into society at much the same age, she bestowed her sweetest smile on them, partly out of an impulse of generosity but also from a desire to snub that dreadful woman.

Lady Brocklebank was concentrating her attentions on Richard. "This is my oldest daughter still at home. Her sister is now Lady Chase, you know. Honoria, come forward." Honoria in a gown of pale green that failed to make the most of what bust she possessed, bobbed a polite curtsy to Richard and Isabella, keeping her eyes demurely downcast as an obedient and chaste girl should. Not so her twin sisters.

"And these are my youngest daughters, Imogen and Cecilia." Their mother gestured them forwards. They came, giggling with excitement and casting longing eyes over Richard's person. They must be as aware as their mother of the attractions of an unmarried duke. As plain as their more staid sister, these two had the rebellious look about them of girls itching to escape their mother's apron strings.

"Honoria came out last Season," their proud mother said. Noticeable that she hadn't mentioned Honoria's engagement. "And both Imogen and Cecilia will be out in the new year. Looking for eligible husbands."

As if any girl coming out in Town would not be. Silly woman. She couldn't have been more explicit if she'd tried. Clearly she was of the opinion that as she possessed three marriageable daughters, she was in with three chances of a daughter as a duchess. Isabella recognized the look in Lady Brocklebank's eyes. It was just like her father's had been. She had to feel sorry for the three girls. If only someone had felt the same about her and rescued her before Marcus had got his claws into her.

"I'm so pleased your mama has brought you," Isabella said, glad that she now had their names. "It's a shame that we are such close neighbors, and yet we have never been properly introduced."

All three girls' eyes widened as though in shock, although both the twins also managed to look suitably impressed. Those were definitely naughty twinkles she saw in their eyes. Good luck to her mother in the new year trying to keep a watch over these two with all the young men likely to recognize those twinkles as the light of encouragement.

What had their mother told them about her? Nothing good, she'd wager. She continued to smile, relishing how that lady would be annoyed if she were to make friends with her daughters, especially these younger two. "Come, let us go into the drawing room and take a glass of ratafia." Holding out her arms for the twins to link with, she whisked them off into the drawing room, a feeling of smug satisfaction coursing through her, abandoning Richard to reception duties alone. The much more strait-laced-looking Honoria remained resolutely at her mother's side.

Isabella felt smug. She might have a reputation as a woman who preferred men, preferably those already married, but she could also be as nice as the next person, and she intended to allow that side of her personality free rein this evening. For a while, at least.

The thought arose that if Richard were to choose one of these two plain but rebellious girls as a wife, she might not be able to mold them to her own design. She brushed it away with confidence. No, these girls were not ones she would choose for him. The fact that she might not be able to find any suitable girl she acknowledged with a small smile. As far as she was concerned, he could stay a bachelor forever.

※

CHAPTER SIXTEEN

RICHARD WATCHED ISABELLA depart with the two younger Brocklebank girls with a wry smile. How typical of her to find an excuse to shrug off her duties as hostess and escape. With a silent sigh, he turned his attention, with a little trepidation, to the girls' sister and parents, and the object of Isabella's hatred, Lady Dangerfield.

Not that the woman had been included in the invitation he'd had Philip Sanders send out over a week ago. No chance of that, as they'd been working from a list of invitees provided by Isabella and Dora. Of course, he'd unofficially met Lady Dangerfield in that dressmaker's in Newbury, but at the time, unaware of the reason for Isabella's hatred, he'd not taken nearly as much notice of her as he was doing right now. He'd been too amused by Isabella's catty putdowns of the woman and obvious dislike of her. Now he knew more about their history, he regarded her with a lot more curiosity.

Dora, he noted, had a mulish expression on her face, but whether it was due to the blue gown she'd been coerced into, Isabella's sneaky departure, or her disapproval of this uninvited guest, he couldn't be sure. It could well have been all three.

"Your Grace," Lady Dangerfield purred at him. Good heavens. Did she talk like this all the time? Obviously not, because he'd already seen the unpleasant manner in which she'd spoken to Isabella. Most likely she reserved this particular tone of voice for gentlemen. Well, it wasn't going to work with him. Even if he'd been susceptible to her all-too-obvious charms, he would not have wanted to hurt Isabella's feelings by succumbing to them, even for a moment. Beside Isabella, which thankfully she wasn't at this moment, she looked what she was—an ageing courtesan, long past the flower of her youth. A courtesan indeed. She might be a lady by title, but that didn't have to also be a description of her.

Oblivious to his internal condemnation of her, Lady Dangerfield extended an elegant, gloved hand, and he was obliged to take it in his and kiss it, making the brush of his lips on her glove as perfunctory as possible. "Lady Dangerfield, how nice that you could accompany the Brocklebanks. This is a pleasant surprise." At least Isabella wasn't able to hear him being mendaciously polite to her, although why he should be bothered what she thought of his actions, he still wasn't quite sure. He only knew that he was bothered, and the happiness of Isabella, no matter how difficult, capricious, and determined she could be, was of great importance to him.

Lady Dangerfield batted her eyelashes in the most obvious of manners and he couldn't miss the sharp intake of angry breath from Dora. Good God, was he spied on from all sides? Could he do no right?

Lady Dangerfield either didn't hear Dora or had decided to ignore her. "How could I resist an invitation to meet a newly minted and extremely handsome duke?"

Hard to place her age, but he suspected she must be a lot older than she looked. Older than he was, that was for sure, and older than Marcus had been. No gray hairs as yet in her lustrous chestnut locks, although she might have had her maid excise them, but small lines radiated from around her eyes that not even judicious application of powder and paint could disguise. Yet she was undeniably beautiful, in an overblown way that was nothing compared to the fresh beauty Isabella possessed. No surprise that his cousin, who'd from an early age been drawn to older women, starting with the servant girls, had fallen for her charms. Although... with the possibility of a woman like Isabella in his bed every night, why had Marcus even felt the need to stray?

Richard was well aware that many men, many happily married men, kept mistresses as well as wives, as if it were de rigueur. And yet, having seen Isabella tricked out in all her finery, he couldn't help but wonder what had gone on between her and Marcus that had driven them apart, and Marcus into the arms of another. Even though he knew what Marcus was like, he still couldn't quite find it in himself to believe maturity hadn't changed his cousin for the better. Even though it clearly hadn't.

There was nothing much he could say in reply to such a gushing compliment about his looks from a lady. "You are too kind," was about all he could muster. If she thought she was going to worm her way into his affections through flattery, she was deluded. What might have worked on Marcus was not going to work with him.

She smiled, her tongue darting out to lick her lips in a most suggestive manner. "Although, of course, we already encountered one another in slightly awkward circumstances at that provincial dressmaker's, did we not? I must apologize for my precipitate departure from that establishment. It was not you who caused that but your choice of... company." She ran her eyes up and down his body as if assessing a prize stallion. If he hadn't known her history, he might have begun to feel hot under his collar. As it was, though, a sense of disgust began to trickle through him. He did not like this woman one bit.

This was quickly followed by a desperate wish to be rescued from her clutches.

Providence provided his escape as a second carriage rumbled in to replace the first. Atkins leaned in close, his voice low. "The Earl and Countess of Manville are just arriving, Your Grace."

Richard heaved an inward sigh of relief. "Perhaps, Lady Dangerfield, you would like to accompany Lord and Lady Brocklebank into the drawing room. My duties as host tonight must, I'm afraid, impose on our conversation. Perhaps we can continue it later?"

Not if he could help it.

Thankfully, the Brocklebanks were well versed in the etiquette of receptions and could be relied upon to know the part they had to play, even if he was only learning his. Their whole party did as it was bid, with obliging smiles and many bows and curtsies. He watched their departure for a moment, with the older Brocklebank girl following her stately galleon of a mother like some small outrigger. Lady Brocklebank was gazing about herself in avid curiosity, no doubt at being inside so notorious a house that might have hosted a murder, but Lady Dangerfield had about her an air of familiarity as though she considered Stourbridge part of her own domain. A pity the absent Lord Dangerfield wasn't here. She certainly needed the heavy hand of a husband to keep her in line more than most women he'd encountered.

Pushing those thoughts to one side, he turned to greet his new guests, acutely aware that Isabella should be by his side to do the same but had somehow escaped. However, he had Dora in her place, and, as if she guessed his nervousness, she gave him a quick reassuring smile as the Manvilles headed their way.

IN THE DRAWING room Isabella was in the unhappy process of discovering that Imogen and Cecilia Worthing were as empty headed as a pair of chickens. Rather a let down, as she'd initially assumed them to have more to them than this. But no, two more feather-brained young ladies it would have been hard to find, and, as Isabella was not blessed with any degree of patience, she was fast becoming annoyed with them. Like so many other young ladies, all they seemed to want to talk about was clothes and what they would wear when they made their debut at the start of the next Season, and how many handsome men they could expect to come calling on them, and what fun they would have.

Not that clothes didn't interest Isabella, because they did.

However, she had no desire to talk about them other than to remark on what other ladies were wearing. And as the only other ladies present so far were Lady Brocklebank, the twins' older sister, and the ghastly Lady Dangerfield, even she drew the line about sharing her opinion of those ladies for fear of offending her new companions. Especially as anything she could have said would have been unflattering in the extreme.

As the white-haired Earl of Manville and his new young countess, who could hardly be much older than Imogen and Cecilia, entered the room and one of the footmen supplied them with glasses of ratafia, she excused herself and made a beeline for Lord Brocklebank. What better way of annoying his wife than some healthy flirting with her husband, even though he was not in the least bit attractive? Although her son, Giles, would have been more fun, as Lady Brocklebank would have been suspicious that Isabella intended him as her next husband. But as Giles was not here, his father would have to do.

"Lord Brocklebank," Isabella said, smiling her most ingenuous smile, one that so often got her just what she wanted. "I declare that you look younger every time I see you. You must share with me your secret—an elixir you imbibe daily, perhaps?"

She had prior experience of Henry Worthing, Viscount Brocklebank, and his susceptibility to flattery. It worked. Again. He puffed out his chest at her flattery and ran a self-conscious hand over his thinning hair, which his valet must have spent considerable time arranging to disguise the expanding bald patch. "And may I say that you look quite charming, Your Grace, as usual. So nice to see you out of mourning at last. I always think it a demmed shame when young ladies like you have to go about swathed in black and are not allowed to have any fun."

Isabella, well aware of the dimples that would be appearing in her cheeks because she'd practiced them often enough in front of the mirror, cast her eyes down in mock modesty. "I did worry that people might think me fast…" She had to bite her tongue, for she well knew that was exactly what his galleon-in-full-sail wife would be thinking right now, and unable to say. She was otherwise engaged talking to the Manvilles, but Isabella hadn't missed how she kept casting her eyes in their direction.

"Nonsense, nonsense," Brocklebank said, putting a hot and clammy hand on the exposed flesh of her upper arm and making her want to shake him off. "No one could possibly think that of you. You're far too young and pretty to have to stay in black too long." He had pudgy fingers and, for a moment, it crossed Isabella's mind to wonder what it would be like to have those fingers fumbling with her in passion. She controlled the impulse to shiver, and smiled instead, while out of the corner of her eye catching his wife's frown deepening.

Satisfied, she leaned in close enough to whisper in the viscount's ear, a strong smell of overly applied gentleman's cologne nearly causing her to gag and cough. "You might think that, but others here don't share your opinion, I fear." Her eyes slid sideways in the direction of his wife, giving him no opportunity to mistake her implication. What fun it was to stir trouble with those she disliked. Dora would have scolded her for being so naughty, but Dora was not here.

His bushy gray brows met in a heavy frown. "Have no fear, my dear. I shall put Maria right about that." Then he leaned closer, as well, his hot breath on her neck making her want to pull away. "In truth I think she is envious of your youth and beauty."

Of course she was. Isabella let out a peal of laughter and all eyes turned her way.

"Is something amusing you, Your Grace?" Lady Brocklebank asked, her tone frosty.

Lady Dangerfield looked as though she'd swallowed a lemon.

Good on both counts.

Isabella managed to stop laughing as Richard and Dora came in with Colonel Jarvis, the elderly magistrate who'd dealt with Marcus's death on that terrible day, and Sir Algernon and Lady Chase. This lady was Verity, the oldest Brocklebank daughter, a scrawny old hen of a woman unlike either her stout parents or sturdy younger sisters, and in possession of a face like a withered prune. They had been invited because they also were near neighbors to Stourbridge and, as Dora had so sagely pointed out, would have been offended had they been excluded from this select gathering before the ball.

Isabella met Richard's eyes, and gave an eloquent shrug. "Just an amusing anecdote dear Lord Brocklebank was telling me about one of his tenants. Nothing anyone else would find amusing, I can assure you." She shot him her most dazzling smile, which made his eyes widen, and a frown settle on his brow. The suspicion that he might not like her flirting with Lord Brocklebank arose. Good to that as well. No better way to keep a man interested than to show interest oneself in a rival. Not that Lord Brocklebank could ever be considered a rival to anything or anyone.

The footman, Robert, carried a tray round, offering more ratafia, then retreated to stand at attention by the sideboard. How boring this must be for him. Was he taking a surreptitious look at her, sideways, as she took another glass from the sideboard? She flashed him an appreciative smile, just because she could, and was rewarded by the blush that suffused his face.

Dora sidled up to her. "If you will excuse us, Lord Brocklebank?" She kept her voice low as she drew Isabella to one side. "I didn't know Lady Dangerfield was to attend."

Isabella kept a smile on her face despite the wish to scowl. "Neither did I. She must be visiting the Brocklebanks and that was why we encountered her in Newbury. I would wager she heard about the ball and decided to stay on and take advantage of their invitation out of pure spite." She took a sip of her ratafia. "If I'd known she was staying with them, I wouldn't have suggested Richard should invite any of them. And those girls…" She waved a hand in the general direction of the twins where Richard was politely engaging them in conversation under the self-satisfied gaze of their ever-hopeful mama. Ten years ago, Lady Brocklebank had wanted Marcus for Verity and been forced to settle for a simple baronet as a son-in-law. No doubt she fancied catching his successor for one of her empty-headed twins. Not if Isabella had a say in the matter.

Lady Chase wafted towards them. Two years older than Isabella, Verity had been a debutante in the same year. But she hadn't aged well, and her sallow skin was dry and dull. That was what churning out babies every year did for you. How many did she and her husband have now? Nine, wasn't it? And by the look of it, another on the way. Shocking, really, to be treated as some kind of brood mare by one's husband. Thank goodness Marcus had never expected that of her. That was one thing that had been in his favor.

The thought was bittersweet though. Isabella couldn't help a pang of sorrow for her own lost baby. She so rarely allowed herself to think of the child nowadays, it was as if it had all happened to someone else or in another life. She bit her lip as a lump formed in her throat. If Marcus had married Verity instead of her, as Lady Brocklebank had wanted, would he now have nine children in the nursery rather than one dead baby in the family graveyard and perhaps not even be dead himself? No, she would not think about her dead daughter. Not here, anyway. Even after nine years, the memory was too painful.

"Your Grace," Verity said, eyeing Isabella up and down as slowly as she could, with just the faintest of curl to her lip. "How very charming you look."

That she didn't mean a word of this was obvious. Isabella fixed that false smile more firmly onto her face. "As do you. Motherhood so suits you. I find myself quite envious of your complexion."

Verity's smug smile slipped. She was not such a ninny that she would not have known this to be tongue in cheek. She must see her reflection every day in the mirror. Motherhood, with such frequency, was doing her no good at all. "What a shame you don't share my experiences of it then."

The bitch. Although it was unlikely she knew about the dead

baby. Hardly anyone did apart from Dora and the servants, and the pastor who had buried her, of course.

Isabella kept her smile rigidly fixed on her face. She'd spent a lot of time perfecting it in front of the mirror, as well as the dimples, determined no one should ever know what was going on behind her mask. "I am sure I'm quite glad not to have experienced everything you have."

No. One child, one living child, would have been enough for her. One little girl who should have been nine years old by now, running and playing, laughing and singing. She deployed her fan as she fought not to think of that tiny coffin. This would not do.

From the ballroom came sounds of the orchestra warming up, and Atkins approached Richard, speaking into his ear. More guests for the ball itself must be arriving. Isabella seized the opportunity to escape. "I'm sorry, Lady Chase, but duty calls. Dora and I must join Richard to greet our guests. I'm happy to inform you that everyone we invited will be attending. All of them keen to meet the new duke."

Too late for you to catch him, and your boring sisters won't stand a chance.

She crossed the room to Richard's side, laying her hand on his arm with delicate proprietary, certain all eyes were upon her. Let everyone see she was in his confidence, that he was her friend, not theirs, and that she was the one in charge here. To get to him, people would have to go through her, and she already had a fine wall constructed. "Shall we go back into the hall, Richard?"

CHAPTER SEVENTEEN

THE BALL SEEMED to be going well, although with his limited experience of social events, Richard couldn't be certain. Everyone seemed happy, at any rate, and all had expressed delight in being introduced to him by Isabella or Dora. In fact, he'd been introduced to so many people he couldn't recall any of their names and would have been hard put to have picked any of the young ladies whose acquaintance he'd made out of the crowd. Even the numerous ones he'd danced with, whose faces had blended into one amorphous blur of nondescript facial features. Of course, all their ambitious mamas had been more than keen to present their daughters, all of whom had been groomed to simper and agree with everything he said. Was that what they all thought men liked? Not this one. Most tiresome.

Amongst the jumbled mass of faces, he encountered an elderly, gray-haired gentleman in a rather old-fashioned suit. Isabella, with whom he'd been taking a refreshing glass of lemonade after a particularly vigorous dance with a young lady of ample proportions and two left feet, had seemed somewhat unwilling to make the introduction.

"Oh, he's old and fusty. You don't want to be wasting your time talking to him. Let me find you another delightful young lady to dance with." Was that a hint of sarcasm in her tone? "We can't have our host without a partner for this next dance, can we? It's Sir Roger de Coverley. My favorite." She laid a determined hand on his arm. "In fact, I could dance it with you, if you like?" She batted those long eyelashes of hers at him, but he wasn't fooled. For some reason she didn't want him to meet the old gentleman.

He smiled as though he hadn't divined her purpose. "Much as it pains me to have to turn you down, Isabella, I fear that if I have to dance again without a short rest it will endanger the future of the dukedom, because I might expire from exhaustion and overheating. And my poor feet also need time to recover from their recent trampling."

She frowned. "Well, let us go and get some more lemonade then and prevent that unfortunate occurrence. I promise not to tread on your toes even once." She gave his arm a determined tug, but he stood his ground.

The old gentleman approached. Age had withered and bent him, but once he would have been as tall as Richard, and he still had a head of thick white hair, confined in the old-fashioned manner in a queue tied with a black velvet ribbon. He made a smart bow to Richard and Isabella.

Richard returned the bow, and Isabella, oozing annoyance from every pore, curtsied.

A little huff escaped before she spoke. "May I introduce Colonel Jarvis, one of our local magistrates, Your Grace."

Richard held out his hand and the old man took it. They shook.

"Delighted to make your acquaintance," Jarvis said, his voice a deep rumble. "An admirable idea to get over the problem of meeting your neighbors by inviting them all here at once. Demmed fine idea indeed."

Isabella, who still had her hand on Richard's arm, gave it a little tug. Now, why was she so keen to keep him away from this magistrate? Could it have something to do with Marcus's death? Perhaps this was the magistrate who'd dealt with it. Richard groped in his memory for the information, if he'd ever been given it, and failed. Not a suitable topic of conversation for tonight, though. He made a mental note to call on Colonel Jarvis in the near future and question him.

"I'm afraid the duchess has decreed that I must circulate," Richard said, as Isabella gave another tug, her fingers digging into his arm. "Perhaps we can talk again later?"

The old man nodded. "Splendid, splendid. I shall look forward to that. Ah, there's old Brocklebank. Must go and have a chat to him about this winter's hunting. Until later, Your Grace."

As Jarvis headed off in Brocklebank's direction, Richard turned to Isabella, who had a badly disguised frown on her face. "What was that for?"

The frown was replaced by an expression of such innocence it had to be fake. "What was what for?"

"All that tugging. Why didn't you want me speaking to Colonel Jarvis?" He favored her with a raised eyebrow. "And don't bother to spin me a faradiddle, because I think I already know the reason."

She glanced around herself as though worried someone would overhear, but no one appeared to be paying them any attention. "He is the magistrate whom we sent for on the day Marcus died."

"And why does that matter?"

She pressed her lips into a hard line before she replied. "Bad memories, of course. I wish you would not pester me about that day. I prefer not to think of it." She drew out her dance card. "I'm afraid I must abandon you now, as I see I promised the next dance to Mr. Carlton, who is even now approaching with a most determined expression on his face, even though you are his host and a duke." And she was gone, with an unrepentant smile, and a flurry of gold silk and auburn curls, to meet the young gentleman who was making his way towards her.

Richard watched as she was whisked out onto the dance floor by someone who was clearly deeply enamored of her, as, it seemed, were most of the gentlemen he'd seen her with tonight. It might well be possible, he reflected, that Colonel Jarvis brought back bad memories for her. Or, if rumor were true, a combination of bad memories and a fear that, as a magistrate, he might work out what she'd done if she spent time talking to him.

The urge to have further conversation with the colonel increased, but Richard was to be thwarted. Just before supper was announced, he caught sight of the colonel leaving. Perhaps, at his age, an early bed was to be advised. Nevertheless, he could visit him in his home at some point, as he'd already planned. Although his questions would have to be circumspect. The last thing he wanted to do was give away more than he received in return and alert that gentleman's suspicions.

Apart from that brief respite from dancing, he found it impossible to get near Isabella again, as she was as surrounded by eager gentlemen as he was by eager young ladies. He'd never felt so popular, although knowing it was his title and new-found wealth they were finding the most attractive of his traits did go some way to bursting his bubble of self confidence. What it was to be so sought after. His fellow officers in the Rifles would have been most amused.

DORA HAD SPENT the evening keeping herself out of the way of as many people as possible. The beautiful blue dress felt as though it was a beacon announcing her disregard for her brother's death. If she'd had her way, she'd have stayed in mourning for the rest of her life. Yes, she'd been terrified of him, but he'd been her brother, and the way he'd died... No, she wouldn't think about that. Not tonight.

Philip Sanders eventually sought her out. As land agent, he'd been invited to the ball, although he'd expressed surprise at his inclusion. Marcus would never have invited him, which he pointed out to Dora as they stood in a shadowy corner, away from the frivolous dancing that Dora insisted she was not going to take part in.

"I have no idea why you've been invited," Dora whispered, keeping her voice down low as she was wont to do most of the time. "I can only conclude that Diccon has done so because he is a much nicer person than Marcus ever was. Something I can vouch for."

"Goes without saying," Philip said. "Picked that up straightaway when I met him. Seems an honest, upright sort. Typical of an army officer."

Dora nodded. "He was always so kind to me when we were children. My only friend."

Philip caught her hand in his. For a moment, Dora froze, then relaxed, his touch sending a warm feeling through her body. A feeling that could have been of safety. Only she wasn't safe, was she? Not now. Not ever.

"How could anyone not be kind to you?" Philip whispered, moving a little closer. "My heart broke every time I saw the way your brother treated you. Every time he did something cruel. Every time he returned here from London, in fact."

Dora gazed up into his face. Everything about him exuded calm reassurance, and yet, she wasn't reassured at all. If he only knew… "I'm safe now," she lied. "Safe with you."

He took her other hand, as well, drawing both up to his chest, clasped between his. "Dare I hope, dearest Dora, that, with your cousin now in charge here at Stourbridge, I might press my suit? I've waited so long to do so. I feel my heart will burst if I have to wait any longer to make you mine."

Dora swallowed. She and Philip had spoken in the past of marriage, but it had all been just in theory, as both of them had known Marcus would never have countenanced it. Philip, in a moment of madness, had even offered to run away with her, to leave Stourbridge behind them and make a new life for themselves elsewhere. He was a land agent, an educated man, and he could find work anywhere, he'd said. But she'd always refused. Leaving Isabella alone at Marcus's mercy had not been possible. "Diccon is yet very new in his position, Philip." Her voice wavered. How to tell the man she adored above all else that she couldn't marry him? Not now, even though both she and Isabella were free of Marcus forever. "Let me choose the time." Only there never would be a time.

Philip glanced about himself. "I would steal a kiss from you, if you will give it."

Oh, how she longed to be kissed, passionately and without anything to prevent their love. And how she longed to be married to Philip and leave Stourbridge and all its memories far behind. But she couldn't do that to him. She stood on tiptoes and pressed her lips to his for a fleeting moment. That would have to do. Anything more and she wasn't sure she'd be able to stop. As ever, he didn't try to take more than she offered. He knew her too well for that.

She cleared her throat, trying to shut out the longing on Philip's face. "Can we perhaps go and find refreshment now? It's so hot in here, and I have a raging thirst."

Emerging from their hiding place was to prove a bad move.

Lady Dangerfield was lying in wait in the refreshment room, and as Dora and Philip headed to the tables of lemonade, she homed in on them like a hound upon its prey. In a short moment she'd separated Dora from Philip, whom she plainly saw as insignificant, like a sheepdog cutting out the one sheep the farmer wants, and was whisking her away into one of the other rooms.

Dora, helpless as a fish in a net, and hampered by her own good manners, could do nothing to escape. Where was Bella when she needed her? Nowhere in sight.

Lady Dangerfield almost frog-marched her prey into one of the curtained alcoves and sat her down on the couch it held. With only enough room for two, Dora found herself far too close for comfort to someone she both hated and feared. A woman who, on her visits to Stourbridge with Marcus, had not held back from following her lover's lead and been as scathing and unpleasant as he had been. Her scent hung heavy in the air around them, thick and cloying and far too sweet. Enough to make Dora have to fight not to gag.

"Now, Dora, my dear," began Lady Dangerfield, a predatory

look in her cold eyes, and oblivious to Dora's need to cough. "I have a few pertinent questions for you."

Dora swallowed. Never once in all the times she'd encountered Lady Dangerfield had that lady addressed her as "dear." This did not bode well. She peered over Lady Dangerfield's shoulder, hoping against hope that Isabella might appear. Or Diccon. But no one came.

"You need have no fear in answering me truthfully," Lady Dangerfield went on, a steely glint now in her eyes. She looked as though she could be as determined as Isabella, which was in no way encouraging.

Dora clasped her hands in her lap to quell the tremble in them. "I never speak anything but the truth," she managed, although it was a lie, and she knew it. The truth here would never do.

Lady Dangerfield bared her teeth in what might have been a smile, on the face of a wolf. "Good girl. That's what I like to hear. Now, tell me everything that happened on the night Marcus died."

Dora's mouth went paper dry, her tongue adhering itself to its roof. Everything she knew about that night flew out of her head, except the worst bits of course, and all she could do was gape at her interlocutor. Only the knowledge that she must never, ever breathe a single word of what had happened to anyone kept her still sitting there, struggling to maintain a calm façade. And praying Bella would find her.

Lady Dangerfield patted her clasped hands. "Don't be afraid to tell me. I can be your friend and confidante. Nothing you tell me will go any further."

As if. Even Dora, ready to see the good in anyone, knew not to believe that. "M-Marcus shot himself," she whispered, her words coming out as a throaty rasp.

Lady Dangerfield's smile dissolved into an angry scowl. "Come now, Dora my dear. We all know that's not true, don't we? Have you not heard the rumors? Marcus most certainly did not die by his own hand. We know who did it, don't we? He enjoyed life far too much. Just tell me. Say the words. Give Isabella up so she can face justice."

Fear edged around Dora, threatening to swallow her whole. She must not give in to this. She must not. "The truth is," she said, her voice gaining strength, which surprised her, "that we none of us know if he did it on purpose or by mistake." Her confidence grew, and she raised her eyes to stare Lady Dangerfield, her brother's despicable mistress, in the face, her heart hammering so hard she couldn't have counted the beats. "As you are well aware, he was accustomed to practice shooting in the library of an evening. We were all used to the loud reports his pistols made. I will allow that it is more than likely that he died by accident, rather than intentionally." She could almost believe what she'd said herself. Isabella would be proud of her.

Seizing the momentum and suddenly feeling as though Isabella were standing beside her and making her brave as a lion, she rose to her feet, snatching her hands back from Lady Dangerfield's grasp. "We have nothing more to say to one another, so I must wish you good evening, my lady." And channeling Isabella for all she was worth, she swept out of the alcove and headed for the ballroom, heart still hammering so fast she feared it might come leaping out of her mouth at any moment. She would find Philip again and he would help her hide.

RICHARD HAD SOUGHT solace in the shadows. Supper, in the company of a rather vapid young lady with little or no conversation, was over and done with, midnight was long past, and dancing was continuing in the brightly lit ballroom apace. None of the guests showed any signs of flagging, despite the lateness of the hour, and the heat in the room was oppressive, redolent with the sweat of many over-exerted bodies. Right now, Richard was relieved to have been able to snatch some peace and quiet from the attentions of all those ambitious mamas. Who would have thought so many existed within striking range of Stourbridge

Park, and that Isabella would have insisted on inviting them all?

He was engaged in watching her as she danced with a handsome young buck who seemed quite awestruck by her beauty. Not that Richard could blame him. She had been at her vivacious best all night, tripping through the dance steps with elegance, laughing up at every one of her partners as though each was the most important person in the world to her, and chattering away to them to the annoyance of their womenfolk in between each dance. If anyone could have been said to be the belle of this ball, it was her. No matter how much any of the other ladies present might have liked to shine, she eclipsed them all. If he could find a girl like her, somewhere, then maybe he might find marriage not quite so tedious as he anticipated.

The heat was making him uncomfortable. His shirt was sticking to his back and he would have liked to have been able to remove the expertly tailored coat that was now feeling far too restrictive and tight. Maybe if he went outside into the cool night air he could do just that. But how to evade the eyes of this ever-watchful pack of slavering mamas?

At that moment, one of the footmen emerged from a door camouflaged in the wall behind him, carrying a tray. Before he had time to regret the idea, Richard retreated back further into the shadows and let himself out of the ballroom. He found himself in a narrow corridor that led into the service areas of the house. Immediately, he was aware of a welcome coolness in the air. With relief, he wriggled out of his coat and slung it over his shoulder.

A few quick right-hand turns and he was emerging from yet another service door into the chill night air. Oil lamps had been lit in the brackets along the side of the house and on stands at the edge of the balustraded terrace, but they threw only small pools of golden light across the ancient flagstones. Nobody was out here in the darkness that he could see. Thank goodness. He didn't want to run into any young ladies who might be eager to claim he'd compromised them so he could be forced into marriage.

Isabella had warned him about that hazard, and that probably a few mamas had come with just that in mind. One girl in particular had seemed overly keen to get him to show her the library, which could have been from a desire to see the scene of Marcus's death, or could just as easily have been at prompting from her mama to get herself alone with him.

He strolled across the flagstones to the wide stone steps down into the ornamental gardens. Long hedges ran away to left and right, as well as flower beds, trees, and a network of paths. He smiled. There might well be a few liaisons already going on within the shadowy recesses of this garden. The scent of late roses wafted through the cool air. Maybe a walk along the paths he'd played on as a boy might soothe his admittedly frazzled nerves. No one had told him hosting a ball would be such a stressful undertaking, or he might have said no to it. The thought of ever having to host another, or even attend one at someone else's house, horrified him. Returning to his regiment had never looked so alluring a prospect.

He descended the steps and glanced to right and left. Nothing and no one. He went right, wandering aimlessly along path after path, breathing in the scents of the garden that threatened to transport him back in time to his childhood. Such different scents to those in distant Portugal.

But he was not destined to be allowed to travel far down the lanes of nostalgia. From up ahead came the sound of voices, the low rumble of a man's, and the higher cadence of a woman, her tone demanding. He glanced about himself, anxious not to be found alone down here. Who knew what the consequences might be?

To his left, along a short path, lay the old summerhouse. The moonlight glinting across its windows caught his eye. The voices drew closer. With nowhere else to go, Richard retreated down the path, but didn't go into the summerhouse. Instead, he edged around behind it to where a small shed, overgrown with creepers, had used to nestle. It had been used by the gardeners for their tools as well as a spot to eat their meals while on duty, and he and Dora had spent many a happy hour chattering to them in there as children.

It was still there, a little more dilapidated, but in place. He didn't go inside, but retreated into the shadows behind it, the summerhouse on his left, the shed on his right.

Just in time. The door of the summerhouse opened, and whomever he'd heard talking went inside. As it was summer, all the higher windows were propped open, and their voices carried to him with clarity. He couldn't help but overhear them.

"You're certain no one is about?" came the man's voice, a little rough around the edges. Not one he recognized. Well, it wouldn't be, unless it was Atkins, as everybody here tonight was new to him. And it wasn't the measured, polite tones of his butler.

"Quite certain," snapped the woman. Something about her voice sounded familiar. It was terse and sharp, but nevertheless, he'd heard it before somewhere. Whoever it was, though, it was neither Isabella nor Dora, both of whom he would have recognized in a heartbeat. That was a relief. At least he wasn't going to have to eavesdrop on a tryst involving either of them. That would have been far too embarrassing.

The man grunted. "I don't like this sneaking about." He was not a gentleman, that was certain. So he couldn't be a guest, could he? Richard had met everyone present, and none of the men had struck him as not being gentlemen.

"You think I do? I might be missed at any moment. I've taken a risk to come out here to meet you."

The man snorted. "Excuse me, your ladyship, but if I'm caught in the gardens someone is bound to ask questions. I'm supposed to've stayed with the carriage. That driver's going to notice if I'm gone long." Was this a lady on an assignation with one of the male servants? A groom or footman perhaps? If only he could see through the back summerhouse wall.

The woman sighed. "You worry too much. What did you

find out?"

Find out? This didn't sound like an assignation any longer. At least not one that involved a couple of illicit lovers.

Another grunt from the man. "Almost everyone's tight as a clam. So far, no one in the servants' hall's been ready to talk. I couldn't press anyone much. I didn't want to make them suspicious."

What? Someone, a servant of one of his guests, had been in the servants' hall asking questions of his staff? About what, he didn't have to wonder. But was this idle curiosity or something more?

"That's not good enough. What am I paying you for?"

"I know, I know. No need to get up on your high horse. You know I'm the best, and I'll get the information for you somehow. Just not tonight. If it's there, I'll find it. You can be sure of that. There just might be one servant I can get to talk. To say what you want to hear. Seemed as if they had a grudge they might want to act on."

"The longer I have to wait, the more likely it is she'll get away with it. You know that. She's got away with it this long. It has to stop. You have to get that servant to talk."

Richard caught his breath. Not just idle curiosity at all. "She" had to be Isabella. This was someone out to find evidence to condemn her. Someone convinced she had murdered her husband. But whom? A woman. A woman who was paying someone else to do her dirty work.

"I can't force people to talk." The man sounded annoyed. "They needs persuading."

"Pay them then." Her voice hissed out, heavy with venom. This was a woman on a mission. A mission to topple Isabella. "I have plenty of money for that. You'd be surprised what people are ready to say if you grease the wheels of their memories. I'll supply you with the necessary. And you will return and continue your enquiries. Make promises to the servant you've found. Offer them more than they could ever earn."

Another grunt. "Very well, your ladyship. If that's what you want."

"And if they still won't say what you want them to say, offer them more money until they do. You know what I want to hear. I'll see that smug bitch hanged and damned in hell if it's the last thing I do. She killed my Marcus and she'll face justice for what she did, or I'll die trying. Whatever it takes, do it."

"Yes, milady."

"Now go. Get back to the carriage before you're missed. We can't be seen together."

The door of the summerhouse opened and closed, but the grass muffled whatever footsteps there were and Richard couldn't be sure if both of them had left or not. Not wanting to run into the mysterious woman, he remained where he was another ten minutes, mulling over what he'd heard. Whoever was paying this man wasn't only after proper evidence. They were already convinced of Isabella's guilt, and it sounded as if they weren't averse to paying for someone to give false witness.

It was a good thing he'd waited, because, just as he was thinking of moving, he heard the door of the summerhouse a second time. Peering around the corner he spotted the blur of a figure hastening up the path back towards the house. Impossible to tell who it was at this distance, although the rustle of skirts told him it was the woman.

He gave her another ten minutes just to be on the safe side, put his coat back on as he was by now feeling chilly, and started back up the path to the house.

Entering through the French doors from the terrace, he found everything in the ballroom was much as he'd left it, with the dancing still going on. None of the women he could see showed any hint of having been the woman he'd overheard in the summerhouse. All of them were either involved in the present dance, cheeks pink with the effort, or clustered in small groups, chattering together. No one had the cloak of guilt about them.

But she'd come this way. She was not a servant but a guest.

So she had to be here.

"Richard, where have you been?" He almost jumped out of his skin. Isabella was standing beside him. "I was looking for you as I've been saving a dance for you all night. I was just about to give in and let Lord William Cholmondeley have it, when I saw you return from the terrace. Is that where you've been hiding?" She batted her long lashes at him, which in her was a far more alluring prospect than when Lady Dangerfield had done it.

Richard couldn't help but smile. "I was overcome by the heat and needed some fresh air. I've been here all night, doing my duty, as I saw you were with all our male guests."

"Oh, those gentlemen who were pressing me for favors?" She laughed. "It's always that way for me. I find myself the center of attention without ever having to do anything." She sounded complacent, but was she, or was it all an act? Perhaps. Her voice held that brittleness again. Was one of the men here her lover? Somehow, he doubted it. She didn't have the air about her of a woman with a secret lover. Richard might never have been in love himself, but he'd seen enough of his fellow officers when they'd been infatuated to recognize a lack of infatuation in her.

"You said you'd saved me a dance?"

She nodded. "The very next one. Shall we?" The orchestra were striking up again.

Richard looked down into her face. Was it the face of a murderer? Could a murderer be that beautiful, that ingenuous, that fragile? For fragile he saw she was. Beneath her outer shell of incorrigible flirt and devil-may-care duchess, there lurked a frightened little girl. More frightened even than Dora. He took her proffered hand. "I would be honored to dance with you, Isabella."

And he spun her out onto the dance floor.

CHAPTER EIGHTEEN

RICHARD WOKE LATE the following morning with a thumping head and bleary eyes. A little unfair, as he'd not touched a drop of anything stronger than lemonade last night, thinking it wisest to keep a clear head in the face of the onslaught of all those ambitious mamas. Instead, it must be due to the combination of the late night, or rather early morning, the hubbub of noise and heat at the ball, and the stress of having to deal with such an unaccustomed and demanding situation. Not to mention the fact that thinking about what he'd overheard in the garden had kept him awake long after he'd retired to bed. If he never had to host another ball in his life, he would be happy.

He rolled over in bed and peered through half open eyes at where pale light was edging its way in around the thick drapes. The morning was already well on, from the look of things, and too late to have joined Isabella for her early morning ride. If she'd been up to going herself. She'd been throwing herself into her enjoyment of the ball last night with more energetic gusto than he'd been able to muster. Knowing her, though, she probably had been up and out early. He couldn't imagine much existed that would stop that young lady doing what she wanted. Not even an earthquake.

For a few minutes he remained lying in bed, thinking about the events of last night. Again. What he should have been considering was the identity of the woman who wished Isabella ill, but what he was actually thinking about was that dance with her after he'd returned to the ballroom. Having watched her all evening, he wasn't foolish enough to think that her charm was anything but deliberate, and yet... she had that knack of making a man feel as if he were the only one in the room of interest to her. Visions of her lissome body in that golden gown, of her sparkling eyes, of the rise and fall of her alabaster breasts... Of the feel of her slender waist under his hands... Well, a man could dream. However, she'd been just as flirtatious with every other man she'd danced with. He had no reason to think he meant anything more to her than any of her other conquests. A list he'd been sure she intended to add him to from the moment he met her. But somehow, he couldn't stop thinking about her...

A tug on the bell produced Baxter, looking annoyingly chipper and smart in his new uniform of valet, although he'd had to stay up just as late as Richard to assist his master in retiring to bed. While Baxter had been helping him prepare for the ball, Richard had offered to sort himself out after it so Baxter could go to bed at a reasonable time. "I'm an adult, Baxter, and I don't need nannying. If you take a good look at me, you'll find I'm exactly the same man for whom you were soldier servant all those years." But Baxter had insisted that as he was now no longer just a soldier servant and had been transformed, by a miracle, into a valet, it was his duty to attend to his master's every need. In his own way, he could be as determined as Isabella. In the face of such determination, Richard had acquiesced.

Baxter now set down a tray containing a fortifying cup of the strong black coffee Richard had grown used to on campaign, and drew back the curtains. A disappointing vista presented itself. Gray clouds filled the sky, and rain streaked the windows. Would Isabella have ridden even when it was like this? Again, the conclusion was in all probability. He couldn't see a bit of rain putting her off. And bang, his thoughts were of her again.

"Good morning, Major," Baxter said with studied aplomb.

He'd evidently been doing his homework about becoming a valet, although addressing his master as "Your Grace" hadn't yet sunk in. Hopefully it never would. He passed his master the coffee. "Would you like me to fetch you breakfast in bed this morning?"

Richard shook his head. "I hope that was said in jest. I might be a duke in name, but I refuse to adjust my habits to fit the title. So, no, thank you very much. I'll get up when I've drunk this and go down to breakfast. I've a few pressing things I need to do today." He did indeed, and was slightly annoyed at himself for having wasted time sleeping. If someone was intent on making enquiries about Marcus's death—unscrupulous enquiries—then it was imperative to be one step ahead of them.

Half an hour later, washed, freshly shaved, and dressed in the least formal of his new clothes—a navy coat and buff breeches with a plain waistcoat and shining top boots—Richard descended the oak staircase into the hallway. Empty of any sign even of Atkins. There must be a lot of clearing up after the ball going on. Perhaps Atkins was supervising it, although he, and the rest of the servants, must all be as tired as Richard was.

No one was in the breakfast room. Dora, who'd retired last night looking like a wilted bluebell after a hot day, must still be in bed, and Isabella… well, she might or might not still be riding. Not his concern right now. Food was. Even though he was worried about what he'd overheard last night, he wasn't about to go out without sustenance.

He ate a quick meal of kedgeree, his favorite, more coffee, and toast and marmalade, and, when Atkins at last appeared, looking flustered, asked him to have the carriage brought round to the front of the house. No point in riding in the rain when he had a perfectly good dry carriage to ride in. Isabella would be shocked, in all probability.

He glanced at his fob watch. Time was getting on, and if he weren't careful it would be afternoon before he arrived at his destination. Irritation arose again at how late he'd woken this morning when time was of the essence.

He was just going out of the front doors, his cape over his arm, when Isabella, a decidedly damp Isabella, appeared in the hallway, her curls drooping forlornly about her pink-cheeked face. His heart performed a little, unexpected leap. How young and girlish and innocent she looked. Surely that couldn't be the face of a murderess.

"Richard!" She sounded pleased to see him.

He stopped. "I did wonder if you would still ride in the rain." He chuckled. "I should have realized that you are completely mad, so of course you would."

She laughed back. "You have assessed me correctly. Nothing would prevent me from riding, unless it was a broken leg, and even then I think I would hoist myself up into the saddle and make an effort." Her gaze ran over his attire. "But I think you are on your way out? Despite the rain."

He nodded, having no intention of telling her where he was intending to go. "I find I must attend to some boring estate business. I'm not like you, and I'm not used to the rain, hailing as I do, most recently, from somewhere hot and dry. I'm taking the carriage."

She made a moue, but he could see she was curious and wanted to delve deeper into his reasons for going out. "And I suppose I must go upstairs and change out of these wet things or I might have offered to accompany you. If only for my amusement. However, I have a hankering for a large breakfast before the servants clear it away, and dry clothes must come first, I fear. Shall I see you later on?"

"Perhaps. I have no idea how long this will take me."

She gave him a little curtsey, her eyes sparkling in a most disturbing fashion. "Until later, then, adieu, mon duc."

He swallowed an awkward lump down. "Yes, until later." Why did he not want to go now she'd returned? She was like a powerful magnet, drawing him in, making escape difficult if not nigh on impossible. With a struggle, he lifted a hand to her and turned away before the draw of her pulled him in. That wouldn't have done at all. Not when he had important matters to attend to. Matters that affected her.

He went outside, an uneasy sensation of guilt at lying to her settling over him. Dickens, wearing a voluminous greatcoat, was waiting on the gravel with the landau, its hood up. "Colonel Jarvis's house," Richard said, as he got in.

Was that a look laden with suspicion Dickens shot him? Were all the servants in on whatever secret Stourbridge Castle was hiding? No doubt the rest of them would find out from Dickens on their return that Richard had been to see the local magistrate. Colonel Jarvis; the man who'd overseen the process following the discovery of Marcus's body. He shied away from calling it Marcus's murder. He had no way of knowing yet if it had indeed been a murder or just an unfortunate accident or suicide. And besides which, he'd reached a point where he'd been forced to acknowledge that he didn't want Isabella to be guilty of it.

He liked her too much. She might be vain and an incorrigible flirt, determined to the point of bossiness, and a sight too inclined to speak her mind to those she didn't like, but the sense that beneath the brittle public exterior lurked a hurt and frightened girl wouldn't leave him: that almost everything about her was an elaborate sham, a mask, a disguise of who she really was. A once-innocent girl damaged by ten years of marriage to Marcus. If she'd been forced to adopt any less attractive character traits, then he held Marcus responsible for every single one of them.

The landau moved off, the gravel crunching under its wheels, passing a rider in a shabby brown coat heading around to the stables. A tradesman, perhaps. Richard had other things to think of. Was he being a fool? A fool taken in by a pretty face? Perhaps. He sat back against the upholstered interior as the horses ate up the road across the park, still not sure he was doing the right thing. That old adage his nurse had been wont to remind him of surfaced. *Let sleeping dogs lie.*

He shook his head to dispel his doubts. If he didn't do this investigating, then the man in the employ of that woman was going to, and neither he nor his employer seemed to have any scruples about falsifying evidence if they had to, and paying for it. The fact that he was sure evidence must be frequently falsified in courts across the country in order to gain a conviction did nothing to improve his confidence. He closed his eyes for a moment, hoping his headache would begin to improve. It didn't.

He soon discovered that Colonel Jarvis, the elderly magistrate who had eventually been called to the castle on the morning Marcus's body had been discovered in the library, lived some seven miles distant, to the west of Newbury. A good hour's drive. He owned a substantial Palladian style mansion set in a small park on land that gently sloped down towards a river, by way of a mound that might well have been the motte part of an ancient motte and bailey castle. At any other time this glimpse back into history would have fascinated Richard, but not today.

Dickens brought the landau to a gentle halt outside the porticoed entranceway of the house, and Richard wasted no time in descending and hastening under the shelter provided by the elegantly peaked roof. The door was already being held open by the colonel's butler, so he hurried up the wide stone steps and into a spacious front hall.

The butler closed the door behind him and bowed. "Your Grace."

Did everyone in this blasted place know who he was? The thought that it would be nice to be able to go incognito surfaced, only to be brushed away. His likeness to the previous incumbent was never going to allow that. Being a duke was to be almost constantly in the eye of the public. The only thing worse than that would be to be a member of the royal family. Which brought back to him the Prince of Wales's interest in Isabella.

Richard addressed the fellow, who looked as venerable as his employer. "Good morning." If it still was morning, of course. Richard didn't bother to check his fob watch. "I wonder if Colonel Jarvis might be at home?"

The butler bowed again. "If you would be so kind as to wait in the drawing room?" He indicated a pair of double doors to the left, one slightly ajar. "I will go and enquire about the colonel's availability, Your Grace."

Richard obliged and went into the drawing room, the butler discreetly closing the door behind him as though he feared such a rare creature as a visiting duke might escape before he returned. A pleasant room, it was somewhat in need of redecoration and possessed a decided aroma of old tobacco. A thick Turkish rug covered the floor, and some of the furniture had a dilapidated look to it. Yet it was a comfortable room that seemed to fit with the persona of a retired soldier. It had the effect of making him feel more at ease with his mission.

He walked over to one of the long windows and peered out into the rain washed world. This would have afforded him a pleasing view of the park, had not it been obscured by the misty drizzle.

He didn't have long to wait.

The door opened to admit the elderly gentleman he'd so briefly met the night before. Colonel Jarvis's military service must have been long behind him now, as surely he had already attained his three score and ten and possibly a bit more than that. Even though the hour was now late, he was dressed as though he'd not long arisen. On top of his white hair, he wore a small round hat liberally decorated with embroidery and sequins, and an ornately patterned silk banyan covering his shirt and breeches gave him the appearance of an Indian potentate. If Richard had been forced to guess, he would have hazarded that the colonel had come by his rank in India some time in the last century.

"Your Grace." He presented a welcoming smile, courteous, but not overly familiar. A man who kept people at a distance. His bow was formal.

"Colonel." Richard returned the bow. "I hope you don't mind me calling upon you without notice."

The colonel shook his head, curiosity in his gaze. "Not at all.

An honor. I'm feeling very popular this morning. Please, take a seat, and I'll ring for refreshment. What will you take? Brandy?"

Richard, who was not a big drinker, particularly not in the mornings, shook his head, at the same time as a tiny nagging thought arose about why the colonel would call himself popular today. "Tea would be most acceptable. Thank you."

Was that a look of disappointment on the lined old face? "Tea it is then." He did have the sort of red nose, covered in broken veins, that indicated he might be a tippler.

Richard had already decided to take the bull by the proverbial horns. No point in being coy. When the tea had been ordered and they were alone again, he leaned forward in his seat. "I gather you were the attending magistrate when my cousin killed himself." Best to avoid any suggestion he'd died a different way.

The colonel's rheumy old eyes sharpened. "I wondered how long it would take you to come over here and ask me about it." He harrumphed. "Did think we might have had the chance to talk a little more last night, but I noticed all those matchmaking mamas were keeping you busy meeting their daughters." He chuckled, which made him cough. "What it is to be young and supremely eligible. Glad no one's likely to think that about me any longer."

Richard smiled in agreement. "It was a little tiresome at times. I imagine, though, that you must understand that I have a natural curiosity about what has led me to my new position in life."

"I daresay you have. The old duke, although one can hardly call him old, just a whippersnapper really, cut down in the prime of his life. Most unexpected. Most disturbing."

"Indeed. Maybe you could tell me what happened that day from your own point of view? The official view of it, as everyone else I've spoken to has either been a servant or a female, and we know how inclined to emotion they can be. A sensible, man's view is what I need." Flattery might get him everywhere.

The colonel leaned back in his chair, with an air of being the required sensible man, and rubbed his chin, his fingers rasping over a goodly amount of stubble. He didn't look as though he'd found time to be shaved that morning. Who had been here earlier, disturbing him? "I'm afraid I didn't arrive until the middle of the morning, so I can't speak for what went on before that, you know. I can only tell you what I saw when I arrived, and how I organized things. There's a fair amount to do after an unexpected death, I can assure you."

"As a soldier, I'm not unused to the prospect of sudden deaths. Although in battle, they are at least to be expected from time to time, although that never makes them any easier."

The colonel nodded. "As you say. As you say. Military man myself. Well, as I was taking my breakfast that morning, I received a groom from the castle bearing a message. It was about a quarter before nine, I'd say. Told me there'd been an accident at Stourbridge Castle, and I was required. I questioned the lad a bit further and discovered it was a death I was to be dealing with, but he didn't know whose." He harrumphed again. "Well, I was hungry and, if the fellow was dead, he wasn't going to be running off anywhere, so I had the groom wait while I finished my meal. No use going off half-cocked."

Richard had to suppress a smile. The colonel didn't strike him as the sort of man who would venture far without either sustenance or lubrication. He was sipping at his tea as though he feared it might contain poison. "And what did you find when you arrived at the castle?"

The colonel shook his head. "I wasn't there until at least half past ten. It's quite a way from here to the castle, you know, and the roads are not of the best. Might even have been eleven. Yes, I think it was. Now I think about it, I recall hearing a clock somewhere strike the hour."

Richard couldn't help a raise of his eyebrows. So the old man hadn't even bothered to consult his fob watch. Not very efficient. But that might bode well for Isabella.

The colonel shifted a little in his seat as though his old bones pained him. "That land agent fellow, Sanders, I think he's called, told me it was the duke and took me into the library. Seemed keen to get me in there. They'd had the sense not to move the body, which was a good thing."

"What position was it in?"

He scratched his head for a moment. "Near the desk, on its back, arms out to the side. But I can do one better than that. I'm not a total fool, you know. I had my man, who's gifted in the artistic department, draw a sketch of the scene. I can show it to you." He heaved himself out of his chair and went across the room to where an escritoire stood against one of the walls. "You're in luck. It's in here." He rummaged about. "You're not the only person who's come asking me about this today, you know. Seems a popular subject around here all of a sudden."

Richard's ears pricked, and his stomach did an awkward roll. "Really? Who else has been asking questions?"

The old man turned, something in his hands, and gave a shrug. "Let me think. Not so good at remembering names nowadays, I'm afraid. Ah. I know. Said his name was Barker. Made me think of a dog I had once by that name. That's it. Silas Barker. Asked me all about that day, same as you're doing." He wrinkled his sizeable nose. "A rather low-class individual. Not a gentleman by any means, but very keen to find out what I could tell him. Very keen indeed. Even though I couldn't see what it had to do with him."

He frowned at the memory as he handed a sheet of thick, good quality drawing paper to Richard. On it, someone had sketched the layout of a room, presumably the library at Stourbridge, in plan, as though seen from above, with the body sprawled beside the desk. The colonel was right. His man did have an artistic flair, and an eye for detail that his master lacked, too. Clearly marked, beside the outstretched right hand, lay a pistol, with an arrow leading to a remark at the side of the sketch—"*dueling pistol, one of two recovered—probable cause of death.*" Even if the colonel was not particularly efficient, it seemed his man was.

However, one thing about the sketch had already struck Richard. Enough to set his heart pounding with anxiety. He glanced up at the colonel. "And this was exactly how you found everything. No one had touched or moved anything after he was found?"

He nodded. "I daresay. Evers, my man, takes his job seriously, you know. A boon to me. Insisted on doing a plan of the whole room and questioning the servants, even though it seemed obvious to me it was either an accidental death or suicide." A puzzled expression slid over his face. "Don't know why, but the man Barker seemed very interested in all of this too. Wanted to take Evers's drawing with him, but I said he couldn't. Evers needs to keep it filed in his office. So he made a ham-fisted copy. Not as gifted as Evers, though. Which reminds me—I need to put it back or he'll be scolding me for losing it." He harrumphed again.

Richard had the distinct impression that Colonel Jarvis would not be providing anything more of use here. His presence at the castle had been nothing more than a formality. Evers was the man with the information. "Would it be possible for me to speak to Mr. Evers, do you think?"

The colonel nodded, a look of unmistakable relief on his face. "Of course. He'll be in his office doing something useful, no doubt. He seems to find a lot of things to do he deems useful. I don't interfere. He's very efficient and a great help to me, so I leave him to it. I'll get my butler to show you the way." He smiled. "And if you could give him back the drawing, I would be grateful."

CHAPTER NINETEEN

MR. EVERS TURNED out to be quite the opposite of his employer. In his very early twenties, but with the round, guileless face of a boy, he nevertheless wore thick-lensed reading glasses on the end of his long, aquiline nose and was in possession of an acute brain as well as a natty dress-style. He was well-spoken and clearly well-educated, possibly at the grammar school Philip Sanders had mentioned, and Richard found himself wondering if he was perhaps the son of a local clergyman.

He was relieved to have his sketch returned. "I like to keep all of the colonel's cases complete," he said, as Richard laid it on the desk. "But he does have a tendency to take papers out from time to time and then forget he's had them. I have to keep quite an eye on him."

Richard nodded. "I'm not here only to deliver you your sketch. I was rather hoping you might be able to tell me something of what happened the day of my cousin's death. The Colonel tells me you would know more than he does."

Mr. Evers frowned. "How very odd. You're the second person who's come to me today wanting to know just that. I hope you're not about to try to bribe me, as the first fellow did. I can assure you that I am not open to such a thing. I was quite offended when he drew out his wallet and sent him on his way with a flea in his ear."

That was good news. Perhaps Silas Barker had not managed

to glean anything much before he'd been sent packing. Richard's spirits rose. And it did give him cause to think that if it came to it, Mr. Evers could give evidence that Barker was not above offering bribes.

He smiled. "I'm a duke. I don't need to bribe people." He might as well use his title for something. "I just want to ascertain the truth, as I'm sure you do. Did. Perhaps you could tell me about your discoveries that morning."

Mr. Evers nodded. "Of course, Your Grace, but I didn't find a lot in the way of discoveries, I'm afraid." He frowned. "I'd far rather tell you about it than I would that despicable man." He drew out his notes from a drawer and ran his eye over them. "Let me see… We arrived at nine minutes to eleven." He patted his waistcoat. "I checked my watch on arrival. I always do. In the hall to greet us were Mr. Atkins, butler to His Grace and now to you, Mrs. Barnes, the housekeeper of long standing, and Mr. Rowan, head groom, who told me he'd been employed at the castle since he was a boy. No other servants were present, and the library door was closed and locked. Mr. Atkins was in charge and had the key. He informed us he'd sent Her Grace and Lady Dora up to lie down as both ladies were suffering from acute shock. He'd sent them up together, to give one another comfort."

All well so far. This tallied with what Richard had already learned. "What first struck you when you went into the library?"

Mr. Evers's brow furrowed. "As far as I could tell, very little was out of place. Save for the body on the floor, of course." His eyes took on a faraway expression, as though he were seeing the scene again. "His Grace was lying with his feet towards the door, as if he'd fallen backwards onto the rug. He was wearing silk breeches and stockings. One of his shoes had come off. If you look at my sketch, you'll see I've included that." He tapped the paper, perhaps more than a little proud of his own attention to detail.

Richard nodded. "And the weapon? Where was that?"

Mr. Evers nodded. "I'm coming to that. I have a particular

way of working, if you don't mind, Your Grace." He cleared his throat. "Now. Where was I? Aha. He must have removed his coat. It was lying on the back of the seat on the far side of the desk. There was an empty brandy glass and a half full decanter on the desk. Just the one glass."

So Marcus had been drinking. Nothing new there.

"His Grace was still wearing his waistcoat, which was unbuttoned, and his cravat, which was still done up. His right arm was thrown out to the side, his left bent with his hand up near his head." He cleared his throat again, as though not liking his task. "His head was slightly to one side, as though he'd been looking to the left when the trigger was pulled. There was a small hole in his right temple, a larger exit wound on the left side of his head. Very little blood or brain matter on the rug. I concluded that the fatal shot had come from the right, while he was standing nearer to the door, as the blood and brain matter was scattered over some of the furniture and bookshelves at head height."

Luckily Richard was well acquainted with violent death and this description didn't bother him. "The weapon?"

Evers nodded. "It was lying close to his right hand as though it had fallen from his grip. It was one of a pair of dueling pistols which Mr. Atkins identified for me as belonging to His Grace. He told me his master kept them in the study. To hand for when he liked to use them of an evening. For target practice, apparently. Indoors. Something I must admit I found a little strange, but then, he was a duke."

Richard ignored the implication that dukes were not normal. "Did you find the other pistol of the pair?"

Mr. Evers nodded.

"And was it loaded?"

Another nod. "It was. I asked Mr. Atkins and he told me that His Grace was in the habit of keeping them loaded in case of burglars, and in case he needed them in a hurry for any other reason. Although I have to say that I have no idea what other reason for which he could have required them. Mr. Atkins was the one who ascertained that it was not unusual for His Grace to practice target shooting in the library in the middle of the night. With those two weapons. I have been led to believe that His Grace has been involved in at least two duels in the last few years. I concluded that he must have considered it wise to be a crack shot. Just in case. Mr. Atkins confirmed this."

Richard suppressed a smile. Much as Marcus, as a boy, had constantly practiced with his bow, intent on reaching the standards of a Robin Hood or William Tell. Marcus had always insisted on being the best, and the animals on the park had suffered for it.

"Can you tell me anything about what happened before your arrival?"

Mr. Evers nodded. "Mr. Atkins informed me that he'd heard the shot at about three in the morning. He'd been in bed. Their Graces, and Lady Dora Carstairs, had returned from an evening engagement an hour before that and His Grace had informed Mr. Atkins he could retire to bed. They were going to take a glass of brandy in the library, something Mr. Atkins said His Grace often did after he'd been out for the evening."

"Did Mr. Atkins think my cousin was drunk?"

Mr. Evers shifted a little, perhaps not wanting to speak badly of the dead. "He did."

Richard nodded. "And when he heard the shot, what did he do?"

Mr. Evers consulted his notes again. "At first he assumed it was His Grace practicing with his pistols, but then he heard a scream, and this alerted him to the possibility that all was not well. He put on his trousers, knocked on the housekeeper's door, and hurried upstairs from the servants' quarters. When he arrived at the library, he found Her Grace, the duchess, and Lady Dora with the body of the duke. Both of them were in a state of severe distress. Mrs. Barnes arrived a few moments later, and Mr. Atkins sent both the ladies off with her to see if she could calm them down. He informed me he wanted to get them away from the gory sight."

He turned a page in his notebook. "He then proceeded to take a quick look around the library in case there were any lurking burglars, and checked to see if His Grace was alive. He was not. He then closed the door and locked it and informed Mr. Rowan, the groom, who had also heard the shot, that someone would have to call the magistrate. The colonel. Realizing nothing more could be done for the duke, he didn't call Mr. Sanders, the land agent, until he deemed it a reasonable hour. Mr. Sanders then took over and set up a guard, one of the grooms, over the library door. They sent for the colonel when they deemed it a polite time to disturb him. I gather they saw no point in sending for him sooner, as His Grace was clearly dead."

"And no one touched the pistol until you arrived?"

"Mr. Atkins assured me no one went into the library after he closed the door. Other than Mr. Sanders, of course."

Richard frowned. Someone was lying here and it wasn't Mr. Evers. A more upright young man he had yet to meet. And a thorough one with all his observations and careful note taking.

"Did you tell all this to your Mr. Barker?"

Mr. Evers pulled a disgusted face. "He is not 'my Mr. Barker,' Your Grace. Far from it. If I never see that scoundrel again, I shall be a happy man." He paused. "I did tell him most of that though, before he tried offering me money. I am a servant of justice, Your Grace, not someone who can be bought. I was deeply offended that he thought I might be."

Richard nodded. "Most commendable. But what was it he wanted you to say?"

Mr. Evers frowned. "I would really rather not divulge that."

"I'm afraid I'm going to need you to."

"Putting it into words offends my sensibilities."

"It won't offend me. Just tell me."

Mr. Evers swallowed. "He wanted me to say that I thought His Grace had been murdered. That he could not have killed himself."

Richard regarded the young man for a long moment. So Barker had wanted Mr. Evers to tell what he assumed to be a lie. The only problem was, Richard knew without a doubt that it would not have been a lie at all. Given the evidence he'd seen today, Marcus could definitely not have killed himself. Someone, and there were very few suspects, had murdered him. Granted, it might have been some kind of accident, and he hoped it was, but there was no way Marcus had done this himself. Thanks to the evidence he'd seen, Richard knew that without any doubt. The question was, who had done it?

He kept his face expressionless and nodded to Mr. Evers. "Thank you very much for your assistance. If this Mr. Barker returns, you have it on my authority to have him kicked out of the colonel's property, or better still, arrested. Do the same to anyone else who wants information, as they will only turn out to be scandalmongers. You were very wise to send him off like that." He held out his hand.

After a tiny pause, as Mr. Evers accustomed himself to shaking the hand of a duke, the young man took the offered hand. "I hope I was of some use to you, Your Grace."

Richard nodded. "You were indeed."

ISABELLA PEERED INTO the drawing room but was disappointed. No sign of Dora. Was she still in bed? It was most annoying that both she and Richard were not about. He'd had about him a furtive manner when she'd encountered him in the hallway, on his way out. Business in town. Poppycock. There was definitely something afoot with him. Dora might know more than she did.

The clock on the drawing room mantlepiece declared it to be nearly midday. Surely Dora couldn't still be asleep, even after her late night. She'd have to go upstairs and find her.

Hitching her skirt up a little so as not to trip, she mounted the stairs and headed towards Dora's bedroom, which wasn't far from her own.

She'd maligned Dora. She was not in bed but sitting on her

cushioned window seat gazing out at the rainy landscape. She still wore her nightgown, and over it a delicate silk peignoir. Her mousey hair hung down her back in a long plait. How a man as striking in appearance as Marcus had once been had managed to have such a plain sister was beyond Isabella. But whatever Dora looked like, she was Isabella's dearest friend, and she loved her.

Dora turned her head as Isabella entered, eyes wide with fear, face pale and drawn. Her lower lip trembled as though she might be about to burst into tears. That would never do. She really had to hold herself together or all would be lost.

Isabella fixed a determined smile onto her face and marched across the room to join her. "There you are. I was getting quite lonely downstairs. Richard had already taken breakfast by the time I returned from my ride, and now he's gone out on some sort of business. Most tiresome of him when I wanted some company. Why aren't you up and dressed yet?"

Dora drew in a deep, steadying breath. Yes, ignoring her potential fit of the vapors was the best way of dealing with it. She had past experience with Dora and her nerves. Good heavens, as if living with Marcus all her life would not have rendered her a gibbering wreck. She could hardly blame the poor girl for her tendency to allow her nerves to get the better of her. Although with Isabella's encouragement and support, she'd done her best to overcome it while Marcus was alive. It was only now, with him safely in his grave, that her nerves seemed to be resurfacing. Little wonder, really.

"What are you going to wear?" Isabella gave her a perfunctory pat on the hand, instinct warning her that to show any sympathy was a sure way to reduce Dora to tears, and went to her large armoire. She flung open the door. On one side hung Dora's pre-Marcus's-death gowns, none of them particularly cheerful, despite Isabella's influence, and on the other hung the one black mourning dress Isabella had not managed to remove, mainly because Dora had been wearing it at the time of her raid on her wardrobe. She lifted out the least dreary of the gowns and held it up. "What about this one?"

Dora seemed to have herself back under control, for the moment. "I can't wear anything as colorful as that. I think I'd like to wear the black still, if that's all right with you." She sounded apologetic.

Isabella looked down at the gown she was holding up to herself and shook her head in despair. It was a rather dull green. "I don't think you can go back to black now you've been seen out of it." She tried to sound as sure as she could, although she wasn't herself certain of the technicalities of mourning. She'd worn black for papa for six months, but that had been because she'd wanted to.

Dora's brows met in a worried frown. "I wasn't at all happy last night with wearing the gown you chose for me, you know. I felt like a terrible hypocrite all evening, and I'm sure our guests thought the same. They kept staring at me."

"Wearing black would make you an even bigger hypocrite," Isabella rejoined, with some asperity. "Don't you think?"

Guilt swept over Dora's face and her lip trembled again. Isabella frowned. Had she gone too far? Keeping Dora calm involved walking a veritable tightrope. It was far too easy to say the wrong thing to her, especially as she herself was given to speaking her mind.

"I didn't mean that," Isabella said in a hurry, before Dora could dissolve into the ever-threatening tears. "You aren't a hypocrite at all. I'm sorry. My tongue runs away with itself sometimes. You know it does. But I really think you should wear something other than black, which is so ageing."

Dora sniffed. "But I am a hypocrite," she whispered. "And I'm a liar. And I'm an old maid, so I might as well wear black and look like one. And every time I have to lie to Diccon, I feel myself creeping closer to the mouth of hell." Her eyes brimmed with anguish as well as the unshed tears.

A little over dramatic. But then, Isabella didn't believe in heaven or hell herself so didn't fear the latter. Perhaps she should.

For if Dora was right, she was surely headed there.

She threw the offending gown onto Dora's bed and came over to the window seat. Sitting beside Dora, she took both her bony hands in her own. They were icy cold. "We've talked about this before, dearest Dora. We are not being hypocrites. Neither of us. We could have done nothing else. You know we couldn't have. You have to put it behind you and try not to think of it, or it will eat you away to nothing."

Dora shook her head. "I've tried, oh, I've tried, Bella darling. But every time I close my eyes I see him lying on the library floor with… with his eyes just staring up at the ceiling as though he's so surprised at what's just happened to him."

Isabella tightened her hold. "I should jolly well think he was surprised. But you mustn't think of it. I've told you not to. You can't let him blight your life when he's dead, as he did when he was alive." She gritted her teeth and scowled her hardest. "He deserved to die, Dora. He did. There can be no buts about it. And I for one refuse to mourn him or feel in the least bit guilty." She gave a shiver. "He would have killed me if he could. I know he would have."

Dora shook her head. "It's all right for you. You're so much stronger than I am." She sniffed again. "And you weren't with me last night when that ghastly Lady Dangerfield tried talking to me. It was awful. I didn't know what to do. She cornered me, and no one was about to save me. I looked for you, but you weren't there."

Isabella's hackles rose. "Lady Dangerfield? What did she want?" Thoughts of what she herself would like to do to Lady Dangerfield arose.

"She wanted to know about the night he… he d-died."

Of course she had. Marcus had been her lover. Maybe in her own way she'd even loved him, although Isabella doubted anyone could have done that. But then, Lady Dangerfield's personality was very similar to Marcus's, so perhaps they had indeed loved one another. Who knew? "What did you tell her?"

Dora swallowed. "Nothing. I told her nothing. I told her Marcus killed himself."

Which of course wasn't true.

Isabella nodded. "Well done."

Dora's hands turned over under Isabella's hold and gripped hers tightly. "Oh, Bella, she's not going to give up until she finds out. I'm sure of it. She had mad eyes, like you have sometimes when I know you're not going to drop a subject. She means to find out the truth."

Isabella scowled. "She's never going to find out, Dora, I can assure you. All we need to do is remain silent. Nearly two months have passed. We're safe. He's buried and we have our new duke here. He won't let anything happen to us."

But would he? She might like him, but did he like her? She couldn't tell. And if he did like her, would it be enough to make him want to keep their secret if he ever discovered it? Perhaps, on reflection, she ought to make herself be a little more friendly towards him. Which wouldn't, in truth, be difficult. What she didn't want to admit to herself was that she liked him rather too much. To the point of it perhaps being dangerous.

"Everything will be all right," she said to Dora, false confidence filling her voice. "Don't worry about it. We'll come through this."

CHAPTER TWENTY

ISABELLA, WHO HAD been lying in wait with ever-increasing impatience, at last spotted the returning carriage from the windows on the galleried landing. She watched it sweep up the drive and come to a halt close to the front doors. The rain had died away, but a heavy, threatening sky overhung the park, as though betokening gathering doom. From where she stood, she couldn't see Richard descend from the carriage and head indoors, so she abandoned her post and hurried towards the stairs.

Richard was already in the hallway, handing his rain-splattered hat and coat to Atkins, so she slowed to a more decorous pace, mustered all her elegance, and descended, her gown swishing behind her. She'd been careful with her selection of what to wear, and had settled, after several false starts that had probably exasperated Hawkins, on a pale-cream muslin embroidered with small blue flowers. It was one of the simplest of her gowns, and in its simplicity lay its allure. The vision she'd presented in the cheval mirror had met with both her own and Hawkins's approval. Although Hawkins would have had no idea of her intentions.

Richard must have noticed her approach out of the corner of his eye, because he looked up, a concerned frown on his face. Shoving aside any worry at his expression, she bestowed a welcoming smile on him. It was not, of course, difficult to do as he was so infernally handsome. At least, as she got to know him, his resemblance to Marcus had begun to diminish. That was one blessing.

The object here was to get him to like her enough to be on her side if a crisis were to arise. Not to fall under his spell. She would have to keep reminding herself not to succumb.

She paused several steps above him so he had to look up at her. "Richard, how happy I am to see you returned and your tedious business completed." She batted her lashes at him. "At least I hope it is?"

How deliciously dark and smoldering his eyes were, even when anxious. What would it be like to allow him the liberty of stealing a kiss? For an instant, the sobering and somewhat melancholy thought that she'd never been kissed out of love reared its head only to be shoved back down where it belonged. She would not think about the way Marcus had used her.

That look of concern remained on Richard's face. "I think it is..." He banished the look with a smile, albeit a forced one, which only served to make him look more handsome and less than ever like Marcus, who had never in his life looked concerned about anything, not even his own death. "But I may have to attend to it later."

"Is it something I can help you with?"

He shook his head. "I don't think so. But thank you for the offer."

She descended the last few steps and now had to look up to him. He was so tall—at least a foot taller than she was. Taller than Marcus had been, and with a look about him of latent strength that Marcus had never possessed, not even when she'd first known him as a twenty-eight-year-old. For the last few years of his life, her late husband had chosen to wear a gentleman's corset to hold in his growing paunch. She wasn't supposed to know that, but Hawkins, who'd had it from Hopkins, Marcus's valet, had divulged the secret. She and Dora had laughed hysterically about it in private. Not that she'd ever seen it herself. No, she'd not seen him in a state of undress for a long time before he died. Thank goodness.

She frowned. For someone who had set out with the intention of drawing her prey closer to her, she was doing a poor job of it, when all she could think about was how it might feel to press her lips to his. Heat threatened to rise to her cheeks.

She spoke in a hurry, anxious to distract him from her blush. "I was about to go for a stroll in the gardens, now the rain has stopped. Would you care to accompany me? I have quite missed your company today." If she was going to firstly win him and secondly keep him on their side, then the sooner she began, the better. And the sooner she stopped having silly ideas about loving him.

What? Had she really just thought that? She must be addle-pated. The blush increased. Drat it.

She looked down at her feet. Was he going to turn her down? No. Manners got the better of him, but she could see he didn't want to come. Annoying. A little insulting, in fact.

"Of course." He held his arm out to her, and she slipped her hand into the crook. Had he even noticed how beguiling she was looking in this gown? How her maid had done her hair to look artless and a little untidy, with stray auburn curls cascading onto her shoulders? What kind of a man was he that her charms seemed to be having no effect? Or was she wrong in her perception of him?

She steered him through the drawing room and out onto the terrace. "I often like to take a stroll in the gardens in the afternoons." A lie, but he wasn't to know this. Probably not, at any rate. She liked the gardens well enough, but only when it suited her, and she had nothing else to do. Or when she fancied working her wiles on someone with a little privacy.

He matched his pace to hers. "I used to play here with Dora when I was a child."

She pricked her ears. Perhaps it would be a good idea to get him to tell her more about his childhood. In her experience, men liked to talk about themselves to ladies, and if a lady feigned interest in a man's tedious conversation, it was a sure way to winning his heart. As the possessor of a number of men's hearts, she'd had enough practice at this. She could do it with Richard. With Diccon. A sudden overwhelming urge to call him by his nickname swept over her. She fought it off. "You must have at least a few happy memories of Stourbridge."

He nodded, and they descended the wide steps into the gardens, where paths opened off to left and right, winding between ornamental bushes and flowerbeds. Impossible to see far thanks to their intricacies. The scent of late-flowering roses was strong, and here and there autumn camellias were coming into bud. She must get one of the servants to pick some of the roses to put in the hallway before it was too late and they were over.

"Of course I had some happy times," he said, steering her towards the center of the garden where the summerhouse lay. "But I also had some terrible ones."

Having sufficient of her own, she didn't want to hear the bad ones. "You and Dora must have been very close."

Birds were singing in the trees and a patch of blue sky had appeared, hopeful amongst the gray clouds. Perhaps the day was about to improve.

Richard nodded again. "We were. From the moment we met, we were friends." He sighed. "And nine years later, I cruelly abandoned her without a backward glance. Something for which I feel eternal guilt." He hesitated. "She is not the girl I used to know. And I feel it's all my fault."

Maybe not all his fault, but he wasn't to know that. Still, she might be able to learn a few things, after all. "What do you mean?"

He stopped beside a statue of a naked cupid, and turned to look down at her, an odd expression in his eyes. The urge to stand on her tiptoes and plant the kiss she longed for on his lips emerged. "I mean," he said, seemingly oblivious to her longing, "that when I took up the commission my grandmother persuaded Marcus's father to purchase for me, I didn't for one moment think how Dora would suffer with me gone."

"Oh." It had never before occurred to Isabella that Dora's life could have been any different to the way it was when she'd first met her. Although she had to admit that right now Dora was far worse than she'd ever been. Understandably.

He gave a shrug of his broad shoulders. "We were friends. One united entity against Marcus. Together, we were strong. She could rise above his treatment, as could I. But I left her. And look what it's done to her. All my fault." He shook his head. "She should be married, with a brood of children, not withering away here at Stourbridge, turning into an old maid. Marcus did that to her. Out of spite."

Isabella frowned. That Dora was wasting her life away had also never occurred to her. Dora had always been Dora, the sister of her hated husband, her friend, her ally. She'd never existed independently. Only she must have. Once. "She didn't used to be quite so timid," she said, feeling her words to be on the inadequate side. True, but inadequate and making excuses.

"She's a shadow of her former self."

This was awkward. Isabella bit her lip. How to imply Dora's fragile nerves were only recently acquired without making him suspicious? "I think the loss of Marcus has hit her hard." There, that wasn't too incriminating. And it was true. The truest thing she'd said so far.

Richard's stare intensified. "I can see that for myself. She's a bag of nerves, Isabella, and I fear for her sanity. I really do."

Good heavens. Fear for Dora's sanity was a third thing that hadn't occurred to Isabella, possibly because her own sanity had never been in question. Now he'd pointed it out, though, she could see it with clarity. She should have seen this coming. She'd always known Dora was not as strong as she was, despite having had to live with Marcus far longer, or perhaps because of that. Why had she not seen that Dora's fragile grip on sanity was what had caused this in the first place? Or had it? Had it not been her own fault?

For want of anything else to say, she resorted back to her customary dismissive response. "Nonsense. Given time, Dora will get over this. She's still upset about Marcus's death, that's all. He was her brother, when all's said and done." All of which was true, if not quite enough of the truth.

He frowned down at her. "But is she really upset about his loss? Are you sure of that?"

The skepticism he'd loaded those words with cut Isabella to the quick. Could he not use his eyes? Did he not believe Dora upset?

"Of course she is." She kept her own voice light and airy, as though discussing nothing of more import than the weather. "She will be better shortly, I can promise you." With a good talking to from Isabella herself, that was. Dora needed to learn to hide her feelings, or they'd both be lost. She had to be more like her determined sister-in-law and less of the frightened mouse.

Richard caught hold of her hand. "Tell me what happened that night, Isabella." The intensity in his voice sent a chill down her spine. Hadn't he already been told what had happened? Hadn't he asked everyone but her already? Perhaps he was unaware she knew about all his questions to everyone but her. Might his steering clear, until now, of questioning her point in one direction only—showing that he believed the rumors? For once in her life, she didn't know what to think or how to react.

"Marcus killed himself," she said, and clamped her lips together, her whole body stiffening and thoughts of snatching kisses flown.

His dark eyes bored into her very soul. "So everyone says, but I know, and so do you, that isn't true." He paused. "Is it?" His words fell leaden in the damp air.

The chill clutch of fear closed around Isabella's entrails. She wrested her hand free of his. "Of course it's true. He was drunk. Maudlin. Whether he did it by mistake, playing with his dueling pistols, or not, he did it himself. I can assure you. The magistrate, whom I know you saw today, declared it so. I have no idea where the vile rumors have come from that suggest otherwise." She tossed her head. "But people do like to gossip about their betters whenever they can, I find. Only a fool listens to rumor."

"No, Isabella. We both know he didn't do it himself."

The conviction in his voice sent further chills running through her. How could he be so certain? How did he know?

The best thing was to ask him. She gave a little laugh, trying to infuse it with casual interest and failing. "Whatever makes you think that?"

He was gazing into her eyes as though searching for something. "Isabella, just answer me one question, if you don't mind. Tell me if Marcus was right-handed or left-handed? You were married to him for ten years. You must know."

Fear trembled through her and for a moment she thought her legs might give way. He knew. He'd spotted what no one else had done. She could lie, but he would know her for a liar if she did, even if no one else did. He'd been brought up with Marcus, after all, shared a schoolroom with him, watched him write and shoot and eat. Best to be truthful. She met his gaze with a challenge. "He was left-handed."

Richard nodded. "Correct." She couldn't read his expression but was glad she hadn't lied.

Determined to stare him out, she stiffened her backbone. "Why? What does it matter?" She could brazen this out.

Richard sighed. "Because he'd been shot in the right side of the head, and afterwards, someone had put the pistol in his right hand. He couldn't have done it himself. Not with him being left-handed. It would have been impossible for him to do so."

He knew. The one thing they'd not been able to change. He'd spotted it where no one else had. For a moment, she was lost for words, but not for long. "Why could he not have done so? I'm sure if I wanted to, I could shoot myself with my left hand, even though I'm right-handed."

He shook his head. "You couldn't."

She fell silent, still staring into his eyes. She concentrated hard on what they looked like, refusing to think about what he'd just said. Right now they'd lost the gentle expression they'd held before when he looked at her.

"Did you kill him, Isabella?"

It took a huge effort not to tremble at his words. He believed the rumors. He thought she'd killed her husband. What should she say? Seeking wildly for words, she opened her mouth to speak, to tell him the truth. Surely he would understand and forgive her if she did so.

But she was not going to need the words. Footsteps sounded on the gravel path, her head swung around and she saw five people coming into view: Atkins, hurrying behind two men and two women. The women were Lady Dangerfield and Lady Brocklebank, galleons in full sale, determined expressions on their triumphant faces. The men were of a different class altogether. One was Hooper, the local constable who'd attended with the colonel on the day of Marcus's death. The other she didn't know. Short and wiry, with stringy brown hair streaked with gray, he wore a countryman's brown wool suit of matching frockcoat, breeches, and waistcoat, and a look of satisfaction on his cunning, ratty face.

"That's her," Lady Dangerfield said, pointing at Isabella, as though she might be unrecognizable. "Seize her."

"Your Graces, I couldn't stop them," Atkins, breathless with hurrying in front of them, spluttered, his honest face full of anguish. "They demanded to see you immediately."

Hooper, as a local man whose own father had worked on the estate, had the grace to look embarrassed. Not so his cocky companion. He stepped forward as bold as brass, shouldering Atkins out of the way as though the elderly man didn't matter. "Lady Stourbridge, duchess, I'm arresting you for the murder of your husband. You'll have to come along with me and Constable Hooper now and answer some questions." His ratty face was smug with self-satisfaction. As were those of the two ladies.

Isabella's heart gave an unruly lurch. She glanced back at

Richard. Too late now for the truth, if it had not always been too late. She leaned in close to him. "I did it. I killed him by myself. Take care of Dora for me, Diccon. Please."

His frown deepened and she recognized the shock in his eyes, but whether it was due to her confession or this arrest, she had no idea. "Bella…"

She shook her head at him and stepped away.

The man grabbed her arm as though he thought she might try to flee.

She shook him off. "Unhand me. I am offering no resistance." She shot an icy stare at the two ladies. "Satisfied, my ladies?"

Lady Dangerfield's cruel mouth curved in a triumphant smile. "Not quite yet. I shall only be satisfied when I see you hang for what you did to Marcus."

Lady Brocklebank's piggy eyes were cold. "I always said he was making a huge mistake in marrying her for her money. Class will out, and this proves that she has none."

Richard held up his hand. "Wait. On whose authority are you here?" His voice rang out across the garden. He had fixed the ratty man with a furious glare.

The ratty man quailed just a little. "On the authority of Mr. Theodore Dawes, Justice of the Peace." He held out a piece of paper. "See. I have here the warrant for the duchess's arrest in black and white."

Isabella raised her eyes to meet Richard's. "Please leave it. I will go with them willingly. There's no need to make a fuss."

That he wanted to say something was obvious, but he remained silent, only his eyes fixed on hers trying to give her some kind of message. What it was, she had no idea.

"Come along-a-me then," the ratty man said, reaching out for her again. "We'd best get going."

Isabella turned away from Richard and Atkins and stepped towards the house without a backward glance, head held high. Let no one say she did not leave with dignity.

Behind her, Richard called out, fury edging his voice. "I will put a stop to this ridiculous accusation. You're all making a mistake, and I'm going to make sure you regret it."

"The mistake is yours," Lady Dangerfield snapped, "in being taken in by a tradesman's daughter with a murderous heart. You will thank us for your lucky escape when she goes to the gallows."

Isabella shut them out of her head, concentrating on setting one foot ahead of the other, and keeping her back ramrod straight, for if she didn't, she would surely faint from fear.

CHAPTER TWENTY-ONE

RICHARD FOLLOWED THE party escorting Isabella back up the steps, across the terrace, and through the house, Atkins in his wake. All the while his mind was churning with the revelation of Isabella's whispered confession, her entreaty to him to take care of Dora, and the certain knowledge that even had she done what she'd just admitted, he didn't want to lose her. The conviction had also seized him that the confession wasn't what she'd been going to tell him just before they were interrupted.

Outside the front door stood a carriage bearing the coat of arms of Lady Dangerfield's absent husband. It was into this that the two men hustled Isabella, as though she was a common criminal, and there seemed to be nothing he could do to prevent it. He could hardly overrule a justice of the peace, even though the fellow's colleague had come to a different conclusion about Marcus's death. Now it was in the hands of the law, a proper process would have to be undertaken to free Isabella and absolve her of guilt.

He ground his teeth in impotent frustration. What was it she'd been about to say to him before they were interrupted? After her arrest her demeanor had changed completely. There'd been such an air of resignation about her, as though she were giving up, unable to fight against the odds any longer. As though she were resigned to her fate.

Hooper climbed up to ride beside the driver, which would

give more room inside. Presumably, they were taking Barker inside the coach in case Isabella gave in to the murderous tendencies of which they'd accused her.

Lady Dangerfield turned to face him as she was about to mount the step into the carriage, her face ugly with satisfaction and smugness. "You must think yourself lucky you have been saved from a similar fate to your predecessor," she said with the air of someone convinced that whatever she was doing must be right. "I can only say that it is with great relief that the man I hired to investigate His Grace's ruthless murder has succeeded in finding the necessary evidence to convict her. You may rest in peace in your bed tonight, Your Grace."

Richard glared at her. "I think you will find, my lady, that you have made a grave error here."

Her eyes widened. Did she imagine he approved of this? She must have been blind to his earlier reaction. Either that or she was stupid. Possibly both. She recovered herself quickly enough, though. "I think not. A witness has come forward who is prepared to swear that they saw her carry out the murder."

She couldn't resist playing what she saw as her trump card. However, as Richard was now certain she was the woman he'd overheard in the garden last night, he was also doubtful as to the veracity of this "witness." Money had probably changed hands, as she'd implied it could. Everything in him fought against believing Isabella's confession. Everything. She simply wasn't a murderess. Maybe he was a fool for thinking this, but he did.

From inside the carriage came a grunt of annoyance. Perhaps Barker disapproved of her ladyship disclosing her hand so early in the proceedings.

Lady Dangerfield gave him a smile that would have looked well on the face of a shark, Richard having once seen one of them close up, with all their ferocious teeth. He was quite surprised to note that hers were not sharp and pointy. "She will find it impossible to wriggle her way out of this."

Unable and unwilling to answer that, Richard stared into the carriage, his eyes meeting Isabella's. She looked away with calm deliberation, as though she couldn't meet his eyes, her face paper pale. Her lower lip wobbled for a moment, before she had it back under control. Richard's heart, already seriously involved, broke for her. The desperate longing to be able to snatch her out of that carriage and into his arms nearly overwhelmed him.

Lady Dangerfield, unaware of his reaction, climbed in behind Isabella and Lady Brocklebank and, having closed the door, pulled down the blind aggressively. Her driver cracked his whip, and the horses moved off. Richard was left standing alone on the gravel forecourt, his heart, most uncharacteristically, in shattered pieces.

He stared at the retreating carriage, while the whirl that was his mind gradually began to settle into some sort of shape. It was only after a full minute had passed that he became aware of Atkins standing beside him. A discreet cough alerted him.

Richard turned to the butler. "Where will they take her?"

Atkins, his face as pale as Isabella's had been, gave a shake of his head. "I don't know, Your Grace." The old man's voice shook. "There is a jail in the middle of town, in the marketplace, I gather, beside the courthouse. And of course there's the Bridewell, but that is beside the workhouse and reserved for the indigent poor. They wouldn't take her there, would they? Surely they wouldn't, Your Grace? She is a duchess. Our duchess."

Richard's turn to shake his head as despair welled. "I don't know." He glanced back towards the house, but it afforded him no answers. Its blank windows stared back at him in stony silence. If only the walls could talk and could tell him the truth of what had happened on that fateful night. If he knew that, he would be in a far better place from which to defend Isabella and secure her rapid release. "You heard what they said, Atkins. They have a witness ready to swear he saw the murder. Do you think that's even possible?"

Atkins shook his head with positivity, as though glad to be able to answer a question. "No. They couldn't have one. Whoever it is, they are lying."

Exasperation swept over Richard. The biggest problem here was that everyone was lying, even if it was with the best of intentions. No one wanted to tell him the truth. And now look what had happened, all because everyone was being so secretive. He banged one fist into the other palm. "It must be one of the servants. It has to be. Who else is there they could have bribed to say this?"

Atkins nodded. He seemed to have shrunk in on himself more than ever, his clothes hanging off him, making him resemble some withered old scarecrow and not a duke's butler. "None of the servants would betray the duchess, I'm sure. We've all seen what she's had to put up with. We all love her." It seemed this had untethered the old man's tongue at last.

Richard squinted up at the topmost windows, to the attics, where most of the servants had their rooms. "Money is a great invitation to imagination."

Atkins shook his head. "None of the servants could have seen anything, Your Grace, and would not have pretended they did. I'm certain of it. Only myself, Mrs. Barnes, and Amos were present that night. The others remained asleep in bed. It's not me, and I can vouch for Mrs. Barnes and Amos. They've worked here most of their lives and owe this family so much. We all hold Her Grace in the highest esteem. Neither I nor they would have been tempted by a fat purse. Rest assured."

A chill breeze blew across the gravel forecourt. "I know you wouldn't have, old friend. You have no need to tell me that. I believe you. So, only you three were there at first, with Isabella and Lady Dora?"

Atkins nodded. "That is correct. No other person was involved."

"So their witness has to be a liar. There's no fear anyone could have seen anything."

"No, Your Grace. No one saw anything. I am quite certain."

From the kennels at the back of the house came the sound of dogs having a group howl. Perhaps they knew their mistress was gone, or it was just time to be fed. Richard glanced back at the house. Best to continue this conversation out here, where no one could overhear it. Especially if there was a spy lurking somewhere in the household. "Then you'd better come clean and tell me exactly what happened. I think I deserve the truth. Hold nothing back, this time, or I'll be able to do nothing to help Her Grace. This truly is a matter of life and death, my old friend."

DORA, WHO HAD retired back to bed once Isabella had left her, was awoken by the sound of wheels crunching on gravel. She yawned and stretched, for a moment far away in her dreams still. Then the import of the sound sank in. She sat up on the bed and listened. A vehicle, by the sound of it a sizeable one, was driving away from the house.

Drawing her peignoir more tightly about her body, she slipped off the bed and approached the window. Sure enough, a carriage was just breasting the rise heading north towards the Winchester Road. Impossible to recognize at this distance, but clearly the vehicle of someone of importance. Who could have been calling on them this afternoon, so soon after the ball? All their friends had been present last night, so no one had any reason to visit today.

She pressed her forehead to the cool glass and peered down into the driveway. Who was that standing there? Diccon, tall and upright, close by Atkins, who seemed more bowed and bent than usual, as though the weight of the world was bearing down on him. She well knew that feeling. Difficult to see their faces from here, but by their demeanor, she guessed they were deep in conversation. Or at least, Atkins was talking and Diccon, darling, wonderful Diccon, was listening. Diccon, to whom she longed to open her heart and tell the truth. An inescapable sense of foreboding crept over her. Something bad had happened.

Without stopping to put on any more clothing, nor even slide her feet into her slippers, she ran across the room and out onto the galleried landing. The house was silent. No sign of any of the servants. At the top of the stairs, she paused, heart hammering against her ribs so hard it hurt. Where was Isabella?

She turned her head to right and left, questing like a hound. Nothing. Light spilled in through the open front door, but the house remained mute. This house was well versed at holding its secrets to its bosom.

On bare feet, she sped down the stairs and across the hall, her peignoir trailing behind her in gossamer strands. At the door, she halted, hand on the jamb. Diccon and Atkins were still deep in conversation and hadn't seen her. For a moment, all she could do was watch them as she fought to catch her lost breath. She could see Diccon's face, his beloved face, as emotions flitted over it: anger, disgust, impotence, and finally compassion. Atkins was telling him the truth. The truth she'd so wanted to share but been too afraid to. As she watched, he ran a hand across his eyes as though he could wipe away what he was being told. Impossible. She'd tried it often enough herself and failed. Nothing could ever wipe this away.

He knew. The secret was no longer just theirs.

With a little, frantic cry, she felt her legs fold beneath her as the ground seemed to come rushing up to meet her body. With a bang, her head hit the flagstones, she saw stars for a moment, and then merciful darkness enveloped her.

Sound returned first. Voices, but she couldn't make out what they were saying because they were echoing as though in a huge bell chamber, the sound reverberating and hammering on her pounding skull. She blinked open her eyes. At first, all was blurry, and then she saw the familiar ceiling of her bedroom, with its decorative plaster and the crack that ran across one corner.

"Dora." Diccon's voice, gentle, comforting, compassionate.

She remembered.

She blinked some more and his anxious face came into focus.

He knew.

She turned her head away as tears of shame welled, screwing

her eyes tight shut against the light. She couldn't look at him. Not ever. What must he be thinking?

His hand covered hers, warm and reassuring. "It's all right, Dora. I know."

She kept her eyes screwed tight shut. "Go away. I don't want to see you. Please. Just leave me alone." A sob broke through. "Oh God, I want to die. Let me die."

"Shall I fetch Mrs. Barnes, Your Grace?" Atkins's voice, low as though he were in the sick room. Of course. He was the one who'd betrayed them all to Diccon.

"No. We don't need her." Diccon's voice again, kind, gentle still, as though what he'd just discovered didn't matter at all. He tightened his hold on her hand and she let herself take a peek at his beloved face. "I'm here, Dora. I know what you did, and I don't blame you for it. You couldn't have done anything else."

The import of his words began to sink in. He didn't blame her. But that didn't count, because she blamed herself. What she'd done was too terrible for words.

No. She screwed her eyes tight shut again. In an instant, she'd left the safety of her bedroom behind and was back on that fateful night.

CANDLES LIT THE gloomy library. Marcus, standing beside the large oak desk, was pouring a generous measure of brandy for himself. Not his first by a long chalk, and he'd already been well foxed when they returned from the party. The oppressive silence magnified the sound of the brandy slopping into the glass. Isabella stood in front of the desk, upright and rigid, dressed in her cream evening gown, fury contorting her face. From the door, her hand on the ornate knob, Dora watched, transfixed by a fear that seared through her body from her toes to the top of her head. Not again. Please don't let him hurt them. Please. Her lips moved in silent prayer.

Isabella's words cut into the silence like a hot knife slicing through butter. "If you must disport yourself with that slut, kindly do so in private, or keep it to the salons of London where I cannot see it. Do not bring her into our circle of friends and expect me to tolerate your peccadilloes without saying anything."

Marcus knocked back the brandy. "I had no idea she'd be there. Not that it's any of your business."

"Oh really? No idea? When she is an especial friend of that dreadful Brocklebank woman who you know hates me? I wouldn't be at all surprised if you hadn't asked her to invite the slut."

Marcus laughed. If a laugh could ever have been called menacing, then this would have been it. "So what? I can do whatever I like and you can't prevent me. And don't you call her a slut. That's a bit rich coming from the daughter of a shopkeeper." The sneer in his voice was unmistakable. He laughed some more as he poured himself another measure of brandy, some of it slopping over the glass's rim and spilling onto the polished surface of the desk.

"A shopkeeper's daughter whose fortune allows you to live the life you seem to prefer," Isabella, upright as a young sapling, snapped back at him. "A fortune which allows you to support a mistress, to gamble at high stakes, to indulge every whim you fancy." Her lip curled. "You think I can't prevent you?" Isabella's fists were clenched. "I refuse to have you show me up in public the way you did tonight."

Marcus, who had been well on the way to being drunk even before he'd broached the brandy, swayed a little and put a hand out to steady himself. "Don't make me laugh. Me, showing you up? What about you with your coterie of tongue-lolling men, all anxious to get a hand up your skirts and your hand on their cocks. For how many of them have you spread your legs and cuckolded me? For that fop Wyndham, who can't seem to leave your side? I'd have his throat slit in a dark alley if I even cared. But I don't. Has old Brocklebank had you yet? He was slavering to get his hands on you all night, so I think you haven't let him in yet, but give it time. A bitch in heat like you won't be able to wait long.

You're ready enough to give them what you won't give me. And you have the gall to wonder why I look elsewhere for what I should be getting at home." He laughed again. "I can tell you now that Barbara Dangerfield knows how to please a man in bed—not like you, just lying there with a look of scorn on your pretty face, waiting for it to be over."

Dora clapped a hand over her mouth. She wanted to leave, but didn't dare. And besides, she couldn't leave Bella when Marcus was like this. She'd seen the bruises far too often. Worse than any he'd ever given her. She had to stay, for Bella's sake.

Isabella's hand shot out, fist still clenched, striking Marcus on the jaw. He staggered backwards but remained upright. His hand went up to rub his jaw. "Got a sting in your tail, have you?" And he lunged forwards. But he was drunk, and Isabella dodged his grasping hand. Instead, he caught the skirt of her gown. The delicate fabric ripped.

Isabella laughed. "You've drunk too much to catch me, husband." Her lip curled in a sneer every bit as malicious as his. "I'll leave you to rot your insides a little bit more, I think. Much more of that and you might do me a favor and turn up your toes." She turned away from him.

Even half cut, he could be fast. This time she couldn't have seen him coming. He caught her by the shoulders and wrenched her round to face him, the top of her gown ripping this time. His left hand came back and he struck her hard across the face. He was a lot stronger than she was. She fell, catching her arm on the edge of the desk, and he followed her, looming over her in threat.

She curled herself into a ball in an attempt to protect herself. "No one will miss you if you're gone," he grunted. "I'm a duke. No one's ever going to dare to question me about your disappearance." He leaned over her. "I'll tell them you've gone abroad for your health." He laughed again. "No one'll look for you. Mark my words."

Dora cowered back in terror. He meant it this time. She'd seen his violence to Isabella so many times, but this time there was something terrifyingly different about it. He was far too drunk, and his eyes were mad, madder than usual, the pupils dilated. Had he taken something more than just brandy?

Dora glanced about herself in desperation. On the side table near the door lay his two dueling pistols, left ready for him by his valet so he could indulge his whim of target practice whenever he wanted.

Marcus kicked Isabella. She was scrabbling away across the floor, now, and he was following her, towering over her, the light of bloodlust hot in his eyes, his hair awry, spit drooling from his mouth. He'd never looked so ugly.

Dora blinked. She was beside the desk but had no idea how she'd got there. Her hand was reaching out of its own volition to pick up the nearest of the dueling pistols. It felt heavy in her hand as she lifted it.

"You little bitch," Marcus snarled at Isabella. "I don't know why I ever married you. Oh yes, it was for your father's money. Well, I've got that now, and I don't need you any longer. And you couldn't even give me the heir I needed. You had to have a useless girl. A girl that didn't even live. Thank God. A useless girl I didn't want. That was all you were ever good for."

Dora floated across the library on legs that worked without any effort on her part. She was beside Marcus, on his right as he glared down at Isabella. He raised his foot above her beloved friend's head, ready to stamp it down. Isabella glared back up at him, her face bloody, defiant to the last.

Dora pulled the trigger.

The pistol's report brought her back into the present with a jerk.

"I didn't mean to do it. I'll tell you everything," she whispered, and burst into tears.

✦

CHAPTER TWENTY-TWO

HALF AN HOUR later, with Dora having finally cried herself to sleep with the aid of some laudanum, and Mrs. Barnes stationed on a chair in her room to keep careful watch over her, Richard and Atkins repaired to the scene of the crime.

Richard found Marcus's decanter of brandy, which someone had refilled in the intervening period, and a couple of glasses, and poured two large measures. He handed one to Atkins. "I think you'd better sit down."

They both sat and, for a moment, neither spoke, but the brandy was consumed. As Atkins set his empty glass down, without saying anything, Richard refilled it. They both needed its fortifying properties after today's events.

Richard sighed. "This is a pretty pickle we find ourselves in, my friend."

Atkins bowed his white head. "I must apologize for my part in this, Your Grace. I had no idea it would go this far or cause such trouble. In fact, I cherished a hope that it was all done and dusted." He sounded old and exhausted. And he looked it. "You must understand that none of us could say anything to you about how the duke died. We would never have betrayed Lady Dora." He shook his head in despair. "And yet look at how she is now. I don't know how we can help her. I really don't. Perhaps it would have been better to have admitted she shot him in defense of the duchess. I just don't know. But it's too late to change our story now, I fear."

Richard sighed. "If it weren't for the infernal tenacity of Lady Dangerfield, I doubt that it would have mattered. She hates Isabella with a vengeance, and is determined to see her punished for a crime she wants to believe she's committed. Even if it means sending an innocent woman to the gallows. Her jealousy is the root cause of this, mark my words."

Atkins frowned. "That woman, if I may be so bold as to refer to her in such a way in front of you, is a bad lot." He licked his lips. "I have had occasion to encounter her many times. Your predecessor often brought her here when Her Grace and Lady Dora were in Town. Sometimes when Lady Dora was actually present." He downed the second brandy with the look of a man convinced he needed extreme fortification. "If Her Grace goes to trial for this, I fear for what it will do to Lady Dora's sensibilities."

"I think I know most of it now," Richard said, setting his own glass down only half consumed. He needed to keep his wits about him and formulate a plan if they were all to escape from this unscathed, or as unscathed as it was possible to be. It was going to have to be a good one.

Atkins wiped a rheumy eye. "I'm so sorry we had to keep this from you, Your Grace. It wasn't my secret to reveal. Her Grace was of the opinion the fewer people who knew, the easier it would be to contain."

Richard sighed again, wishing that nagging headache he'd had all day would go away. The brandy probably wasn't helping any. "Please stop calling me 'Your Grace' every time you speak, Atkins. I was Master Diccon to you for long enough. Think of me as that lost boy if you can. We must work together here, and rank counts for nothing." He paused. "If it ever did."

"Thank you, Your—Master Diccon."

Richard managed a taut smile. "We've known each other a long time now. So please don't be offended if I have to ask you a question you might not like."

Atkins bowed his head.

"Who was it put the pistol in Marcus's hand?"

"I did. Lady Dora still had it in her hand when I came into the library. Her Grace was on her knees on the floor near the duke's body. I could see he was dead. No one could have survived a wound like that." His voice shook as though he were recalling what must have been a horrific injury. "He was lying in a pool of blood from a bullet wound in the right side of his head."

"In the right side of his head."

"Yes."

"That ties up with the sketch Colonel Jarvis's man showed me. With the pistol lying close by Marcus's right hand."

"That was where I put it after I'd taken it from Lady Dora's hands, and Mrs. Barnes had arrived. We could both see what had happened, so I helped the duchess to her feet and told Mrs. Barnes to take them upstairs and put them to bed. It was obvious they were both suffering from shock. We had to get them away from the body. Lady Dora was hysterical."

"You put the pistol beside his right hand?"

"I did…" Atkins's voice trailed off. Was realization dawning at last at the terrible mistake he'd made?

Richard held his gaze. "Marcus was left-handed in everything except eating. He shot his bow left-handed. He fired his guns left-handed."

Atkins, his face even paler now, smacked his hand against his forehead and groaned. "How could I have been so stupid?" He hesitated, raising anguished eyes to meet Richard's. "But what else could I have done? The wound was in the right side of his head. That was where she'd shot him. It seemed to play into our hands. It looked like a self-inflicted wound. With a little adjust-ment of the scene, we could make it look as though he'd done it himself. I put the pistol in that hand because I could see where the wound was." He shook his head. "I didn't think. It was automatic. I know no one but His Grace who is left-handed, and I forgot." His hand went to his mouth. "Do they know? Is that some of the new evidence they've discovered? I was so relieved when the colonel declared it an accidental death. I believed we'd come through it safely."

This was not a question Richard could answer. He shrugged. "I don't know what they know or what they could've guessed. The Dangerfield woman was quick to claim they have an actual witness ready to swear they saw Isabella pull the trigger. Which we know is a lie, but we cannot refute it without condemning Lady Dora. And we can't do that. You say you're certain there were no witnesses, and you and Mrs. Barnes found the pistol still in Dora's hand. No one could have seen Isabella do anything. It all has to be a pack of lies concocted by those two women who hate her." He shook his head. "And they must hate her far more than anyone could have guessed."

Atkins's lined old face had gone from waxy pale to an unhealthy gray. "Might I trouble you for another glass of brandy, Your Grace, just to steady my nerves? I can feel my heart fluttering." He put his hand to his chest as if to feel its beat.

Richard obliged. He didn't want the old man dying of a heart attack before they'd sorted out this problem. If it was possible to sort out. The real fear that it might not be loomed large. Isabella might not be responsible for what she'd confessed to, but Dora was. That Isabella was protecting her sister-in-law was obvious. But what could they do about it? He felt as if he'd entered a dead-end street and was up against the blank wall at its end.

He needed time to think, to work out what to do, but he didn't have any. This, the trial of a duchess, was a crime local magistrates would not want to touch. That man Barker would be sending for the Bow Street Runners forthwith, if he hadn't already done so. Isabella had to be saved before she found herself incarcerated in some terrible London prison and dragged before a hanging judge.

He leaned forward in his seat, resting his elbows on the desktop. "I will be blunt, old friend, and this is strictly between the two of us. Marcus undoubtedly deserved to die for his sins, and I'm not sorry he's dead. He was drunk, and possibly also under the influence of opium when he attacked Isabella. We'll never know that for sure, though. Dora had spent her life subjugated and bullied by him, and witnessing Marcus about to kill his wife, she snapped, as any human being would have done. Somewhere other than the library, she might just have attacked him with her fists to save Isabella, but that didn't happen. A pair of loaded pistols lay on a table where she could see them. She picked one up and shot him before she had time to think about it. It was an almost involuntary reaction to seeing him kicking Isabella so viciously." He paused. "I strongly believe, as Dora must have, that he would have kicked Isabella to death had she not intervened."

Atkins nodded. He was starting to look bleary eyed. Probably didn't often drink three large glasses of brandy one after the other on an empty stomach.

"Did Mrs. Barnes examine Isabella for bruises?"

Atkins nodded again. "She did. It was Her Grace's own idea. She's a brave one, and was not as shocked by what she'd seen as Lady Dora. Mrs. Barnes said she wasn't even crying. Just calm and cold and practical, as though she'd distanced herself. When she and Mrs. Barnes had got Lady Dora upstairs and into bed, she asked Mrs. Barnes to help her take off her ruined gown. It was torn and she'd knelt in some of the duke's blood." He seemed, despite the influence of the brandy, to have realized the importance of any evidence they could find. "She was anxious her bruises should be witnessed. She showed them to Mrs. Barnes again on the following day, when they'd darkened. She was heavily marked, but not on the face. His Grace was usually careful not to mark her where the bruises would be seen. I myself saw the bruises on her arms where he'd grabbed her. Mrs. Barnes can vouch for the truth of the story."

Of course, they would have faded to nothing by now, but at least she was alive. For now.

"Tell me," Richard said. "Why did you decide to do what you did? To cover it all up the way you did?"

Atkins's hand shook as he placed his empty brandy glass back on the table, but at least the awful grayness had gone from his face. "It was a spur of the moment decision made by me and Amos Rowan. He wasn't asleep, and he heard the gunshot and came to find me. I think perhaps we both guessed it wasn't the duke's normal target practice because it was only the one shot instead of several. And there'd been the scream." He indicated one of the long windows. "He had a habit of opening this window and setting up the targets on the ledge or trying to shoot rabbits on the lawn. He was proud of his marksmanship."

Richard could vouch for that. A vivid memory of Marcus, full of glee, shooting the chickens in the yard of one of the tenant farmers leapt into his mind. And the cats. An unpleasant memory he'd thought packed away and forgotten.

Atkins went on. "Amos came in, you understand, after Mrs. Barnes had taken the ladies upstairs, and I told him what had happened. We neither of us knew what to do, but both of us wanted to protect Lady Dora." His voice shook as much as his wrinkled hands. "I saw where the duke had been shot and put the pistol beside his right hand, so it would look as though he'd done it himself. I didn't think. I was in a panic. I knew he was left-handed but until you pointed it out, it completely slipped my mind. I should have thought of it, though. I've known him all his life, so I should have known." He shook his head again. "Then we came out and locked the library. We waited until first light before we sent a footman to knock on Mr. Sanders's door and report to him what had happened. We both wanted him to take over responsibility."

"Was he a party to this deception?"

"No. We didn't tell him. We showed him the body and he seemed to accept it for what it appeared to be. He asked a few questions only. But now I come to think of it, they were about where the gun was. Do you think it's possible he guessed as well?"

Richard shrugged. "If he did, then he's kept the secret. He

gave nothing away when I spoke with him."

Atkins went on. "We waited again until a more hospitable hour for disturbing the gentry and then sent the footman, Robert it was, to fetch Colonel Jarvis. He brought his man who questioned everyone and made a sketch of the scene. Then he allowed us to move the body and make the necessary arrangements. And clean up the room. I had the gardeners take out the rug and burn it. The colonel was satisfied with our deception. Fooled, I should say. We thought we'd succeeded."

"Colonel Jarvis is one of three magistrates for Newbury, is he not?"

"He is. Mr. Theodore Dawes is the second—the one who signed the arrest warrant for Her Grace. The third is Sir Oswald Peverel."

"I think I need to visit Sir Oswald with some urgency. If two of the magistrates disagree with the third, we might prevail. It seems Mr. Dawes might be in Lady Dangerfield's pocket. Her deep pocket."

Richard recounted what he'd overheard in the garden on the night of the ball. Last night, or rather earlier this morning. Was it such a short time ago? A lot had happened since. Too much. It felt as though more than a week had passed since he'd stood hidden behind the summerhouse, not just a few short hours.

Atkins listened, his face paling further, if that were possible. Richard began to feel a real concern that the old man might keel over from the stress.

When he'd finished, he reached out and covered the old man's bony hand. "The first thing we have to do is find out which of the servants, for a servant it must be, they have paid to lie."

Atkins's face brightened a fraction, as though hope had arisen in his breast. "Indeed. I would vouch for all the older ones, for they've been here for years and all of them care deeply for the duchess and Lady Dora. It can't be any of the kitchen staff, the below stairs servants, for they never come up to the main part of the house so would have no excuse to say they saw anything. Of the above stairs servants, only a few are not of long-standing. And of course, there are the stable staff who would perhaps have reason to claim they were awake at that time and peering in a window. Some of them are more recently employed, so perhaps not so loyal."

"Which ones? We need to speak to them. Now." Richard paused. "I think we will need Mrs. Barnes as well, and Amos. All of us will interview these servants. The more of us to intimidate them, the better. Can you arrange it?" He rubbed his eyes. "Our only chance of saving Isabella is by proving their witness to be a liar." He glanced towards the door. "For we can tell no one the truth. We have to protect Dora."

Atkins got to his feet, a trifle unsteadily, it had to be said. "I will have them sent for immediately, Your Grace." They were back to being butler and master again, the camaraderie gone. As it should be for this.

THE COACH BEARING Isabella drew up outside the Guildhall, a building in a rather sorry state of disrepair standing in the middle of the marketplace in Newbury. The ratty man, whose name Isabella gathered was Barker, descended first, then reached up and took hold of her in a pinching grip on the upper right arm as she climbed out. Did he think her about to make a break for it, here in the center of the town? With late passersby staring at her in open curiosity.

He must have forgotten she was a duchess.

She held her head up high and made an attempt to shake him off, but this time, when Richard was not present, he hung on, his strong fingers digging into her flesh. Constable Hooper climbed down from the driver's seat and took up a position on her other side as though he, too, thought her a dangerous captive.

Isabella glanced over her shoulder, but neither of the ladies, if you could call them that, which she swore she never would again, had made any move to exit their carriage. However, Lady Dangerfield was leaning forward, her stony eyes brimming with malice. "I warned you not so long ago never to cross me, tradesman's daughter. You would have done well to have paid more attention to my words." Her upper lip curled in a sneer, which made her look very ugly indeed.

Despite her erratically pounding heart and the weakness in her knees engendered by real fear, Isabella mustered her most cutting of stares. With reluctance, she dismissed the impulse to warn Lady Dangerfield that the wind might change and her face would be stuck like that, and turned sharply back to look where Barker and Constable Hooper were about to take her.

She'd seen the Guildhall on a number of occasions. A large building with a belltower on the peak of its sagging tiled roof, one half of it rested on sturdy pillars under which she'd often seen market stalls sheltering on market day. Perhaps luckily, it was not market day today. Outside it stood the currently unoccupied pillory and whipping post. No doubt that woman would have liked to have seen her make use of them. Above the pillared section lay she knew not what.

She was soon to find out.

Constable Hooper and Barker marched her up a wide flight of sagging wooden stairs on the northwest side, where Hooper opened the door into what must have been the Council Chamber. Isabella had a vague idea that this was used for the Quarter Sessions and other public purposes, but right now it was empty, their footsteps echoing as they crossed it.

A door on the far side swung open and a man emerged, his face familiar, but not one she could put a name to.

Barker and Constable Hooper, who had hold of her left arm, pushed her toward this man. They seemed to be enjoying having control over a duchess, but she was a veteran of far worse bullying than either of them were capable of.

"We have her here, Mr. Dawes, sir," Constable Hooper said. "As requested."

So this was Mr. Theodore Dawes, one of Newbury's magistrates, and a colleague of Colonel Jarvis, who'd attended on the day of Marcus's death. She would not think of it as his murder. No, it had been more like the putting down of a rabid dog.

Mr. Dawes gave a slight bow to her, perhaps intimidated by being in the presence of a duchess, even though she was his prisoner. He was an elderly man whose sizeable paunch was straining the buttons of his waistcoat in an alarming fashion. His plain face was notable in the main for the size and color of his nose—a sort of mottled purple resplendent with livid veins. Not unlike Colonel Jarvis's own proboscis. Isabella knew the signs of a heavy drinker when she saw them. Perhaps being a magistrate inclined one in that direction.

"Your Grace," Mr. Dawes said. To do him credit, he appeared to be more than a little discomposed at having to take a duchess into custody. "I'm sure we can sort this little misunderstanding out with alacrity."

That sounded promising. Her spirits rose a little and the feeling that she might be about to disgrace herself by collapsing in a heap lessened. She lifted her chin.

To her right, Barker stiffened. "We have a witness, sir, what says as she was seen in the act of killing her own husband. You know we have. A witness as is prepared to swear to it. On oath."

Mr. Dawes nodded, his lack of conviction evident. "That's as may be, but she's a duchess. I can't try a duchess. Not for murder."

Mr. Barker had this under control. "We thought as much. She'll have to go to London and stand trial at the Old Bailey. I already sent for the Bow Street Runners to come down and take charge of her before we even made the arrest. They should be here in the morning. Meanwhile, she needs to remain secure under lock and key, lest she does a runner."

Isabella bit her lip. How dared this upstart order a magistrate about in this way? And yet, Mr. Dawes seemed inclined to be obedient. She'd had no prior dealing with magistrates, apart from Colonel Jarvis, so had no idea if this was the normal way of doing things. Instinct told her it was not.

Isabella fixed Dawes with a hard stare but his eyes slid sideways as though he was too embarrassed to look at her. Had they paid him off?

"Very well," he said, resignation in his voice. "Hooper, take Her Grace to one of the cells. Neither is occupied. She'll have to remain there overnight." He turned away, like Pontius Pilate washing his hands of Jesus. Considering she was pretty certain forty pieces of silver or their equivalent had changed hands somewhere, a Biblical comparison was not out of place.

There turned out to be two cells in the Guildhall. The best thing anyone could have said about them was that they were large. And empty of other inhabitants. Human ones, at any rate. Considering it was September, the one Isabella was consigned to was both damp and cold. The stink made her gag as Constable Hooper pushed her inside the door, but she fought to control herself. Nothing would let her show distress to either of those bullies. She'd had ten years to practice hiding distress.

The door banged shut behind her and the key grated in the lock. She was shut in.

The source of the worst stink turned out to be the privy in the corner. She could only hope she wasn't going to need it, because nothing would induce her to go near it. However, the one good thing was that the cell possessed a window in the back wall. Grimy, barred, and covered in cobwebs, it nevertheless let in light so she wasn't confined in total darkness. At least it possessed glass, although cracked and missing here and there, so it kept out the worst of the cold.

When night fell, though, she would be in darkness, so she'd best explore the cell while she had the chance. Its size indicated it was meant to house more than just the one prisoner, and half-a-dozen pallet beds suggested a maximum of six. Was Newbury the sort of town that might have to house so many felons at one time? It had always seemed so peaceful whenever she'd ventured in. Thank goodness she was the only one here right now.

What was that? She froze, eyes straining wide as she scanned the cell. Something was scuttling across the floor. Something black with legs. Good heavens. A cockroach. And not just one.

Isabella shivered. The thought that, when night fell, she wouldn't be able to see any of the creatures with whom she might be sharing this cell horrified her. But she'd stood worse. Well, not cockroaches, nor rats, which she didn't even want to think about, but worse treatment than she'd had here. She could do it. If she could survive Marcus nearly killing her, then she could survive anything. She sat down on one of the pallet beds and, leaning forward, rested her chin in her hands.

The most frightening part of this was that things were only going to get worse, and she could see no way out of it without implicating Dora. And she would never do that.

CHAPTER TWENTY-THREE

IT TURNED OUT that Atkins had a list of only five servants who were relatively new to the castle and whom he suspected, albeit unwillingly, might have been either foolish or desperate enough to have taken a bribe and told a lie. All of them were young and had been only a matter of months in the castle's employ. Two of them were young parlor maids, one was a recently arrived underfootman, and two were grooms.

"We'll have to treat them as though we suspect them of having seen something," Richard said to his assembled senior servants. "Even though all three of you feel certain they couldn't have done this, and that whoever it is, is lying for money. Whatever it is, it's not a wild goose chase."

Mrs. Barnes pursed her lips. "If it was one of those girls then I'll know them for liars the moment they open their mouths. Although, as it's hard enough getting these new girls out of their beds in the morning to do their chores, I can't believe either of them would have voluntarily risen at three even if they heard someone shouting 'fire.'"

Amos chuckled. "And my two lads from the stables would've been tucked up in their beds, exhausted. They'd had to wait up and deal with the carriage when Their Graces returned from their dinner party. That takes a while, and with having to be up again by six they wouldn't be wanting to hang about in the stableyard."

Atkins frowned at his fellow servants. "The underfootmen all sleep upstairs in the attics, same as the housemaids, so it seems to me the most likely that the grooms would be ideal candidates to fabricate a story about having seen something that night. We have to remember that whoever it was is lying. They didn't actually see anything, which means it could be any of them, regardless of the chance of them having been up at that hour of the night."

It seemed from this, though, that each one of them didn't want to assign guilt to any of the suspects under their own command.

Richard rubbed his bristly chin, trying to dispel the unwelcome image of where Isabella might currently be finding herself without success. His imagination was working overtime, even though he was supposed to be organizing an interrogation. "Mr. Atkins is correct. It could have been any of them. It could just as easily be one of the maids as the footman or grooms. We must not allow ourselves to harbor any preconceived ideas at this point." He surveyed his assembled would-be inquisitors. A rather formidable bunch. "But we'll start with the two maids, then the footman, as they are indoor servants, and leave the grooms until last."

The four of them abandoned the library and repaired to the room Richard had known as his uncle's study. He'd elected not to include Philip Sanders in this matter, as the less people who knew the truth, the better. If questioned at some point in the future, Philip would quite legitimately be able to claim ignorance, even though it now seemed as though he might know more than he was letting on. With the nature of his job, it seemed likely that if anyone were to spot the pistol having been in the wrong hand, it would have been him.

Atkins had co-opted Robert, the head footman, who was absolved of suspicion due to his long service and seniority and the trust Atkins had in him, to fetch each of their suspects to them without alerting the others. At least, that was the idea.

Maud, the youngest and newest parlor maid was the first arrival.

She was a small girl for her eighteen years, with a pretty face liberally scattered with freckles and sandy brown hair confined under a mobcap. She'd put on a clean apron for her interview and, as she stood before the desk in the study, behind which her interrogators had seated themselves, her hands gripped that apron as though she were trying to screw water out of it. Guilt about something exuded from her every pore, but not necessarily the kind of guilt they were looking for.

"You may sit down, Maud," Mrs. Barnes said, keeping her tone kind. They'd decided, as she was in charge of the female servants, that she should be the one to question the two housemaids. The theory was that they wouldn't be so frightened of her, but this might have been negated by the presence of not only the butler and head groom, but also her employer.

Maud perched herself on the edge of the chair Atkins had put in front of the desk, clasping her reddened hands together and staring down at them as though they were fascinating. She was trembling.

"Can you look me in the eye please?" Mrs. Barnes said.

Slowly, Maud raised her head and peeped up at them out of wide, frightened eyes. She reminded Richard of a deer he'd once seen Marcus shoot. But he couldn't afford to feel sorry for her. He had to remember Isabella.

"Now, Maud," Mrs. Barnes said, her voice softening a little more. "I want you to tell me the truth and you will not be in any trouble. Do you understand?"

Maud nodded. "Yes, Mrs. Barnes." Her voice came out as a terrified whisper. This was a girl with something to hide. Richard watched her closely. Had they struck lucky the first time? Could this mouse of a girl be the one they were after?

"Think about last night. I want to know if anyone approached you asking questions about the night the previous duke died."

A brief look of relief shot across Maud's face. Clearly this wasn't the question she'd been expecting. Did she have something else to feel guilty about? Who knew what young servant girls got up to that they didn't want those in charge of them to find out about. Richard's hope of early success dissipated.

"Yes, Mrs. Barnes. They did that. Last night, at the ball, a man come into the servants' hall and was asking us all questions." She blushed, almost falling over herself in her haste to answer. "One of they visiting grooms, I think he said he was. What come with the carriages to the ball. He was a bit familiar, like." More blushing. Probably he'd used flattery on her. "He was asking if any of us could tell him what he called 'the inside story.' He asked everyone the same thing."

"And did you tell him anything?"

She shook her head with mounting enthusiasm. "No, Mrs. Barnes. I didn't tell him nothing. I didn't know nothing to tell him, for a start. I was asleep in my bed when it all happened, like a good girl, and I didn't know nothing till I got up in the morning to do my chores." She leaned forward in her seat, eager to help now she'd realized she wasn't going to be in trouble. "And he kept trying to put words in my mouth that I wasn't saying. He was, that. Real cheeky like. Kept asking me to say yes to things. Over'n'over again. I told him I had work to do and couldn't be talking to the likes of him. Put him straight, I did. Cheeky so and so. He went off to ask someone else after that. I think."

"Very sensible of you," Mrs. Barnes said, with a smile that must have been meant to be reassuring. It worked, because Maud smiled back, suddenly brimming with confidence.

"Thank you, Mrs. Barnes."

"And that was the only contact you've had with this man?"

"It was, Mrs. Barnes."

Richard exchanged glances with Atkins who gave Mrs. Barnes a nod.

"Thank you, Maud," she said with real kindness in her voice now. "You may go."

As soon as the door closed behind her Mrs. Barnes spoke. "She's telling the truth. I know my girls. It wasn't her."

Richard nodded. "I agree. Did you see how relieved she was

when she found out what she was being questioned about?"

Atkins nodded, a hint of reproval in his eye and voice. "No doubt she has some other small crime she feared would be discovered, Your Grace. Mrs. Barnes will need to keep a better eye on these girls, I fear. They are inclined to foolish behavior if given half the chance."

Mrs. Barnes snorted at his tone. "Girls will be girls. I do my best, but it's not easy. But it's those handsome young footmen you'll have to watch, Mr. Atkins. They're every bit as bad as my girls." She tutted her tongue. "But at least I don't have to worry about the duke chasing after the maids any longer." She glanced at Richard. "Begging your pardon, Your Grace. I don't mean you, of course."

Richard smiled. "I know you don't, and I consider it very flattering that you haven't classed me with my cousin in that department."

"Let's have the next girl in now, shall we?" Atkins said.

The second girl, Betsy, a year younger than Maud and the newest addition to the staff having only been employed for a bare month before Marcus's death, appeared just as innocent of having been bribed as her fellow parlor maid. She was a more cocky young lady and less inclined to fear, so perhaps she was not hiding any misdemeanor of her own. She answered the questions readily, and departed with a spring in her stride and a peek over her shoulder at Richard. Innocent of the crime, but perhaps not innocent in other ways. A good thing he wasn't inclined in the same direction as Marcus. This wasn't the Middle Ages.

That left the three male servants.

Thomas, the underfootman, came in next. He was a handsome young man with a secret he plainly didn't want divining, that might or might not have had something to do with young Maud. But he too knew nothing about money exchanging hands and had been on duty in the ballroom when Silas Barker had come asking questions in the kitchen on the night of the ball, so had never even crossed paths with him. Of course, he could have been lying, but all four of them concluded that if he were, he must be the best liar any of them had ever met. "And I've met a lot of them," Atkins said, after Thomas had left.

It was looking more and more likely that the culprit was one of the grooms, a fact that Amos seemed inclined to take as a personal insult.

"Can you tell us anything about them?" Richard asked him, before they had Robert go and fetch the first one in.

Amos rubbed his whiskery chin, deep in troubled thought. "I don't like to think ill of either of them, but young Jack Watkins has been here the shortest time. He only started working six months gone. He seems a good lad and a hard worker, but he's not quite the full ticket, I'm afraid." He frowned as though he didn't want to malign the boy. "A bit slow, you might say. Suggestable. If anyone were to try to get him to agree to something that wasn't true, I think they might succeed. Probably get him to believe it was true, too, if they told it to him enough times. About the yard I give him one task at a time to do, and he manages, but if I try to give him any kind of list, the lad's lost."

Interesting. And if he turned out to be the false witness, his reliability could be easy to call into question due to his slow wittedness. But his poor memory and slow wits might be something that would make him a bad liar for the prosecution.

Well, according to his three companions, whoever had agreed to give evidence was indeed lying, and Richard had no reason not to believe them. They were all adamant no one could have seen what went on that night, and besides which, if anyone had seen anything, they'd have been naming Dora as the murderer, not Isabella. He began to feel more hopeful. "What about the other lad?"

Amos pulled a wry expression. "Jem's the older of the two and been here longest. A couple of years now. He's a lad from one of the tenant farms, which is where he used to work. His pa's been ill this last year or more, and Jem's older brother's running the farm. From what the lad's told me, all his wages go back to his ma and brother to help keep the farm afloat." He paused as if reflecting. "Bit of an eye for the ladies, I've noticed, and he's a sight better looking than young Jack, and about five times cleverer. Might be him that lass Maud's been philandering with, if it ain't young Thomas. If she's been up to anything, that is."

"If she has, she'll be in trouble," Mrs. Barnes put in.

Atkins sighed. "Both of them sound possible."

Mrs. Barnes nodded. "That lad Jem's been hanging around Nellie the kitchen maid too. Got too much of a wandering eye, that one. Likes all the girls. I've warned him off more than once but he's got perseverance, I'll give him that. And I've overheard him moan that he never has any money because he has to give it all to his family." She shook her head. "That's never good for a lad his age. He needs a bit to spend on a girl. He might well have been swayed in return for money."

"Let's see Jem first then," Richard said. "My instinct is telling me he's our best bet if the other boy is a bit simple."

Robert was dispatched to fetch Jem to the study.

He arrived, cap in hand, a big, blustering, confident youth with rough good looks any housemaid or kitchen maid might fancy. Richard had seen him about the stableyard. It was he who'd been eyeing Isabella. That was enough to raise his hackles, but he shouldn't hold that against him. Noticing how beautiful Isabella was didn't mean the man was guilty of anything else, or he, Richard, might have to accuse himself.

"Jem, isn't it?" Richard said, keeping his voice level and non-committal. "Sit down."

Jem seemed unfazed at having to face his lord and master. "Yes, Your Grace. Thank you, Your Grace." He sat down, an altogether more relaxed individual than even young Betsy. A bit overly confident. Money in one's pocket could do that to a lad, as Richard well knew. Jem reminded him of one or two of his own riflemen after payday shenanigans.

He studied the young groom in silence for a few moments, weighing him up. He couldn't be much more than twenty, so would have been a baby when Richard left to join his first regiment. That in itself made Richard feel old. "We have a few questions to ask of you, Jem. We're asking them of everyone." Best not to let him feel singled out, as that might put him on the defensive.

"Yes, Your Grace." Despite his apparent politeness, a current of rebellion underlay his words. This was a young man who didn't like to doff his cap to authority. Richard had met enough young men like this during his time in the army. A few years as a soldier would do Jem a lot of good. If he turned out to be the guilty party, that was where they would send him. Off to take the king's shilling.

"Good," Richard said. "We'd like to know if anyone came asking you questions on the night of the ball."

Jem might be overly confident, but he was not practiced at hiding things. He would have been terrible at playing cards. "I don't think so," he said, after a telltale momentary pause.

"Are you sure?" Atkins asked. "Others have told us that someone did. All of them have told the same story of a servant from another house come asking impertinent questions."

Richard kept his eyes fixed on the lad.

Jem's eyes darted to left and right, the bluster evaporated. He had the appearance of a man who would like to leap up and flee. "Now I recall," he said in a hurry. "I'd forgot. Some man from one of the carriages—a groom, I think—he came and chatted to us in the stableyard. Bit over friendly, I thought." A glisten of sweat had formed on his forehead.

He'd clearly decided that he would have to come clean about Barker's presence, but not give away too much. In his lap, his hands had clenched in fists, the knuckles whitened.

"Did you speak to him?" Richard asked, his voice stern. "And do not forget that we already have the testimony of others." Not quite true, as so far they'd only heard from a few of the indoor servants, but Jem wasn't to know they hadn't already spoken to the other stable staff. He might even think he'd been overheard speaking to Barker, if they were lucky.

Jem took on an even more hunted demeanor. His overconfidence must have all been a show. "I might have done. I don't rightly remember. I was busy in the stableyard with my chores. There was water to take out to the horses what'd brought the guests to the ball, and sweeping up to do." Now he sounded sullen, as though he resented having had to work.

Richard's gaze never wavered. The lad was on the back foot now, making any excuse he could think of. They probably weren't going to have to talk to young Jack. With every word he uttered, Jem was digging himself in deeper. Had it not crossed his mind, or Barker's, that they would search for whoever claimed to have witnessed the murder? Perhaps he was no brighter than poor Jack, after all.

"Well, think about it a bit harder and tell us what was said to you." This was Amos, his bushy gray brows lowered over fiercely angry eyes, enough to quail the most cocky of young grooms. And Jem might already be in awe of his boss.

Jem swallowed. "Some bloke came asking me if I worked here," he mumbled. "I said as I did." He had balled his cap up in his hands.

"Go on," Richard said. "I want the truth, mind."

A war was going on, clearly written across Jem's face. "He wanted to know if I'd seen anything on the night the old duke died." He dropped his gaze to his hands.

"And what did you say?" Richard asked, menace in his tone now.

Jem shifted on his seat. "I said as I didn't know nothing."

Richard glanced at his fellow inquisitors. Amos shook his head, the scowl still on his face. Mrs. Barnes's lips were pressed in a thin line of reproval. Atkins was glaring at Jem. "Did this man offer you money? Think carefully before you answer this. We want the truth."

Jem kept his head down and stayed silent, as if that wasn't a dead giveaway.

"Answer His Grace," Atkins snapped. "You are in grave danger here, young man. And if you lie, the danger will only increase. Believe me. Giving false evidence is a serious offence punishable by a long sentence and perhaps transportation."

Jem's face blanched. "He did," he mumbled.

Atkins pounced. "For what? You had seen nothing. What could he possibly have wanted you to say?"

Jem lifted terrified eyes, tears glistening in them. "He wanted me to say I'd seen the duchess shoot the duke. I said I couldn't, because I hadn't, but he was... he was forceful, like. He kept telling me I must've seen it, through a window or something. I said as I hadn't, but he said if I said I had, he'd pay me." Red spots flared on his ashen cheeks. "He said as he'd come back later on and see me right if I'd sign a statement for him. He come back this morning. With a piece of paper."

"Can you read?" Richard asked.

Jem shook his head. "No, Your Grace, I can't. I can sign my name, but can't write nor read. I never went to school, see, but my ma, she learned me to sign my name."

"So you didn't even know what you were signing?"

Jem shook his head. "I didn't sign it. He wanted me to, but I wouldn't. I said as I'd changed my mind and the duchess was a lovely lady what I couldn't tell lies about. Not for anything." His hand went to his trouser pocket. "I was going to send most of it back to my ma. She needs it now my pa can't do nothing on the farm no more, and the rent's due on the next Quarter Day, and it's gone up this year, and my brother don't have the money to pay it." He paused, and a couple of the tears escaped and ran down his cheeks. "I thought as I could help them stay on in the farm if I did what the feller wanted. But in the end, I couldn't do it."

Richard's anger, which had been mounting, subsided a little. "You wanted the money for your mother?"

Jem nodded. "I was going to keep just a little bit back and buy my girl something pretty."

Richard exchanged glances with Atkins, who raised his eyebrows in question. For a moment, Richard did nothing, digesting the idea that one of the tenants, his tenants now, was in such dire straits that their son had been forced to resort to dishonesty to raise the money for their rent. Although this reflected harshly on Marcus, it also did so on him.

"I'm sorry your family is in such dire straits," Richard said. "And I will endeavor to help you and them. I believe you when you say you refused the temptation of the bribe, and I praise you for it. Now. Think hard. When you turned him down, where were you?"

"In the stableyard, near the tackroom."

"And was anyone else about who could have overheard your words?"

Jem's brow puckered as he thought.

Richard waited.

The boy was clearly trying to go over the events of the morning. Eventually, he lifted his eyes and looked Richard in the face. "There was. Mr. Hopkins was there, what used to be the duke's valet but he's now just a footman. He was there polishing his shoes. Cook don't let the servants do that in her kitchen. She makes 'em do it outside, even if it's raining."

"Mr. Hopkins?" Had Richard even laid eyes on this man? He was ashamed to admit that in the ten days or so he'd been at Stourbridge he'd not taken an awful lot of notice of the individual servants. Another thing to chide himself with.

Atkins spoke. "He stayed on after the duke's death because he hoped that when a new duke arrived he, I mean you, would be in need of a highly trained valet." He cleared his throat. "He has been most discontented since he discovered you had brought Mr. Baxter with you from your army days."

Mrs. Barnes nodded. "Moans about it every day, down in the servants' hall."

Richard swallowed. "What sort of a man is he? I mean, is he vengeful."

Silence met this question. Only Jem seemed brave enough to answer it. "That he is, Your Grace. He's a man scorned, and he's said it hisself more than once."

"Thank you, Jem. Go and wait outside the door with Robert," Richard said.

Jem nearly fell over his feet in his haste to leave.

When he'd gone, Richard turned to the other three. "The boy isn't the callous, greedy villain I thought he was going to be. It seems apparent he only considered doing this to get the money his family needed to pay back to me on the Quarter Day at the end of the month. His is a family in difficulty because of the sickness of the father. Was my cousin such a monster that he had no sympathy for the problems of his tenants?"

More silence.

Atkins broke it. "Best ask Mr. Sanders about that, Your Grace. I'd not like to comment on what I don't know for sure."

Richard nodded. "I will speak to Mr. Sanders as a matter of priority. I should have enquired more about the tenants already. I'm ashamed to say I was too busy preparing for that damned ball. I should have put the people who depend on me first, and look what's happened because I didn't. But before I speak to Mr. Sanders, we have to get Hopkins in here. It has to be him. He needs to recant his statement and sign another to say he was coerced into the first by that man Barker. And then we have to get to the jail and try to get the duchess released."

Right now he couldn't think about Dora, the true perpetrator of the crime, if it even was that. The French would have called it a crime of passion as she'd killed him in fury at seeing what he was doing to Isabella. She'd done it only to protect Isabella. If she hadn't, her sister-in-law would have been dead, and no one would have lifted a finger to find out where she'd vanished to. He, Richard, would still have been in Portugal with the Rifles, and no one would be here to protect Dora from Marcus. Right now though, she needed protecting from herself.

He'd think about what to do about her later. How to help

her. But only after he'd rescued Isabella. Right now, his whole being was focused on doing just that. The thought of her locked up in some jail in Newbury turned his stomach. A vision of her pale, anguished face as she'd taken the blame for Dora's crime rose before his eyes, twisting his heart. If only he'd been the one who'd married her ten years ago, not Marcus. How different he could have made her life.

He rose from the table. "Have Robert call Hopkins in, Atkins, and we'll see to his confession. Amos, can you have the grooms prepare the carriage. I'll be going to see both of the other magistrates before I attempt to secure the duchess's release. We have to go about this the right way, or we'll fail. And we need to make haste." The thought of Isabella having to spend a night in a jail cell chilled his heart.

CHAPTER TWENTY-FOUR

COLD, DAMP, CLOYING blackness, so thick she could almost touch it, pressed in on Isabella from all sides, with not even a hint of light being thrown by the prison cell's dirty windows. No matter how much she strained her eyes as wide as they would go, she could see nothing. But that wasn't the worst thing. No, the worst thing was that with the fall of darkness, the prison cell had sprung to life. All around her, it seemed, the sound of scuttling across the floor and up the walls grew louder and closer with every passing moment. She'd already swept her long skirts, the skirts of the gown she'd chosen especially because she'd thought Richard would like it, up above her knees out of fear that something heard but unseen would try to climb them. Now she lifted her feet off the floor as well and hugged her knees to her chest on the hard pallet bed.

Only that was of no comfort at all. She'd removed the one tatty and stinking blanket to one of the other beds and for a while had sat on the thin straw mattress. Until she'd begun to itch. Unseen small things were crawling on her now, despite having thrown the mattress aside and sitting on just the hard base, and there was nothing she could do about it. Scratching herself only made it worse and the more she dwelled on it, the more she became convinced that her body and hair were seething with unwanted visitors. She'd never be clean again. The feel of little feet, real or imagined, on her skin, made her want to rip her clothes off and hammer on the door. But she was a duchess. That would never do.

Someone at last went around lighting Newbury's streetlamps, such as they were, and a faint glow managed to enter the cell from the filthy window, but not enough to see much by. Not enough to see what it was that scuttled across the floor on tiny feet. Her imagination provided for that. Nervous exhaustion washed over her in ever increasing waves, but she couldn't bring herself to lie down on this dreadful bed. Who knew what would come crawling over her if she dropped her guard.

She had to keep her spirits up. Richard would do something, wouldn't he? The expression of anxiety on his face as she'd been taken had given her hope. She refused to consider that there might well be nothing he could do. After all, she'd confessed to him that she'd done it. He would have believed her. He must never know it was Dora who'd pulled the trigger and killed her brother. Never.

His face danced before hers as she'd first seen him in the stables, his hair tousled, his sleeves rolled up above his elbows revealing his well-muscled arms. She'd thought him handsome then, but his resemblance to Marcus had been enough to make her shy away from allowing herself to like him. It was only later, when that likeness seemed to have dissipated, and he'd stood out to her as an individual distinct from his cousin, that she'd dared to admit to herself that she was attracted to him. He was like the mirror image of Marcus—the good version, the antithesis to her late husband, opposite to him in so many ways. How would it have been if Marcus had never existed and Richard had always been the duke? If he'd been the one her father had set his sights on? The one she'd married? Would she even now be at home with a brood of children of her own, like Grace? Would Dora be married as well? Happy, contented women, fulfilling their roles in life, unmarred by their relationships to Marcus.

What would it be like to be married to a man like Richard? This was the first time she'd truly allowed herself to consider this possibility. She'd said she'd help him find a wife, with the intention of taking her time—a lot of time. Had she really intended to do so? To see him married one day to some other undeserving woman? Her own arrogance remained, an arrogance that had been nurtured by Marcus's treatment of her, an arrogance she'd had to foster in the face of his cruelty, or she would have crumpled to nothing. Did Richard even like her, with all these character traits she suspected he might despise? He'd given nothing away. But that look... the horror in his eyes as she'd been taken away. Had it been something more than friendship? Could she hope for a miracle?

Something larger ran across the floor close by her pallet bed and she tightened her hold on her knees in fear.

That people were kept like this, and she'd known nothing about it, horrified her. Had that woman known this was the way she'd be treated when she'd departed with that smile of smug self satisfaction? Surely not? Isabella wouldn't have wished this on her worst enemy. Not even on Marcus. Well, maybe on Marcus if she were honest. His death had been an altogether too merciful and quick affair, and she was not ashamed to admit that thought. She had, on many occasions, considered suitable ends for her late husband, none of which had included a quick death by shooting.

Outside, the town clock struck the hour. Nine times. How long had she been here? She'd lost track of time. Been too preoccupied to have noticed the clock striking earlier. Too wrapped up in her own fears.

But she was made of stern stuff, and she refused to give in to despair, close as that enemy was lurking. Surely, in the morning they'd be taking her up to London where the conditions would be better. Surely.

Discomfort weighed down on her. She didn't dare lean back against the wall for fear of the cockroaches. She kept her feet off the floor for fear of the rats. Sagging a little in weariness, her lids drooped and almost fell. This jerked her awake. No. She would not give in and lie down on this awful bed. A shiver of disgust ran through her at the thought of how many people, possibly wrongly accused like herself, had already sat where she was sitting. Suffering the same despair she was feeling.

Her one consolation was that she was here and not Dora, with her fragile grip on her sanity, courtesy of a lifetime of bullying by her brother. Dora, who had finally cracked when Marcus had been about to commit murder himself, could not have stood this, but she, Isabella, could and would. Dora had done what she'd done only to save her life, and in return, Isabella determined to save her. There was no argument here. Isabella loved Dora as the older sister she'd never had, the island of normality in her turbulent marriage, the succor in her storm. No, she would never let Dora come to this. She would die for her if she had to, or suffer transportation to the colonies. Anything to save gentle, fragile Dora.

Thinking of Dora brought a wetness to her eyes. She swiped away the unshed tears. She would not cry. If she did, she would be giving in. She was Isabella, Duchess of Stourbridge and the daughter of Josiah Hope, and she would never give in, not even if she were sent to the gallows. To the very end she would be dignified, and prove to all those doubters that you didn't need to be born into nobility to be noble and proud.

The night crept past on slow feet. Or was it still the evening? Much later, or she thought it must be so, the sound of revelers perhaps returning from one of the inns after a night of carousing came from outside. Shouts, carefree laughter, someone singing a drunken song. People who were free and unaware how easily they could be brought down, as she'd been. Later still came the clatter of hooves and rattle of coach wheels on the cobbles as a mailcoach passed through. Ostlers shouted from a nearby inn, voices of passengers carried. All of them free as the birds of the air but unappreciative of it. Perhaps it had brought the promised Bow Street Runner to take her up to London. Then, even later, although for all she knew it could only have been minutes, came the drum of rain on the cobbles outside and the jail's tiled roof.

It leaked. The steady drip of water in more than one spot joined the scuttling of unseen creatures.

The fresh damp fueled the chill, and the chill ate into her bones. For September, the prison cell was colder than she could ever have expected. She squeezed her hands between her thighs in an effort to warm them. If only she'd thought to bring her warm shawl, some gloves, a clean blanket. But it had all been so sudden. So unexpected. With the passing of two months since Marcus's death, she'd made the mistake of thinking both of them safe, despite the persistent whispered rumors. No doubt they'd been fueled by Lady Dangerfield. His mistress. A woman intent on revenge just because she couldn't have become duchess herself. She and Lady Brocklebank, who'd smiled and smiled and remained her hidden enemy since the day Marcus had chosen her instead of Verity as his bride.

What could they possibly have in evidence? Nothing. No one knew what had really happened save herself, Dora, Atkins, Mrs. Barnes, and Old Amos. And none of them would breathe a word.

She bit her thumbnail, a habit she'd had drummed out of her as a child. A habit that was returning with a vengeance. All her nails were now bitten to the quick. So what possible evidence could that woman have seized upon? Nothing that was true. This was her only hope. If she stood trial, could she prove they were lying without incriminating Dora? Could Richard help her do it?

And she was back to thinking about him again. She would be hanged for this, and he would go on living at Stourbridge without her. Perhaps Dora would marry Philip Sanders now she'd no longer fear abandoning Isabella to Marcus. Instead of running off to find employment elsewhere, Philip would be able to remain at Stourbridge. Yes, Dora needed Philip's solid stability. If anyone could help her overcome her guilt, he could. But he would have to be told. She needed to tell Richard that Philip should be told the truth. If he came to visit her, she could do that. Then Dora might have a chance at happiness, and, one day, she and Philip might have children. Long after she, Isabella, was gone.

But what of Richard? Dear, kind Richard. He would forget about her and marry some young debutante he met during the Season. If not the one approaching, then the one after that. He'd have children. An heir. And then he might go back to his regiment as he'd said. If he'd married her, she'd have made sure he didn't do that. She'd have wanted him by her side forever. Safe from harm.

She frowned. What was she thinking? He didn't love her, and surely she was mistaking her own maudlin feelings for love when they couldn't be? You couldn't fall in love like this. Could you? Not with someone you hardly knew.

She drew in a deep, steadying breath. She was going mad. That was it. Madness was taking her over, fueling her imagination, making her think things that could never be true.

Something squealed and feet scampered close by the bed. She drew her knees closer still to her chest and hugged them tighter. This was going to be a long night.

IT WAS LONG after dark when Dickens drew the coach up outside Colonel Jarvis's house and Richard, Sir Oswald Peverel, whom Richard had snatched away from his dinner, and a reluctant and cowed Mr. Hopkins descended from it. Sir Oswald, a rotund man whose very appearance spoke of his fondness for his dinner, was in a bad humor. The unfortunate Mr. Hopkins, who'd spent the journey trying to sink into the shadows of one corner in the coach, looked as hangdog and guilty as it was possible for someone to look. He'd waited in the carriage, under Dickens's watch lest he turned chicken and fled, while Richard went inside Wormstall House and apprised Sir Oswald of his mission.

With bad grace, as he hadn't yet reached his dessert, which he declared was to have been his cook's specialty, a plum pudding, Sir Oswald had agreed that it was indeed an emergency, and a duchess could not be allowed to suffer such an indignity as being locked up for a crime she hadn't committed. With nearly as much reluctance as Mr. Hopkins, he agreed to accompany Richard to the Colonel's house.

When they arrived, it was late, but lights still shone in the downstairs windows of Hampstead Manor indicating that the owner had not yet retired to bed. His butler, a little surprised by the lateness of their arrival, escorted them into the colonel's library, where they found that gentleman ensconced before a blazing fire, his stockinged feet on the fender, and accompanied by a half-empty decanter of brandy. His nose was notable by its shiny redness.

Richard did not beat about the bush. With every hour that passed, his anxiety had been rising, although he realized there would be nothing gained by racing to the jail and trying to see Isabella unless he held the right cards. The confession of Mr. Hopkins alone, who had at first insisted that he had indeed witnessed the murder and had only caved in under severe threat from Richard, would not be enough. He needed the power of the magistrates behind him.

He explained once again, just as he had to Sir Oswald, but only what he wanted them to know rather than what was strictly true. He couldn't allow Dora to be exchanged for Isabella's freedom. He had to gain her release without implicating his fragile cousin.

When he'd finished, he handed the signed statements of his three servants to the colonel. Each of them had sworn that they had been the only ones involved that night, and Atkins had attested to having been first on the scene after the duchess. No one else had been up and about at that time, and neither had any of them had reason to be.

The colonel listened without saying anything until Richard had finished. Then his gaze moved to Mr. Hopkins, who'd been standing, twisting his fingers together in anxiety, near the door as though poised to flee. "And who is this fellow?"

There was no getting around it. Richard had to reveal Mr. Hopkins's part in this. "This is Albert Hopkins, who was valet to my cousin. He was motivated to give false witness due to his demotion from valet to under footman. You see, I brought my own man with me from the army, so there was no place for a second valet at Stourbridge." He glanced at Mr. Hopkins, who was looking most un-valet-like. "The investigator whom the Ladies Dangerfield and Brocklebank hired bribed him to lie for them. To say he witnessed the duchess shooting her husband. He has owned up to being bribed. We have his signed confession." He paused, seeking to soften the implication if he could. Poor Mr. Hopkins, whatever the consequences of his lie, didn't deserve to be transported. The poor man had lost his position in the house and he, his employer, had not even noticed.

"The investigator, a Mr. Barker, preyed upon Mr. Hopkins's dejection, which I must confess is partly due to the fact that I knew nothing of his predicament. Had I been made aware, I would have sought to help him to a new position of similar standing, and he would have had no need to nurture thoughts of revenge. But I've not been back long, as you know, and I've yet to find my way about my estate and gain an understanding of the way it's run. Although that is a poor excuse for all the mistakes I've made." He glanced back at Mr. Hopkins. "I can assure you that this is a lesson learned, for me as well as for Mr. Hopkins, and one of the things I shall be doing in the near future is talking to all my servants and asking about their situations. My tenants as well. I do not intend to be a harsh master or landlord. There are things going on at Stourbridge, of which Marcus approved, that I intend to change."

Whether this little speech would have any mitigating effect on Mr. Hopkins's or Jem's problems he had no idea, as undoubtedly both magistrates present would also themselves be landlords. In Richard's experience, landlords everywhere put their own incomes before the situations of their tenants. They may well not be sympathetic at all to a servant who had born a grudge against his masters. Both of these magistrates might even disapprove of his sentiments to the extent of wishing to make an example of the poor man. A risk that had to be taken.

Luckily for Richard, as the colonel clearly wasn't at his sharpest with half a bottle of brandy in him, Sir Oswald interrupted. "The fellow has recanted his statement and declared he made it under undue pressure. He's already confessed to me in the carriage on our way here. That is why he's here, so that you and I, Jarvis, can hear his confession and present it to Theodore. I already have it on paper but the fellow's own words should carry more weight. He, it seems, was taken in by this man Barker, who, in turn, was keen to earn his reward from Lady Dangerfield. This is a sorry mess and has resulted in one of our own, a delicate lady of the highest order, at that, being incarcerated in the town jail. I say she must be removed from there with alacrity."

The colonel nodded, blustering. "Good God. They've put her in the jail at the Guildhall, or even worse, the Bridewell? I wouldn't wish that on my worst enemy. No fit place for a lady for even an hour. We must get her out of there immediately."

"She'll be in the Guildhall cells," Peverell said. "Being as she's accused of a capital crime. They only put the vagrants and drunks in the Bridewell cells."

Richard nodded. "I believe that is where she's been taken." His anxiety rose. He'd never seen the inside of a jail. Was it as bad as these two were painting it? The thought of what Isabella must be suffering tore at his heart. "Can we go now, straightaway, and have her released?"

The colonel lost a little of his angry bluster, and shook his head. "I'm sorry, Your Grace, but I happen to know that there's no turnkey at the jail overnight. No warder. The prisoners are left to themselves until seven in the morning. The Guildhall will be deserted and locked but for any prisoners being held there. We won't be able to get in."

Good God. Was she stuck there until the morning? Richard fished out his pocket watch. It was already past eleven and heading for midnight. Seven or eight hours before anyone came on duty at the jail. "We can't just leave her there. Someone must have a key."

The colonel and Sir Oswald exchanged worried glances.

"We can't leave her there all night," Richard repeated, his anger rising by the moment. If he had to, he was ready to break down the doors of the prison to get to her.

"I think the warden at the Bridewell might have a key," Sir Oswald said. "He lives on site, as the Bridewell is beside the workhouse of which he's in charge. You could go there."

"Me?" Richard snapped. "I'm not risking going alone in case they turn me away. You're both coming with me. I need the weight of your positions behind me. And I need something signed right now agreeing to the duchess's release without prosecution. With Hopkins's confession to having been coerced into lying, then no evidence exists against her. I want it in writing. Now."

The colonel and Sir Oswald once again exchanged glances. They'd probably never before been asked to sign release papers in the middle of the night for a duchess accused of murder.

Richard glared at them. "And you'd better send out a warrant for the arrest of Mr. Silas Barker for coercing false evidence and bribing witnesses while you're about it." He clapped a hand onto Mr. Hopkins's shoulder, feeling the fellow flinch. "Hopkins will be giving evidence against him. I'll see the venal snake transport-ed for his crime." If only his prosecution would result in the transportation of the appalling Lady Dangerfield as well, but that was too much to hope for. Likely she would get away scot free of this crime. The nobility so frequently did.

Sir Oswald, more compos mentis than the colonel by far, even though he was without his plum pudding, nodded with vigor. He was probably a lot happier about pursuing a member of the working class than he was going after a lady. "A damned good idea, Your Grace. We'll set the wheels in motion for nipping that fellow's career nicely in the bud. He'll enjoy the antipodes not one jot. I promise you."

Richard heaved a sigh of relief. "Now, can we go and rescue the duchess please? I feel it should be done forthwith. As a matter of urgency."

CHAPTER TWENTY-FIVE

ISABELLA HUGGED HER knees and shivered, both from the cold that was eating into her bones and from the continued scuttling of unseen creatures across the floors and walls. She'd already concluded that her imagination was worse than not being able to see what was making the noises. More cockroaches? Mice? Rats? Probably all three and in large numbers by the sound of things.

She kept her head hunched between her shoulder blades, the fear that something might drop down her neck from the ceiling all too real. Spiders, possibly. If she'd had a shawl she could have put it over her head and had some protection, but they'd taken her into custody in what she'd been wearing to walk in the garden and charm Richard. For a moment, she was tempted to go and retrieve that stinking blanket from where she'd thrown it, even though she had no idea how many people had used it before her. But the thought of having to set her feet on the floor and risk having something run over them, or worse, up her legs, put her off.

Plus, her whole body itched, and the blanket might be harboring any amount of creatures intent on infesting her. Even without it, she was certain she could feel things crawling over her skin and biting her. Was this what her life was going to be like from now on? Mired in dirt and the sort of horrible parasites she'd only heard tales of from her nurse as a child.

The temptation to give in and let herself cry mounted, but with it so did the determination not to. She had to remember who she was, even though by now it was an uphill struggle. She was not just an ordinary young woman; she was a duchess. Surely those who had her in their power couldn't leave her like this? Surely once she was in London she would be held in a more salubrious jail. They didn't put members of the nobility in with common criminals, did they? She pushed aside the fear that they might not care and would do just that. She determined not to think about the future. Instead, she would comfort herself by thinking of Dora, safe and not incarcerated, but being looked after by Richard. Yes, he would take care of Dora for her. He was a man of his word. She'd asked him to, so he would. And perhaps, just perhaps, he might be able to get her out of this. Thinking of him warmed her frozen heart just a little. Although dwelling on how different her life could have been had she met Richard instead of Marcus promptly lowered her spirits once again.

The town hall clock struck once. How long would she have to wait for someone to come? Maybe they'd just leave her here for another day. Well, it was another day now. Perhaps the Bow Street Runners would take their time to come down from London and collect her. She glanced at the corner; she was going to have to use that noisome privy soon, even though they'd given her nothing to drink. At least she'd got a little more used to the stink, but the thought of having to go anywhere near it had her ready to gag. Plus, she was back to not wanting to set her feet on the floor in the dark and all that threatened.

Outside, the town was now silent. As though a heavy cloak had fallen over it, muting its life blood, she could hear nothing. No voices. No footsteps. No more mail coaches. Not even the familiar call of an owl. She wasn't used to being in a small town at night. In London, when she was at the townhouse, there was never total silence, because London never slept. Not totally. At night there was always something going on: people returning from balls or soirées, men on their way back from gambling dens, dogs barking, owls and the occasional nightingale, more than a few carriages even in the middle of the night. But not here in this small market town. Here, there was nothing. She could have been immured in the underground dungeon of some ancient castle, were it not for the faint glow of light from the nearest streetlamp.

The loneliness of it pressed in on her, threatening to squash her flat against the hard wooden pallet, like a fly.

She buried her head against her raised knees and closed her eyes. Perhaps she could snatch a little much needed sleep in this position. Perhaps if she thought about Richard... Diccon. How she wanted to possess the familiarity with that nickname that Dora had. How she wanted to call out his name, and have him turn to her, smiling with those kind eyes that were nothing like Marcus's hard and cruel ones. How had she ever thought him like his cousin? He was cut from a different mold. He was a man she could willingly have spent the rest of her life with. A man with whom this would now never happen.

Time ticked past.

She couldn't get Richard out of her head. If she went to the gallows, she'd close her eyes as they put the noose around her neck and visualize his face, so it could be the last thing she saw in this life. Sitting here, afraid to sleep, she let her imagination furnish her with images of what it would have been like to have had him love her. A tear trickled down her cheek, to be swiped away. She refused to let herself cry.

The sound of hooves and wheels on the cobbles at last broke into her troubled doze. She lifted her head and listened. Another mailcoach? The hour must be very late. By the sound of it, more than one coach. They did pass through at unsociable times, of course. They had to, in order to make their times. These were stopping, and from the sound of it, right outside the Guildhall rather than nearer to the big coaching inn on the east side of the marketplace.

Voices carried on the damp night air. Men's voices raised in anger.

Wait. She knew one of the voices. The loudest and angriest. Was that, was that... *Richard?*

Her heart leapt as hope burgeoned, and she sat up straighter, alert now, ears straining.

Footsteps sounded on the stairs outside the cell. A key rattled in the lock. The door swung open so hard it crashed against the wall, and light from a handheld lantern flooded inside, blinding her. Rats scurried for cover, as did the cockroaches. She'd been correct in her imaginings.

For a long moment nothing happened, and then Richard was across the room. His strong arms went around her, scooping her bodily up off the bed, as though she were light as a babe in arms, clasping her to him, pressing her close, careless of how she must smell after all these hours in this cell. His breath was hot on her cheek, the feel of his arms tight around her, holding her as though he never wanted to let her go, so much more than just comforting.

All her previous determination flew out of the window. She wrapped her arms around his neck and clung onto him like a drowning woman, burying her face in his shoulder, a shoulder that smelled clean and fresh, despite the musky aroma of his sweat. She clutched him to her as though he were a living pomander, sent just to dispel the stink of the jail, breathing him in, taking great lungfuls of him deep into her core. "Diccon," the name came out as a whisper against the bristles of his unshaven neck. "You came. I knew you would."

WHEN THE TURNKEY from the Bridewell, dragged most unwilling-ly from his bed, and swearing that even a duke ought to wait until a man was awake of a morning, had unlocked the cell door, and the light of the colonel's torch spilled inside the fetid room, Richard had for a moment thought it empty. The terror that they were too late, that somehow a Bow Street Runner had arrived this quickly, and Isabella was already on her way to London to another, bigger and more impregnable jail, washed over him. And then something in the far corner, close to the filthy window, moved.

She was hunched, small as a child, on a narrow wooden pallet, devoid of mattress or blanket, her knees drawn up to her chest, her wide eyes blinking in the light. She couldn't see him.

He stepped into the cell, the stink hitting him like a solid, malodorous wall. He almost hesitated, only the sight of Isabella so vulnerable, so small, so pathetic, drove him on. In a few short strides he was across the damp flagstones, insects he couldn't see crunching under his boots, and before she could move or respond in any way, he had her in his arms, clutching her to him as though he never wanted to release her. Which was true, because he didn't.

He could not have held her more tightly had he tried. Her breath was against his neck as she turned her head towards him, his lips in her hair. Out of instinct, he kissed the top of her head as he turned back to the others, fury on his face.

"What sort of a place is this?" he snarled, as a rat dashed away from the light and vanished into one of many holes in the wooden wall. Beneath his feet, the carapaces of more cockroaches crunched.

"The-the jail," Colonel Jarvis said, holding a handkerchief to his mouth, his own rheumy eyes wide with shock. Perhaps he'd never seen the inside of where he was consigning those presumed guilty to languish before their trials.

The turnkey, a little rat of a man, shrugged his scrawny shoulders. "Same as the inside of any jail I've ever seen. Same as the Bridewell, an' that's got half a dozen vagrants in it right now." He grunted. "She's lucky she weren't put in there with those doxies. None of them'd've taken kindly to a duchess being in with 'em. This 'uns the best of the lockups we've got in Newbury."

Richard reached the door and the others moved hastily out of his way. Isabella's fingers clung onto his coat, her body trembling in his hold, her face turned into his body as though she couldn't bear to see the place in which she'd been confined. Heedless of the two magistrates, he carried her down the wide stairs and out into the fresh night air of the market square. His carriage stood waiting, Dickens on the driving seat, Mr. Hopkins up beside him, a man shrunken in on himself with shame. The colonel's coach stood behind it.

"You're safe now," Richard murmured to Isabella. "I have you now, and you're safe. It was all a lie. I won't let them take you again. You're safe."

For answer she clung on more tightly to him and his heart swelled so much he feared it might burst. The feel of her in his arms, her warm breath on his neck, her desperately tight clinging hold; all of these filled his heart with something more than immense relief, something he couldn't quite define. All he knew was that he never wanted to let her go.

He didn't wait for the magistrates and turnkey. With a strength born of urgency, he climbed into his carriage with Isabella still in his arms. No mean feat. He set her down on the seat and leaned out of the door again. "Take us home, Dickens. As fast as you can."

The two magistrates were at the bottom of the stairs, illuminated by the turnkey's lantern.

"Are you just going to leave?" Sir Oswald called. "What about Dawes? And the investigating fellow?"

"You'll have to deal with them yourselves," Richard called as he swung the door shut. "I have other more urgent matters to attend to."

The horses sprang into a trot, as Dickens set them on the dark road back to the castle.

Richard leaned back in his seat. The single lamp burning inside the carriage showed him Isabella, stiff and upright on her side of the carriage, all the limp vulnerability vanished as though it had never existed. Her composure had returned. She was, after all, a duchess. A duchess who had weathered ten years as Marcus's wife and had the sangfroid to cover up his killing by her sister-in-law. Would he have expected anything less of her?

"Thank you for my rescue," she said, polite as though they were both at a soirée and just casual acquaintances.

"I could do nothing else."

She licked her lips. "How…?"

He told her about Hopkins's role in her apprehension, observing her eyes widen in shock and then in acceptance. When he'd finished, he watched her for a moment or two longer as she took time to recompose herself. She'd had a very traumatic day. It was a miracle she could look so calm. Perhaps her years of marriage to Marcus had engendered that ability.

She smoothed the skirts of her filthy gown. Her hair was awry, with loose curls falling to her shoulders and across her forehead, and her face was smudged with dirt. The hands she was now clasping on her lap were grubby as a canal navvie's.

"I know what happened," he said, keeping his voice gentle. "I know why you let them think it was you who killed Marcus."

And now her eyes did widen. He'd shocked her. Perhaps she'd thought it a secret no one would ever dare disclose. After all, her faithful servants would never have betrayed her or Dora.

She licked her lips again. Had they given her anything to drink in that place, and if they had, would it have been palatable? He drew a hip flask of brandy from an inner pocket of his coat and handed it to her. What he really longed to do was to take her in his arms again and hold her close, but she seemed to have decided the time for that had passed. He wouldn't press her. Independence exuded from her every pore, and perhaps she needed to cling onto that for her own sanity.

Without a word, she unfastened the lid of the flask and put it to her lips. She gulped down a goodly measure, paused, then drank again. When she offered it back, he took it and did the same. After the day's adventures, he needed it. He was becoming quite a toper.

"You will not give her away?" she said, her voice a little hoarse.

"Of course not. You were prepared to give up everything for

her. I would do the same. We both of us love Dora above all else." Well, not quite above all else.

She nodded. "I am sore afraid for her."

Richard couldn't disagree with that. "It's a terrible thing to take a life." He paused. "I have done so on many occasions as a soldier, and it never becomes any easier. For a young lady raised to gentility, it is enough to derange. She is suffering for it."

She nodded. "I know. She's not like me. I am strong, and she is not. Not in the way I am." She brushed a strand of hair out of her eyes. "She has certain strengths, or she would not have survived at Stourbridge under Marcus's tyranny, but her power is to bend to the wind, to give in, to apologize rather than to fight." She gave a little, brittle laugh. "Whereas my strength is a fighting strength. I refused to let him defeat me."

"And yet she was the one who killed him in the end."

She nodded. "Ironic, isn't it? The mouse has saved the falcon from the wolf."

"She was as brave as you, in the end. She saw that he would kill you if she didn't try to save you, and because of his position, he would get away with it."

She fell silent, but he could see how uncomfortable she was. He ventured a smile. "You should have a bath as soon as we're home. You look as if you need one."

And now she did laugh. "Don't worry. That is the first thing I intend to do. And I shall have Hawkins comb through my hair to check for lice and any other unmentionable creatures that might have hitched a lift with me. That cell was crawling with creatures that have no place on a human body." She frowned. "Will you take it upon yourself to improve the jail? No one, innocent or guilty, should have to put up with incarceration in such a hole."

"Is that all you can think of?"

She shrugged. "Believe me, that is foremost in my mind and will be until I've taken off these clothes and seen them burned. Only decorum is preventing me from doing so right now. The sooner we are back, the better."

Their knees were almost touching. He reached out a hand and took one of hers. "Isabella, I didn't know this was going to happen."

"I know you didn't. It was that creature, Lady Dangerfield. I should have realized when we met her in my dressmaker's, and then later on when she came to the ball. I should have known then that she refused to accept Marcus's death. She was the source of all the rumors, I'm sure." She sighed. "She wanted him, but she knew she could never have had him. Not properly. Perhaps she hoped to usurp my position at Stourbridge one day, although she could never have become his duchess unless I died…"

Her voice trailed off as realization must have dawned. "Do you think…?"

It had struck Richard at exactly the same time. "That he intended your death that night so he could replace you? That is very possible. But she has a husband of her own, does she not?"

Isabella nodded. "A hunting man, and old and gouty, or so I've heard. Perhaps someone who could have been disposed of easily when an opportunity arose. Who knows? I doubt we ever will." She frowned again. "Although I've always wondered if Marcus had something to do with my own father's death. Again, we will never know now. His secrets have gone to the grave with him."

Richard squeezed her hand. "You have no need to worry now, Isabella. I know everything, and I will do all in my power to protect you and Dora. You may sleep easy in your bed tonight. Barker will be the one residing in that jail tomorrow. For causing false witness by coercion and bribery. I will press for his transportation to the colonies."

She gave a little, it had to be said satisfied, smile. "And now, if you don't mind, I would like to close my eyes for a few minutes. I didn't dare fall asleep in that awful prison for fear of my fellow cellmates."

Oh, how Richard longed to suggest she sat beside him and

used him to lean her weary head on. But of course, he didn't. Instead, she leaned her head against the upholstered side of the coach and closed her eyes. Her exhausted, drawn face relaxed as sleep rapidly took her.

All he could do was gaze at her and drink her in. The realization that he need look no further for the woman he wanted to marry swept over him, along with the fear that after Marcus, she might never want to marry again.

CHAPTER TWENTY-SIX

I SABELLA WOKE LATE for the first time in her life. And for the first time in her life she appreciated that she was clean, and in a soft feather bed, and warm. And, also for the first time in her life, she realized that there were people who were not waking up as safe and secure and comfortable as she was. Of course, she'd always known that the estate tenants and the servants didn't have such a luxurious life as she did, but they had homes, they were warm and well-clothed as far as she could see, and well-fed. None of them suffered want.

Now, as she lay in bed on the morning following her incarceration, as rays of warm sunshine streamed in around the edges of her window drapes, she had time to reflect on how lucky she was: lucky to have been born her father's daughter, to have never known poverty or want, to have always had fine clothes and big houses, to have eaten well all her life, and to have been, despite Marcus, for the most part happy. Well, only unhappy when he was about.

She sat up in bed. What time was it? The sunlight suggested quite late. She needed to get up. A ride on Sultan was what she needed. A ride to clear her head and make her appreciate her own freedom. Her own hard-won freedom. Won for her by Richard. Diccon. As if she weren't appreciating everything enough right now. She buried her nose in her pillow for a moment, taking deep breaths. Oh, the scent of clean sheets and her clean nightgown, the feel of clean hair and skin. She would never take that for granted ever again.

A tug on her bell rope brought Hawkins hastening to her bedroom.

An hour later, smart in her green riding habit and feeling very much herself again, and after a breakfast in her room of toast and hot chocolate, she descended the stairs into the hallway, intent on heading to the stables. No one seemed to be about, so she could make her escape with alacrity and be gone before anyone noticed. Her longing to be out in the fresh air burgeoned ever further.

Her progress down the rear passage past the kitchens to the stables went unnoticed, and in a minute or two she was entering the long stable block, where the horses greeted her with soft whickers in the hope of treats. Today she'd brought nothing but a caressing hand though, as she hurried towards Sultan's loosebox, the delicious aroma of hay and horses seeping into her every pore.

She reached the door and set her hand on the bolt, and as she did so, someone stood up from behind the stable wall. Someone who must have been waiting inside the stable with Sultan for her to arrive.

Richard.

With a little gasp of surprise, Isabella took a half step backwards, her hand to her mouth. Her heart did a little excited flutter, and heat rose to her cheeks.

He was dressed much as he'd been on the first day she'd met him: his old boots and breeches, a white shirt, clean today, open at the neck to show his darkly curling chest hairs, sleeves rolled up to reveal his powerfully muscled arms, and braces keeping up his breeches. As he was brushing straw from his clothes, he must have been sitting down. In Sultan's stable.

"Good morning, Bella." He smiled, a wide, friendly smile, as unlike Marcus as he could possibly be. Another flutter of the heart.

She had to smile back. "Good morning... Diccon." She gestured at Sultan. "What on earth are you doing in Sultan's box?" As if she didn't know the answer.

His smile widened and his dark eyes danced. Her heart did an involuntary flip of pleasure and she was aware of the pounding of her pulse in her throat. "Waiting for you." He chuckled. "And it was a long wait. You must have been very tired to sleep in so late."

"You surmised that I would come straight out to ride?"

He nodded. "I did indeed, and I was right, was I not?"

Excitement buzzed through her. "You seem to think you know me well."

"Not as well as I would like to."

Her mouth went dry and her unruly heart began to beat even faster, a queer feeling beginning in her belly. Could she deny that she would like to know him much better, as well? That maybe now she was free to? She opened the stable door. "I see you've groomed him for me." She glanced around. "That was very kind of you, but where is your horse? I don't see Douglas standing ready to be ridden out."

He moved towards the door. How tall he was, standing over her now, looking down at her out of those gentle, peaty eyes. "I thought to take out the horse on which I traveled here. Amos thinks he has the makings of a good hack, and he's had over a week of good food in him now, and plenty of rest. He'll be a different horse to the one I paid a few guineas for in Maidstone."

She smiled, her heart fluttering like the wings of a captive bird. "Be careful he's not grown too full of himself on Stourbridge oats." How short a time ago she'd been right here, dismissing Richard as just her late father-in-law's by-blow, come looking for work.

He grinned a little irrepressibly, perhaps at the same memory. "We'll have to see. I'll fetch your saddle for you."

Half an hour later they were riding up the long track to the downs, both Sultan and Richard's horse full of the joys of spring, despite it being quite the opposite end of the year. Although

Richard's horse was, in truth, mainly full of the joys of the oats he wasn't used to receiving. He fairly bounced along under Richard, as though the oats and good treatment had changed his personality and turned the nag of ten days since into a blood horse raring to go at the start of the Epsom Derby. As she watched Richard struggling with so fiery a mount, Isabella couldn't help but wonder if it had been a wise decision to ride this particular horse. She herself would have found the beast a challenge, and Richard wasn't that good a rider.

She had to laugh at his expression, though, as the horse, whom she'd declared should have a name and chosen Mercury for—"Because he so clearly has winged heels"—skipped sideways at a fluttering leaf. It was certainly on its toes, but, so far, Richard appeared to be coping.

"Do your grooms never turn out the horses into the fields so they can stretch their legs? Or exercise them?" Richard asked, hanging on for dear life as Mercury lived up to his new name by leaping into the air, as though he had pretensions of flight, as a pheasant carked in the bushes on the right. An occupational hazard on an English country estate.

Isabella, who was finding herself more and more at ease with Diccon as the ride progressed, mainly, it had to be said, because she was finding his predicament so amusing, laughed out loud. There was nothing like seeing him in difficulties to make her feel more in sympathy with him. "I'm sure they do turn them out, and they do exercise them too, when I'm not at the castle, but your Mercury is a new horse, and there were no instructions about him, I imagine. I fear the grooms just might have left him in his box this last week or so, while filling him up with oats." She patted Sultan's warm neck. Mercury was doing a good job of making Sultan look like an old plodder, which he was not. "He does seem a trifle over enthusiastic about being out. Are you sure you're all right on him? We could go back, if you prefer?"

Richard shook his head, possibly because he didn't want to lose face. "He'll get it out of his system once we've had a gallop, I should think."

They passed the folly gatehouse where the Crumps lived, luckily for Richard with no frightening washing adorning the bushes, and turned out onto the ridgeway path across the top of the downs. A warm breeze ruffled Isabella's hair. The downs stretched away green and open to the south, heading towards Winchester. The urge to just let Sultan gallop and not stop until they were off the Stourbridge estate, away from all the troubles of the last weeks, rose. Common sense took over, though. It would have been a long ride back.

Instead, she shot Diccon a challenging smile. "Shall we run Mercury's high spirits out of him then? And see if that improves him a bit?"

Doubt flitted across his face, as Mercury had just performed a creditable buck combined with a sideways leap when he caught sight of a scarecrow in one of the arable fields to the left. Best not to give him time to think. She gathered her reins. "I'll race you." A slight tap of her heel to Sultan's side, and her horse was off, springing forward from walk to gallop in a matter of moments, the wind whistling in her ears. This was true freedom. Only on the back of a horse had she ever felt it—the exuberance, the vitality, the being at one with all those who'd come before her who'd galloped over these open downs, back down the countless years into the mists of time. She crouched forward, Diccon forgotten, urging Sultan ever faster, as though her speed might carry her back into the past herself.

Sultan was fast, but he was pure Arab and only fifteen hands, and Mercury was a good six inches taller, with longer legs. Who knew but that he didn't have gallopers in his ancestry? Derby winners, perhaps. He certainly looked as though he might have, right now, as he came alongside Sultan. Diccon was hauling on his reins to no effect because the horse had his mouth wide open, evading the bit, his neck outstretched and his eyes wild and dilated. This was a horse that might have been trained to run at some point. He'd fallen on hard times, ending up being sold off as a hack, but now, after all that good living and those buckets of

Stourbridge oats, he'd found his feet again. With a vengeance.

"Give him his head," she called out, and Richard seemed to take her advice because he stopped fighting to slow his mount down.

With all caution thrown to the wind by their riders, both horses flew along the grassy track, neck and neck, their riders now crouching forward to encourage even greater speed. Hooves thundered on the turf, and the rapid snort of the horses' breathing was loud. Isabella turned her head again to look at Richard, and at the same moment he turned and their eyes met. His dark hair had blown back from his face, and his eyes were alight with enjoyment, as he bared his teeth in a grin.

But neither of them had counted on the sheep.

From behind a scrappy hawthorn bush, half-a-dozen sheep, disturbed in their peaceful afternoon nap by the imminent arrival of two racehorses, erupted, bleating in panic, to flee away south across the downs. Isabella glimpsed them a fraction of a second before Sultan did, barely enough time to grasp firmly onto the pommel with one hand as her horse leapt sideways. Her foot came out of her stirrup, and, for a moment, she she had to cling on as Mercury crashed into Sultan's quarters in a panic, then they were galloping on again.

Only Richard was no longer astride Mercury.

Isabella found her flapping stirrup and hauled on Sultan's reins, ignoring Mercury who was showing no signs of slowing. She had to saw on Sultan's mouth and swing him from left to right to slow him down, but at last he did. Ahead of her, no longer encouraged by his friend's speed, Mercury also slowed to a trot, his broken reins trailing. She swung her head around to look back for Richard. She couldn't see him.

Panic seized her. Whipping Sultan around, she trotted him back up the track towards the bush where the sheep had been hiding. Nothing. Where was he?

Then she spotted him. He lay in the grass, on his back, motionless.

Her heart must surely have stopped beating. No. Fate could not be so cruel. The thought that she was being punished by God for her part in Marcus's death shot into her head and almost made her vomit.

She slid down from Sultan onto legs that didn't want to support her and staggered the last few yards, flinging herself down on the grass beside Richard, heedless of where the horses went.

He lay quite still, eyes closed, one arm outthrown. Was he dead? Was this the retribution she suddenly feared she deserved? Was fate stacked against her?

With tremulous fingers she felt under his jaw for his pulse. His skin was warm to the touch, and there, faint but present, she found his pulse. He was not dead. She heaved a deep sigh of relief, and sat back for a moment on her heels, fighting to quell the tears of relief that threatened to come cascading down her cheeks.

His eyelashes, unfairly long and thick for a man, fluttered on his cheeks.

"Diccon!" She caught him by the shoulders and would have shaken him had she not suddenly remembered it might be a bad thing to do. Instead, she put her hand against his rough cheek, something she'd wanted to do for so long. "Diccon." Her voice broke with emotion.

His eyes opened and he blinked up at her, at first unfocused, confused. She'd fallen off herself a few times when she'd started riding, so was well aware of how it could affect you. He must have hit the ground very hard.

"Diccon, tell me, does it hurt anywhere?"

His eyes focused, and a slow smile spread across his face. "Bella…" The sound of her name on his lips…

"See if you can move your arms and legs." She was being practical, but he was gazing at her like a lovesick schoolboy. Good heavens, could he have feelings for her that she'd never dared to hope for? The sensation that he might washed over her in a wave of heat that had her putting her hand up to hide her hot cheeks.

Apparently not noticing her discomfiture, he moved one arm then the other, his legs just a little. "All in working order." He made to sit up, but she pushed him back.

"No. Stay lying down. You've had a nasty fall. Does your head hurt? Or your neck?" She'd seen a man fall out hunting who'd moved too soon and been left paralyzed. Well, in fact he'd died within days. That couldn't happen to Richard. It couldn't.

"My neck is fine. I think I have a bit of a headache coming, though."

She sat over him, staring down into his soft brown eyes. They were almost hypnotic in their intensity, devoid now of any confusion. Brimming with something that could only be love. Were hers the same? Did she need to speak or would he read them as she was reading his? How she longed to bend forward and press her lips to his.

His hand came up to touch her arm, feather light. "You might think this an impertinence, but will you kiss me, Bella? I feel it might improve my head."

What? Was he a mind reader? She swallowed.

He didn't move, just lay there, gazing up at her, eyes twinkling with something that might be mischief. Something she'd never before seen in the eyes of a man. "I find that I don't think I could return to the castle unless you kiss me. I might lie here and die if you don't."

She wanted to tell him that of course he wouldn't die if she didn't kiss him, but she didn't. Because, of course, she wanted to kiss him. So badly. And it was most definitely not an impertinence.

Two could play his game, though. "If I do, will you live?"

His lips curled in a mischievous smile, rendering him more boyish than ever. "I think a kiss from you would revive me."

"Just one kiss?"

He frowned. "I fear just one might not be enough. Perhaps you should try. I have a headache, but I'm sure a kiss from you would cure it."

Excitement bubbled up in her, mingling with something that had to be real happiness, a new emotion for her, or one that she'd not experienced in years. She leaned over him. "Close your eyes."

He did as she'd bidden him.

She let herself hover his face as she gazed down at him, taking in the little laughter lines around his eyes as he relaxed, the small scar she'd never before noticed on his chin, the alluring curve of his lips. Now, at this moment, all resemblance to Marcus had flown. He was his own man, and she… she loved him. Yes, she loved him, and not just because he wasn't Marcus, nor because he'd saved her life. She loved him for himself, and she was ready to acknowledge it.

Bending closer, one hand on either side of his head, she pressed her lips to his.

Under her pressure, his mouth opened and his tongue stole into her own. She didn't draw back, though, but instead let her own tongue dance with his, as a myriad of feelings cascaded through her body, the foremost an almost overwhelming longing for this never to end.

As if he'd read her mind, his arms came up and encircled her body, pressing her against his chest as the kiss deepened still further. Her core was on fire, burning for his touch as she'd never burned for a man before. Was this true love? Was this what her life could be, free at last of Marcus?

One of the horses blew down his nose, close by, and she drew back, still within the circle of Richard's arms, gazing down at him again, as though she'd never truly seen him before. Sultan nudged her shoulder, and she burst out laughing. "He wants to know what we're doing."

He cupped her cheek with one of his hands, his thumb sliding over her chin and up towards her mouth. A little gasp escaped her lips at the intimacy of such a simple touch, and a quiver ran through her to her starving core. Overhead a buzzard wheeled against the blue of the sky, its mewling call plaintive in the now still air. The sound of the horses ripping up the grass as they grazed filled the silence.

"You can tell Sultan we're loving one another," he whispered. "Two people who should have met long ago. Two people who were meant to be together, but were kept apart by fate." His other hand slid down to her waist. The heat of his touch burned through to her skin, and brought another gasp. How could he be doing this to her? How was he making her feel as though she was wanton enough to spread her legs for him here and now, under the arching blue of the sky with only two horses and a buzzard as witnesses? Because that was what she wanted to do. Right now. Something she'd never wanted to do before, but only done out of duty, at the start of her marriage.

"You love me?" she whispered, partly because she wanted to hear him say so, but also because she wanted to be sure. She'd had enough men after her body in the past to be well aware that some men just saw women as conquests. She'd thought all men…

He smiled again. "You need to ask me? Bella, my love, my sweet innocent girl. I love you with all my heart, and I want you to be my duchess. I could marry no one else and be happy. It has to be you. I think I knew it almost from the moment I met you." He paused. "Tell me you love me and you'll be my wife, and you'll make me the happiest man alive."

Her eyes widened. She'd never allowed herself to dream of this. Not, at least, until the night she'd spent in that cell. But that had all been nothing but fantasy, a child's game to keep her spirits up and prevent herself from falling asleep. A fairy story with a happy ending she couldn't see. And now that fairy story was being offered up to her. Surely there was a trick in it somewhere? How could she be deserving of a happy ending?

"You wish to marry me?" She couldn't keep the shock out of her voice.

"If you'll have me. If you love me. I could never force you into a marriage you didn't wish for."

His fingers caressed her face, sending shock waves down her body. She couldn't think. Her whole self was twisted up with the feel of his touch, only able to think of his hands on her, wanting him to touch her all over.

Could she say the words? Words she'd never used before. She licked her lips. "Diccon… of course I will marry you." The words came tumbling out. "Of course I love you."

The answer to that was another kiss, long and deep, that made the world spin under her and time stand still.

All too soon, though, it came to an end. He chuckled. "I suppose that wasn't a very good proposal as proposals go. I love you, Bella." His brows met in a worried frown. "But I must be sure you're not just saying yes to please me. I won't force you into anything you don't want to do. If you don't love me enough, or prefer to remain as friends, and don't wish to marry me, you won't have to. I don't want you to feel you're under any obligation. You have the power to say no to me if you wish it."

She licked her lips, a tiny doubt resurrecting itself. Might he turn out to be like Marcus? Her experience of marriage had not been good, and that was a gross underestimation. She'd only known Richard a little over a week. Was she feeling all this for him out of gratefulness that he'd saved her? He clearly thought she might be. Was her body responding to his only as a reaction to the long years of loneliness she'd suffered?

"I-I do love you," she whispered. "But I'm afraid."

His hand slid down from her cheek to her throat, his touch electric. Oh, how she was aching for him. "What are you afraid of, my love?"

"That love might not be enough. I-I'm damaged goods, Diccon. I always will be." There, it was out.

He stroked her neck. "I have enough love for the two of us."

"So I've noticed."

He burst out laughing, the tension between them vanishing. "Damn it, Bella, but I'm hot for you. Right now, with only our horses as witnesses. I could take you now, here on the grass under the sun with no one around for miles. But I won't. We shall be married in the estate chapel, before God."

She joined in his laughter, her fear melting. "A feeble excuse. I fear with your recent fall you are too unwell to perform anyway."

He swore under his breath. "Temptress. You are playing with me now. I find my headache has cleared away entirely. Your kiss has quite recovered me."

He made to try and rise but she pushed him back, her old determination returned. "Then let us see how much this one reinvigorates you." And she kissed him again.

His lips were indeed hot. Demanding too, and against her body she felt his hard arousal pressing against her until she was panting with a desire she'd never felt before. But he was right. They had to wait. Instead of giving in to hot temptation, she would do it properly this time, when she married the man she loved. She would be a proper duchess.

She sat back on her heels, the breeze ruffling her curls, her cheeks warm. Sultan and Mercury were grazing close by still, as though nothing untoward had just occurred. "I can wait, so long as it is not for too long."

Richard sat up, none the worse for his fall, it seemed. He put up a hand to caress her cheek. "I'll get a special license, have no fear. We'll be married within the week if I can manage it. But you're right, it will be hard to have to wait for both of us, but when we're married, the wait will be worth it."

She had the distinct feeling he was speaking the truth.

He scrambled to his feet and helped her up. "And now I think we'd better catch our horses and head for home. I'm not even sure Mercury is rideable, as I think he's broken his bridle. The reins, at least. It's a long walk, but the sooner we're back, the better, as we have a wedding to prepare for."

His words snatched Bella back to normality. "But what about Dora? How can we help her?"

"I've already thought of that. We'll make it a double wedding. She will marry the man she loves, and he will keep her safe. We'll have to tell him your secret, but I'm certain he'll be ready to help her. I have the feeling he's already guessed Marcus's death wasn't as it seemed—I'm sure he knows about the gun being in the wrong hand but has kept it to himself. And perhaps marriage and becoming a mother will chase away the guilt Dora feels about her brother. I hope she'll be able to come to terms with her conscience. We have to convince her it was the only thing she could have done."

Isabella nodded. "If anyone can bring her back and make her happy once again, Philip will. He's loved her for years, but they had to keep it secret from Marcus, who would have given him his marching orders had he found out." She smoothed down her skirts. "I have more than once suggested to her that she should elope with him, but she wouldn't leave me alone with Marcus."

Richard brushed the grass off his clothes. "We don't want anyone to guess what we've been doing, now do we?" He chuckled. "But I feel these two weddings had best be very soon, because I won't be able to wait long to have you in my bed." And he folded her into his arms once again.

"Oh, Diccon." She let herself relax, her whole body weak with relief that this was finally over. That she wasn't locked up in a cell or on her way to London to stand trial, that only Richard knew their secret, that Dora could be helped, and she could allow herself to love Richard. She lifted her face to his, and their mouths met in another kiss.

THE END

About the Author

After a varied life that's included working with horses where Downton Abbey is filmed, riding racehorses, running her own riding school, owning a sheep farm and running a holiday business in France, Fil now lives on a widebeam canal boat on the Kennet and Avon Canal in Southern England.

She has a long-suffering husband, a rescue dog from Romania called Bella, a cat she found as a kitten abandoned in a gorse bush, five children and six grandchildren.

She once saw a ghost in a churchyard, and when she lived in Wales there was a panther living near her farm that ate some of her sheep. In England there are no indigenous big cats.

She has Asperger's Syndrome and her obsessions include horses and King Arthur. Her historical romantic fiction and children's fantasy adventures centre around Arthurian legends, and her pony stories about her other love. She speaks fluent French after living there for ten years, and in her spare time looks after her allotment, makes clothes and dolls for her granddaughters, embroiders and knits. In between visiting the settings for her books.

Social Media links:
Website – filreid.com
Facebook – facebook.com/Fil-Reid-Author-101905545548054
Twitter – @FJReidauthor